continued . . .

"An adventure-type fantasy, of epic nature with lots of bloody scenes and characters full of personality and imagination . . . much like *The Lord of the Rings* . . . a great adult look at the world of dhampirs, and the always-constant battle, in any world, between good and evil."   —MyShelf.com

"Complex and bloody. . . . Interspecies distrust, grand ambitions, and the lure of dangerous secrets protected by the undead drive the action in this neat mix of horror with more traditional fantasy elements."   —*Publishers Weekly*

"Fantasy and magic blend with vampire lore in another spellbinding story in the Noble Dead series. This may be book six, but new readers will get caught up quickly. Brilliantly conceived characters face danger and inner conflict in a vividly imagined world that's full of violence and gore. Readers will be on the edge of their seats."   —*Romantic Times*

Rebel Fay

"Entertaining . . . a hybrid crossing Tolkienesque fantasy with vampire-infused horror . . . intriguing."   —*Publishers Weekly*

"A real page-turner."   —*Booklist*

Traitor to the Blood

"A rousing and sometimes creepy fantasy adventure . . . this is one of those books for which the term 'dark fantasy' was definitely intended."   —*Chronicle*

"A unique tale of vampires and half-vampire undead hunters set against a dark fantasy world ruled by tyrants. The personal conflicts of the heroes mirror the larger struggles in their world and provide a solid foundation for this tale of love and loyalty in a world of betrayal."   —*Library Journal*

Sister of the Dead

"[A] wonderful addition to the Noble Dead series . . . *Sister of the Dead* leads us on an amazing adventure that will keep you engrossed until the final chapter. . . . This is a series that will appeal to both horror and fantasy fans."   —SF Site

"The Hendees continue their intelligent dark fantasy series by cleverly interweaving the sagas and personal demons of their heroes with rousing physical battles against the forces of evil. Much more than a medieval 'Buffy does the Dark Ages,' *Sister of the Dead* and its predecessors involve readers on a visceral, highly emotional level and fulfill a craving for nifty magic, exciting action scenes, and a strong heroine who defies genre clichés."   —*Romantic Times* (4 stars)

Thief of Lives

"Readers will turn the pages of this satisfying medieval thriller with gusto." *—Booklist*

"Fans of Anita Blake will enjoy this novel. The characters are cleverly drawn so that the several supernatural species that play key roles in the plot seem natural and real. Supernatural fantasy readers will enjoy this action-packed strong tale because vampires, sorcerers, dhampirs, elves, fey-canines, and other ilk seem real." *—Midwest Book Review*

"*Thief of Lives* takes the whole vampire slayer mythos and moves into an entirely new setting. The world the Hendees create is ... a mixture of pre-Victorian with a small slice of eastern Europe flavor.... Magiere and Leesil are a really captivating pair.... [The Hendees] handle the ideas and conventions inherent in vampires really well. While, thanks to the clever setting and characters, they make it feel like a very different twist on the subject." *—SF Site*

"The Hendees unveil new details economically and with excellent timing, while maintaining a taut sexual tension between Magiere and Leesil. The multifaceted personalities of these two are what make this series so enjoyable. The mysteries ... add texture and depth." *—SFX Magazine*

Dhampir

"*Dhampir* maintains a high level of excitement through interesting characters, both heroes and villains, colliding in well-written action scenes. Instead of overloading us with their world building and the maps and glossaries typical of so much fantasy, the Hendees provide well-rounded characters that go a lot further than maps in making a lively fantasy world." *—The Denver Post*

"An engaging adventure that is both humorous and exciting."
—New York Times bestselling author
Kevin J. Anderson

"Take Anita Blake, vampire hunter, and drop her into a standard fantasy world and you might end up with something like this exciting first novel ... a well-conceived imagined world, some nasty villains, and a very engaging hero move this one into the winner's column." *—Chronicle*

"An altogether compelling and moving work.... These are characters and a world worthy of exploration."
—Brian Hodge, Hellnotes

IN
SHADE
AND
SHADOW

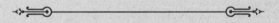

Barb & J. C. Hendee

A ROC BOOK

ROC
Published by New American Library, a division of
Penguin Group (USA) Inc., 375 Hudson Street,
New York, New York 10014, USA
Penguin Group (Canada), 90 Eglinton Avenue East, Suite 700, Toronto,
Ontario M4P 2Y3, Canada (a division of Pearson Penguin Canada Inc.)
Penguin Books Ltd., 80 Strand, London WC2R 0RL, England
Penguin Ireland, 25 St. Stephen's Green, Dublin 2,
Ireland (a division of Penguin Books Ltd.)
Penguin Group (Australia), 250 Camberwell Road, Camberwell, Victoria 3124,
Australia (a division of Pearson Australia Group Pty. Ltd.)
Penguin Books India Pvt. Ltd., 11 Community Centre, Panchsheel Park,
New Delhi - 110 017, India
Penguin Group (NZ), 67 Apollo Drive, Rosedale, North Shore 0632,
New Zealand (a division of Pearson New Zealand Ltd.)
Penguin Books (South Africa) (Pty.) Ltd., 24 Sturdee Avenue,
Rosebank, Johannesburg 2196, South Africa

Penguin Books Ltd., Registered Offices:
80 Strand, London WC2R 0RL, England

Published by Roc, an imprint of New American Library, a division of Penguin
Group (USA) Inc. Previously published in a Roc hardcover edition.

First Roc Mass Market Printing, January 2010
10 9 8 7 6 5 4 3 2 1

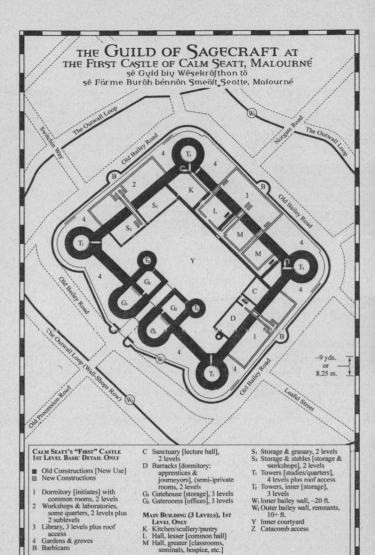

THE GUILD OF SAGECRAFT AT THE FIRST CASTLE OF CALM SEATT, MALOURNÉ

sê Guild biy Wêsekrâfþan tô sê Färme Burôh bénnôn Smeält, Seatte, Malourné

~9 yds. or 8.25 m.

CALM SEATT'S "FIRST" CASTLE
1ST LEVEL BASIC DETAIL ONLY

■ Old Constructions [New Use]
▨ New Constructions

1 Dormitory [initiates] with common rooms, 2 levels
2 Workshops & laboratories, some quarters, 2 levels plus 2 sublevels
3 Library, 3 levels plus roof access
4 Gardens & groves
B Barbicans

C Sanctuary [lecture hall], 2 levels
D Barracks [dormitory: apprentices & journeyors], (semi-)private rooms, 2 levels
G₁ Gatehouse [storage], 3 levels
G₂ Gaterooms [offices], 3 levels

MAIN BUILDING (3 LEVELS), 1ST LEVEL ONLY

K Kitchen/scullery/pantry
L Hall, lesser [common hall]
M Hall, greater [classrooms, seminals, hospice, etc.]

S₁ Storage & granary, 2 levels
S₂ Storage & stables [storage & workshops], 2 levels
T₁ Towers [studies/quarters], 4 levels plus roof access
T₂ Towers, inner [storage], 3 levels
W₁ Inner bailey wall, ~20 ft.
W₂ Outer bailey wall, remnants, 10+ ft.
Y Inner courtyard
Z Catacomb access

PROLOGUE

Well past sunset, Elias hiked up the hem of his gray sage's robe and rounded the avenue's next corner. Jeremy was close on his heels, but at his stumbling footfalls Elias glanced back. Jeremy had tripped over his too-long robe yet again.

"Will you slow down!" Jeremy grumbled.

"Let's get this finished!" Elias shot back. "I don't want to miss Elvina at the Bang-Tankard Inn. And neither should you . . . if she brought a friend, as promised."

Jeremy grumbled again but quickened his pace.

Elias hurried on through sparse pools of lantern light cast upon the wet cobblestones of Calm Seatt, the king's city in Malourné. So much remained uncertain for his future in the Guild of Sagecraft.

He and Jeremy had only recently achieved journeyor status, having completed their years as initiates and then apprentices. Now they needed only be given assignments somewhere in the provinces, maybe even in neighboring Faunier or Witeny. Up to five years of duty abroad would follow, and then perhaps their skills would be recognized. They could at least petition and test for master status. One of them might even one day gain a post at a guild branch with the coveted title of domin. But Elias was worried.

Tonight he'd have to tell Elvina that he would be leaving for a while. She wasn't the kind to wait. And why hadn't he and Jeremy been given assignments yet—instead of errand duties? How insulting for a pair of journeyor sages. And why?

All because of Witless Wynn Hygeorht and her half-rotted tomes from abroad!

"Is she smart . . ." Jeremy panted, "aside from pretty?"

"What . . . who? Oh, of course she's pretty . . . she's gorgeous! You've seen Elvina."

Trotting the last city block to their destination, Elias hopped up the steps of a small shake-wood shop. He barely noticed the hand-painted sign above the door—THE UPRIGHT QUILL. Dim light was seeping through the shop's shuttered windows, and then something thumped sharply on his back.

"Not Elvina, you bits a' brain!" Jeremy hissed. "The other one . . . her friend!"

Jeremy slapped at him again, but only the cuff of his too-long sleeve connected. Elias fended it off.

"I don't know!" he whispered back.

His friend buckled over, hands on knees, trying to catch his breath. Jeremy finally straightened, his plain face slack in astonishment.

"You haven't even met her? Do you even know her name?"

"Of course I do," Elias returned.

The last thing he needed was for Master Teagan—or worse, Master a'Seatt—to catch them in some petty argument outside the scribe shop.

"It's . . . it's . . ." he began.

But the name of Elvina's friend escaped him—or had she even told him? Either way, he wasn't about to let Jeremy ruin his evening plans. Not after all the work it'd taken to avoid Elvina's father.

"You ass!" Jeremy whispered, about to swing again.

A sharp creak of old hinges rose behind Elias.

Warm light spilled around him, illuminating Jeremy's suddenly abashed features. Elias spun about and came face-to-face with old Master Teagan.

The elder scribe glared at him from the shop's open doorway, and Elias shrank back.

"What's this nonsense?" Teagan creaked. "And where's that timid cohort always following behind?"

"I . . . um . . ." Jeremy began.

"We're not doing anything," Elias answered. "Just here for the latest transcription folio . . . as instructed. And Nikolas wasn't assigned to come with us."

Fortunately, as far as Elias was concerned.

As much as Elias liked the shy young man—in a general way—Nikolas had barely achieved apprentice status. He was a bit old to have advanced so little. Besides, Elvina wasn't very fond of Nervous Nikolas.

Scrawny, shriveled, and half-bald, old Teagan peered at Elias through round thick-lensed glasses. His amplified pupils above his extended nose gave him the look of a gaunt hound sniffing out a fox beneath a chicken coop.

"Get in here," he ordered in a crackling voice, "before all the heat leaks out."

Elias didn't wait for Jeremy and stepped briskly into the scribe shop's warmth.

The front room was little more than a wide and shallow space. Its long and worn counter blocked off two doorways to the shop's rear—and behind that counter stood the tall and dour Master Pawl a'Seatt.

Shining black hair hung straight to the shoulders of his charcoal suede jerkin. And although a few strands of gray graced his locks, not a single wrinkle showed on his face. It was hard to guess his age. His features were a bit squarish and never seemed to show emotion, but his brown eyes, too bright for that color, were cold and intense.

Elias didn't care for the shop's owner any more than for Master Teagan, but a'Seatt was well regarded at the guild. Elias had to be polite in all dealings with this establishment.

"Aren't you done fussing?" Teagan called.

Elias glanced back. Jeremy had sneaked in behind him, but the old master scribe wasn't looking at either of them. Teagan closed the door and impatiently watched the shop owner behind the counter.

"Another error," Master a'Seatt returned flatly.

"What?!" Teagan squeaked, and quickly hobbled over.

Pawl a'Seatt never looked up. He scanned page after page in a stack freshly transcribed by his staff.

"Not in the scripting," a'Seatt replied, "in the translation."

Teagan grumbled under his breath. "Enough already. You think you know more than sages?"

"An error nonetheless," a'Seatt answered.

Elias watched the shop owner dip a quill precisely in a stout ink bottle. As he scrawled something on a spare parchment sheet, the right door beyond the counter cracked open, and a small head peeked out.

"Ah, no," Elias muttered.

Imaret was barely tall enough to peer around Master a'Seatt's back and over the counter. Her kinky brown-black hair was tied back, but too many errant strands bounced around her caramel-tinted face. And her eyes lit up at the sight of Jeremy.

Elias scowled, but Imaret didn't notice.

Why did grim Master a'Seatt have a thirteen-year-old girl working in his scriptorium?

Imaret was known on the guild grounds and had suffered more than once as she tailed Jeremy about. Instead of attending one of the four public schools run by the guild, someone, somehow, had paid for her more intense tutelage. Certainly not her father, who was only a retired sergeant of the regulars.

"Hello, Imaret," Jeremy said politely.

Elias rolled his eyes, but again no one noticed.

Imaret dropped her gaze bashfully, opening her small mouth to speak.

"You have finished cleaning up?" Pawl a'Seatt asked, not looking up from the pages.

Imaret raised her eyes, her mouth still open.

"It's late, girl," Teagan added. "And I don't need another sharp word from your parents."

Imaret's pout turned to a vinegar scowl, and she backed through the door with a last lovesick glance at Jeremy.

Pawl a'Seatt finished another notation. When he set down the quill, Teagan snatched up the sheet of notes.

"Seven?" the old scribe moaned. "Seven corrections to

the translations? I can barely read half the sages' symbols in what we transcribe, let alone know what they mean. Our task is to provide clean copies for their master codex—not to correct their work. How would you know what's an error or not?"

Elias wondered how, indeed. Translating scattered passages from Wynn Hygeorht's texts had been a slow and tedious process, from what he'd heard. Whatever pieces could be completed with certainty were recorded in the sages' Begaine syllabary. Occasionally this might include certain untranslated words or phrases carefully rendered in the original symbols and languages.

Neither Elias nor Jeremy had actually seen the contents of any folios sent out to select scriptoriums. The whole project was hushed and secret, and only guild masters and domins were directly involved. Yet Master a'Seatt, mere owner of a private scriptorium, had the presumption to correct work he knew nothing about.

"That is all," Pawl a'Seatt said, and he lifted a more worn collection of sheets from under the counter. "Now for your corroborating count."

Teagan paged quickly through the first crisp stack. "All of our work is present."

"And the guild's note sheets?" Pawl asked.

Teagan reviewed the second stack more slowly, its sheets wrinkled and creased by repeated handling. He accounted each against the inclusions list sent with the folio.

"All present," he confirmed.

The old master scribe began wrapping both stacks in a larger sheet of russet paper, but he stopped as Pawl a'Seatt held out his corrections list. Teagan blew an exasperated snort, but he took the sheet and placed it upon the stacks before wrapping them all.

Master a'Seatt brought out a blue wax stick and the shop's heavy pewter stamp, and he sealed the package closed. He then slipped it into the same leather folio in which the sages' work had been delivered that morning.

"Finally," Jeremy whispered.

Elias was no less eager to be on their way. Elvina was waiting.

Pawl a'Seatt held out the folio, and his brilliant eyes settled coldly on Elias. But as Elias took hold with both hands, Master a'Seatt didn't let go.

"You will return immediately to confirm delivery."

Elias slumped in dismay as Jeremy groaned.

They were going to be very late to the Bang-Tankard inn. For an instant he thought to argue, but a'Seatt's hard gaze made him quickly reconsider. He nodded again.

"Come on," he grumbled, and pushed past Jeremy for the door. "We'll have to hurry."

He was already trotting the wet cobblestones by the time he heard Jeremy close the shop door.

"Wait up," Jeremy called.

Elias had no more patience. When he came to the first side street, he skidded to a stop. Only then did Jeremy catch up. Elias could barely make out the crossing alleyway at the side street's end.

"No, you don't," Jeremy warned.

"It'll be faster," Elias countered. "We can cut through to Galloway Street, then the main alley behind the northwest market, and out to Switchin Way."

"No!" Jeremy snapped. "We're supposed to stick to the main streets, where it's well lit."

"Damn you, I'm not missing the whole evening. Elvina's only—"

"Elvina this, Elvina that . . . Blessed ink and sand! Are you going to let that girl run your life?"

Elias stammered for a few breaths. "Well, at least I have someone I'm leaving behind when we finally get our assignments!"

Jeremy flinched as if slapped, and his face clouded over.

"Fine!" he growled. "Go bumble around in the dark. I'm not slipping and sliding on chamber pot leavings in some alley. Not for some girl . . . when you don't even know her name!"

Elias slumped, the folio dragging down in his arms.

Jeremy had never been any good at holding a girl's . . . a woman's attention—not counting Imaret. Either tongue-tied or babbling about whatever he was currently studying, he was lucky if any companion lasted through a whole meal. But Elias wished he could take back the low blow he'd struck his friend.

Someone moved beneath a shop awning down the way. The indistinct figure halted and seemed to be looking their way.

Oh, that was all they needed—to have the local constabulary set on them for disturbing the peace with all their shouting in the street.

"Just this once, trust me," Elias urged. "It'll be worth it; you'll see."

Jeremy didn't answer.

"We'll stop at the inn on the way back," Elias offered. "You can wait with Elvina and her friend . . . and I'll go give Master a'Seatt his damn confirmation."

"Fine," Jeremy mumbled.

Elias turned into the side way, but he glanced once down the main street.

Whoever had been standing outside that one shop was gone. Hopefully the constable had simply moved on. But the sooner he and Jeremy were away from here, the less likely they'd have to deal with another on patrol. At the side street's end, he turned southeast into the alley. And Jeremy followed, muttering the whole way.

"Stay clear of the center gutter," Elias advised, "and keep your robe up. You won't have time to change if it gets soiled."

"Yes, yes," Jeremy grumbled.

They made their way past the back doors of shops, around crates and ash cans and less identifiable shapes in the dark space. Three side alleys passed by before Elias heard a sharp snap of cloth. Jeremy had stumbled again, and he paused.

Jeremy came up short to keep from running into him. Elias could barely make out his friend's face.

"What?" Jeremy asked.

"Nothing," Elias uttered. "I thought you slipped."

"I'm fine!"

Ready to press on, Elias started to turn, but Jeremy backstepped, his eyes popping wide.

"What was that?" he whispered.

Elias froze, staring at him. "What are you talking about?"

"Ahead," Jeremy whispered, "between us and the light of the far street . . . something crossed."

Elias looked down the alley. At the far exit into Galloway Street, a lantern around the corner spilled light across the opening. But he saw nothing more.

"A stray dog scavenging garbage," Elias assured him. "Come on."

A shadow filled the alley, blotting out the far light.

Elias backed up one step, bumping into Jeremy.

"Who's there?" he called.

The shadow shifted slightly, hesitant movements beneath a voluminous cloak. The far avenue's light rendered only its silhouette filling the narrow space. It was so black he could barely make it out. And the wide hood's opening was only a pocket of night.

"We've no coin," Elias called, trying to sound forceful as he clutched the folio to his chest. "You'll gain nothing by robbing sages. . . . Be off!"

But the figure didn't move.

"Come on!" Jeremy whispered, tugging the shoulder of Elias's robe.

Elias retreated three steps. As he turned, Jeremy bolted. They were halfway to the side street's entrance near the scribe shop when Elias glanced over his shoulder.

The alley was empty. The dim glow upon Galloway Street was plain to see in the distance.

Jeremy squealed sharply.

Elias barreled blindly into his friend's back, and they both stumbled. Still trying to right himself, he looked ahead.

A shadowed silhouette stood at the alley's head, where it spilled into the side street. Light from the street barely reached it, but its full form showed clearly.

It was so tall that Elias would've had to reach up to grab the neck of its hood. And still he saw nothing within it. Its cloak wafted softly, though the night air was still and breezeless. Beneath those flexing wings of the black cloth, there was nothing but night's darkness.

"Come on!" he hissed.

Jeremy only whimpered.

Elias snatched the back of his friend's robe as he fled down the alley. He'd almost made it past the final side alley when the distant light of Galloway Street suddenly winked out.

Elias shuddered, sliding to a halt.

Jeremy snatched his arm and pulled him into the side alley. He didn't even have the wits to pull back nor to realize their mistake, not until they swerved two corners, straight into a dead end.

Someone else tried to grab him from behind.

Elias whirled away and heard his robe sleeve tear as he stumbled deeper into the alley's end.

"We have a few coins!" Jeremy shouted. "Take it. . . . Take it all!"

A tinkle of scattering coins filled the blind alley. But Elias kept his eyes on something else as his back met a brick wall. He couldn't see it clearly at first, that black fist gripping a piece of his gray robe. Then it opened, and the scrap of gray fell.

Elias thought he saw long fingers wrapped in shredded strips of black sackcloth.

The shadow figure drew closer, seeming to grow in height.

It didn't lean down for the cast coins, and he heard no footfalls in its approach.

"Help!" Jeremy screamed. "Someone . . . guards! Help us!"

But Elias couldn't take his eyes off the figure towering over him.

Its cloak folds spread, seeming to climb the alley walls. He heard Jeremy pound on wood, maybe the back door of some shop. But he was shuddering even before the air turned frigid.

The smell of dust choked Elias, just as an overpowering scent of strange spices thickened in his head.

CHAPTER 1

Wynn Hygeorht knelt on the narrow bed of her small stone chamber and stared out her window. She watched the square inner courtyard of the first castle of Calm Seatt, home of the Guild of Sagecraft.

A few sages came and went in yellow pools of light cast by hanging lanterns and the torches on the gatehouse's inner wall. The last sages reached the great double doors at the courtyard's rear and slipped from sight into what had once been the feasting hall in bygone days.

Wynn crawled across her bed to the floor, and settled cross-legged upon a braided cloth rug.

She was not exactly hiding. Rather, she called her recent tendencies a "preferred privacy."

But in the two seasons—summer and autumn—since her return, she'd shied away from her brethren more and more. At times she even wished she were still on the arduous long journey that had brought her home to the king's city in Malourné. And though the Farlands lay half a world away, her memories of the eastern continent were still so clear.

A plate of green grapes and a fluted tin mug of water sat on her bedside table. She sighed, deciding to do something more constructive than wallow in the past.

Wynn closed her eyes, clinging to the image of water within the mug.

Nearly two years had passed since she'd first attempted a small thaumaturgical ritual. She'd tried to give herself mantic sight in order to see the element of Spirit in all things—an arrogant choice, considering she was no mage. Her companions at the time, Magiere and Leesil—and Chap—had been desperate to track an unfamiliar undead. And Wynn had succeeded in her small ritual, helping her friends save a village, but the repercussions still plagued her.

As a journeyor sage, but one with no new assignment and few duties, she had too much free time. She spent some evenings secretly working to expand the ever-present taint of the mantic sight still trapped within her. To date, she'd had very limited success—and one quite painful mishap.

Wynn held to the image of water as she evoked a memory of Chap . . . that wise old Fay-born dog now gone from her side. Focusing upon his image had assisted her more than once in summoning mantic sight. She thought of his brilliant crystal blue eyes, his shimmering silver-gray fur, and even the derisive way he licked his nose at her. As a Fay, an eternal entity of the elements, Chap had chosen to be born into living flesh.

In the form of a majay-hì, the rare breed of guardian wolf-dogs found in the Elven Territories of the Farlands, he had watched over Leesil and Magiere—and Wynn. And then he left her. She missed him in more ways than one.

The only times she had sure control over her lingering mantic sight was in his presence. But tonight she wasn't seeking the element of Spirit.

With the image of Chap and that of Water lodged in her mind, Wynn opened her eyes . . . to nothing.

Just her room, her little table-desk piled with scattered books, paper, and quills . . . and the plate of grapes and mug of water on the bedside stand. All of it was lit by the glow of her cold lamp's crystal.

Wynn slouched, and her back thumped against the bed's side.

Whenever she awakened her mantic sight to Spirit, that element showed as a blue-white mist permeating all things, strongest where life existed but thinner where it waned—or where it never was—for the five elements were part of all things, living or inert.

And a few times she'd seen black spaces amid that mist. Places where there was no Spirit at all, or perhaps its unknown opposite. Permeating mist would shift ever so slightly, flowing into those voids—to be swallowed by the presence of a Noble Dead.

Wynn wasn't certain how Water would've appeared compared to Spirit, but obviously she wouldn't learn tonight. Then a thought occurred: What if she evoked sight of Spirit, as she'd done a few times, and then tried to shift it to something else?

Wynn closed her eyes once more.

In a small inn within the Warlands of Leesil's birth, she'd sat alone with Chap in their room. It was in the early days, when her malady was still a mystery. With that memory of Chap's face, Wynn recalled the feel of his fur, her fingers curled in his thick coat, and she opened her eyes again.

Nausea welled in her stomach.

The room turned shadowy beneath the overlaid off-white mist just shy of blue.

Everything, even the stone walls, became doubled, as if variegated blue-white shapes of things overlaid and over-whelmed their real forms. She'd grown accustomed to the queasiness and the vertigo, but they were no less unpleasant for being familiar. Luckily she hadn't eaten yet, and she glanced at the bedside table.

Strongest in the grapes' small nodules, the mist waned within the table's wood and the bed's wool blanket. Only a thin trace showed within the stone walls and the tin of the fluted mug. When she glanced down at her own hands, Spirit glowed strongest within her living flesh.

To see the element of Spirit was part of her curse, if and when she could make it come at all. But if she had to accept this condition as more than just a malady, she needed more from it.

Wynn lifted her eyes to the fluted mug, whispering, "Give me . . . water."

Nothing happened—then a flicker passed. Or had it?

Was that color shift real? Did the blue-white in the grapes melt for an instant . . . to blue-green . . . to a deep teal?

The mist's color surged into cascading shifts as vertigo swelled in Wynn's head.

Blue-white swirled to a yellow-white. She hadn't seen such a color before. Then it turned rapidly to dark amber-red.

Wynn sucked in a sharp breath. "Oh, no . . . not again!"

The mug's shape overlaid with deep black, for the water it held chilled the tin vessel. A dim umber-red blotch covered the bed's blanket, showing the remnants of her body heat from kneeling upon it.

Once before Wynn had briefly glimpsed the element of Fire.

She panicked, flinching away, and turned too quickly. Before she could shut her eyes, her gaze lit upon the desk— and the glow of her cold lamp's crystal.

Searing pain welled through nausea and vertigo, spiking through her eyes into her skull.

Light was a manifestation of Fire.

Wynn grabbed her aching head. Tears leaked through her clenched eyes, as if she'd stared into the sun, and swirling blotches of color played across the backs of her eyelids. Vertigo sharpened, and she knew mantic sight was still with her. She dared not open her eyes.

The last time she'd seen Fire, half the night passed before her altered sight faded on its own.

A knock sounded at her door.

Wynn whimpered under her breath. "Ah, damned dead deities . . . not now!"

She nearly fell over as she shifted. Her head ached so badly she found it hard even to think. A baritone voice called softly from beyond the door.

"Wynn, are you up?"

"Oh, no," she whispered.

The one person in this place who even knew of her malady stood outside. And he was the last person who should see her in this state. He would know exactly what she had been up to.

"Wynn, I can hear you," the voice called, strangely accented and already less than patient. "Enough solitude. Open up!"

Covering her eyes with one hand, she crawled across the cold floor. Her knee suddenly pinned her robe's gray skirt. When she tried to jerk it free, she toppled to her elbows.

In the Farlands she'd worn everything from breeches and hand-me-down shirts to elven pants and tunics. The bulky robe was one more thing to which she hadn't readjusted. She finally reached out blindly for the door, but the latch clacked and the iron hinges grated softly. Something heavy struck her shoulder—the door, of course—and she toppled sideways with a grunt.

Shuffling footsteps followed, then a pause, and then an angry exhale. Someone grabbed her robe's collar and half dragged her across the room. Before she cried out, she was dropped into a sitting position upon the bed's edge.

"You obstinate little fool," his deep voice barked. "I have told you never to do this without my supervision."

Wynn was very tired of being called obstinate, among other things. Before she could spit back a retort, slender fingers peeled her hand from her clenched eyes and settled over her face. With them came the smell of parchment dust and the lingering odor of olive oil and spices she couldn't quite name. A low and breathy chant filled her ears and ended with an exhausted sigh.

"Open your eyes."

Wynn's head still ached and her eyes still burned, but she carefully parted her left eyelid and peeked out.

Colored blotches swam over everything. Then she made out the front of a midnight blue robe and dusky tan hands. She opened both eyes and stared up into the hard glower of Domin Ghassan il'Sänke.

He was tall for a Suman, and, standing so close, he towered over her. His short, glossy hair, the color of pure chocolate, waved slightly upon his forehead where it peeked from beneath the lip of his cowl. The barest flecks of silver showed in those locks. A straight but beaked nose separated his thick eyebrows above bright eyes with irises darker than his skin.

He had become a master among sages long before Wynn was born, and yet his true age was a mystery to her. Only hints of lines showed at the corners of his lively eyes. His cheeks were rough, as if exposed to blowing sands of the great desert separating the northern Numan Lands from the great Suman Empire to the far south. And he didn't wear the light gray of Wynn's Order of Cathologers, those who studied in the Realm of Knowledge.

Domin Ghassan il'Sänke was garbed in midnight blue, for he belonged to the Order of Metaology.

As the smallest of the orders, and perhaps the most enigmatic, they focused upon the Realm of Existence. They gathered and recorded information concerning metaphysics and cosmology, cultural religions and myths, and even magic.

Il'Sänke made most young sages uncomfortable, even those attending his seminars given as a visiting domin of note. But not Wynn—or at least not often. No one knew him well, for his guild branch lay half a continent south in Samau'a Gaulb, the capital of the Suman Empire and that of il'Dha'ab Najuum, one of its nations. Il'Sänke was a mage of thaumaturgy—by spellcraft, ritual, or artificing— and was well acknowledged for his skill.

His mouth tightened, and he didn't look pleased.

Despite her state of suffering, Wynn couldn't help a wave of anxious anticipation. It sharpened when her gaze fell upon a narrow bundle of plain muslin cloth lying on the bed beside her.

"It's finished . . . finally?" she asked without even greeting him.

She reached for the bundle, but il'Sänke grabbed it first.

"Premin Sykion will have harsh words," he said in his smooth accent, "when she sees the final accounting of resources and funds—at least those I listed. Then, of course, there's Premin Hawes."

Wynn didn't care what her order's leader or the head of metaology had to say on the matter. She fidgeted impatiently until il'Sänke unrolled the bundle, and she drew another quick breath.

Resting in the opened cloth was a six-sided crystal, pure

and clear as polished glass. Two fingers in thickness, it was longer than her outstretched hand.

Wynn was still holding her breath as she grabbed the crystal from his hand. She instantly began rubbing it furiously, as she would to initiate a cold lamp crystal.

But nothing happened.

"Contain yourself!" il'Sänke chided. "Even when it is finished, friction's heat will not be enough to awaken the 'sun crystal.'"

Wynn's mouth turned dry at those final two words.

It didn't matter if il'Sänke thought her foolish, or that most sages here viewed him as a mysterious outsider. He had listened to her wild tales of the Farlands without judgment—the same tales that Domin High-Tower and others dismissed as nonsense. Many of her peers now viewed her as an outsider as well. Ironic, considering she'd grown up in this branch of the guild.

Staring into the lightless crystal was like looking at an open blank book. And across its unmarred pages she could see words she didn't wish to write.

Not names, places, and events of her time in the Farlands, but words for the fear that made her desperate for il'Sänke to finish what she'd asked from him.

Years ago as an apprentice she'd taken leave of her home to follow her master, Domin Tilswith. They traversed their continent and crossed the eastern ocean to the Farlands, where Domin Tilswith intended to found a new guild branch in the city of Bela. The prospect had been thrilling, and she'd been pleased with this adventure—until the day her life tangled with two hardened strangers and a dog. In that city, Magiere, Leesil, and Chap had come to the old barracks, claiming to be hunting an *upír.*

A vampire, in their language—one of what they called the undead . . . the Noble Dead.

All too soon Wynn had faced realities she'd never imagined nor wanted. When this trio left Bela in search of an ancient artifact sought by a powerful undead, Domin Tilswith had sent her with them—as a journeyor on her first solo assignment. Their travels took them through the dank lands of Droevinka, and through Stravina and into the Warlands on their way to the Elven Territories of the an'Cróan. The journey's last leg ended far south in the Pock Peaks' high, desolate range. There they'd finally uncovered the artifact—the "orb."

Hidden within an ancient castle, it was guarded by a female vampire so old that she'd forgotten the sound of spoken words. Li'kän had waited there for a thousand years or more, and was perhaps one of the first Noble Dead of the world.

In that place locked in ice and snow, Wynn and Chap had dug through a library filled with ancient texts written in languages or dialects either dead or long forgotten. Some of the writings were garbled mixes of tongues that echoed the chaos and madness of Li'kän's fragmented mind. Wynn and Chap had struggled to choose what to carry away amid an overwhelming amount that was left behind. Upon their return to Bela, Domin Tilswith gave Wynn the task of bearing those texts safely back to Calm Seatt.

She accepted willingly but with sadness at leaving her old master—as well as others she might never see again.

Magiere, Leesil, and Chap had sailed with her, bringing the orb. The ocean voyage was long, and traveling the middle continent even longer and more dangerous. The entire journey encompassed the better part of a year. Her friends remained by her side until the city of her childhood was within sight—then they parted ways, to Wynn's pained regret.

She'd thought they were bringing the orb to her guild's home branch, at least to seek counsel from her superiors. But something had changed along the way, something she hadn't been told—and which had likely been all Chap's doing. He, Magiere, and Leesil were to take the orb into hiding, someplace safe from those who might still seek it out.

Wynn tried to deny their concerns. Magiere remained adamant that none of the sages would be safe with the orb in their midst. That had been a very bitter argument. But in the end Wynn reentered the city of her youth, alone among the caravan.

She'd delivered the ancient texts to the guild's first branch; she believed they were penned by ancient vampires from the time of the Forgotten History and the mythical great war. She sought solace among like-minded scholars.

But nothing had turned out as she expected.

The texts, as well as all of her journals, were taken and locked away. She was most stunned by the confiscation of the latter. She hadn't seen them since. And no one believed even the lesser of her tales.

When she grew insistent, the other sages kept their distance, as if she were sick in the mind and contagious. Domin High-Tower, a master of her order, chastised her and insisted she stop telling "wild tales" of undead, dhampirs, and superstitious nonsense.

For a while Wynn had tried to remain obedient.

She'd never been—felt—so alone. Eventually she couldn't stand it any longer.

She pressed her accounts of powerful undead, of subterfuge and meddling from the Anmaglâhk, and Most Aged Father's obsession that a long-forgotten Ancient Enemy was stirring in the world. And the more she said, and the more she was denied and shunned, the more her fears overwhelmed her from within.

Memories came as nightmares that wouldn't ease, but no one listened to "Witless" Wynn Hygeorht anymore. No one except quiet, watchful, sardonic Ghassan il'Sänke, another outsider in a place she thought was home. But even that didn't keep her from dwelling on her inadequacies compared to the strengths of her missing friends.

Magiere, a dhampir born of a mortal mother and a vampire father, had a nature akin to a Noble Dead. Leesil, half-elven with the sharp senses of his mother's people, had been trained as an assassin. And Chap, a born-Fay in a majay-hì's large form, had awareness like no other living being. Each had their way of dealing with the undead, and together they had sent many to ashes.

What did Wynn have to match them? Nothing.

So she had gone to il'Sänke with a wild notion.

She asked—begged—for his help, as he was the only one who might achieve her request. Rather than the cold lamp crystals made by her guild with notable effort and cost, she needed light of a different nature.

Wynn wanted sunlight—to shield herself from the dark and all that moved in it, including the Noble Dead that no one else here believed in.

That night, Domin il'Sänke had just stared at her.

The look on his dusky tan face made Wynn's doubts eat her up inside, until she nearly broke into tears. Was what she asked even possible? It had never been done, to her knowledge, at least not by the few sages with skill in alchemy, a practice of thaumaturgy via artificing.

To make a crystal that could emit light of the same nature as the sun . . .

Waiting upon il'Sänke's reply had been the heaviest silence Wynn could remember. But he never looked at her as if she were mad. When he finally nodded, narrow-eyed and scowling, Wynn almost broke into tears again.

Finally someone believed in her.

Now, sitting upon the bed with the dark-skinned domin, Wynn held up the long crystal.

"Show me . . . how to activate it."

Another disapproving scowl darkened il'Sänke's face. He shook his head with a huff and took the crystal.

"First, it must be properly mounted for handling. I do not think it safe to hold when activated—and it is not yet ready. I and my chosen aides have only completed its physical making . . . after quite a few unsatisfactory results. Now I must work upon it myself . . . prepare it . . . and only then teach you its use."

Wynn's mouth dangled open. "How much longer?"

Il'Sänke arched one thick eyebrow.

"Sorry," she said. "It's just taken so long, but I'm grateful for your effort and faith in me."

Domin il'Sänke rewrapped the crystal and slipped it inside his robe. "Then as repayment, you will come out among your peers. Play at cards, discuss local politics, drink tea, anything besides this self-imposed cloister."

Wynn quickly shook her head. "No, no, I'm . . . I have things to work on privately."

"No, you do not!" he answered sharply. "Not without my supervision. If only I could find a way to remove your . . . talent."

At that Wynn turned narrow-eyed herself.

He was the only one here who knew of her malady, and she noticed the glistening of his brow. Shutting off her mantic sight hadn't been easy on him, even as an adept mage. Not as it had been for Chap, with his Fay nature.

When she'd first told il'Sänke, he'd seemed anxious and angry, immediately suggesting he try to "cure" her. She'd hesitated, and then refused. That didn't please him, and he insisted she not tamper with her sight except under his supervision.

He'd said "could" and not "should" concerning removing her mantic sight. Had he been trying something behind her back?

Il'Sänke placed a hand behind her shoulder and propelled her toward the door.

"Your *work* can wait. Come."

Annoyed at being forced from privacy, Wynn couldn't think of a polite refusal. Not after all his efforts on her behalf. She allowed herself to be escorted into the outer stone passage.

Along the hallway they passed other doors to small chambers of other apprentice and journeyor sages. They headed down the far narrow stairs and out an old oak door. Entering the castle's inner courtyard, il'Sänke herded her to the same double doors she'd watched from her window. When the domin pulled one door wide, warm air with a thin taint of smoke, and the sounds of voices, spilled out around Wynn.

Even in her hesitation, il'Sänke waited patiently until she stepped into the entryway. She followed as he headed left down the passage leading into what had once been half of the castle's old great hall.

In spite of everything since Wynn's return, she loved this *place*—this old fortress. Over four centuries past, the first rulers of Malourné had resided here, when Calm Seatt had barely been a city. But they'd embarked upon plans for a new and greater castle. The royal court moved in, and this first castle became a barracks for the country's armed forces.

Two centuries later, Queen Âlfwine II saw a need for

something *more*. Several scholars of history thought she desired a more lavish residence, while others claimed that—like her descendants—she wanted a place where she could view the sea. Those of the royal bloodline had always shown a strange attraction to the open waters, even unto tragedy. To this day no one knew why the sea called to the family of Âreskynna. Even their name meant "kin of the ocean waves."

Âlfwine II oversaw designs of an elaborate castle closer to Beranlômr Bay. The nation's armed forces, including a newly established city guard to augment the constabularies, moved to the vacated second castle. The first castle—by far the oldest and smallest—was given over to the early beginnings of the Guild of Sagecraft.

And since that time, with the help of the dwarves across the bay in Dhredze Seatt, who had lent their legendary stonecraft to the building of all three fortifications, the first castle was modified to meet the sages' needs. New buildings were attached to the main keep's exterior in its inner bailey.

The keep of the guild's castle was a hollowed square, its inner courtyard surrounded by the outer walls, with inner buildings flush against them. The round corner towers were now used for the offices and studies of domins and premins. Wynn's room was located on the second floor of the old barracks to the courtyard's southeast side.

"Perhaps some cinnamon bread is left over from this morning?" il'Sänke mused, stepping ahead of her.

Wynn almost smiled. The Suman sage had a fondness for spiced cakes and breads, perhaps missing his homeland more than he acknowledged. Down the passage, they rounded a main archway into a great hall.

Here the royals of Malourné once entertained guests of high birth and visiting dignitaries. But the space was now the guild's common hall, filled with a variety of mismatched tables and chairs, stools and benches. It was used for everything from off-hour meals and light studies to leisure pursuits and social gatherings. As a child Wynn had spent happy evenings here, with the enormous hearth in the back wall blazing with piled logs. The royal family was generous in increasing the guild's yearly budget.

Tonight, twenty-plus sages of lesser rank milled about the hall. Most were initiates in their plain tan robes, while others were likely apprentices, garbed in the colors of their chosen orders. It was difficult to know if anyone was a journeyor like Wynn, but few such remained at the guild unless awaiting assignment abroad.

Nearly everyone looked up as Wynn entered with Domin il'Sänke. No one called a greeting, and Wynn wished she'd stayed in her room.

Aside from those who thought her somewhere between addled and half-mad, others considered her "above herself" as a journeyor. Even sages weren't beyond envy, considering that she'd returned home bearing the greatest scholarly find in the guild's history. And worse, no one but the domins and premins even knew what the find entailed.

Wynn had few, if any, friends here, and privacy was becoming a standing habit. Her gaze settled for an instant upon a stooped young sage wearing the gray robes of a cathologer.

"Nervous" Nikolas Columsarn sat reading by himself in the hall's near right corner. Even sitting, he kept his shoulders turned inward, as if he curled into himself. Straight, unkempt brown hair fell forward to nearly cover his eyes and shadow his sallow features.

How could he read like that? Wynn knew his name only from hearing it, but she'd noticed him a few times. His only companions were two young journeyors he occasionally tagged along behind. More often he kept to himself, as Wynn did.

Il'Sänke ignored all the staring or averted eyes and headed straight through for the hearth.

"We shall pull chairs by the fire," he said, "and arrange for tea. Hopefully something other than the weak stuff you drink here in the north."

Wynn sighed, about to follow, and a voice like grating granite rose behind her.

"Ghassan, you are back."

Wynn flinched, reluctant to even turn about.

There in the arched entryway stood the broad form of Domin High-Tower. It wasn't his family name; dwarves preferred to be called by their given names, usually translated into Numanese to keep inept humans from bumbling over the Dwarvish language.

Wynn had read ancient folklore of the Farlands that spoke of dwarfish beings as diminutive. She knew better firsthand, having grown up in Calm Seatt.

High-Tower, like all of his people, was an intimidating hulk compared to such myths. Though shorter than humans, most dwarves could look her directly in the eyes. What they lacked in height they made up for in breadth. High-Tower had to turn sideways to get through any standard human doorway. His shoulder width was more than half again that of a man.

Stout and wide as he was, even under a gray robe he showed no hint of fat. Coarse, reddish hair laced with gray hung to his shoulders, blending with his thick beard braided at its end. His broad, rough features made his black-irised eyes seem like iron pellets embedded in his pale and lightly freckled face. Wynn always thought of a moving column of granite whenever she heard his voice or heavy footsteps.

Though she would never say so aloud, she thought that long, straight-cut wool robes were hardly flattering to the dwarvish form. High-Tower's people were more impressive in their breeches, iron-shod boots, and thick leather clothing.

"Back?" il'Sänke replied politely.

High-Tower entered like a war machine, moderate but steady, and no one would dare step in his way. He glanced at Wynn with scantly concealed disapproval and folded his barrel-like arms to look up at il'Sänke. The master cathologer made no secret of his dislike for the visiting Suman sage.

"Yes, I saw you go out earlier," High-Tower said, "and was wondering if you had seen Jeremy or Elias about. They were due back a while ago with a folio."

Il'Sänke blinked once and seemed to contemplate his answer, and Wynn wondered why he'd gone out after dark. Upon returning he must have gathered the crystal and come straight to her room.

"I saw no one from the guild while out," he answered. "I was hurrying to reach the docks with a letter to my home branch. But I arrived too late. The port office was closed, and there was no way to find any ship going as far as the Suman coast."

Domin High-Tower frowned. "You waited to take it yourself? Why not send an apprentice earlier?"

Il'Sänke didn't need to answer. He'd been called to assist with translating Suman passages of the texts Wynn brought back, but he'd come to Calm Seatt with no apprentices or attendants. High-Tower knew this but goaded him just the same.

Il'Sänke smiled with another cock of one eyebrow. "The walk was welcome after a long day in stillness. You might consider it yourself—or even a night's row in the bay."

High-Tower snorted, and Wynn glanced away.

Really, such a jest was in poor taste. Dwarves walked everywhere they went, as few mounts could hold them up. As for a leisure boat trip, no dwarf cared to be on water. Even without armor or weapons, they sank.

Before either could exchange another barb, two apprentices in gray bolted through the entry. Wide-eyed and panting, they never got out a word before someone strode in purposefully on their heels.

Tall with long tangled hair, the man wore a red tabard over his chain mail vestment and padded hauberk. As frightened as the apprentices appeared, his expression was twisted somewhere between anger and anguish. The man's sword sheath was embellished with an inlaid panel of silver engraved with the royal crest and a panorama of Calm Seatt.

His red tabard marked him as military, but the silver plate suggested more. This one was an officer in the Shyldfälches—the "People's Shield"—the contingent of the city guard.

Wynn had no idea why he was chasing two apprentice sages of her order.

"Where is the premin of cathologers?" he demanded.

Both young sages stepped aside as Domin High-Tower closed on the officer.

"Why do you seek the premin?" the dwarven sage demanded with twice the officer's force.

The man calmed slightly. "Pardon . . . I'm Lieutenant

Garrogh. Captain Rodian sent me to bring either the premin . . . or a domin of the cathologers. Two bodies were discovered in an alley. The master of the nearby scribe shop
identified them, but only knew their given names . . . Elias
and Jeremy."

Murmurs of shaky voices rose in the common hall, and
Wynn heard a stool scrape as someone stood too quickly.

"Bodies?" High-Tower growled. "They are dead?"

Wynn's mind blanked as others in the hall drew nearer.
She barely noted the varied degrees of shock and fright
on their faces. She didn't recognize the names mentioned,
even when a frightened, breathy voice repeated them.

"Jeremy . . . Jeremy Elänqui . . . and Elias Raul?"

Nikolas surged from his corner stool, his face paler than
usual. At the lieutenant's continued silence, his gaze wandered and he began to shiver, backing toward his corner.
When he dropped upon the stool he teetered, nearly slipping off. His jaw clenched as tears rolled down, shaken out
of him by his shudders.

Wynn's thoughts cleared. Nikolas knew them both, likely
the same two she had seen him with. But try as she might,
she couldn't remember their faces.

Lieutenant Garrogh licked his lips nervously at all the
attention he'd drawn in his haste.

"My condolences," he said quickly to High-Tower. "But
the captain requires an authority from the guild. By your
robe, you'll do as well as the premin."

High-Tower's dark glower broke. He turned his iron eyes
on one apprentice who'd led the lieutenant inside.

"Find Premin Sykion immediately. She may be in the
new library. Inform her where I have gone . . . and why."

He waved Garrogh out and followed.

Without a word, Domin il'Sänke went after High-Tower,
and Wynn didn't hesitate to tail him. But when they reached
the wide doors into the courtyard, High-Tower realized
they were following. He planted himself, and a vibration
shuddered through the courtyard's stones.

Wynn pulled up short as the lieutenant slid to a halt. But
she had no intention of being left behind.

"One of us is not enough," il'Sänke said quietly. "I am

the only other of rank at hand. There will be much to deal with in this grave matter."

It made sense, though Wynn knew that if High-Tower were less pressed, he would've chosen someone else.

Lieutenant Garrogh backed toward the castle's gatehouse tunnel. Still seething, High-Tower resumed following. Wynn sneaked along behind il'Sänke, a little more than relieved. Trying to get past a dwarf, once he was planted upon the earth, was harder than battering through a stone wall with one's own head.

Two young sages returning a translation folio had been found dead in an alley. And that folio had contained material from the texts she'd brought back. She didn't *want* to see the bodies, to learn how they'd died or why.

She *had* to—her fears demanded it.

CHAPTER 2

Siweard Rodian, captain of the Shyldfälches, rocked on his heels as he stared down into a young, ashen, dead face. Another body lay crumpled nearby in the dead end's corner. Neither victim bore any cuts or bruises, and he saw no signs of a struggle, except a piece from the robe's shoulder of the nearest body had been torn off.

The eyes of both young sages were open wide, and their faces . . .

Both expressions were locked in similar twisted fear—no, outright terror—with mouths gaping, as if their last scream had never come out. Their hair looked faintly grayed, aged in an instant. Though he'd seen sudden fright and trauma produce such symptoms in men, particularly after the worst of battles, he'd never seen this in ones so young.

Rodian was at a loss for where to begin. He wasn't even certain how much he should disturb the scene.

Murders happened in most large cities. Unlike petty crimes, left to district constabularies, the dead always fell in his lap. At twenty-eight, he was notably young for his position. He knew it, though he'd certainly earned the honor. And in the three years since taking command of the Shyldfälches, he'd learned that most murders were motivated by revenge or passion. Only a few came from panic, when some unfortunate stumbled upon a culprit engaged in criminal undertakings.

Serious poverty wasn't rampant in Calm Seatt. Even pickpockets and muggers were less common than elsewhere. The royal family kept the people's welfare at heart. Funding to help the poor and homeless was made available whenever possible.

But Rodian had never seen anything like this.

He would have to report these deaths by dawn to the minister of city affairs. By noon at the latest the king and queen would hear of it. Malourné's royals took pride in the guild, founded by their ancestors.

Shaken, angry, even anxious, he felt overwhelmed. He needed to resolve this quickly.

And where was Garrogh?

Guards of the local district's constabulary had blocked both alley entrances. Two of his own men stood at the turn into the dead end. And one more stood close, holding a lantern to light the scene.

There were also two civilians present.

Master Pawl a'Seatt, owner of the nearby scriptorium, had found the bodies. Behind him, clinging to his arm, was a dark-haired girl named Imaret—in his employ. She wept in silence, her eyes locked wide as she stared at the bodies. Now and then she looked up to her tall employer, who ignored her.

Rodian felt sick inside that he had to keep the girl this close for so long.

"You found them . . . just like this?" he asked. "You didn't move or touch anything?"

Master a'Seatt seemed neither shocked nor unsettled by the sight.

"I touched nothing," he answered. "I found them and sent word to the constabulary. In turn, they called for the guard."

Rodian lowered his head, studying the bodies in their long gray wool robes. They wore the color of an order as opposed to the bland tan of initiates. But he couldn't remember which order. Too young to be masters, they were still old enough to be apprentices, perhaps even journeyors.

And as to how they had died . . .

His best guess was poison. Something quick, but cheap and common, considering they'd died in such agony. But why would anyone poison two would-be scholars? And why poison, if this was murder spawned by the culprit's panic at being discovered? It wasn't done with some toxin-laced weapon, since he could find no wounds.

"Sir?"

Rodian lifted his head at the familiar voice rolling along the alley walls. Garrogh pushed through, ushering in three robed figures.

Lieutenant Garrogh was a good man, quick and efficient, though waiting here had eroded much of Rodian's patience. Perhaps now he could begin finding answers. Then he spotted Pawl a'Seatt watching the newcomers.

The hint of a serious frown spread across a'Seatt's features—the first real expression Rodian had observed on the man's face.

A determined, solid-looking dwarf in a gray robe led the new trio, followed by a tall, slender man with dark skin in a deeper-colored robe. As the latter entered the lantern's light, Rodian spotted him as Suman, and his robe was a blue shade near to black. The last of the trio was a young woman in gray. As the dwarf's gaze settled upon the bodies, sorrow broke his stern features, then quickly turned to frightened anger.

"*Bäynœ, vastí'ág ad,*" he whispered like a prayer.

The Suman released a long sigh and held his arm back.

"There is nothing for you to see here," he said, beginning to turn.

But the young woman shoved his arm aside and peered into the alley's dead end.

"No . . . not here!" she breathed, each word rising in force. "Not so far from . . ."

She lunged into the dead end and fell upon the first body before Rodian could stop her. Grabbing its head, she tore back the robe's cowl.

"Wynn, no!" the dwarf commanded.

Everyone flinched at his thunderous voice in the alley's small space—except for the young woman. Rodian reached for her as she wrestled to tear open the robe's neckline. The instant he touched her shoulder she lashed wildly at him, striking his hand away.

"Wynn!" the Suman snapped. "This is not the way!"

Rodian glanced at the man, but his attention shifted to Pawl a'Seatt.

The scribe master had stepped closer. As he peered around the two elder sages, his stoic expression filled with intensity. He watched the young woman's furious struggles with the body, and her actions seemed both to surprise and fascinate him.

Rodian reached again for Wynn as Garrogh closed in on her other side. To his shock she rolled the victim's head from side to side, pulling down the robe's collar as she pawed at his throat and chest.

"No blood?" she whispered between rapid breaths. "No wounds . . . no blood?"

Rodian halted Garrogh with a raised hand. He'd already memorized every aspect of the scene, so what was the young woman looking for?

"Did you find them like this?" she blurted suddenly, but she didn't look up. "Did anyone see what killed them?"

"They were found by Master a'Seatt and one of his scribes," Rodian answered. "And neither saw . . ."

He never finished, for his answer wouldn't have matched her question.

She hadn't asked *who*—but rather *what*—had killed members of her guild. There was something telling in her strange choice of words. In her frantic pawing, was she looking for a cause of death, something she'd expected but hadn't found?

Master a'Seatt stepped yet closer, watching her every move. Imaret remained half-hidden behind him.

"No teeth marks," the small sage whispered.

"Wynn!" a deep voice grated. "That is enough!"

The dwarf hurried in and grasped her upper arms from behind.

"No!" she shouted, struggling in his grip. "Look at them! I told you! Can't you see? Domin il'Sänke, look!"

The sage in dark blue only whispered, "Come away from there."

The dwarven sage heaved her up like a light bolt of cloth. He turned fully around before setting her upon her feet, and then Rodian got a clear look at the young woman's face.

Wispy brown hair hung loose past her shoulders. Her round olive-toned face was streaked with tears, and her small mouth quivered under quickened breaths.

The dwarf sputtered in embarrassment. "Shush . . . shush now."

Wynn's brown eyes were wild and manic.

"Forgive the outburst," the Suman said to Rodian. "It is the shock of losing our own. . . . I am Domin il'Sänke, and this is Domin High-Tower. Young Wynn is clearly distraught."

The Suman glanced once at Wynn before his eyes returned to the bodies. Beneath a mild sorrow he seemed annoyed, as if some other issue troubled him beyond these deaths.

"Yes," Rodian acknowledged, "but she was searching for something . . . and what was that about teeth marks?"

Domin High-Tower cocked his head.

"She is overwrought," he growled, and then frowned so deeply his face wrinkled from forehead to chin. "She should not have come."

But his gaze roamed the alley floor.

"Did you find a folio?" he suddenly asked, and then he twisted toward Master a'Seatt. "Did they come for it?"

"I put it in their hands," a'Seatt answered. "You have my sympathies."

"What folio?" Rodian asked, for he'd found no such thing in this place.

"Their task," Master a'Seatt answered. "The guild sends us pages of draft work to be copied into final versions. These young men were carrying such back when—"

"Time enough for that later," High-Tower cut in. "Two of ours are dead, and another is beyond herself."

"The pages are missing?" Wynn demanded, and she whipped around, her wild eyes searching the alley floor.

"We do not know what happened yet!" High-Tower growled.

"What more do you need from us?" il'Sänke added. "This is not a place for lengthy discussion."

All of these reactions struck Rodian as bizarre, from the blustering dwarf, to the panic-stricken young woman, to the disturbingly composed sage in blue, who now showed no emotion at all. Behind them stood Pawl a'Seatt, his attention still fixed on young Wynn.

"I will take the bodies for further examination," Rodian answered.

He had many questions, some he hadn't even fully formed as yet. And he wished he had more time to study everyone present. Too many strange reactions had passed too quickly.

"I will arrange interviews at the guild," he added.

"Interviews?" High-Tower echoed. "For what?"

"For a formal inquest. Both victims currently resided at the guild, correct?"

High-Tower opened his mouth as if to argue.

"Yes, come tomorrow morning," Wynn blurted out. "We will expect you."

High-Tower swept her back with one massive arm, and il'Sänke pulled her farther up the alley. A moment of uncomfortable silence followed. But as Wynn back-stepped past Pawl a'Seatt, she cocked her head slightly, looking at him.

The scribe master met her gaze steadily, as if he were the one studying her. Grief-stricken Imaret was still shocked into stillness, except when her eyes flicked nervously up at her employer.

All three sages paused near the alley wall, perhaps waiting to see how the final few moments here played out.

For another breath Rodian watched the scribe master, who passively turned his attention from Wynn as if he'd seen nothing of note.

"I will arrange interviews at your scriptorium as well," Rodian told a'Seatt.

Master a'Seatt glanced his way. "Business will keep me from the shop all day, but Master Teagan will be in. I will not be available until evening."

Rodian frowned but nodded. Hopefully Master a'Seatt

fully understood he was connected to a murder investigation.

"At dusk then," he replied.

Pawl a'Seatt began turning away; then he paused. "Captain, I have some things to attend to at my shop. Could you arrange an escort to take Imaret home?"

"Of course," Rodian answered. "Have her wait with one of the constables at the alley's entrance, and I'll see to it directly."

"My thanks."

Pawl a'Seatt reached down to usher Imaret along. She jumped slightly as his fingers slid across her shoulders. She turned, walking close at his side, right past the three sages.

Rodian didn't bother to watch them go. He had too much to deal with this night.

"Lieutenant, have a cart brought in."

Garrogh was staring at the ashen bodies, and Rodian stepped closer.

As officers of the Shyldfälches, they were uniformed much alike, with their contingent's red tabards over clean chain vestments and padded hauberks. But while Garrogh paid only passing attention to his appearance, Rodian was meticulous, with clean hair cropped short and a close-trimmed beard sculpted across his jaw. In Calm Seatt, appearances counted for much—if one were ambitious.

"Lieutenant," Rodian repeated. "The cart?"

Garrogh finally nodded. "Yes, sir."

He was a hardened soldier, late of the regulars, and it bothered Rodian that his second in command was so unsettled by dead sages. Finally Garrogh turned away from the eerie scene.

"Would you like an escort back to the guild?" Rodian asked Domin High-Tower.

The dwarf blinked. "No, we need no escort."

Il'Sänke nodded politely, ushering Wynn out, and all three headed back toward where the turn into the dead end joined the main alley back to the street.

"I'll arrive before noon tomorrow," Rodian called after them, but no one answered.

As much as he shared his lieutenant's shock over these

ugly murders, he had other concerns. The royals would hear of this soon enough. Ambition and devotion had taken him far, but if he didn't settle this matter quickly and thoroughly, it might ruin him.

Rodian stood alone, but for the guardsman holding the lantern. The closest body lay at a crooked angle with his robe's collar torn open, exposing his throat.

What had Wynn Hygeorht been looking for?

A figure crouched low upon a candle-shop roof.

He watched a cart with two bodies in gray roll from the alley, pulled by city guards in red tabards. Another guard with a close-cropped beard led the way, obviously their superior. All of them paused upon reaching the constables waiting at the intersection. The officer appeared to give orders. With nods, the constables went their way, escorting a young girl, and the guards headed off with the cart. But the officer remained.

Looking one way and then the other along the street, he froze, perhaps watching something farther off. And the cloaked figure upon the roof lifted his hooded head, peering in the same direction.

The bundle he held pinned to the roof suddenly began to slide, and he quickly pressed his hand down on it.

The bearded officer below looked up, and the figure flattened low and still.

He waited in silence, listening. He could hear the officer's breath pause, the click of chain and creak of leather as the man turned around twice. Finally boots clapped slow and steady upon the wet cobblestone, until the sound all but faded. Only then did the figure rise, searching along the street below.

Down the far way, three figures were nearly out of sight: one small woman in gray, a dwarf in a like robe, and a taller man in midnight blue.

And the figure leaned forward, overhanging the eaves, as his gaze fixed on the woman.

That distant glimpse was not enough, but fear of being seen smothered his urge to drop down and follow her. He looked to the bundle he held pinned against the roof's shakes.

And he lifted the leather folio in his gloved hand.

He had barely gotten it out of the alley before the scribe master and the girl arrived. Pulling the strap from its buckle, he whipped the folio's flap open and peered inside. He froze for an instant, then dug furiously about inside of it.

The folio was empty.

Sagging in stunned confusion, the figure reached behind and pulled forward one of two canvas packs. Opening its flap to shove the folio inside, he paused, glancing over his belongings.

Tucked within the pack were old books, some coming apart with age. Two boxes as well, one bound in leather and the other wrapped in cloth. Several short rods of various metal lay askew, leaning against a large hoop of smooth steel with hair-thin etchings. And for an instant he remained fixed upon an age-marred, tin scroll case.

The figure lifted his hooded head, listening a moment for anyone nearby. Then he quickly shifted his belongings, with clinks and clatters, and wedged the empty folio into the pack. Rising up, he hefted both his packs over one shoulder and gazed down the street.

Those three robed sages—man, woman, and dwarf—slipped from sight around the road's gradual curve. And the cloaked figure pulled back his hood, letting raggedly cut red-brown hair swing freely around his narrow pale face.

Chane Andraso stood high in the dark, staring after Wynn.

But she was beyond his widened sight as much as beyond his reach.

Ghassan il'Sänke lingered outside the main archway of the guild's common hall, watching the commotion play out. Half this branch's population was now crowded into that large space. A small sea of initiates in tan robes pressed in toward the mammoth hearth at the hall's far end. Among them were the teal, cerulean, gray, midnight blue, and sienna of apprentices and perhaps a few journeyers of the five orders. Domins and masters of the guild were present as well. And the thrum of agitated voices echoed out over Ghassan.

He had no wish to answer questions, either those of the premins or the curious and fearful gathered about. High-Tower could face that task. The dwarf's sharp brevity, though unsatisfying to some, might quell morbid fascination and fear among the guild's populace. And more likely, High Premin Sykion would not let things go too far. Discussion of unpleasant details would be held until privacy was achieved.

But still, Ghassan wanted to know what was said—and thought.

And how much anyone suspected regarding the deaths of two young sages and the missing folio of passages from the ancient texts. How would the sages of this guild branch react?

Frustration cracked his self-control in a sharp exhale.

If only he had found a way to remove the texts and taken them to his branch far south. These Numans were ill-suited for protecting the ancient writings, regardless that this was the guild's founding branch. Compared to his own branch, this castle was still a tiny place in the world.

High-Tower was hard to spot amid the crowd, but he was somewhere near the hearth. Wynn would be close by as well. Then one of the dwarves' broad hands rose above the thickened forest of cowled heads as he bellowed for silence.

Ghassan pitied him—almost.

The stout domin was the perfect example of a solid, pragmatic dwarf, who preferred each day's schedule to follow an ordered and efficient regimen. The potential for chaos in the hall would be torture for him—as much as for those behind him.

All five of the Premin Council, leaders of the five orders, stood scattered along the great hearth's front ledge.

Premin Sykion looked uncomfortable, even a little shaken. She raised a narrow hand, echoing High-Tower's gesture, and her reedy voice lowered the rumble in the hall.

"Please, we have told you all we know. We hope to learn more tomorrow. But for now there is nothing more."

Some of the crowd drew back, taking up seats at benches and stools, while others drifted toward the exits with low and fervent murmurs.

At more than sixty years, Sykion was as slender as a solitary palm tree on a grassy shore, and perhaps slightly bent like one under the wind of a gathering storm. The gray robe of a cathologer suited her serene demeanor, as well as did her long and braided silver hair. Il'Sänke respected her position but otherwise had no opinion of her. As premin of cathology at Calm Seatt, and high premin of the branch's council, she had been the one to request his extended stay.

Môdhrâfn Adlam, premin of naturology, stood closest to her. At a break in the crowd il'Sänke saw a handful of brown-robed apprentices gather near him, as if seeking his protection.

Ghassan snorted.

Môdhrâfn's given name meant "proud raven." Odd as it was for a Numan name to refer to an animal, he supposed it suited the head of naturology here, those who studied the natural world. Still, "prideful" would have been a better translation.

"How did they die?" young Nikolas asked, his voice trembling.

Ghassan hadn't even noticed him before. In general, Nikolas Columsarn never warranted much note. He was usually hiding in some corner with hunched shoulders, like a mouse watching for a cat. As he had been now, before stepping into sight around the archway's side.

High-Tower cleared his throat. "The captain of the guard has made no determination, but with no visible injuries ... it appears they may have been poisoned."

"Poisoned?" a clear voice called too loudly.

There was a hint of contempt behind its fear, and Ghassan shifted his gaze to Wynn.

She stood just beyond High-Tower at the hearth's left end, her arms crossed as if she were cold.

Domin High-Tower glared at her. "No one needs to hear any more of your nonsense!"

He had tried to say this under his breath, but the words still carried. Wynn straightened and held High-Tower's eyes with hers.

"They weren't poisoned," she said. "Even so ... whoever killed them took a folio completed this day at Master a'Seatt's shop. What did you send to have copied? What was in those pages?"

"Their deaths had nothing to do with their task!" High-Tower snapped. "Some thug killed them, and merely took anything found."

"A common thug . . . using poison?" Wynn returned coldly. "Where's the sense in that?"

Premin Sykion stepped along the hearth toward Wynn.

"You are tired and overwrought, my dear, and it grows late." She looked around at the remaining hesitant faces. "Everyone should rest. There is nothing more to discuss."

Sykion's hazel eyes grew sad in her gaunt, lined face.

"A great tragedy happened tonight, but as Domin High-Tower suggests, we may yet learn it was a random act that took our brothers from us."

Muttering softly, the last of the initiates, apprentices, and masters began to break apart, heading out in small groups. Some passed Ghassan on their way to the front double doors and the courtyard, off to their quarters elsewhere.

Premin Sykion gently steered Wynn toward the main archway.

Ghassan had noted more than once how the premin handled Wynn's outbursts—with sympathy and compassion, versus High-Tower's fuming frustration. But the premin's method had done more to discredit Wynn than the dwarf's ever had. Perhaps Sykion did pity Wynn—as some poor, addle-minded girl, not up to the journey her domin had given her in a faraway land.

But Wynn did not inspire sympathy in Ghassan.

She made him anxious, almost wary, and fear was unusual for him.

He watched Wynn approach, her olive features defeated and disturbed. What did she know, and how much? She stopped when she saw him standing beyond the arched entrance.

"You didn't even come in?"

"I was not needed."

"They're all fools," she whispered. "And yet I'm the wit-less one? Tell me . . . if you're the last sane person in a world of blind lunacy, what does that really make you?"

Ghassan saw no point in playing at intellectual conundrums.

"Is it not possible that Elias and Jeremy were poisoned?" he asked. "Can you not grant that much?"

Wynn's small mouth tightened, and Ghassan thought she might accuse him of being a fool as well. For in a world of fools, the sane and rational were always labeled idiots and madmen.

"I suppose," she said low in anger.

He nodded once. She passed him by, heading silently toward the entry chamber and the great doors.

Ghassan took two silent steps after her, just enough to take him beyond sight of anyone still in the common hall. And he blinked slowly.

In that sliver of darkness behind his eyelids, he raised the image of Wynn's face in his mind. Over this he drew the shapes, lines, and marks of blazing symbols stroked from deep in his memory. A chant passed through his thoughts more quickly than it could have passed between his lips.

Poison indeed! Blindness . . . all of them blind to what I know!

Ghassan il'Sänke finished his blink as the cacophony of Wynn's conscious thoughts erupted in his mind.

They were killed by an undead. . . .

He took care not to sink too deeply. Searching for anything more than surface thoughts could arouse a target's awareness. Even if she wouldn't know what startled her from within, he had no wish to fuel her paranoia—not yet.

I wish Magiere were here. Or Leesil . . . yes, he'd get a good laugh at such a notion . . . as poison for a mugging.

It was difficult to catch anything coherent in her overwrought mind.

How could this thing feed without leaving marks? And why steal the folio? Chap would figure this out. Where are you when I need you?!

Ghassan heard Wynn lift one of the iron ring handles on the double doors—but he did not hear the door open.

How did il'Sänke hear about the poison . . . if he wasn't inside the common hall?

His right hand trembled, perhaps from the strain, and he

reached across to stop it with his other. Wynn believed the deaths were related to the texts . . . those texts that never should have been brought here, never placed in the Calm Seatt branch for translation.

I thought il'Sänke would . . . at least he should've believed me . . . I thought . . . I am so alone.

Ghassan heard the heavy door creak open, and its thud upon closing echoed back down the passageway. Even in Wynn's scattered thoughts, he sensed determination. How far would she go to uncover the truth—either what he already knew or had yet to learn?

How far must he go to stop her?

CHAPTER 3

Just before noon the following day, Rodian urged his exquisite white mare up Old Procession Road toward the bailey gate of the Guild of Sagecraft.

Slender aspen trees now grew inside the castle's inner bailey wall, their high branches overhanging its top. At one time the royals had suggested that the entire wall be removed. The prospect of clear sight of the guild's keep might enhance the impression of accessible knowledge in the city. But the sages had already converted the inner bailey into narrow groves and gardens and natural conservatories—except where additional buildings had been added to the keep's exterior. They feared too many people traipsing through their precious accomplishments. Or so they said.

Rodian had his own perspective. These discomforting scholars coveted secrecy, and he wasn't looking forward to this morning's interviews.

He passed through the inner bailey's gate and headed for the fortification's hulking gatehouse. Before his mount entered the long tunnel to the inner courtyard, a stout young female in a gray robe scurried out.

"Premin Sykion and Domin High-Tower are expecting you, Captain," she said. "I'll see to your horse."

He looked into the young sage's face as he dismounted and handed over the reins. Her eyes struck him as dull and vacant, yet somehow she'd proven adequate enough to become an apprentice. Rodian shook his head as the girl led off his horse, and he headed into the gatehouse tunnel.

All three portcullises were open, not that this place needed such anymore. His footfalls on mortared stone echoed around him until he stepped into the wide and square inner courtyard. Today he wore a cloak over his uniform and kept his sword covered. Had it been possible, he would have sent Garrogh here instead.

Sages, so misguided in their ideals, but Rodian knew the truth of higher learning. Something they did not.

Knowledge belonged to the blessed.

Only those with the highest sentience were suited to the use of the highest knowledge—all for the betterment of those less endowed. Anything else was letting a mule drive the cart, while the carter donned halter and harness. And such knowledge had to be coupled with sound moral reasoning versus blind adherence to codes of ethics. Yes, there were laws and rules to be upheld, for such was his calling, but it wasn't the same thing.

If only more sages, particularly their masters, domins, and premins, would join his own brethren, their service to humanity might one day achieve a greater glory. But there were no sages in his own temple congregation. As much as this was a sorrow to his faith in the Blessed Trinity of Sentience, it was a greater loss to them.

Rodian headed swiftly across the courtyard to the main doors of the large keep. And another young sage opened one door before he'd even touched it.

"Please follow me, sir."

The warmth inside felt welcome, but Rodian steeled himself for a private audience with the premin of catchologers, head of the entire branch. Perhaps any masters or domins who knew the victims would be present as well.

The young sage led him through the entryway, and then turned left down a long passage. A low buzz of voices, footfalls, and other noises carried from ahead, leaving him puzzled. At a wide archway on the right, the boy turned in.

Rodian stepped into a vast common hall where a fire blazed in a great hearth at the rear. Numerous robed figures milled about rough tables, benches, and stools, with books and parchments spread about. Two boys were finishing an early lunch, and everyone looked up.

Rodian exhaled sharply. This wasn't the proper place for questioning.

He ignored curious faces and glanced around until he spotted Domin High-Tower at one long table. The dwarf was muttering gruffly with the tall Suman named il'Sänke. A slight woman in a gray robe stood at the table's head.

Rodian had taken time to review the structure of the guild's orders before setting foot in this place. A long silver braid hung down the woman's back, dangling over the folds of her downed cowl. She was so slender that she might almost disappear from a sideways view. When her head turned, following High-Tower's thick pointing finger, her calm hazel eyes fell on Rodian.

He approached with a respectful nod, expecting her to speak first, but she only held his eyes with her penetrating gaze.

High Premin Sykion—for all the naïveté of sages—had the presence of a calculating intellect.

He cleared his throat, suddenly feeling a need to apologize for the intrusion, but that was a foolish impulse.

High-Tower rose to his feet. "What have you learned?"

Rodian ignored the question, facing only the premin. "I expected a more private meeting. Could we speak in your office?"

Her composure appeared to waver just slightly. "Surely you can give us your report here."

"I think you misunderstand," he offered politely. "I'm here to obtain information regarding the victims, not to make a report."

"What can we possibly tell you that you do not already know?" she asked. "They were attacked in an alley, not here. Would your time not be better spent looking for the murderer?"

Rodian didn't blink nor take offense. Even in his scant years as captain of the city guard, he'd faced such opposition before. Family and friends—even those of superior intellect—rarely understood how a victim's personal life had anything to do with a crime.

"Your office, Premin?" he repeated.

"My study, then," High-Tower intervened.

"Yours is as high up as mine," Sykion returned.

"But closer," he added, then looked to Rodian. "Will that do?"

Rodian nodded, though his attention had drifted elsewhere.

Domin il'Sänke remained silent where he sat. His dark brown eyes, nearly black in the alley, were just as observant now as then. Something about the foreigner's intense dusky features put Rodian on edge, as did the color of his robes—the midnight blue of the Order of Metaology.

Meddlers in the beliefs of others, dabblers in the arcane, who thought they understood a higher reality.

"You come, too," Rodian said.

Il'Sänke cocked his head in acknowledgment, but Premin Sykion intervened in a smooth voice.

"Domin il'Sänke knows nothing of the young cathologers you found dead, as he is not of their order. He is here to provide *me* with additional understanding of what he observed last evening."

"I insist," Rodian returned, "because he *was* there last night." He looked quickly about the hall, scanning those present. "Where's the young woman? I'll speak with her as well."

"Wynn Hygeorht is resting," the premin said. "She is easily troubled and should never have been allowed to witness last night's tragedy."

Sykion's steady gaze cast subtle reproach at High-Tower.

"Very well, later then," Rodian said, stepping back. "Which way?"

High-Tower's habitual scowl deepened, but the stout dwarf turned to lead.

They passed out of the hall's north side, walking in silence through long passages and one turn. When they reached an end door somewhere along the keep's rear, Rodian's best guess was that it opened into the castle's old north tower. They entered the tower's lower chamber.

To his surprise an inner wall had been constructed; the curving stairs ran upward between it and the outer wall. They climbed all the way to the third level, where High-Tower paused before a stout oak door. The domin pushed it open, waiting for others to enter.

Rodian stepped inside.

In older times the room had probably been weapons storage, when the keep housed the earliest royals and their armed forces. From Rodian's brief encounters with the domin, he expected the office to be a disorganized mess. He was not wrong.

The age-darkened old desk was nearly buried in books and papers, and even a few small wooden boxes. One hefty volume with a frayed cloth cover lay open atop the pile. A large cold lamp, its crystal still holding a dim glow, sat on one corner near an old mug filled with stained quills. Stacks of parchment or paper were piled on the floor below short oak bookcases, equally as aged as the desk.

Somewhat somber though not gloomy, the study's inner wall appeared to run flush with the tower's outer one beneath the rising stairs. Three sides of the room had narrow, paned windows set deep into its thick walls. These had once been arrow slits for archers to defend the keep. Through one Rodian had a clear western view of the city over the keep's wall and that of the inner bailey.

The dwarf likely expected perfect order from everyone—including himself—outside this room. But here he did as he pleased. Rodian knew the type.

Not wishing to be seen as herding the others, he stepped aside and waited as Sykion and High-Tower entered. Il'Sänke softly closed the door behind all of them.

"Only two chairs," High-Tower grunted.

Rodian gestured for the premin to sit. He remained standing and pulled a small journal from his belt.

"Have you determined a cause of death?" Sykion asked.

Rodian was careful with his answer. "A healer from the city's hospice examined the bodies this morning." And he had specifically sought one outside of the guild's influence. "His findings are not yet complete," he added.

This was a half lie, and he didn't add that the healer could provide no conclusive findings. If the victims had died by some fast-acting poison, inhaled or absorbed through the skin, the healer found no such evidence. However, Rodian couldn't allow this interview to turn around, making him the one being interrogated.

"Does either young man have blood relatives in or near the city?" he asked.

"No," the premin answered. "Jeremy's family is from Faunier, but his parents have both passed over. Elias's family resides on the western coast, near the free town of Drist. I believe his father is a fisherman. We have already sent word of this tragedy."

Rodian nodded and took a few notes. "I'll need the names of the victims' friends and immediate acquaintances, anyone of close personal attachment, and what their daily routines involved and with whom. Particularly if there were any noted contentions, whether of a personal or professional nature. Also the whereabouts of all such individuals last night."

The premin stared at him.

"This is routine, but necessary," he assured her.

Her thin lips parted once and then closed as she turned her gaze on High-Tower.

The dwarf walked around behind his desk and dropped heavily into a wide chair suitable to his people's bulk. It seemed a bit calculated to make Rodian feel like an initiate or apprentice summoned for a private lecture. High-Tower huffed once.

"All apprentices and journeyors here are friends," he growled. "But they are too busy to be close ... or sweethearts who form attachments. They are here to *study*—not chase each other about like goats in spring." He cleared his throat. "And they do not contend with each other, except in betterment of our pursuits. Proper debate is encouraged as the crucible from which we extract truth. You will get no such list of names here ... as we cannot provide one."

Rodian warmed with an edge of anger.

If these pretentious scholars thought they could stone-wall him, they were seriously mistaken. When he took command of the Shyldfälches, he'd already solved four murders long considered unsolved by his predecessor. He hadn't climbed to his position by being easily waylaid.

"The names will help limit the investigation's scope," he replied dispassionately.

"Are you asking for alibis?" the premin demanded, though the barest hint of worry leaked into her reedy voice.

"Of course," he replied. What had these people expected in a murder investigation? "I assume all three of you were in residence last night?"

"This is outrageous!" High-Tower growled, loudly enough that it reverberated from the walls. "Offensive insinuations . . . and a waste of time!"

"I could ask Lieutenant Garrogh to bring several men to gather this information," Rodian said. "Though that would be more time-consuming—and invasive—they will speak with everyone who lives here. No matter how long it takes. I would prefer to be . . . expedient."

No one spoke for several breaths.

"I was in the new east library with several apprentices," Sykion said, "instructing them in proper tutoring of initiates. Domin High-Tower, I believe, was overseeing cleanup after supper. We do not employ servants here and equally share all daily tasks. Domin il'Sänke—"

"I was out alone," the Suman interrupted, adding with a shrug, "and I have no one to attest to my whereabouts."

Rodian studied him. "You were out after the supper hour? Why?"

"I took a letter to the courier's office at the docks. Just a note to my home branch of the guild."

"The courier's office isn't usually open past dusk."

"The day passed too quickly," he replied. "I lost track of time and hurried but was too late."

"Why not wait until morning?" Rodian countered. "It could take days or more before finding a ship leaving for the Suman coast."

"I heard of one already in port," il'Sänke answered. "I wanted to be sure my letter was aboard for its return trip."

Rodian made another quick note in his journal. It would be easy enough to check whether any vessel was headed that far south. As he was about to press the matter, High-Tower cut in.

"I am certain you can locate citizens who saw il'Sänke near the docks—which are *always* busy, Calm Seatt being the most major port to the north! Now, if there is nothing else, I suggest you—and your men—get to the streets with your questions."

"What were Jeremy and Elias doing out after dark?" Rodian asked. "You seemed anxious last night concerning a 'folio' they'd been carrying."

The room sank into silent tension. Il'Sänke's eyes narrowed slightly, and Rodian caught the slight shift of Premin Sykion's slim shoulders.

"The folio has nothing to do with their deaths," the premin said, calm and poised. "And any regret at its loss is meaningless compared to the lives of our own. The work it held can be redone."

Rodian listened politely to the barest rise of pitch in her voice. He'd struck a sensitive spot.

Perhaps the folio was only a happenstance theft. Perhaps it had nothing directly to do with these deaths. But it did have to do with something of serious concern to these three.

"Last night," Rodian continued, "Master a'Seatt said that you've been sending draft work to his shop for transcription. He handed over a folio to Jeremy and Elias to carry back. What did Master a'Seatt's people copy for you yesterday?"

Domin il'Sänke shifted one step closer. His dark fingers laced together across the front of his waist.

"None of us would know from memory," he answered. "Master a'Seatt's scriptorium is one of several employed in such work. Drafts are sent to multiple scribes' shops in the city."

"Every evening?" Rodian asked.

"At dawn," Sykion answered, appearing too satisfied with il'Sänke's explanation. "The guild is working on a large-scale project. We do have some sages who are skilled in scripting, but we prefer the expertise of the private scribe shops for materials to be added to our libraries and archives."

She paused, pivoting in her seat to face him fully.

"Captain ... this work has proceeded uneventfully for almost half a year, so I see no reason why anyone would now kill for such a theft. Elias and Jeremy were in an unfortunate place at an unfortunate time ... and taken by chance."

A large-scale translation project, going on for nearly six moons?

"What is being translated?" Rodian asked.

"We cannot release that information," il'Sänke answered.

"You will release whatever I ask," Rodian declared. "This is a murder investigation."

Premin Sykion's stern frown deepened the lines of her face.

"If you confer with the city minister to the royal family, you will find the project is under exclusive guild authority. The work is of a sensitive nature. Until we are told otherwise by the monarchy, no information concerning the project will be shared with anyone outside the guild."

Her gaze hardened, as if those politely blunt words were all she need say.

Rodian suppressed frustration.

The guild was highly favored by the royals, as it had been for generations. If the king and queen stood behind the sages, it would be dangerous for him to force the issue, even under rule of law. But the more these three evaded speaking of this project and the folio's content, the more Rodian began to wonder.

How little—or how much—did it have to do with the deaths of two young sages?

"If you can't tell me what is being translated," he tried, "at least you can tell me where and how the materials in question were acquired."

High-Tower rolled his lips inward, turning his eyes on il'Sänke. The Suman seemed uncertain, and Sykion finally shook her head.

"Surely *that* cannot be confidential?" Rodian asked. "If the work is so important, every initiate and apprentice in the guild would know where it came from. Rumors are unbridled things."

"Do not attempt to badger any of them," High-Tower warned, "or I will present a formal complaint . . . and not to the high advocate but to the monarchy itself!"

Rodian was at an end. A tangle of suspicion and frustration choked off any reply. For the moment nothing could be learned here, and he turned to the door. For the span of a breath il'Sänke's darkening expression made him hesitate—then it was gone. Rodian gripped the door latch.

"Have someone send for Wynn Hygeorht—now. I will talk to her alone."

And he pulled the door open.

"Unacceptable!" High-Tower shouted from his desk. "We will not have her bullied by the likes of you! One of the masters will be present."

The dwarf's clear anger brought Rodian a wave of relief.

He much preferred open hostility. Angry people made mistakes, always saying much more than intended. Premin Sykion rose, stepped past him through the door, and headed silently downward.

Rodian glanced back to find both High-Tower and il'Sänke waiting behind him. Obviously they weren't going to even give him a chance at seeking Wynn on his own. He stepped out with both domins close on his heels.

When Sykion reached the turn made on the way to the tower, she motioned to a passing apprentice garbed in the teal of the Order of Conamology, sages who studied in the field of trades, crafts, and practical matters. They also managed the few public schools established by the guild in the king's city. Sykion bent like a willow, whispering in the boy's ear, and the apprentice rushed off with a quick nod.

"I have sent for Wynn," the premin said calmly. "But I agree that she should have someone else present."

She led them out to the entryway, before the large double doors to the courtyard. And Rodian stopped, holding himself in check.

This visit hadn't played out as expected. Misguided or not, he'd believed the sages would want these murders solved—would offer him what assistance they could. Yet they hobbled him, shielded by their favor in the royal court.

All four of them stood in uncomfortable silence until the apprentice burst through the doors.

"Premin . . ." the boy panted. "Journeyor Hygeorht is not in her room. And no one knows where she is."

High-Tower shoved past Rodian toward the boy. "What? Who did you ask?"

Rodian tucked his journal back into his belt, not waiting for the boy's reply. "I will speak with my liaison to the royal family about this—and I'll be back."

With that, he walked out into the courtyard.

For some reason these sages didn't want him speaking with the young woman, obviously driven by desperation beyond protecting a member of their guild. They could hardly be unaware how much more this drew his attention. But before he reached the gatehouse tunnel, a smooth voice called from behind.

"Captain."

Rodian turned to find il'Sänke standing just outside the keep's main doors. Stiff with anger, he stopped and waited.

The tall Suman seemed to float across the flagstones, the hem of his robe barely swishing with his steps. His expression was far too composed for the standoff that had just occurred, and Rodian's instincts cried out in warning.

"What?" he asked sharply.

"Wynn truly is not here. If you wish to stop her from interfering, I suggest you visit the scriptorium of Master a'Seatt. By her nature, I fear she may be looking into this matter on her own."

Rodian paused, absorbing the words. "Why would she do that?"

Il'Sänke shrugged, and his dark hands, fingers still laced before him, separated in a smooth gesture of empty palms.

"Who can say why another does anything? But I would hurry . . . if I were you."

Gritting his teeth, Rodian turned and jogged into the gatehouse's long tunnel, shouting for his horse.

*   *   *

Wynn stood in the street outside the Upright Quill, the scribe shop of Master Pawl a'Seatt. An autumn breeze pulled strands of hair across her eyes. She had always liked this street and could see why Master a'Seatt would choose it for his place of business.

Lined with squares of red stone, worn by years of foot traffic and coastal weather, when wet with rain the cobble glistened like deep burgundy. All shops here bore brightly painted shutters and signs. Rather than a street for needs, it was a place for pleasant wishes.

Citizens could buy a variety of items within the span of a few blocks, from scented candles and ornate stands on which to place them to finely crafted teapots and serving sets. One little bookstore down the way did business in conjunction with the scribe shop, and she could smell aromatic oils sold by a perfumer across the street. Cardamom and lavender were so rich in the air she could almost taste them.

Wynn wished she were sixteen once again, that this were nothing more than another errand for Domin Tilswith. And that she possessed no knowledge of unnatural things that lunged from the dark.

There was still time to abandon her present course. She could return to the guild's warmth and the safety of her room. She could leave all of this to premins, domins, and the city guard.

Wynn took a deep breath and climbed the three steps to the scriptorium's door. A little bell tinkled as she cracked it open.

Amid the warmth inside, a hint of parchment dust tickled her nose, and by comparing the chill outside she realized how quickly autumn was passing. No one was present in the entry room, not even behind the old counter, with its two heavy doors to the shop's rear. A few wooden stands about the room held open books on display with ornate scripting as examples of the shop's work.

"Hello?" she called.

Wynn was trying to decide if she should sneak into the shop's back when the left door behind the counter swung outward.

A small, wizened man wearing round spectacles emerged, looking tired and strained. Startled by the sight of her, he closed the door and looked her up and down.

"Can I help you?" he asked.

His tone didn't suggest eagerness to assist, and Wynn mentally translated his words as, *What do* you *want?* Now that she was here, she hardly knew what to say.

"I'm from the guild . . . ," she began weakly.

He raised one eyebrow, as if to say, *Obviously*.

"I need to speak with someone . . . a scribe," she added. "A girl with dark brown hair, slightly frizzed and curled and—"

"Imaret?"

Wynn didn't know the name but she nodded. The old man's face softened with something close to sadness.

"Come," he said, and opened the other door behind the counter. "I'm Master Teagan. Imaret is working in back."

Wynn had seen Imaret crying last night, which suggested the girl knew Jeremy or Elias. Sages in training occasionally made friends with working scribes, as such connections could be useful later. And it wasn't uncommon for apprentice scribes to seek schooling with the guild.

Master Teagan must have assumed Wynn was another companion come to offer condolences. He flipped open a hinged panel in the counter to let her through, and she suppressed a pang of guilt at her deception.

The scriptorium's rear was quite different from the front. The large back room was filled with tables and desks, chairs and tall stools. Bright lanterns stationed about the room provided ample light as scribes worked upon sheets amid scattered quills, blotting pads, and trimming knives. Shelves lined the back wall around the stout rear door with its iron bar. These were filled to the top with stacks of blank parchment, bottles of ink, jars of drying talc and sand, and other sundry supplies.

Only a few scribes sat at work, and Imaret was easy to pick out.

She sat at the room's far corner behind a short table suitable to her stature. That by itself showed she was an exception here, aside from her surprising age. What professional scriptorium would have such a young girl working as a scribe?

But Imaret wasn't scribing anything.

She stared blankly at her tabletop, quill poised in stillness above a blank sheet. She seemed locked in a moment other than here and now, as if time had stopped.

Wynn approached, and Imaret finally looked up. Her eyes widened with two blinks. On instinct Wynn lifted one finger to her lips. She didn't wish for Imaret to gasp.

Master Teagan hung nearby, but he leaned over to check the work of another scribe.

"You were there . . . last night," Imaret said loudly enough to be heard throughout the room.

Master Teagan glanced over with a confused frown.

Lying didn't come easily to Wynn. "My name is Wynn . . . and Jeremy and Elias were my friends at the guild."

Imaret's dark eyes turned glassy and wet. One tear spilled down her brown cheek.

"I thought so, when you became so . . . They were my friends, too. And Nikolas. Is he all right? I thought he'd come today."

Wynn didn't know how Nikolas fared, but she stored Imaret's question for later.

"Much of the guild is in mourning. We'd like to know more of what happened last night, to try to ensure the safety of our messengers. Were you here when Jeremy and Elias arrived?"

"Yes, just me and Master Teagan . . . and Master a'Seatt."

Imaret spoke the last name so softly that it caught Wynn's attention the most. Her next question was risky, but she blurted out, "How did Master a'Seatt come to find Jeremy and Elias in the alley?"

The bell over the door in the front room tinkled.

Imaret lowered her voice. "He asked them to verify the folio's delivery, but after they'd been gone a short while he seemed . . . bothered. He kept pacing, and . . ."

Wynn waited, and Imaret glanced at the back door. "And?" Wynn finally said.

"He kept looking at the back door, but he never opened it. Then he just stopped suddenly and stared at the wall."

Imaret's gaze shifted, and Wynn glanced along the girl's line of sight. But she saw nothing except the back room's far wall beyond the end of the storage shelves.

"Then he grabbed his cloak and told me not to leave the shop." Imaret trembled slightly. "He rushed out the back . . . and didn't even stop to lock the door."

"What's this all about?" Master Teagan sputtered.

Wynn straightened. She'd learned a thing or two about keeping up a lie from watching Leesil.

"Two of our people are dead, and the folio in their charge is missing. Domin High-Tower wishes to know the events beforehand."

"Then why didn't he come himself?"

"We are in mourning, and he has greater matters to attend. I'm Journeyor Wynn Hygeorht."

Teagan blinked, his pupils exaggerated by his thick-lensed glasses. And Wynn could tell he recognized her name.

Perhaps he knew she was the one responsible for the current wealth of scribe's work—and good payment. Domin High-Tower and Premin Sykion had warned her against speaking to anyone concerning what she'd brought back. But of course there were many at the guild who already knew she was the one who had caused so much "fuss" for the last half year.

Teagan's scraggly eyebrows wrinkled, but he finally grumbled off to check on the other scribes. Wynn turned her attention back to Imaret.

"So . . . Master a'Seatt became worried about the length of their absence and went after them?"

"Yes," Imaret said, her eyes growing distant. "I knew Jeremy and Elias had plans to meet up with . . . other friends. I thought they might deliver the folio and ignore Master a'Seatt's request for confirmation, so I decided to go after them. And I left the shop."

Wynn sighed. Aside from Imaret disobeying her employer, a young girl shouldn't be wandering about alone at night.

"Then I heard a scream," Imaret whispered. "I didn't know where it came from until I heard footsteps . . . in the side street down the way."

Imaret choked off, and Wynn put her hand gently on the girl's shoulder.

"I went to look . . . and saw them," the girl whispered, "but he was there . . . Master a'Seatt was already there."

"That is quite enough!" Master Teagan sputtered. "If Domin High-Tower wants any more morbid details, he can damn well—"

"Speak with me," a deep voice cut in, "after my investigation is complete."

Wynn jerked upright.

Captain Rodian stood in the workroom's doorway, glaring at her.

How long had he been listening? He wasn't due at the shop until evening, as Master a'Seatt had requested. Rodian strode across the room, his swinging cloak dragging a few parchments from an unattended table.

"Mistress Hygeorht, is it?" he demanded. "What are you doing here?"

In last night's fear and sorrow, she hadn't taken much note of him.

At first nothing about him stood out. Of medium height and build, he wore the typical garb of the Shyldfälches, but beneath his open cloak his red tabard was carefully pressed. His cropped hair was an almost colorless shade of dark blond, but the slightly darker close beard along his jawline was perfectly trimmed. His eyes struck her the most—large for the rest of his face and a light shade of blue.

Wynn swallowed and calmed herself. He would be just like Premin Sykion or Domin High-Tower—another obstacle to the truth.

"I'm asking after dead friends and our lost folio," she answered. "Is that against the law?"

"That depends upon circumstances . . . or any interference in my investigation."

He glanced once at little Imaret, then turned his heated suspicion past Wynn to Master Teagan. The old scribe returned it in kind for another unwelcome outsider. The captain appeared to compose himself.

"Forgive the intrusion," he said, but it hardly sounded apologetic. "I've just come from the guild, though no one there seems able to tell me what was in the folio that Jeremy and Elias carried. Perhaps one of you can help."

And his gaze settled back on Wynn.

Both Teagan and Imaret frowned in unison.

"Did the sages not explain about their script?" Teagan asked.

"No," Rodian returned, but he never took his eyes off of Wynn.

Wynn grew nervous, then agitated, and then angry over being scrutinized. As usual she started babbling.

"Even if the scribes were allowed to speak of their work—which they are not—only a few have enough experience with our Begaine syllabary to read any of it. They are concerned only with aesthetics and precision of copying and are trained to carefully rescribe a draft. Only journeyors or higher among the guild are fluent in this writing system, which is more than some standardized set of letters."

Master Teagan ignored her and spoke to Rodian. "No work from the guild was delivered today. I didn't pay attention to pages scribed yesterday and have nothing to say regarding their content. By our contract with the guild, you'd better have a court order before you ask that again. I was under the impression that you would be visiting us this evening. We have work to do. Master a'Seatt should be present tonight for any sort of . . . interrogation."

Rodian's eyes flicked only once to Teagan, with a mild twitch of annoyance.

Wynn knew he wouldn't likely question scribes right in front of her. So why had he come here unannounced?

The captain finally nodded to Teagan, but he settled a strong hand on Wynn's shoulder.

"Wynn Hygeorht . . . please come with me."

Instead of waiting on her answer, he pushed her with slow, steady force toward the door to the front room. Wynn wished she had some way out of this place other than in the captain's company.

Imaret stood up, and her stool scraped sharply across the floor. The tears had already dried on her cheeks.

"She's only asking after friends," the girl cried, and her small voice filled with hysterical anger. "The sages are like a family! I only wish that I knew . . . that I could remember more, but when I saw Jeremy . . ."

Poor Imaret broke, and Wynn's guilt overwhelmed her. Her interest lay only in what had killed the messengers. She tried to turn back to the girl but couldn't get out of the captain's grip.

"If you think of anything else," Wynn said to Imaret, "will you send for me?"

"No," Rodian ordered. "She will send for me."

He shoved the door open and propelled Wynn out. Once they passed through the counter's hatch and stepped outside, he took his hand away and pointed toward his horse down the street.

"Over there."

Wynn followed beside the captain, noting the point of his sword's sheath trailing beneath his cloak's hem. Heading for Rodian's white mare, they passed the very side street leading to the alley of last night.

Wynn was lost in resentment when a skittering sound reached her ears, like the click of claws on cobblestones, and she turned her head.

At the side street's end something dark darted away into the alley.

Wynn slowed, almost turning aside, but then thought better of it. It was probably just a dog scavenging behind the shops. For some reason that brief glimpse wouldn't fade from her thoughts, though she hadn't seen it clearly.

Suddenly she missed Chap so much her chest ached.

"What's wrong?" the captain asked.

Wynn found him paused in the street, studying her again. She shook off the strange melancholy remembrance. Part of her wondered if Premin Sykion, High-Tower, and others weren't right about her. Was she losing her wits?

"Nothing," she answered.

He rounded the horse, motioning Wynn to follow, and they stood out of the chill breeze between his white mount and a pottery shop.

"Do not interfere," he began. "Every question you ask may change an answer I seek later, when someone thinks they've already mentioned something of importance. I'll find who murdered your brethren, but only if I'm able to gain information untainted or second-guessed. Do you understand?"

She glanced down at the street stones, wondering if he would be of any use at all to her. At least he now spoke to her as an equal.

"Yes," she answered.

"Last night, when you began searching the body . . . what were you looking for?"

The sudden question took her off-balance. She peered up, again trying to estimate his nature. If there was an undead in the city, she would need help when the time came to deal with it. At present she had no one except Domin il'Sänke.

In Rodian's cold blue eyes, meticulous appearance, and zeal for order, she saw a man determined to advance himself. He bore no title other than rank and had probably worked his way through the military by effort rather than favor. But he might still tell the royals and their officials exactly what they wanted to hear. How would he react if she told him an undead had attacked Jeremy and Elias, drained the life from them, and taken a folio for some purpose of its own?

"I was simply shocked by their condition," she half lied. "Your lieutenant didn't warn us."

"You were looking for wounds," he said flatly.

"And you didn't? With their faces so twisted, skin paled too quickly . . . yet they bore no wounds, did they?"

His jaw didn't even twitch at her challenge, so she knew he had checked the bodies. But he also said nothing at her insinuation concerning the mysterious way they'd died. No, she couldn't look to this captain for any help.

"So, have you been sworn to secrecy as well," he began suddenly, "concerning this project of your guild?"

Wynn sighed. "I am only a journeyor. I have no part in the translation project."

"Even if you did know, would you tell me?"

"No," she answered honestly.

This time his jaw clenched. He put his foot in the stirrup and swung into his saddle.

"I don't understand your people. You all claim to want these murders solved—the killer or killers caught—yet your project seems to mean more than two lives."

"Perhaps you should stop blaming my guild for your shortcomings," she answered. "You are the captain of the Shyldfälches—the People's Shield—established by the monarchs of Malourné. Where were you when two of my people died?"

Rodian pulled his horse around, and his calm broke. "Even with my full complement of guards, we cannot be everywhere at all times. Nor can the constabularies. We are few compared to the breadth of our responsibilities."

"You know less than you presume concerning my guild," Wynn countered. "We have our own duties and limits, some dictated from the same sources as yours. We fulfill our responsibilities, but it's your duty to solve these murders—not ours."

Rodian looked down upon her, and she watched his breaths deepen. He shifted uncomfortably, settling both hands upon the saddle's pommel with the reins still wrapped between them. Wynn was tired of this arrogant soldier.

"It's not always easy . . . what is asked of us," he said quietly.

"Yes, remember that." And she turned away down the street.

"Where are you going?" he called after her.

"Home."

Wynn heard the clop of horseshoes. Rodian's mount appeared beside her, and she hopped aside in surprise. The captain flipped his cloak back and reached down an open hand.

In truth, the afternoon grew cold, and in her hurry she'd worn no cloak. The sun had been out earlier, but the sky was now overcast and rain would likely come. Rodian's horse craned its head at her, a pretty white creature with round gentle eyes.

Without a word, Wynn grasped Rodian's hand.

He heaved her up behind himself. As the horse lurched forward, Wynn quickly wrapped her arms around the captain's waist. For a short way the ride was unnervingly quiet.

Wynn tried to watch the people in the streets going about their daily lives.

"You are a journeyor, yes?" the captain suddenly asked.

Sitting behind him, she couldn't see his expression. "I said as much," she replied.

"And, as you said, I know little of the guild's ways," he answered. "I was merely curious."

She said nothing to this.

"As such, you have . . . an assignment? Or so I've heard. Some duty you perform outside the guild, now that you've achieved journeyor status?"

"Yes—no . . . not anymore."

"Yes, no, which is it?"

Wynn leaned sideways but couldn't quite see his face. What was he getting at?

"I had an assignment, as you call it. It ended about six moons ago."

"So you finished, and now you will advance in rank?"

"It's not that simple . . . and I haven't finished anything. Not enough to petition and test for master's status, not by far."

"I see," Rodian replied. "At times, in the military, we too must point out our accomplishments to our superiors."

Wynn looked up at the back of his head. This captain had ambition if he was bold enough to do such a thing. That wasn't the way things were done in the guild. And she wondered just what he'd done to gain his post as head of the city's honored guard. Even in that, it seemed a strange place to be, if he was a career soldier.

"It's not like that with us," she said. "Our superior, a chosen mentor in our selected order—usually a domin—advises us when it's time to go before the Premin Council."

"And you've not been so advised?"

"No."

"But you have no assignment, as a journeyer?"

"Not anymore." And it was her turn to sigh. "I just sit about . . . waiting."

"I don't understand," Rodian said. "For what?"

Wynn thought she saw him shake his head, and she had no answer for his question.

"What was this assignment you didn't finish?" he asked.

"I went with my mentor and others to help start a new branch of the guild."

Rodian was silent for a long moment. "That seems quite a venture, but I haven't heard of any new branch in the making."

"It wasn't anywhere nearby."

"Then abroad? I know the Lhoin'na, the elves to the far southeast, have a branch. Another is in the Suman Empire on its western coast. It seems there's no need for one more."

"Not here . . . on the eastern continent."

"A lengthy journey. You must've been gone a long while. Yet now you do nothing. So the endeavor failed, and you and your mentor returned?"

"No, just me. The others still strive to keep it going."

"Is this a common pursuit . . . to establish further branches in far-off lands?"

"It's the only attempt I know of—in my lifetime."

"I see," Rodian said, and that was all.

They rode in silence until Wynn spotted remnants of the old outer bailey wall among shops and other buildings along Switchin Way. That wall had opened in many places over the centuries since the guild took over the first castle. The city had flowed in to fill the outer bailey, all the way to what was now called the Old Bailey Road. They turned onto it, looping around the still-present inner bailey wall of the guild's grounds.

"Wynn!"

The thunderous growl carried to her as the captain's horse neared the front gate. Beyond, just outside the gate-house, Domin High-Tower stood with two apprentices in gray. He began striding down the path, and both apprentices scurried after in nervous steps.

"You'd better leave me here," Wynn told the captain.

He reached back, bracing her as she slid off his horse. Before she could thank him for the ride, Domin High-Tower came at them.

"Get back inside!" he barked at her, but his outraged expression was aimed at the captain. "And you were told no interrogation without supervision."

Baffled, Wynn looked up, wondering what Captain Rodian had done to earn such ire. And what interrogation was the domin referring to?

"By the Trinity, I thank you for the tutelage, Journeyor Hygeorht," the captain said. "Knowledge is always a blessing, when it comes. Perhaps you would teach me more at a better time."

Wynn cringed for more than one reason.

Firstly she knew his reference to one of several religions in the land—they called it the Blessed Trinity of Sentience. Though one of the most reasoned, it didn't sit well with her. Captain Rodian was an arrogant, controlling, ambitious man, but she hadn't figured him as a fanatic.

As he turned his horse down the street, Wynn tried to remember all she'd said to this complicated soldier. And the second reason . . .

He had played her, but she wasn't sure how well or for what.

At the first intersection along Old Procession Road, Rodian reined in and turned his horse in time to watch the dwarven sage herding Wynn Hygeorht into the guild's castle. He pulled his small journal from his belt and scanned his notes.

Whatever the sages had in their possession and hid from outside eyes under royal protection, he had little doubt where it had come from. Or at least, who had brought those texts to them.

Half a year, Sykion had said, since translations had begun—and six moons since a young journeyor returned alone from abroad. In that time, the project was still ongoing in small pieces. Whatever Wynn Hygeorht brought back from foreign lands, it was more than just a few old scrolls or an obscure tome. But it wasn't all that she'd brought.

Wynn had brought fear to her guild, though they hid this as well.

It didn't matter that these sages dismissed a connection between one folio and the deaths of two of their own. Their emphatic certainty didn't weigh in the balance.

Captain Siweard Rodian believed—knew—this, as sure as his faith.

CHAPTER 4

After finishing half a supper, alone among the others in the common hall, Wynn carried a wooden crate filled with empty milk bottles out through the gatehouse tunnel.

Everyone living within the guild grounds equally shared regular duties. Tonight Wynn took her turn in the kitchens, and any errand to get away from staring eyes was welcome. Chopping vegetables had been especially unpleasant, considering who'd been in charge of meal preparations. Regina Melliny was a nasty beanpole of an apprentice in the Order of Naturology, and the ringleader for those whispering most behind Wynn's back.

Whether it was snide comments about Wynn being "above herself," or just that she was a fool with all her mad talk of dhampirs, undead, and assassins, Regina had a hand in it. She was like the head of a motley troupe of street players, who picked a passerby to mock for everyone else's amusement.

Perhaps the venom stemmed from a zealous approach to her order's pragmatic pursuits in natural and earth studies. Or maybe it was just her noble upbringing. Either way, Wynn couldn't wait to escape the kitchens during cleanup.

She trudged to the inner bailey's gate and settled the

crates with a note on top, requesting a full wheel of goat cheese with the next delivery. In the morning a dairyman would pick up the empties, leave full bottles, and fulfill requests for goods that were available.

Wynn lingered awhile, breathing the damp night air and watching her own breath billow like fog in the cold. Then a strange thought popped into her head—or rather a memory.

As Captain Rodian had shoved her out of the Upright Quill, she'd glimpsed a shimmer, like fur touched by distant street lanterns, as something ducked into the alley. Again she found herself missing Chap to a painful degree.

Wynn peered down Old Procession Road running straight into the city. She didn't really notice the dim glow from all of the scattered street lanterns. Or rather she peered into each pool of light upon the wide cobbled street, one by one, searching for another glimpse.

She shook her head and scoffed. That was all she needed—to lend more credence to her fame for addled wits, even if only to herself. She reluctantly turned up the path and was nearly to the gatehouse when she froze.

Large torches, their blazing heads girded in iron bands, were mounted to either side of the tunnel. But someone stood in the entrance's darker shadow, just out of the light's reach.

Nikolas Columsarn inched out into plain sight.

Wynn sighed, heart still pounding in her chest. It had been too long a day, and she wasn't up to this. But the closer she stepped, the more his lost expression wrenched her. His straight brown hair hung partly over his face, but didn't quite hide his nervous, shifting eyes.

"I heard the captain brought you back," Nikolas said softly, uncertain whether to whisper or not. "Did he tell you anything about . . . ?"

"Jeremy and Elias?" she finished after he faltered.

"My only friends, except maybe Imaret."

"I saw her today. She asked after you."

He brushed his hair aside. "How is she?"

"Sad. You should go see her."

Wynn stepped past him into the tunnel, but he didn't follow. She should've left him there if he was just going to lurk about, but she reached back and pulled him once by the arm.

His shuffling gait sent the sound of scraping leather on stone rolling around the tunnel until they entered the inner courtyard. Wynn turned aside rather than head for the main hall. Nikolas quickened his step to catch up as she walked around the courtyard.

"Does the captain know anything yet?" Nikolas repeated.

"Why are you asking me?"

"I can't ask Domin High Tower, or the premin ... or anyone else. They wouldn't talk to me. Do you think the captain will find whoever did this ... punish them, execute them?"

Wynn stopped. Clear hatred and hunger for vengeance surfaced under those shaky words. She was already certain the killer was undead, but Nikolas had sought her out for a reason. If he harbored any blame for an innocent, it had to be dispelled immediately.

Then again, she'd known vampires who'd fooled her into believing they were mortal—at least one or two. Welstiel, Magiere's own half brother, fooled her for a while, and as to the other that had once tricked Wynn ...

But she also remembered Rodian's warning not to meddle—or from her own perspective, not to get caught doing so.

"If you know anything," she said, "you must tell the captain."

Nikolas quickly shook his head. "I couldn't, not him. There are things in my past ... But Jeremy and Elias were easy to be with. They might've laughed at some of what I told them, but not to make fun of me."

He paused.

"I could tell you," he said, "and you can tell the captain."

Wynn was a little lost and really not up to this. Nikolas spoke of something more than friendship that he shared with two lost companions. Something out of the young man's own past was tangled in his loss of Jeremy and Elias.

"Tell the captain what?" she asked.

His eyes narrowed, and anger seeped back into his voice. "Elias was courting a merchant's daughter named Elvina."

"Courting?" Wynn blinked. "When would he even find time?"

Nikolas shook his head again, dismissing the question. "Have you heard of Baron Adweard Twynam? Only one generation noble, barely above a commoner, but his son Jason wants Elvina, too. Eight days back Jason cornered Elias behind the soap shop in the eastern district . . . and threatened to kill him if he didn't stay away from Elvina. Jason said no one would miss a useless little sage."

Wynn exhaled slowly. "Why didn't Elias tell the domins?"

"He'd just made journeyor and was still waiting for his assignment. The domins would've told him to stay away from her. And who knows where they would've sent him to make sure of it."

Nikolas was correct, though he still should've told someone about a death threat. But Wynn's own conclusions wavered a bit concerning the deaths of Elias and Jeremy.

What if il'Sänke was right? Was it possible they were killed for such an explainable reason, and not by something out of memories that still plagued her dreams? But it didn't all add up, if this Elvina was interested in a minor noble's son with wealth and means. Sages generally led austere lives, and only a few found their way into some wealth. So why had Elvina given Elias any note?

And if this story was true, why had Jason even felt threatened, unless he was that petty and controlling?

"How could Elias afford to court this girl?" Wynn asked.

"He borrowed coin from Jeremy."

Wynn was losing patience. "So how did Jeremy get the money?"

Nikolas started fidgeting again. "He was working . . ."

Wynn folded her arms and glared at him.

". . . for a moneylender named Selwyn Midton," he mumbled. "I went with him sometimes."

Wynn let out a huff. "Nikolas!"

"I know, I know!" he whined. "It's against guild rules, but the payment was so much. Elias was taking Elvina to all the best inns, and Jeremy wanted to help him. And Jeremy also had his eye on a fine set of calligraphy quills that he wanted before being sent off on assignment. He has—had—a good hand, enough to have been a scribe. But after he took the job with Selwyn, we started learning things. Selwyn didn't have a charter for moneylending, and he was charging ridiculous rates on illicit loans. But that wasn't all of it. . . ."

Wynn couldn't believe what she was hearing. How had this taken place with no one's knowledge? High-Tower always seemed to learn everything about his charges. Or had he been so embroiled in the hushed translation work that he never even noticed?

"I couldn't read all of Selwyn's ciphers," Nikolas went on. "But I think Jeremy may have figured out some of his clients. He was very quiet a couple of times heading back to the guild, like he knew some of them."

Wynn slumped against the keep's side.

Most citizens seeking loans for business went through one of the few banks or chartered lenders under the sanction of the ministry of commerce. But there were people—many others—who didn't have collateral. Moneylending, legal or otherwise, was frowned upon, but it still took place in any major city for those who had no other recourse.

Sages should never be involved in anything so sordid.

Initiates and apprentices were forbidden involvement in private enterprise. Aside from masters, only journeyors were allowed to do so, if whatever assignment they were given was explicitly in a legal enterprise. It wasn't just about protecting them from exploitation. The guild couldn't risk tainting its reputation as a public institution.

"What happened?" Wynn demanded, not certain she wanted to know.

"Selwyn had a partner, Mêthos Smythe," Nikolas answered. "They lent only to desperate people who'd never go to the authorities. But a caravan owner couldn't pay back his loan, let alone the interest—probably half the reason he couldn't clear the debt. He confessed to the high advocate and lodged a legal complaint. A judge ordered Selwyn to turn over all ledgers and entry keys necessary, but Mêthos was the one who handled the books. He vanished that night, taking the master ledgers with him. Selwyn called in Jeremy to make altered copies in Mêthos's handwriting . . . Jeremy was that good."

"Oh, dead deities!" Wynn breathed.

She began rubbing her temples at a sudden throb in her head. A murdered sage had been paid for forgery by an illegal moneylender. If this ever got out . . .

"Maybe Jeremy didn't fully understand at first," Nikolas continued. "But he kept at it, even when he started suspecting. I was scared of what might happen to him when the work was finished."

"You should've told someone!" Wynn exclaimed.

"I am telling someone!" His voice broke on a squeak. "They were my only friends, and I know the domins won't want anyone outside to hear of this. But someone should pay. . . . I can't tell the captain, or anyone, because I can't lose my place here. I have nowhere else to go."

Wynn didn't understand the last part. Perhaps, like herself, Nikolas was an orphan. Pity for him, as well as confused second guesses, overwhelmed her. What had actually happened to Jeremy and Elias? Then another question surfaced.

Among those ledger names, whom had Jeremy recognized and worried over? Who would an overworked apprentice sage even know, who needed money enough to go to the likes of Selwyn Midton and Mêthos Smythe?

Members of the guild came from all regions, including other countries beyond Malourné and the Numan Lands. With some of them far from home, their closest companions were always others within the guild.

Wynn immediately thought of the sun crystal she had begged for.

Premin Sykion had demanded an explanation from il'Sänke when she saw the guild's recent ledgers. Wynn didn't know how Premin Hawes, head of metaology, had reacted. Just how much had the sun crystal cost, not just in money but in time and resources? The night Domin il'Sänke had come with the crystal, he'd said something about "at least those I listed." So how else—and where else—had he acquired what was needed?

There was no doubting il'Sänke's skill, but she'd pressed him to do something never tried before . . . as quickly as possible. He'd agreed, and he was still working on the crystal.

Wynn reached for Nikolas's shoulder to offer comfort but stopped herself.

"I'll speak to the captain," she said. "I'll keep your name out, for now. But sooner or later this will come to the attention of the domins . . . and the premins."

Nikolas stared at his feet and didn't answer. Wynn couldn't bring herself to dismiss him outright, no matter how badly she wanted to disappear to her room.

"Come with me," she said. "We'll get some tea in the common hall."

Nikolas looked up in surprise.

"It would do us both good," she added halfheartedly.

As Nikolas fell into step, Wynn glanced back through the gatehouse tunnel. But she caught no glimpse of shimmering fur in the night beyond its far end.

Evening settled beneath a light patter of rain as Rodian sat at the square table that served as his desk. Unlike that of Domin High-Tower, his office was simple and orderly. He paged through his notes within his office at the barracks for the Shyldfälches inside Calm Seatt's second castle.

The wide grounds around this fortress didn't sport gardens. Instead its inner bailey was filled with stables, barracks, and housing available for officers. A full standing army hadn't been necessary for many years, but Malourné's border cavalry and regulars were still carefully maintained. This second castle of Calm Seatt was the heart of all the military, with the exception of the Weardas—the "Sentinels."

That smallest elite force protected the royal family and was housed within the last and greatest castle of the sprawling city. Placed upon a rise nearer the shore, it looked out over the open sea, the wide port of Beranlômr Bay, and the peninsula at the bay's far side, home of the neighboring nation of the dwarves at Dhredze Seatt.

The Weardas answered only to the royal family.

Rodian's position and relative young age drew envy

among older members of the Shyldfälches. Though most officers in the regulars saw the city guard as a dead-end career, others recognized its advantages beyond military life. Affluence could be gained in many ways, and so much the more within the ranks of the Shyldfälches.

But not half as much as among the Weardas.

Someday Rodian would lead that force. If only the Blessed Trinity continued to cast its lessons into his path, elevating his knowledge and wisdom.

Not long ago he'd resigned his commission in the regulars and immediately accepted a lower rank in the city guard under its previous captain, Balthild Wilkens. After that he rose quickly to first lieutenant by numerous—and correct—arrests, with all the necessary evidence for clean convictions. He gained notoriety in protecting his people and formed strong connections with other officers and a few nobles. He took pride in both his service and his accomplishments.

Unlike his predecessor.

Captain Wilkens had married the niece of Lord Kregâllian, a close confidante of the royal family. By happenstance and some effort, Rodian discovered that Wilkens had set up house for a former prostitute in one of the city's mercantile districts. He visited her whenever possible, and perhaps a bit more than he did his own wife, who lived in a remote fief. After one brief warning from Rodian, Wilkens announced his early retirement. He recommended Rodian as his replacement.

No one else learned of the ex-prostitute, as Rodian believed in keeping his word. To his knowledge she remained well cared for by the former captain, but no such man belonged protecting the people's welfare.

Rodian felt no personal guilt or regret over his tactics. He'd already proven himself much more effective than his predecessor. He didn't gamble nor visit brothels. He didn't indulge in drink, besides one mug of ale but twice in a moon or a glass of wine at a formal dinner. Men who practiced complete abstinence were rarely viewed as trustworthy, and appearances were everything.

But tonight his thoughts turned inward with concern.

Two young sages had been dead for nearly a full day, and he hadn't gained a single sure lead. There were only entanglements and the frustrating shroud surrounding the sages' hidden project.

An oil lantern burned brightly on the table, and he glanced out the window.

Night had come. He'd waited long enough for his appointment at Master a'Seatt's scriptorium. As he headed for his cloak hung upon the perfectly placed peg near the door, the image of a face pushed to the forefront of his mind.

Wynn Hygeorht.

Her uncombed brown hair. Her wrinkled gray robes. The soft tone of her olive skin. The way her eyes pierced him as she said, "It's *your* duty to solve these murders."

Rodian didn't notice pretty girls or women. He had a certain kind in mind for when it came time to marry. Face and form were not primary criteria. Virtue, social position, possible wealth, and most certainly education mattered more for someone who would be his ally for life. But no one had ever spoken to him quite like that little journeyor sage returned from abroad. Criminals cursed him and peers whispered behind his back, but Wynn Hygeorht's quiet scrutiny left him unsettled.

And she knew more of these murders than she said—as did il'Sänke. Perhaps she knew more than even she was aware of. Rodian would find out, as always. But as he opened the office door a shadow moved in the outer hallway.

Rodian shifted back and his hand dropped to his sword's hilt.

The shadow came forward into the doorframe, and lantern light illuminated the form of Pawl a'Seatt.

"Apologies," he said. "I thought we had an interview this evening."

Rodian stepped farther back to let him enter. "Yes . . . but at your shop, I believe."

"I thought to save you the inconvenience."

Rodian wondered at this polite turn. He hadn't forgotten the tail end of Imaret's story. Pawl a'Seatt had gone looking for those two sages. The girl had seen him. And that night, Imaret had said, the scribe master sent her away to rouse the constables.

"Sit," Rodian said, not pressing the matter. He could always visit the scriptorium later.

He stepped around the table, took out his note journal, and sat as the scriptorium owner settled across from him. He studied his visitor's face and found the man hard to read.

Black hair hung straight to a'Seatt's shoulders. A few streaks of dark gray could be seen there. Clean-shaven, his complexion was rather light, possibly from a life spent too much indoors, poring over books and parchments. But Pawl a'Seatt did well for himself, by the cut of his charcoal suede jerkin. His intense brown eyes were calmly watchful, though their mundane color seemed too vivid in the lantern light.

Rodian also considered the man's name.

"A'Seatt" might mean "from" or "of" the seatt—a name of a place, likely referring to this city, rather than any surname of Numan origin. Obviously taken by choice rather than heritage, it couldn't be the man's true family name.

"How well did you know Jeremy and Elias?" Rodian began.

"I had seen them a number of times. They were among those selected to deliver folios and return finished work to the guild."

"Last night how long were they in your shop before you sent them off?"

"A few moments at best."

"Imaret said that you requested they come back with confirmation of the folio's safe delivery. Is that normal?"

Pawl a'Seatt's pause took no longer than a blink, but Rodian caught it nonetheless.

"Imaret told you this?" the scribe master asked.

"Is it normal procedure?"

"At times. The guild pays us well and has asked for utmost care."

"What do you know of the project itself?"

"Nothing. Scribes are not concerned with content, only the perfection of the final copy."

"Can you read what is being copied?"

This time a'Seatt paused so long that Rodian continued rather than give the man time to think.

"I learned that translations are written in shorthand or some code created by the sages. Can you read it?"

"Yes," Pawl answered, "though it is not a code or a short-hand. Most master scribes, in working with the sages, develop some familiarity. But the Begaine syllabary is both complex and mutable. Again, we do not concern ourselves with content. If you are asking what information the folio contained, I do not know. And if I did, I would not tell you ... unless authorized by the guild or court-ordered to do so."

Rodian leaned back. He'd already hit this wall with Sykion and her cohorts. As yet, he hadn't found enough connection between the deaths and the sages' project to challenge any royal backing for secrecy—even with the sanction of the high advocate.

"Why did you go looking for the young men?" he asked.

Pawl a'Seatt's strange eyes blinked twice. Perhaps he wondered how Rodian already knew he'd done so.

"Too much time had passed," a'Seatt began. "They should have returned with confirmation. I grew concerned and stepped out, hoping to see them coming back late. I did not, so I followed the assumed path they would take. But when I passed the side street near my shop, I heard a cry. I went to look and heard more noise down the alley at the side street's end. I had just found the bodies when Imaret appeared. I immediately told her to run to the local constabulary station. I assume they notified you, since you arrived shortly after."

Rodian frowned. So Imaret had followed a'Seatt into the alley and seen him with the bodies.

"You saw nothing," Rodian asked, "and just came upon the bodies?"

"Yes."

"And the folio was gone?"

"Yes . . . no, not precisely. I did not notice its absence until after Domin High-Tower's arrival. I was too shocked over what I had found."

Rodian stalled for an instant—"shocked" wasn't a word he would use to describe a 'Seatt's state that night.

"So . . . you cannot verify that the folio was missing when you found the bodies."

"I do not remember."

Rodian stopped to jot down notes. Pawl a 'Seatt's answers were precise, and thereby offered no more than was necessary. Certain details were still missing. And for all the man's concern over the safe return of a folio, Rodian found it hard to believe the scribe master hadn't once looked for it in the alley.

"You said Imaret came after you?"

Another pause followed, and a slight crease appeared on a 'Seatt's forehead.

"Yes, though I had told her to stay inside the shop."

"An upsetting sight for the girl," Rodian added, but a 'Seatt didn't respond. "How is it that you have such a young girl working so late in your shop?"

His tone was not accusatory, but he knew the words might bite with insinuation.

"She is gifted," Pawl a 'Seatt answered without reaction. "I wish to see that gift nurtured."

"Gifted? How?"

"She can recall any text she sees with accuracy. Her hand is not yet refined but adequate—better than any of her age and experience."

Rodian saw new potential in this. "So she remembers everything she reads?"

"No."

"But you said—"

"Every piece of text she *sees*—not reads," a 'Seatt clarified. "She does not know the sages' script. She understands only contemporary Numanese and its common writing and the western Sumanese dialect. But at a glance she can recall the pattern of half a page of strokes of any kind and render a clean copy. What she can read she recalls with accuracy, but that does not include the Begaine syllabary."

Unfortunate, but it might still be of use, and Rodian turned down a connected side path.

"Imaret obviously has a mixed heritage. I take it her parents paid for her apprenticeship."

This time it was Pawl a'Seatt who stared intently. "I fail to see what this has to do with your investigation."

"Imaret is a witness," Rodian countered, "though after the fact. I need basic information on all involved."

Pawl a'Seatt's eyes remained fixed and steady.

"Her father was a sergeant in the regulars, now retired. Her mother was an apothecary in Samau'a Gaulb, the capital of il'Dha'ab Najuum, one of the nations of the Suman Empire. They offered tuition, but it was not necessary."

Rodian stopped scribbling in his journal. "Unnecessary? Why?"

"As I said, she is gifted. I pay her adequately for—"

"You are training an apprentice for free?" Rodian asked. "And paying *her* for her training?"

"Captain," a'Seatt said slowly, "several of my employees are still at my shop, but recent events have left them shaken. If you have no more relevant questions, some of them must be escorted home."

Rodian found this scribe shop owner troubling, one who took on an unusual apprentice without tuition and yet hadn't noticed a missing folio of importance sent off with two young sages. And again he wondered why Pawl a'Seatt had come all the way to the barracks rather than wait at his shop.

"Visits from the city guard are the fodder of rumor," a'Seatt said, as if catching Rodian's suspicion. "I prefer this unfortunate business be kept as far as possible from my staff and shop."

Rodian had heard such excuses before, as if an interview with the captain of the city guard suggested a taint of guilt. Sometimes it did. For now he could think of no further reason to detain this man.

"I regret any gossip," Rodian offered, "but the killer or killers must be caught. If . . . *when* . . . I have further questions, I will try to exercise discretion."

Pawl a'Seatt looked slowly about the office, taking in its

scant and orderly fixtures. Rodian thought he saw the man nod slightly to himself.

"Good hunting," a'Seatt said softly, and then rose and left.

Wynn stepped through the guild's main doors with Nikolas close behind. At panicked whispers, she paused and spotted a small cluster of initiates and apprentices in the entryway. Nikolas's eyes widened in like confusion.

Journeyors were scarce at the guild, as most were off on assignments, but neither did Wynn note any domins nearby. After supper initiates were supposed to be in their quarters if not in the common hall.

"What's going on?" she asked.

Two apprentices turned eyes on her. As they shifted aside Wynn saw Miriam, a stocky apprentice with a cloak draped over her gray robe. Another cloaked apprentice shivered beside her as if they'd both just come in from outside.

"Oh, Wynn," Miriam said, as if glad to see someone—anyone—of higher rank. "Domin High-Tower sent us to Master Shilwise's scriptorium to retrieve today's folio . . . and Master Shilwise wouldn't give it to us! He said the folio was too intricate, and his scribes hadn't finished. He wouldn't turn over unfinished work."

Wynn was stunned. Nothing sent by the guild was ever to remain overnight. That much, if nothing else, was well-known concerning the translation project.

"What about the drafts?" she said.

Miriam shook her head. "He said they would finish first thing in the morning, and he kept the whole folio. He shooed us out and locked up his shop! What is Domin High-Tower going to say? I don't want to tell him this!"

Wynn rubbed her head again, a persistent ache now growing. First Nikolas's belated confession and now this?

She'd never heard of even one folio left out overnight. The domins and masters sent out only one per day to any of the five most reputable scriptoriums. They seemed paranoid about too many pieces of the texts in the same outside hands or beyond their control for too long. And no one scriptorium should grow entirely dependent upon the translation project—which would end at some point—and thereby build a stronger relationship with the guild than the others had.

Domin High-Tower handled all the arrangements and had made it clear to all that folio contents delivered in the morning must be returned with the final scribed versions that evening. What was Master Shilwise thinking?

"I can't tell Domin High-Tower!" Miriam nearly wailed. "He'll be so angry. He'll blame *me*."

"No, he won't," Wynn said, but her words did nothing to calm the girl. "Very well, I'll inform him."

"You?" Miriam sniffed, wild relief filling her eyes.

High-Tower was already displeased with Wynn. Aside from the usual, he hadn't cared for finding her unsupervised in the company of Captain Rodian.

"Yes," Wynn answered wearily. "Now, you two take off your cloaks. Nikolas, take them to the common hall and get some tea."

Without waiting for a reply, she headed off for the north tower.

When she finally climbed the curving stairwell to the third floor and approached High-Tower's study, the heavy door was shut tight. He did this only when he preferred not to be disturbed. Wynn grasped the iron handle anyway.

Muffled voices rose beyond the door.

She didn't want to disturb whatever was going on inside, but if she waited the domin would be even angrier at not being told straight off. She'd barely raised a clenched hand to knock when someone inside half shouted—in Dwarvish.

High-Tower's home was Dhredze Seatt, the dwarven city across the bay on the mountain peninsula. The journey wasn't long, but she'd never known him to have visitors from home before. And whatever she'd heard passed too quickly for her to translate.

Wynn stood in indecision. She couldn't leave, but she shouldn't stay and listen either.

"You will stop!" someone roared from inside—or so Wynn thought. And the voice had a strange quality, like gravel being crushed under a heavy boot.

She read Dwarvish quite well, but their written terms

didn't change as much as their spoken words. Unlike Elvish, even the old dialect of the an'Cróan, pronunciation of Dwarvish mutated over generations. Yet the dwarves never faltered in understanding one another. When she was a young girl, Wynn's tutor in the language had been High-Tower. She'd enjoyed attempting conversation with him, much as he smirked at her diction.

"It is not within my power!" High-Tower shouted back. "And unfair of you to ask."

"Sages—such foolish scribblers!" the first voice declared. "You will exhume our ruin!"

"Knowledge is not the enemy," High-Tower shot back. "And translation will continue."

"Then you risk betraying your own, to shame and remorse," a third voice shouted, "if you let others know what you find."

Wynn wasn't certain she understood it all correctly, but it was the best she could make out. And that new voice was so much different from the other. More somber and reserved than the first, though equally passionate, it held a strange warning. The first voice demanded that High-Tower put a stop to translating the ancient texts, but the other one seemed less resistant, so long as what the sages learned was shared with only . . . whom?

Footsteps pounded toward the door's far side.

Wynn scurried down around the stairwell's bend. She heard the door jerk open and held her breath as she peeked carefully around the inner wall's rising arc.

A dwarf stood in the open doorway, head turned as he looked back into High-Tower's study. Wynn caught only his profile.

Wide features, with a dim undertone of gray, were deeply lined as well as flushed in rage. He was old, though he stood strong and tall, at least as tall as Wynn but over three times her bulk. At best guess he had to be well over a hundred years old, as dwarves often made it past two hundred.

He swallowed hard, trapping anger down. And his attire was . . . stunning—like that of no dwarf she'd ever seen.

Over chargray breeches and a wool shirt he wore an oily black hauberk of leather scales. Each scale's tip was sheathed in finely engraved steel, and two war daggers tucked slantwise in his thick belt had black sheaths with fixtures to match.

Then another face appeared over his shoulder. Armed and armored like the first, this dwarf had hair of a reddish hue and he was clean-shaven. Something about his face looked familiar to Wynn, though she knew she'd never seen either of these two before.

As the second visitor came up, the first turned back toward the stairwell.

Wynn ducked away, but not before she glimpsed something more.

They both wore *thôrhks*.

Those heavy, open-ended steel circlets rested upon the collars of their scaled hauberks. Each end knob flanged to a flat surface that bore an intricately etched symbol. Wynn couldn't make it out from a distance, but she couldn't help remembering a *thôrhk* of ruddy metal given to Magiere by the Chein'âs—when Magiere and Leesil had visited "the Burning Ones" on the last run to find the orb.

Magiere's open-ended circlet wasn't the same in make as what the dwarves wore. But it had been close enough that "*thôrhk*" was the only term by which Wynn could describe her absent friend's device.

Thôrhks were gifted only to thänæ, those among the dwarves most revered for their accomplishments. They were also worn by the leaders of the tribes and sometimes clans, and a few others of social status. These two dressed like warriors, but skills in battle weren't all that the dwarves found virtuous. And most warrior thänæ took service by their own choice, swearing no allegiances and serving wherever they saw need.

Wynn heard the study door slam shut.

She held her place for a few shaky breaths and then peered around the stairwell's turn. No one stood upon the landing, though she heard voices again inside High-Tower's study. The three spoke too softly, so she crept up the stairs, crouching low near the narrow space between the floor and door to listen.

"The war happened!" High-Tower growled in Dwarvish.

"You know it . . . we know it. But now we have the means to prove it. And something that—"

"You will not find it in those rotted texts!" the gravel voice roared. "All you will find is ruin and—"

"And the shame of the *Hassäg'kreigi*?" High-Tower finished.

A moment of silence followed, but Wynn was already lost in confusion.

She couldn't make out that final word. Was it some kind of name or a dwarven clan or tribe? She struggled to think of root words from which it had been formed.

The root *chas'san*, if she recalled correctly, meant "passage," and *hassäg* sounded like a verbal noun in the vocative. Something about "passages"—no, someone making passage or using a passage—a "walker"? And *chregh*—"stone"—she knew well enough. In the vocative plural it might be pronounced *kreigi*.

"Stonewalkers?" Wynn whispered.

Then she flinched at her own voice, but no one inside seemed to have noticed.

"Even some of our own people are sick of your secretive ways," High-Tower growled, "especially the rare few who still know the myth of Bäalâle Seatt."

"Watch your tongue, brother!" the younger voice countered. "Thallûhearag was no myth!"

Wynn's eyes popped wide. High-Tower had a younger brother? That was why the younger visitor had looked strangely familiar.

"Spare me your misguided faith!" the domin answered. "And don't speak to me again of that *thing*. I do not share your belief. I do not accept you or it. You do not even know that false abomination's real name . . . and no one should, if he ever existed!"

"I believe," the same voice answered.

"Faith that denies fact is fanaticism," High-Tower spit back. "Not faith at all, when it tries to hide from truth. I will find truth. If you have no stomach for it go back to praying in your crypts."

Dead silence trailed on. Wynn finally rose to her knees, leaning an ear close to the door.

"I said get out!" High-Tower shouted.

Wynn recoiled in panic. With no time to gain her feet, she scrambled down the stairs on all fours. One hand slipped and she tumbled over.

Wynn flopped and slid along the stairwell's downward curve until her trailing knee smacked a step. She yelped before she could stop herself, and her back hit the outer wall. Finally at a stop, she rolled to sit up and dropped another step. Her rump hit stone as she grabbed her aching knee. Panic-stricken, she bit her lip and stared up the flight of steps, waiting to be caught.

No one came down. She never even heard the study door open. And another tense moment passed.

Wynn finally found the courage to rise and limp upward, but not as quietly as she wanted. She paused, listening at the study's door, but heard no voices.

"Yes?" High-Tower growled from within. "Well, come in or be off."

With everything else she'd done to lower the domin's opinion of her, the last thing she needed was to be caught snooping about. She gently gripped the handle and slowly opened the door.

Domin High-Tower sat behind his desk, scribbling on a scrap of paper, as if merely at work. But his rough features were flushed, and perspiration glistened upon his brow beneath the wiry tufts of his gray-streaked reddish hair.

Domin High-Tower was alone.

Wynn looked about the room. Where had the other two gone?

The only way out of the room was the door. Even so, no one had come down, and the other way led up to the tower's next level—which was the top. Had they slipped out, and gone up, and she hadn't heard them? But why and to where?

She stepped in, still uncertain if she'd been overheard outside.

It was uncommon for High-Tower's people to join the Guild of Sagecraft—and some even considered it an unworthy choice. He was the only dwarf among sages that she'd ever known. High-Tower never spoke of this, but

Wynn guessed he had suffered over the decision of his chosen path. He finally looked up and let out a growling sigh.

"Well, what is it?" he asked.

Perhaps he'd been so caught up in arguing with his visitors that he hadn't heard her outside.

"News that couldn't wait," she answered quickly. "Today's folio wasn't returned. Master Shilwise's scribes didn't finish, and he refused to turn over work to our messengers . . . he kept the drafts as well."

High-Tower stood up. "What?"

"There is nothing you can do," Wynn said, but he was already rushing for a cloak thrown over the spare chair. "The shop has been closed and locked for the night."

"Closed?" High-Tower's black pellet eyes widened as he set his jaw.

Wynn had no wish to upset him more than he already was. Neither did she care to be the only target available for his ire.

"All the scribes have gone home," she added quickly. "But the drafts should be safe for one night. Master Shilwise's shop is in a good neighborhood."

High-Tower's gaze drifted—not to the stairs or the door, nor did it wander about the room. It fixed upon the study's northwest side, and Wynn followed it.

Through one deep-set window, she saw the keep's northwest wall. But upon a second check she found High-Tower wasn't looking out the window. He was staring at the study's curved wall to the left of it—in a direct line with that outer wall.

"Fools and fanatics!" he hissed to himself.

He seemed to come to his senses, glancing at Wynn. His voice rumbled like a distant sea storm closing upon the city.

"This is the last work Shilwise will ever see from us! I must tell Sykion."

High-Tower headed for the study's open door, sidling sideways to get through it, and Wynn felt his heavy steps through the floor stones. She was lost in her own jumbled thoughts as the domin vanished down the curving stairs.

Thallûhearag . . . Hassäg'kreigi . . . Bäalâle Seatt . . .

That last was a myth that the world had forgotten, though Wynn knew better.

During travels in the Elven Territories, Magiere had seen the distant memories of Most Aged Father, reaching all the way back to the "mythical" war. The Enemy's forces had laid siege to a dwarven stronghold called Bäalâle Seatt. Both sides had perished, though no one then ever learned what happened there. The place itself was forgotten as much as any of the Forgotten History.

But within the domin's chamber had been two who knew it. And what of those other Dwarvish terms?

Wynn studied the wall to the window's left, whispering again, "Stonewalkers?"

Where had High-Tower's two visitors gone?

Chane Andraso woke from dormancy with a start. Dusk had fallen, and he had not even stirred at the eighth bell marking the end of the day. He should gather his cloak and head fast for the Gild and Ink, the scribe shop of one Master Shilwise.

It had not taken him long to map out the pattern of the scriptoriums being utilized. The guild had hired five shops and rotated them on the same daily basis: the Upright Quill, the Gild and Ink, the Inkwell, the Feather & Parchment, and Four Scribes in House. But as he sat up in his shabby bed, his mind still lingered on the previous night.

He had seen Wynn for the first time in well over a year.

His existence had once been so intricately connected with hers that he knew every line of her face. Back in Bela, when she had joined the journey of Magiere, Leesil, and Chap, Chane had reluctantly accepted a kind of servitude to a Noble Dead named Welstiel—Magiere's half brother. And the two of them had secretly followed Wynn and her companions across entire countries, seacoasts, and mountain ranges, all in search of Welstiel's coveted "orb." But in the end, only Magiere could find and retrieve it. And Welstiel lost his head in the ice-trapped castle of the Pock Peaks, his body dropped into the misted depths of a molten fissure.

But Chane survived.

Running a hand across his face, he rose, looking about the faded walls of his small attic room.

When he had first arrived in Calm Seatt, with little money, he had taken the cheapest accommodation he could find. It was a run-down inn called Nattie's House on the outskirts of the city's poorest sector, which the locals had dubbed "the Graylands Empire." Over time he had acquired coins from his prey and could have afforded better lodgings, but he did not care enough to make the effort. Remaining in this obscure, little-noticed shambles suited his needs.

Chane went to crouch before his belongings, all piled in the corner where the ceiling rafters slanted down to the streetside eaves. He reached for the nearest of two packs, opened it, and removed an aged tin scroll case. With this in hand he closed his eyes, drifting back to the night Welstiel had taken his "second death." The same night Chane had walked away from Wynn in the library of the ice-bound castle.

He hated dwelling on the past, but it was not the first time or even the hundredth that his thoughts slipped to events that led him down this current path. . . .

When he had left Wynn in the library of that castle, which housed one ancient undead, he had stumbled out alone onto the snowy plain.

Free for the first time in his undead existence, he had no place to go. In that moment he had no future, no Wynn, and no fantasies of existing in her world. She did not deserve a monster driven by lust for the hunt and the euphoria of a kill. The need to survive, to feed, was the only thing that kept him moving. Wandering to escape the lifeless Pock Peaks, he drifted slowly west.

Bela was the place where his existence as a Noble Dead had begun—and where he had met Wynn and her sages for the first time.

Part of him believed she would leave Magiere and return there, to the newly established branch of her guild. She belonged there, and eventually she would realize this. Even as Chane crossed the Belaskian border, still far from the king's city, he knew he should not try to touch even that small part of her world. But with each step across the homeland of his living days, Chane's mind slipped backward, desperate to erase his past and *live* only as a sage. . . .

Among books and parchments, a cold lamp's crystal lighting the dark, with one companion of choice . . .

Impossible—for he was undead, and the beast inside him would never sleep.

When he finally reached Bela, he stayed clear of the old barracks given to the sages. Instead he took a room in a dingy little inn beyond the city's outermost wall. He still had all of Welstiel's possessions and his own, as well as the books he had saved from the monastery, where Welstiel had killed and raised healer-monks as feral undead. Chane also had the scroll case, the only thing he had taken from the ice-bound castle.

And every time he held it, a part of him wished it had been Wynn he had taken from that place.

He tucked the scroll case from sight, distracting himself with other things.

Welstiel's belongings and books baffled him, for that arrogant undead had been more than Noble Dead. He had been a skilled conjurer, better than Chane in many ways, though the man preferred artificing over Chane's use of ritual and scant spells. Welstiel's journals were written mostly in Numanese—Wynn's native tongue— and took much time to read. Chane was functional in speaking the language, due to Welstiel's tutoring, but not in reading it.

Welstiel's arcane objects, from the steel hoop that conjured heat within its metal, to the metal rods, the life-conjuring cup, and a strange box of vials, were as unfathomable as the man's two arcane texts. Aside from scattered notes, those latter handwritten volumes were filled with esoteric symbols and characters that likely Welstiel had developed himself.

That was the way of all mages, whatever they practiced. Breaching the personal symbol systems of another mage, born from his fathoming of magic, could take long, if it were possible at all. And even with pieces that Chane worked hard to understand, after only a few moons he found himself holding the ancient scroll case once again.

It represented his one remaining connection to Wynn. And one he could not push aside.

The first time he pulled off its pitted pewter cap, carefully sliding its contents out, the scroll was hard and brittle. Made from a sheet of thin hide, it was too pale even in age for any livestock animal. And he could not unroll it without risk of breaking and crumbling.

Chane had much to do before he could glimpse what it held.

He spent evenings skulking around Bela after dusk before all shops had closed. He needed to know how to restore age-hardened leather to a flexible state without destroying whatever was marked upon it. Consulting leatherworkers on the pretense of refurbishing an old vest, he learned to make a cold-filtered mixture of linseed oil and white vinegar. Then he sought scribes and others familiar with inks who could tell him if the solution would affect anything written. One night, back in his room, he took a camel-hair brush and delicately applied the mixture for the first time.

The scroll's tightly curved outer surface darkened suddenly.

Chane froze, fearing he'd ruined the ancient relic. But as the solution dried, the thin leather returned to its pale aged color. Caution took hold nonetheless.

He applied the restoration solution only once per day, just before dawn but keeping it in a dark, cool corner. He gently tested the scroll's flexibility at each dusk when he rose from dormancy. Twenty-seven nights passed before the scroll lay perfectly flat, but it was on the seventeenth night that Chane had caught his first glimpse of its content—or lack of it.

The top end of the scroll's inner surface was nearly black, as if wholly covered in ink that had set centuries ago.

Chane slumped in astonishment, and he almost took the scroll and tossed it in the inn's front hearth. Instead he opened the small room's one window, sick of the solution's stench, and stalked out for the night.

When he returned before dawn, senses enlivened by a fresh kill, he didn't bother testing the scroll's flexibility.

He shut the window, covered the panes with a moth-eaten blanket against the coming sun, and stretched out upon the straw mattress.

A faint odor tickled his nose. Not vinegar and linseed oil, but something else just beneath that.

Chane sat up.

With fresh life filling him, his skin prickled lightly at dawn's approach. He heard someone out in the inn's front room dump a log on the hearth. Chane drew air deeply through his nose.

He got up and went to the stool he used for a worktable, carefully lifting the scroll.

He'd never before noticed the scent beneath the solution's pungent odor. Or perhaps the solution, permeating and softening the hide sheet, had revitalized something else. With the room's air cleared and his senses opened fully, he lifted the scroll, sniffing its black coating repeatedly.

At first he could not place the thin trace, but it sparked a memory.

In that lost mountain monastery of the healer-monks, called the Servants of Compassion, he had fought with Welstiel and bitten into his undead companion's leg. As Welstiel's black fluids seeped through his breeches, Chane's mouth filled with a taste like rancid linseed oil, and he smelled it as well. . . .

That same odor rose faintly from the scroll's blackened surface.

There had been worn and jumbled writings on the ice-crusted castle's walls, made with the fluids of an undead. The same scent had lingered thinly around the writing.

Urgency made Chane's hands shudder, until the scroll quivered slightly beneath his fingertips. He recognized the scent, not from the ink coating itself, but from something hidden beneath that blackness.

Chane smelled a hint of rancid linseed oil.

A Noble Dead had written on the leather scroll in its own fluids or another's—and then blotted it out with painted ink. But then why had the scroll been kept for so long?

And how would he ever find out, with no way to read beneath the coating?

Chane couldn't reason a way to remove the ink without fear of damaging what lay beneath. So he simply continued with his painstaking restoration until the twenty-seventh night, when the scroll lay completely flat, restored to full pliancy.

He had never been alone before—or perhaps not lonely. The scroll's content, blocked from him, much as he was blocked from Wynn's world, began to conjure renewed thoughts of her.

For a quarter moon he lurked outside the old barracks. All he wanted was one glimpse of Wynn, though he still did not know if he should—could—face her again. But she never appeared. Chane saw Domin Tilswith several times, but he could not reveal his presence to Wynn's old master. Tilswith also knew *what* he was. Finally, one evening he could stand the ignorance no longer.

A girl in a gray robe like Wynn's ventured out of the barracks' worn door with empty milk bottles bundled clumsily in her arms. And Chane stepped from the shadows.

He did not often speak, hating the sound of his own voice. During his pursuit of Magiere she had once beheaded him in the forests of Apudâlsat. Welstiel managed to bring him back through some arcane method, but Chane's voice had never healed.

In his brushed cloak and polished boots, he looked again like a young affluent gentleman. But still, the girl almost dropped her bottles in surprise.

"I am looking for news of an old friend," he rasped. "Do you know where I might find Wynn Hygeorht?"

The girl's brow wrinkled at Chane's maimed voice, but then smoothed as her eyes widened in understanding. Though he took no pride in it, he was aware of how his tall form and handsome face affected some women. She spoke Belaskian with a Numanese accent.

"Journeyor Hygeorht? I'm sorry, but she is no longer with us. When she returned with old texts recovered from an abandoned fortification, Domin Tilswith gave her the duty of carrying them back to the home branch in Malourné. She is gone."

Chane stepped back.

The apprentice looked at him with more interest, perhaps even compassion.

"You could write to her," the girl offered, "though a letter would take a long while to reach Calm Seatt. We do send regular correspondence on the eve of the new moons. I could include yours, if you like."

He nodded, still backing away, as if the ground began slipping from under his feet.

"Yes . . . thank you. I will consider that."

Wynn was gone, left for home across the ocean to another continent—another world.

Chane ambled listlessly through Bela's night streets, paying no heed to where he walked. He found himself at the waterfront, standing before the great warehouses and docks. And he stared out over the bay's night water sparked by a star-speckled sky. The only other light came from sparse lanterns hanging along the double-deck piers or on ships out in the wide harbor.

This was where Wynn had boarded and left for the Numan lands, long gone from any chance to catch one last glimpse of her. . . .

"Sir, will you be wanting tea tonight?"

At the voice, Chane was jerked from his reverie in his room in Calm Seatt. He stepped over and cracked the door.

The corpulent innkeeper, who he assumed was Nattie, stood outside. In the Crown Range north of the Farlands, Chane had picked up the habit of drinking tea. And only recently had he begun going out at dusk to track the folios. The innkeeper sometimes still checked in on him. He always paid his bill in advance, and the grease-stained owner treated him with decent manners, following a request not to knock during the day.

"No, thank you, not tonight," Chane said, and closed the door.

Time was slipping away, and he had already wasted too much reliving events he could not change. He grabbed his cloak, sword, and packs, then locked the door and left the inn.

No one addressed him as he walked quickly through the darkening streets. Wearing a long wool cloak, he was nondescript. A few drunkards eyed him as they stumbled from a tavern, but they stayed well out of his way. He headed toward the better-lit and -maintained eastern merchant district.

He knew the location of the Gild and Ink, but cursed himself for not leaving the inn sooner. It was a long way off, even if he wasted energy bolting along back alleys. Any messenger sages may have already come and gone with tonight's folio. Yet he had to be certain, and walked quickly until approaching the correct street.

Rounding a corner, he slipped in beneath the eaves' shadows as he approached the scriptorium. The entire street was empty—no lights in the shops he passed, and he heard no voices—and he silently cursed himself again. Then he stopped one shop away, looking at the front of the Gild and Ink.

Chane slowly stepped forward to the scribe shop's corner.

All its windows were dark, like the other shops along the street, but the front door . . .

Shattered wood shards lay across the cobblestones before the Gild and Ink. In place of the door was only a dark opening into the shop. No scribes, no sages, the shop closed for the night, and someone had broken in . . .

Chane glanced at the door's remains. No, not in—someone had broken *out*.

He crept closer to see inside, but then voices reached him from down the street. Had someone seen this and called for constables? He could not be seen here, especially not now.

Frustrated, wildly wishing to enter the shop and see what had happened, Chane slipped into the shadows, moving quickly away.

CHAPTER 5

Rodian woke the next morning to knocking on his chamber door, adjacent to his office.

His needs were few—a bed, a basin to wash in, a mirror for grooming, and a chest for extra clothes. After spending long hours at each day's end filling out reports and updating log entries, he felt it best to have his personal space close at hand. He'd chosen an office with an empty adjoining room to convert for personal space.

Rodian sat up quickly, instantly alert. No one knocked this early but Garrogh, and not without a good reason.

"Come," he half grunted.

Garrogh poked his head through the cracked door, his long, unwashed hair hanging in a tangled mess. Obviously he'd been roused early as well.

"Sir?"

"What is it?" Rodian asked, wiping sleep from his eyes.

"A break-in at the scribe shop of a Master Shilwise. I thought you'd want to know immediately."

Rodian blinked and looked at his second.

Garrogh was a good man, personal hygiene aside—competent, reliable, appreciative of his position, but most important, not overly ambitious.

"A scriptorium?" Rodian repeated.

"Yes, sir," Garrogh said with a frown of shared understanding. "Master Shilwise arrived at his shop before dawn. The local constabulary just sent word."

"Is his shop handling work for the sages' guild?"

"I don't know . . . but I'd guess, considering."

"What time is it?"

"Just past dawn . . . barely the first eighth of day, by the bells."

Rodian hurried for his uniform. "Have our horses saddled."

With a splash of water on his face and the basin left full, Rodian joined his lieutenant in the second castle's courtyard. They rode toward the eastern and outermost merchant district.

A chilling prewinter wind pulled at Rodian's cloak as the city's streets began coming to life. Garrogh's big bay gelding continually snorted steam and stomped in protest at the early outing. Once it even tried to thrash and turn back for the barracks. Rodian's white mare, Snowbird, was far better behaved, as if sharing his devotion to duty.

Street vendors were setting up carts of meat pies, spiced tea, and mulled wine, along with baked goods. One hauled a handcart filled with late-blooming wildflowers and ferns, headed toward the city center, where people actually spent coin on such things. The street lamps were already snuffed, and the cleaners had long finished clearing the cobblestones of horse droppings from the previous day. Shopkeepers had just begun unlocking their doors, though most patrons wouldn't be out and about for a while.

Why had Master Shilwise arrived so early at his own shop?

Normally Rodian would've made a note of the break-in, studied his schedule, and placed this visit in order of importance. But given the murders so near Master a'Seatt's scriptorium, and the missing folio, this break-in came too soon to be a coincidence. He and Garrogh turned off the wide main road into a narrower street of eateries and inns.

Master Shilwise's scriptorium wasn't as well situated as Pawl a'Seatt's, but still in a respectable neighborhood. Rodian had never investigated a burglary in this district. The only event that came to mind had happened four streets south—a murder. Two years ago he'd arrested a robust woman who'd smothered her husband in his sleep with a pillow. She confessed and then stopped talking altogether. Rodian never learned her motive. The neighbors claimed she and her husband had gotten on well. But domestic crimes occurred in every neighborhood, at every social level, from paupers to gentry.

"Good gods!" Garrogh breathed.

The shop wasn't difficult to spot. A small crowd of gawkers had already gathered in the street front. Gaudy and worn, its painted sign hung askew—THE GILD AND INK.

Whitewashed outer walls were cracked and faded by coastal weather. Two fake-gilded columns on the front porch, carved like the stone ones found before noble townhouses, looked no better than the walls. Broken pieces of the door lay scattered all the way into the street.

Rodian frowned and climbed off Snowbird. "Stay," he told her.

A stocky man with a round bald spot closed on him instantly.

"Look at this, Captain!" he demanded angrily. "Just look at this! Is this what my taxes pay for? Is this your idea of keeping the law?"

Rodian took a slow breath. "Master Shilwise?"

Dressed in a purple velvet tunic over a white linen shirt, the man hardly appeared to suffer from overtaxation. Perhaps he should spend more coin on his shop's upkeep than his wardrobe. From the look of the place, Rodian couldn't see how the sages would employ such an establishment. He'd also heard enough accusations like Shilwise's, assuming that the city guard could anticipate crimes and intercede beforehand.

"Yes, I'm Shilwise," the man huffed. "Look at what's been done to my shop!"

Rodian stepped between the fake-gilded columns, glancing briefly into the scriptorium's front room. He half turned his head to find Garrogh behind him.

"Find out if anyone heard or saw anything."

Garrogh nodded and stepped out into the crowd, but Shilwise remained close at hand, shaking his head as he stared at the empty doorframe.

Rodian fingered some remaining wood shards still mounted to the hinges. The door had been made of oak about three fingers thick, though probably as unkempt as the outer walls. He glanced down, but found few pieces of wood on the inside floor. Most of the remains were scattered from the landing to the cobblestones—even halfway across the street.

"Broken from the inside out," he said. "You didn't happen to lock some employees in last night?"

"Of course not! What are you implying?"

It was a callous jab, and Rodian quickly regained his manners.

"But even so," Shilwise said more calmly, "you'd need a battering log and three men to break through this."

Rodian stepped inside.

Someone had gained access—with or without a key— then had forced his or her way out. How, was one question— more baffling was, Why? The shop's front room appeared undamaged but for the gaudy examples of scribed scrolls displayed on its walls. The kind that attracted those who thought garnishments rather than content marked the value.

"Have you touched anything?" he asked.

"No," Shilwise answered quietly. "I know better."

The shop master grew less accusatory and more attentive. This too was normal, as after a victim's initial outrage they realized Rodian was there to help.

"I did look around, carefully," Shilwise added. "The worst is in the back workroom."

He led the way around the front counter, through a swinging hinged door, and held it aside as Rodian followed.

"Just look at this," he said sadly.

Rodian shook his head at the sight and stepped into the back room. The whole place looked as if a windstorm had ripped through it.

Scribes' writing desks were overturned. Wood-framed canvas dividers were toppled over them. The floor was littered with quills and parchments. Amid the destruction, books and sheaves and one old-fashioned scroll were scattered as if thrown aside. And much of the mess was spattered by toppled and shattered ink bottles. Everything was cast aside in violence, of no interest to whoever had done this.

Shilwise didn't strike Rodian as the kind to leave any coin in the shop, and even desperate thieves would hardly waste effort on a midlevel scriptorium. At hurried footsteps, Rodian glanced back.

Two young men rushed through the missing front door. As they came up behind Shilwise, one gasped loudly.

"My desk! And where are my stylus tips? Master, what happened?"

Their velvet-and-linen-clad master continued to gaze over the mess.

"A break-in," he said. "The captain is here, so don't touch anything."

Shilwise raised puffy eyes to Rodian, and a bit of venom returned to his expression.

"Two of my scribes." And he cocked his head at the younger pair. "More will be coming, and we've a mess to clean up . . . as soon as you give the word."

Rodian ignored the implied demand. "Have you noticed anything specific missing?"

He already knew what it might be, but the question still had to be asked. For the first time Master Shilwise grew nervous, sucking in his thick lower lip between his teeth.

"One folio," he said.

Rodian took another long breath and let it out slowly.

"We're doing transcription for the sages," Shilwise went on. "Just odd bits and pieces. Normally all drafts and finished work are sent back with guild messengers before closing up. But we ran out of time last night. The domins have been quite fussy, but I never send back unfinished work."

Shilwise stepped carefully through to the workroom's near left corner, where two partitions had been knocked aside. One stout desk of walnut sat there, so old it had darkened to near black. Its entire top had been ripped off and lay tilted against the left wall's supply shelves.

"I locked the folio in my desk," Shilwise said. "It was the first thing I looked for when I arrived."

Rodian joined him, trying not to tread on debris. He peered into the desk's remains.

The top drawers on both sides had been shoved outward, their locking mechanisms torn from the desk's front. The deeper bottom drawer on each side was still in place. The right was filled with journals or ledgers, but the left was empty.

He crouched and studied the broken desk, running a finger over the top's outer side, and then he glanced at the exposed edges of the desk's walls. He saw no marks of a pry bar, but he hadn't expected to find any. Whoever had done this had been in a hurry—and had strength to fulfill such urgency.

"What was in the folio?" Rodian demanded.

Master Shilwise's tone changed. "Excuse me?"

"The pages—what did your people copy for the guild?"

Shilwise glanced at his two scribes, who were watching Rodian in equal confusion.

"How would we know that?" one of them asked.

"You were transcribing sages' notes, yes?" Rodian started coldly, and then he calmed. "I take it what they sent was written in their script?"

Shilwise looked at him in surprise. "You know of the Begaine syllabary?"

"Can you read it?" Rodian asked.

Shilwise's face tinged slightly pink. "I fear not. I bought this scriptorium, so my title is master, but it is my business and no more. I hire certified scribes to do the work. I am not . . . a master scribe myself."

"Like Pawl a'Seatt?"

Shilwise snorted with a scowl, and his pink turned to red.

"I can read a bit of it," said one of the young scribes.

"Shut your mouth!" Shilwise barked, and turned back to Rodian. "If you've spoken with a'Seatt, then you know all scriptoriums working on this project have signed contracts of silence, backed by decree of the royal family. Until you have written court orders to counter that, I won't be caught in a breach. I have a reputation to maintain."

"It wouldn't help anyway," added the young scribe. "It's mostly gibberish."

"What did I just tell you?" Shilwise warned.

"Be quiet!" Rodian barked, and pushed past the paunchy shop owner, closing on the scribe. "What do you mean?"

The young man was rather gangly, with oily black locks pushed back from his high forehead. His deep-set eyes flickered once to his employer.

"The syllabary is just a system for recording . . . syllables . . . how things are spoken—in any language. It saves space, and hence paper or parchment, versus all the different letter systems for various languages. But what little I can make out, I couldn't make sense of."

"Why?" Rodian asked. "What languages did you encounter?"

"I couldn't even say. Bits of it seemed like Sumanese, but I don't know. And others . . ." The young scribe just shook his head.

"That's enough," Shilwise warned. "Captain, if you want to know any more, go ask the sages. I've no idea why someone did this to my shop for a folio of nonsense. But if I find out the content was dangerous, my solicitor will file charges with the high advocate . . . for the guild offering work under false pretenses."

Rodian ignored the shop master's blustering threat and looked about the workroom.

"You're certain nothing else is missing?"

"I'm certain of nothing," Shilwise snapped. "Not until we sift through all of this. But it's the only thing I've noted so far. Now, if you're finished, may we start putting things back in order?"

"No." Rodian waved the scribes aside and pushed through the swinging door. "When my lieutenant finishes questioning your neighbors, he will go over the shop. Do not touch anything until he tells you."

Rodian headed out, his gaze fixed on the empty front doorframe.

One massive blow seemed to have smashed out the door, for wood shards lay in a sprayed pattern, suggesting they all fell at the same time. How—and why—would someone who had managed to get inside, ransack the workroom, and steal the folio, then have to break *out* to escape?

How had the culprit gained entrance?

Perhaps someone had let him in. But then why break out?

This was the second folio to have gone missing in the span of two nights. He still had no information regarding the content of either one. Once again Rodian's only option was the sages.

Ghassan il'Sänke slowed in surprise upon entering the guild's common hall for breakfast.

There was Wynn, sitting between two gray-robed apprentices of her order, eating a bowl of boiled oats.

He knew she preferred to eat in her room, but not this morning. Her left-side companion was a young man the others often called Nervous Nikolas.

Wynn looked up, and her spoon halted halfway to her mouth. She nodded politely to Ghassan. Normally he too preferred to take his repast in his quarters or while working elsewhere. But this uncommon sight, of her willingly out among the populace, piqued his interest.

"Boiled oats again?" he said as he approached. "At my home branch there are honey cakes every morning, in case nothing else seems appealing."

Wynn half smiled, setting down her spoon. "Then how do you stay so thin?"

"Oh, ages of living in near-constant distress," he answered.

She smiled openly at this. "You are hardly that old."

No, Ghassan thought, one would not think so. Nikolas and the other one—Miriam was her name—both stared in fright as he sat down across the table.

"I . . . I need to get started on cleanup," Miriam stammered, rising quickly to scurry off.

Such a plain-faced, pudgy girl—her eyes were too small for her face. But apparently High-Tower had found something promising in her. The old dwarf once mentioned that he had rarely known such an apprentice who comprehended the syllabary's complex system so easily. But most apprentices grew uncomfortable in Ghassan's presence.

For one, he was an exotic-looking foreigner, taller than normal for his people, and of distinguished elder appearance—or so he liked to think. Second, he was a domin of metaology.

The Order of Metaology in Calm Seatt was smaller and less prominent than in Ghassan's own branch, but still treated with some reserve—as were all the metaologers. In most cases rumors of the order's abilities were exaggerated. The only true work they did in magic was mostly in thaumaturgy via artificing, which included alchemical processes. They were responsible for making cold lamp crystals and other minor items used by the guild.

In other rare cases, rumors fell slightly short of the truth—something Ghassan kept to himself.

To Nikolas's credit, he kept his seat. Impressive, but Ghassan had no interest in the young man—only in Wynn. In what she knew, what she might share, and what she would keep to herself. She looked pale this morning, as if she had not slept well, but her hair was cleanly pulled back into a tail.

"Would you care for bread with butter and honey?" Wynn asked. "I can go find some."

Her simple offer moved him. Then he hardened himself against sentiment.

She possessed a giving spirit, but under the present circumstances this was not a good thing. If only she were closed off and self-serving, then she would cause him less concern. He had often been forced into cold decisions, doing what was necessary, and regret was not something he could afford.

Ghassan shook his head politely at Wynn's offer. He was about to tell her that boiled oats would be fine when his attention shifted. High-Tower suddenly appeared from the smaller northeast entrance.

The old dwarf's mouth was set in an angry, determined grimace, and his cloak was tied tightly about his wide shoulders. He strode halfway through the hall toward the main wide arch and the passage to the double front doors.

Where was the dour domin going so early?

Symbols and lines of Ghassan's art appeared in his mind, lacing over the sight of High-Tower. He reached for the domin's mind, attempting to pick up surface thoughts.

A loud commotion rose out of the main archway, echoing from the outer main passage.

"Sir! Sir, you cannot go in there. You must have permission first!"

High-Tower came to a sudden halt as Captain Rodian strode in.

Everyone in the common hall looked up to see an initiate scurrying backward before the captain. But the captain's threatening gait quickly backed the boy into a nearby table.

"What do you think you are doing?" High-Tower growled.

Rodian locked eyes with the dwarf. "I assume you're heading out to Master Shilwise's scriptorium to demand your folio?"

The entire hall fell silent, and Ghassan tensed.

Rodian's growing involvement concerned him almost as much as Wynn did. If nothing else, the captain struck him as competent. Not at all what Ghassan needed.

"I'll save you the effort," Rodian said softly, though his voice carried clearly in the silence. "The folio is gone. Someone broke into Shilwise's shop last night, ransacked the place, and took it."

The captain closed another two steps on High-Tower.

"Now, would you care to go to your study," he continued, "and tell me what was in that folio? Or do I still need an order of the court or a decree from the royal family?"

Ghassan glanced at Wynn.

She seemed as taken aback as everyone else, watching the exchange in stunned silence. Nikolas, however, was staring at the captain, and the young man's brow glistened with a sudden cold sweat.

"More unfounded assumptions, Captain," said a calm reedy voice from the smaller north entrance.

All heads turned as High Premin Sykion entered, silver hair tied back and her long gray robe sweeping the floor.

Rodian did not even flinch. "Unfounded?"

"Do you have evidence that the thieves intentionally broke into Master Shilwise's scriptorium . . . for the sole purpose of taking our folio?"

"It's the only thing missing."

"You are certain, without a doubt, that nothing more was taken?"

"With respect," Rodian replied, "two of yours were murdered, and the folio they carried is missing. The following night another is stolen directly from a scribe shop. My duty is to protect this city, including your guild . . . even from itself. You will tell me exactly what was in—"

"Premin Sykion!"

The initiate who had been driven before Rodian came running back into the hall. Ghassan had not even noticed the boy leave.

"Forgive me, Premin, b-b-but . . ."

The boy looked anxiously about the hall, then hurried close to Sykion and whispered.

Ghassan focused upon the initiate, once again stroking the mental symbols and ciphers he needed. As Sykion leaned down, he slipped into the young one's thoughts and heard . . .

Duchess Reine is here! She asks to be admitted immediately.

Before Ghassan could try for the premin's thoughts, the captain whirled about, facing the archway. Nearer to Sykion, he had obviously overheard the boy.

Shifting a spell's focal point was not so easy once a connection to target was established. The captain appeared startled, and all anger and determination faded from his demeanor. By the time Ghassan grasped at the captain's thoughts, all he caught was . . .

Oh, Blessed Trinity! Why is she here—now, of all times?

Sykion straightened with a worried glance to High-Tower.

"Everyone out!" High-Tower shouted. "Any but domins, clear the room!"

Rodian glanced back, frustration plain on his face, but Premin Sykion relaxed where she stood, offering the captain a polite smile. Or was it an expression of relief?

The hall filled with the noise of rushing feet. Initiates, apprentices, and a handful of journeyors hurried for the exits. Some were diverted away to the northeast exit when they tried in confusion to leave through the main archway. Nikolas seemed reluctant, and Wynn pulled him up.

Rodian pointed at her. "You stay."

Wynn froze, staring at him. She gently pushed Nikolas after the others before taking her seat.

With so many in a frenzy about the hall, Ghassan was uncertain whose thoughts to reach for next. As the room cleared, Premin Sykion nodded to the messenger.

"Please show the duchess in."

Before the boy even moved, Duchess Reine Faunier-Âreskynna swept into the common hall with her full entourage.

Three female attendants in rich gowns of varied and dignified hues, and one tall elven male in a white robe, surrounded the duchess. Or rather princess, for that was her true title.

Duchess Reine was niece to the king of Faunier, one of Malourné's neighboring countries and a staunch ally. She had married Prince Freädherich of the Âreskynna, the royal family of Malourné—though he no longer lived. For some reason she preferred her original title rather than the one gained by marriage. And she was guarded by three of the Weardas.

These tall warriors in their polished steel helms, chain vestments, and long crimson tabards each wore a long sword sheathed upon a wide belt of engraved silver plates. They carried short spears with heads shaped more like a leaf-bladed short sword.

The leader, Captain Tristan, walked beside the duchess. An emotionless soldier, there were some rumors that he had trained with the Suman emperor's personal guard. But this was all Ghassan knew of the man.

And everyone in the entourage towered over Duchess Reine.

She was no taller than Wynn, perhaps less, with a tiny waist and slightly wide hips beneath a long sea foam satin skirt. Her matching vestment scooped beneath her jutting bosom covered in a white linen shirt. In the common hall's somber and earthy colors, she stood out like an emerald tinted by a blue sky. Her dark chestnut tresses were pinned back on each side by twin combs of mother-of-pearl shaped like waves— the only jewelry adornments she wore.

By her early arrival and attire, Ghassan guessed the duchess had risen at dawn, putting her three attendants hard at work in order to achieve such a seemingly simple elegance.

Duchess Reine smiled warmly at Rodian and stretched out one hand.

"Captain Siweard Rodian . . . at your duties already. Do you never tire?"

Ghassan watched the pair carefully. He caught a flicker in those matched gazes. And as the captain took the duchess's hand with a slight bow, his formal—yet familiar—gesture suggested a connection between them. She was about five years Rodian's elder, something Ghassan had not noticed at first. Perhaps her diminutive stature conjured the illusion of youth.

And the effect of Ghassan's spell was lost.

He began his mental work again, eager to reach for the captain's thoughts—and those of Duchess Reine.

"Your Highness," Rodian said, clearly confused. "I didn't expect to see you here."

Ghassan finished the sigils, shapes, and glyphs in his mind's eye, but behind Rodian's spoken words he picked up only a muffled sound in the man's mind—like a far-off voice, muted and unintelligible behind a closed door.

He instantly let the spell wane and scanned the room.

Something—or someone—had interfered. It was not strong, and likely he could have broken through. But if it were an active intervention, rather than some emplaced work or hidden device, whoever held it by will might have felt his effort.

Who else here could even have knowledge or skill like his?

Ghassan's attention was pulled back as Duchess Reine spoke to Sykion.

"Lady Tärtgyth, it has been too long. I trust the latest endowment arrived without complication?"

Rodian turned startled eyes upon the premin, as did Ghassan. The duchess referred to Sykion by her first name—and as "lady"?

"Yes, we're honored, and thank you for visiting," Sykion answered. "The captain was inquiring about an unfortunate break-in at a scribe shop."

"I heard," the duchess replied. "Very unfortunate."

Another surprise. How had word of a mere burglary so quickly reached the royal family?

Duchess Reine glanced sidelong at Rodian. "Surely searching among our sages will help you little in finding the criminal."

The captain shifted his weight uncomfortably. "Highness, I believed the royal family would be most concerned over the deaths of two young sages. And certain guild documents have gone missing twice in two nights. I simply wish to inquire about the nature of those documents . . . to guard against another such loss."

"You have evidence that the guild's project is the target of these crimes?" the duchess asked, and she seemed to work too hard at keeping her tone light.

Rodian glanced at Premin Sykion and struggled for an answer. "Not specifically, but it seems clear—"

"The translation project is important to the guild's masters," Duchess Reine went on. "And *they* are important to our land and people, yes?"

At the duchess's turn, the folds of her skirt twisted. A long slit down the front separated, revealing darker breeches and a pair of glistening, polished riding boots.

This attire was out of place for a royal of the Malourné, but not so for a noble of Faunier. Descended from horse people, they were skilled riders, their high-bred mounts prized even in Ghassan's homeland.

"For now, could you not pursue other leads—until certain of a connection?" the duchess asked. "I remain confident you will solve both these crimes long before such invasive tactics are necessary."

"Your Highness?" Rodian asked.

"The royal family would be grateful for your good faith."

The captain fell silent. With a long side glance at Premin Sykion, he finally dropped his eyes and nodded deeply.

Duchess Reine returned a nod of lesser depth. "Thank you, Siweard ... You have my faith as well—in your abilities. Baron Twynam will join us at dinner on the next full moon. I understand he is a friend of yours. We would be most pleased if you could attend as well."

Rodian lifted his eyes and nodded again.

Ghassan had not missed the duchess's slip. She had called the captain by his first name, something far too familiar for the public venue and their disparate social ranks.

Duchess Reine turned back to Premin Sykion. "Lady Tärtgyth, would you and Domin High-Tower favor me with a tour of the new library's improvements? I have meant to come for so long, but ... time has simply passed too quickly."

Premin Sykion tilted her head politely to the captain and then led Duchess Reine's entire entourage toward the northeastern passage. High-Tower was the last to follow, with a derisive grunt at Rodian.

Ghassan watched them leave—with a long study of the tall elf walking close in the duchess's wake. The cut of that one's robe was the same, or nearly so, as that of a sage. But white was not the color of any guild order. And the notion of interference with his spell from that source was preposterous. As much as his art was little known among humans, it was less likely to be found among the Lhoin'na—those "of the Glade."

Guild domins and premins would go to great lengths to restrict specific knowledge of translations from the texts. But royal intervention had come too quickly. Had Sykion asked the monarchy for help? And if not, did Duchess Reine or the royal family know something of the text's content, wishing to keep it hidden, even from the captain of the Shyldfälches?

Ghassan exhaled in frustration. One of the royal family had appeared at precisely the right moment, referred to a premin by a noble title, and betrayed a connection to the one man digging too deeply into guild affairs.

And Captain Rodian came straight at Ghassan's table, his jaw clenched. He was obviously unaccustomed to having his leash jerked in, no matter how politely done by such a gentle hand.

"Journeyor Hygeorht," Rodian said through his teeth. "Would you be good enough to walk me to my horse?"

It was not a request, and Ghassan stood up. While considering these new tangles, he had almost forgotten Wynn sitting right across from him.

"You cannot find your horse alone?" he challenged.

"It's all right, domin," Wynn said, swinging her legs over the bench to rise beside the captain. "I'll walk out with him."

Glowing lines and marks flashed across Ghassan's sight, and he reached for her thoughts.

... and all Nikolas's foolishness ... and all this mess around Jeremy and Elias ...

A wave of anxiety flooded Ghassan. What had Nikolas to do with anything? He tried reaching deeper.

Wynn put a hand to her temple and looked around the hall.

Ghassan immediately severed contact. Had she felt him? No, not possible; she had no training or experience. He watched carefully as Wynn followed Rodian out the wide archway.

Perhaps too many spells, cast too quickly, with lost attempts due to new random pieces he had just gathered. For whatever reason, Ghassan felt a twinge building in his own head.

"You know the duchess?" Wynn asked, taking two steps for Rodian's one.

His position as captain was well respected. But even so, members of the Shyldfälches didn't have dinner with the royal family—certainly not at the invite of the wife of a prince, even a deceased one.

"I assisted her once," he said bluntly, but he stared ahead, focusing on nothing.

Wynn didn't press further. She suddenly realized that she knew part of this story. Even in self-imposed seclusion, rumors reached her. The higher they came from, the more momentum they gathered as they rolled downward through all levels of society.

About two years ago Prince Freädherich of the Âreskynna had died, and his body was never found.

The tale was that he and his wife, Duchess Reine, had gone out in a small sailboat one evening. Not even members of the Weardas had accompanied them. The boat was found adrift late the next morning with only the hysterical Duchess Reine aboard.

As a Faunier, she knew nothing of sailing and had been unable to bring the small boat ashore. It was said that when she was found she was half-mad with grief, and couldn't— or wouldn't—explain what had become of her husband. Strangely, not one of the royal family raised charges against her, but just the same, an inquest was required by law.

A young captain of the Shyldfälches, newly promoted when his predecessor retired, investigated the disappearance. The inquest was held privately in the royal court. No one ever learned what the young captain had uncovered.

Though the duchess was never proven wholly innocent in the eyes of the people, neither was she charged in any way. The king and queen still held her dear, as if she were one of their own children by blood rather than marriage. Prince Freädherich's death was officially cited as accidental. And all because of a report presented by the newly appointed captain of the Shyldfälches.

Wynn glanced up at Rodian.

She'd never cared enough about the rumor to put a face to the city captain who accomplished this feat. No wonder Duchess Reine had invited him to dinner.

"Was anyone hurt during the break-in?" she asked.

"No." He glanced down at her. "It happened after closing."

The captain hesitated, and his brows gathered as he scrutinized her, perhaps judging whether to say more.

"Whoever did it," he finally went on, "got into the shop

and then broke *out*. Would any of your people know how or why?"

Wynn was confused by the captain's brief explanation. So many of Calm Seatt's citizens viewed sages as possessing arcane knowledge rather than just as hardworking scholars.

"I don't think so."

Then she mulled Rodian's words more carefully. The thief managed to gain access, but then had to break out?

"You might ask Domin il'Sänke," she added.

"Why?"

"He is a master of metaology, metaphysics and the like, which includes the scholarly study of magic."

When they reached the courtyard, Rodian's white mare stood waiting near the open inner gate, not even tied to a post. She nickered at the sight of the captain.

"A pretty thing," Wynn said as they approached, and she reached up to stroke the animal's velvet nose. "And so gentle."

"Unless I'm threatened," Rodian said, and then his voice softened as he patted the horse's neck. "Then she is fierce. Her name is Snowbird. I trained her myself."

"Do your people raise horses?"

His expression closed up, as if he'd given away something private. Wynn knew he hadn't asked her out here to discuss Duchess Reine or his horse. She waited quietly.

"What was your real reason for going to Master a'Seatt's scriptorium?" he asked.

Flustered, she wasn't certain how to answer. She'd kept stoutly to her lie of seeking out a grief-stricken Imaret. But the captain had certainly heard too much when he caught up to her.

"To learn what truly happened to Jeremy and Elias," she finally answered.

"So, then you would believe their deaths and the break-in are tied . . . to this project of your guild?"

"Yes," Wynn answered.

"Then help me," he said. "Even if you don't know what was in those folios, what did you bring back from the Farlands?"

Wynn stared at him, remembering their seemingly casual chat on the ride back to the guild. The first words that came to mind were . . . *you conniving bastard!*

She bit her tongue. This was why he'd been so innocently curious about sages and journeyors and assignments. All his polite questions were nothing more than a way to get into her head. She stopped petting Snowbird.

"My first loyalty is to the guild," she replied coldly, "as well as to any agreement of confidence requested of them by the royal family. But I have other information you should know."

"And what is that?" he returned.

"Jeremy was working—without guild knowledge—for a moneylender under investigation by the high advocate."

All the morning's trials and frustration faded from Rodian's face.

He slowly shook his head. Wynn guessed that he might've known of such a case, as head of the city guard. But obviously a link to the deaths hadn't occurred to him—not without the connection she'd just provided.

Rodian patted Snowbird once more. He pointed toward the lone stone bench to the courtyard's left, and Wynn followed to sit with him. She repeated what Nikolas had shared concerning Selwyn Midton and the forged account books. For now she kept Nikolas's involvement to herself. Rodian listened carefully to every word.

"Why didn't you tell me this yesterday?" he asked.

"I just found out last night. But please be discreet. Even you can see how badly this might damage the guild's reputation . . . and the memory of a dead apprentice."

"Even I?" he returned, but he let the barb pass. "Who told you this?"

Wynn shook her head. "I cannot say."

Rodian's ire began to spread across his face again.

"There's more," she said.

She wasn't certain how to begin, as Duchess Reine had mentioned one of the parties involved.

"Do you know Baron Twynam's son, Jason?"

"Why?" he asked cautiously, which implied "yes" to her question.

"He and Elias were courting the same girl, a merchant's daughter named Elvina. Jason caught Elias one night and threatened to kill him if he didn't stay away from her. I think Elias was going to meet her the night he died."

Rodian's blue eyes widened, and his voice rose. "Where did you hear that?"

She shook her head. "I'm not even certain it'll be helpful," she replied. "What you do next is your own business, but remember discretion ... if you expect anything more from me."

Wynn got up and headed across the courtyard, and the captain didn't try to stop her.

Rodian had to investigate all possible leads, but he'd been "royally" warned off of pressing the sages—at least for now.

Wynn fought to remain rational. She had to at least entertain the possibility that Jeremy and Elias had died for some reason other than the folio they'd carried. And the burglary at Master Shilwise's was just a coincidence. But a feeling in the pit of her stomach said otherwise.

Entering the common hall, she found Domin High-Tower and Premin Sykion speaking quietly by the great hearth. Whatever tour they were giving Duchess Reine seemed to have been interrupted, and il'Sänke was nowhere in sight. Wynn willed herself calm as she went to her superiors.

"Thank you for seeing the captain out," Premin Sykion said. "A bit of air has done you good."

Wynn bit down again at this condescension. Treating her like a child was just another way of undermining her. Although she didn't care for High-Tower's cold looks and lectures, at least he was openly hostile.

"Thank you," she answered politely. "I understand that we must keep the translations away from general citizens, like the captain ... but you both know someone may be seeking the contents of our folios."

High-Tower grumbled under his breath with a snort, but said nothing discernible.

"If I had access to my journals," she continued, "and translations, and the codex of all recent work, I might help find what this ... *person* is seeking."

"Wynn!" High-Tower growled, trying to silence her.

"I didn't just carry back those texts!" Wynn snapped, and it came out too loud, echoing around the empty hall. "I handpicked every one the best that I could! I know what I chose and why."

She took a long breath, grasping for calm once more, and appealed directly to the premin.

"Please . . . I can help stop these thefts, or at least offer a motivation for them."

Premin Sykion raised a hand at High-Tower's impending barrage.

"Wynn, do you truly believe you would understand the texts better than the masters of our order, or even those of the other orders helping us? Is that not rather prideful and assumptive?"

Wynn clenched her hands so tightly that her fingernails bit into her palms.

"Please . . . Premin," she repeated. "What harm could there be in giving me access?"

The slightest flicker of anger crossed Sykion's narrow, serene face. "Your place here, as well as your soundness of mind, has been in question for some time. You will keep away from what does not concern you."

Premin Sykion and Domin High-Tower walked away together.

Wynn stared after the pair until they vanished out of the north archway. She turned to the fireplace and crossed her arms, clutching herself tightly, as if it were the only way to hold herself in one piece.

Why hadn't she presented a more reasoned argument? Someone or something was willing to kill for the secrets of the texts—someone who could read the Begaine syllabary. And none of her superiors seemed the slightest bit willing to acknowledge that truth.

She leaned forward until her forehead touched the hearth's warm headstones.

"Oh, Chap," she whispered. "What would you do?"

He'd rebelled against his kin, the Fay, not only to save her life, but to do what he knew was right for those he watched over. In becoming an outcast among his kind, even an enemy to them, he found the courage to bear that sacrifice.

Wynn gazed into the hearth's low embers.

If—when—she ever saw Chap again, how could she look him in the eyes unless she found the same in herself?

CHAPTER 6

At midmorning Rodian stepped from the city ministry hall overlooking the bay with two addresses in hand: one for Selwyn Midton's shop and the other for the man's home. He'd heard of charges filed against an illicit moneylender but never connected this to either deceased sage.

Once mounted upon Snowbird, Rodian turned eastward through the city.

The inner business district was closest to the royal grounds. He passed one small bank with polished granite steps and a fine inn of massive size called the Russet Palace. Visiting merchants and even the wealthier ones of Calm Seatt often retained residency there for a whole season. He should've been relieved to have uncovered anything besides the guild itself to investigate, but instinct told him to focus on the contents of those missing folios.

And yet Duchess Reine had asked him to follow other leads.

He passed through the merchant district's fringe, filled with respectable and utilitarian shops for basic necessities. Then he slowed to carefully guide Snowbird through a bustling open-air market.

Why were the royals, the duchess included, protecting the

sages and their project? He still remembered going before her inquest tribunal in the main hall of the greatest of the three castles. At first he hadn't cared for the arrangement.

The royals of old had established a rule for all citizens to be held accountable in like fashion. Legal proceedings were always held at the city's high court, prosecuted by the high advocate of the people. It wasn't proper for any royal family member to be given exception to the rule of law.

But later Rodian had also broken the law—twice.

Upon his first interview with Duchess Reine Faunier-Âreskynna, he noted how much she differed from those of the royal bloodline. Her brother and sister by marriage, Prince Leäfrich and Princess Âthelthryth, remained close at her side. Prince Leäfrich's displeasure over Rodian's questions was politely plain.

Unlike the duchess's chestnut hair, dark eyes, and small stature, all Âreskynna were tall with sandy hair and an aquamarine gaze. Their irises shone like a disturbingly still sea under a clear sky.

The duchess initially struck Rodian as a shattered woman. Only later did he come to know her as strong-willed, private, and protective of her new family. All she told him of the night's boat ride was that she'd turned to peer through the dark toward the distant docks. Being a Faunier and an inlander, she was accustomed to wide-open plains and lush woods, and had never learned to swim. Nor did she know anything of sailing. Getting so far from shore made her nervous.

When she turned back, Prince Freädherich, third in line to the throne, was gone. She hadn't even heard a splash.

Duchess Reine passed that night in panic and anguish over her vanished husband as she drifted alone until dawn in Beranlômr Bay. A spotty tale at best—perhaps too much so to be a lie—and more than this had left Rodian puzzled.

The royal family's belief that the duchess had no part in the prince's disappearance remained absolute. Later he began to share that belief, though he never came to fully understand why. It took time to uncover the few pieces he learned of Prince Freädherich and the Âreskynna as a whole.

From questioning dockhands, and any crew and ship out and about at the time, to finding those who knew scant bits of the prince's past, Rodian assembled pieces that didn't make sense. This wasn't the first time Prince Freädherich had sneaked off and run afoul at sea. Though it was the first time someone had been with him.

On two previous occasions he'd been spotted too late slipping away in a small boat. The first time, in his youth, he'd made it to the open sea before anyone knew and was later caught by panicked Weardas upon a Malourné naval vessel. Then, a year before he married Reine, he returned alone along the shore, escorted by a trio of dwarven thänæ. His boat was later found adrift and undamaged.

And one night Rodian had listened to the sketchy rumors of an elder seafarer.

The old man spent his days selling his services for mending fishing nets. He said Prince Freädherich wasn't the only Âreskynna to exhibit such strange behavior. Others as far back as the king's great-grandmother were known for a silent and unexplained fascination with the sea.

The royals of Malourné were benevolent, and despite Rodian's ambition he took pride in serving them and his people. He'd heard occasional stories in taverns and common houses of the cursed monarchs of Malourné, but he gave them no credence. Folktales abounded in any country, and his faith in the Blessed Trinity of Sentience taught him better than to believe nonsense that defied reason. When his inquiries ran dry and nothing more concrete could be learned, faith was all he had left to lean on.

And he broke the law for the first time.

He should've gone straight to the high advocate, before the court, reported that his investigation was complete, and testified before the inquest tribunal. Instead he went to Duchess Reine.

Rodian told her he couldn't clear her of suspicion, but that he also believed she had nothing to do with whatever happened on the boat. Princess Âthelthryth was present, quiet and watchful, but open relief filled her aquamarine eyes. When he related tales of the Âreskynna and the sea, neither the princess nor the duchess said a word.

At the inquest's closing session, before the tribunal and high advocate, he reported that no evidence of a crime could be found. Not truly a lie, but then he'd said nothing about the "curse."

Unsubstantiated or not, withholding this was the second time Rodian broke the law. And the very act forced him to remember the day of his acceptance into the Shyldfälches, as well as his promotion to captain, when he'd stood before the high advocate with his sword hand upon an old wooden box.

Within that vessel was the *Éa-bêch*—Malourné's first book of the law. Over centuries, the rules and regulations of society had grown until they filled a small library. But the *Éa-bêch* was still the core of it all. Rodian swore by it to uphold the law of the people, for the people.

When Rodian left the inquest that final day, his sword hand ached.

Moral reasoning had told him no good could come from repeating rumors at the inquest. But truth meant everything to him, by both his faith and his duty. He went to temple that same night and prayed—not for forgiveness of the omission, but for relief from doubt in his reasoned decision.

Snowbird slowed for a tottering beggar crossing the road, and Rodian started from remembrance. He found himself in what the locals called the Graylands Empire.

Dull and worn buildings stretched beyond sight, many with shutters hung at broken angles. Dogs and unwashed children ran about, and most of the street lanterns showed decay and rust, their glass either lost or shattered long ago.

Rodian disliked this shabby sector, but duty often called him here. Through the generosity of Âreskynna, civil ministers had set up charities for the dangerously poor. All cities had their districts of low-end businesses run by those who hoped to move up in the world. Unfortunately, such were patronized only by other unfortunates. Many shopkeepers here couldn't make enough even for nails to fix their shutters. Of those who could, some simply didn't bother.

Rodian refused to pity the latter, those who wouldn't help themselves.

He glanced at the paper slip to double-check the address. Selwyn Midton's shop—the Plum Parchment—was listed as offering "clerical services." He turned Snowbird left down a street of decrepit shops and one tavern. He had to place a hand across his face as the scent of burning meat mixed with the stench of refuse in a side alley.

Smoke-stained people milled about in the streets as they went their way, seeking a meager living. Although he passed numerous pony- and hand-drawn carts, he was the only one on horseback.

Rather than a swinging sign, *The Plum Parchment* was painted across a faded door. Rodian pulled Snowbird to a stop, and as he slipped from her saddle he patted her gently on the neck.

Perhaps there was a third time he'd broken the law.

On an evening less than half a moon after the inquest, a young white horse had been delivered to the military barracks. She was exquisite, a gift of thanks from the duchess, but as captain of the city guard Rodian shouldn't have accepted. He kept silent when comrades asked about this high-bred horse he named Snowbird, but likely all knew where she'd come from.

The Plum Parchment's shutters were intact but tightly closed. Rodian tried the front door's latch and found it locked. When he thought of Wynn's story of Jeremy, he couldn't picture a young sage coming anywhere near this place.

"Been gone for two days," someone croaked.

An old woman with no teeth shuffled up from the dirty street. Her thinned hair stuck out from beneath an age-yellowed muslin scarf.

"You are certain?" he asked.

She nodded, her loose-skinned jowls jiggling. "We heard he was called to the court. Serve 'im right, leech that he is."

Moneylenders were always hated, even when legitimately chartered. Rodian couldn't fathom why people with little coin would borrow more at high interest. He dug in his pouch, looking for a copper penny, but with only silver he handed one to her.

"If he comes back, I wasn't here."

The old woman scoffed, but pocketed the coin as she shuffled on.

Rodian mounted and headed northwest. Strangely, Selwyn Midton's home was a good distance from his shop and the Graylands Empire. And he hadn't been to work in two days.

Eventually Rodian entered a residential sector where the main businesses consisted of food carts, eateries, or bread and vegetable stalls—all the things sought on a daily basis near homes. He was surrounded by small, modest houses, but all well kept, as if the inhabitants took pride in their neighborhood. The farther west he traveled, the larger the domiciles became, until he pulled up Snowbird before a two-story stone house crafted in the cottage style, with a wrought-iron fence across its front. He double-checked the address as he dismounted.

How could a Graylands Empire moneylender afford a home like this? Such parasites fared better than those they fed upon—but not this much better.

A young woman in a slightly stained apron came around the house's side carrying two large ceramic milk bottles. As she tried to shift both to one arm, Rodian pulled the gate open for her.

"Thank you, sir."

He waited until she placed the empties in her cart and moved on before he stepped through the gate.

"Snowbird, come," he called.

She followed him in, pressing her nose into his face. He steered her aside off the front walkway.

"Stay."

He closed the gate and approached the house.

A fine brass knocker hung upon a stout mahogany door. He grew more uncertain that this was the correct home— Selwyn Midton might have given the court a false address. He clacked the knocker, and moments later the door opened. He found himself facing the least attractive proper lady he'd ever seen.

Tall as himself, she was neither plump nor thin, but rather blockish from her neck to her hips. A two-finger-width nose hung over a mouth no more than a slash above her chin. Her skin was sallow, and her hair, once dark, was prematurely harsh gray. Even worse, some unfortunate lady's maid had tried to dress those tresses upon her head. The result was a mass of braids like coils of weather-bleached rope.

However, she wore a well-tailored velvet dress of chocolate brown. Small rubies dangled from her thumblike earlobes. And she peered at him through small, hard eyes.

Rodian realized that his revulsion had less to do with her appearance than the cold dispassion she emanated.

"Yes?" she said, and her hollow voice left him chilled.

"Matron Midton?"

"Yes."

He had the right house.

"Captain Rodian of the Shyldfälches. I've come to speak with your husband."

"Why?"

He thought the mention of his division might melt her ice with a little concern, but she remained unimpressed.

"It's a matter of city business," he returned. "Is he at home?"

The simple annoyance on her face told him this woman knew nothing of her husband's court summons. She stepped back and grudgingly let him in.

The foyer was tastefully arranged with a thick, dark rug and a mahogany cloak stand. Squeals of laughter rolled down the hall as four children raced out of what appeared to be a sitting room—three girls and a small boy, all well dressed. They stopped, struck dumb at the sight of him.

Rodian remembered his cloak was open when one of the girls stared at his sword.

"Go back and finish your game," their mother said, shooing them down the hall, but she stopped at a closed door and knocked loudly. "Selwyn . . . a captain from the city guard to see you."

Barely a blink later the door jerked inward.

A handsome man holding a brandy snifter leaned out with wild eyes—not at all what Rodian expected. He'd met moneylenders before, and the ones at the bottom of society all tended to be small, spectacled, shifty, and wheezy.

Selwyn Midton was tall and slender, with peach-tinted

skin and silky blond hair. He wore black breeches and a loose white shirt. He recovered himself quickly and smiled at his wife.

"Thank you, dear. Please come in, Captain. Has there been a neighborhood burglary?"

Rodian advanced, backed him into the study, and shut the door. Then a wide-eyed Selwyn Midton quickly turned on him.

"I have one more day!" he hissed in a low voice. "The advocate already checked that I'll make my court date. He doesn't need to threaten me again!"

His light brown eyes were bloodshot, and his breath reeked of brandy.

"Why have you been away from work for two days?" Rodian asked.

"Why have I . . . ?" His eyes cleared slightly. "You went to my shop?"

Rodian gestured at the polished maple desk resting on an indigo Suman carpet. "Hardly a fitting place of business for someone who lives here."

Midton backed around his desk and settled in his damask chair.

"I've been preparing documents for my court appearance. What a shame that our legal system puts so much effort into persecuting me. All I do is provide much-needed service to people the banks won't even speak to."

"Service?" Rodian repeated.

"Who else, if not me, gives them enough coin to improve their lives?"

Rodian took a breath through his teeth. The only shame would be if this hypocrite were found innocent tomorrow, and that wasn't likely. There was no charter on record allowing the Plum Parchment to engage in moneylending. But regarding Rodian's visit, there was also no clear proof that Selwyn Midton had a hand in the death of two young sages.

Rodian realized he wanted Midton to be guilty of that crime as well.

It *was* possible that, to keep Jeremy silent, Midton had killed the young sage and his companion, and then taken the folio to make it look like a theft. Perhaps the break-in at Master Shilwise's scriptorium was unrelated. Stranger coincidences had happened. At the moment it even seemed more likely than Wynn's mention of a minor noble's son making threats.

Rodian wanted to solve these murders today, and sending this parasite to the gallows would be so much the better. But he checked himself. Such a course went against duty, let alone reason, and hence his faith.

"When you say 'preparing documents,'" he began, "have you been waiting for a young sage named Jeremy Elänqui?"

Midton's mouth went slack. "I beg your pardon?"

"He was helping you alter your ledgers."

"If that boy's been telling lies, I'll raise charges on the guild!"

Rodian focused intently on Midton's face in this crucial moment. "Jeremy can't tell lies. He was murdered two nights ago."

Midton dropped the brandy snifter.

It hit the carpet and rolled under the desk, likely spreading brandy all over that expensive carpet. But Rodian sank—no, fell—into sudden disappointment.

Midton's bloodshot eyes widened in complete shock; then shock faded, replaced by fear.

"Dead? But that's not . . ." Midton began. "You cannot think . . . I had nothing to do with it!"

"Where were you the night before last?"

Midton breathed in harshly. He couldn't seem to get out a word until he jumped to his feet.

"I was here, at home. My wife, children, our cook, they can all verify I never left the house."

The cook's testimony would bear the most weight, more than a wife or child's. Then again, Selwyn Midton could've easily hired someone else to do the killing. In fact, that was far more likely, if such a special poison had been used. For what would this coin gouger know of handling dangerous concoctions?

And yet, how would he even know where to find the rare individual who did?

Rodian had questioned many who'd committed whatever crime was in question—and many who hadn't. Midton was certainly a criminal, but he'd been taken too unaware by the young sage's death.

"Don't ask my family to testify!" Midton rushed on. "I swear I had nothing to do with Jeremy's death. If a hint of this comes out I will be ruined, my wife, my family—"

"After tomorrow you *will* be ruined. Fines for illegal moneylending are high . . . if a fine is all the high advocate seeks from the judges. But fortunately for you, hearsay can't be used, and Jeremy won't be joining you for your court appointment."

Midton appeared to calm a bit, and leaned on his desk with both hands, pitching his voice low.

"I'll be exonerated, and no one here need know it ever occurred. My wife knows nothing of my business and . . . neither does her father."

Rodian blinked. "Your wife has never seen your shop?"

Midton shook his head rapidly. "She doesn't involve herself. Her family came out strongly against our marriage, but she wanted it. We bought this house with her dowry, but I've managed to give her a proper life. When her father passes she will inherit, unless she is disowned. Any whisper of my involvement in a murder investigation could . . ."

His jaw tightened as he dropped back into his chair.

"I had nothing to do with Jeremy's death," he repeated. "If you pursue me publicly, you will destroy my family for no reason . . . and no gain."

The man's background suddenly became clear. Midton had won the affections of a dour, plain-faced woman against her family's wishes—a family of means. He'd hung on by a thread ever since, faking a lifestyle barely affordable as he waited for his wife's inheritance.

Ruining this man might squash a parasite feeding on the desperate and poor. But ten more would scurry in like cockroaches to fill his place. And Rodian had no wish to destroy the four children playing in their sitting room.

"I require a written statement from your wife," he said, "that you were at home on the night in question. How much truth you tell her to explain the need is up to you. Have it ready for her to sign in the presence of my lieutenant when he comes tomorrow. I will speak with your cook and your business neighbors myself. Your current legal issues with the high advocate are your own problem."

Gut feelings or not, Midton still had a strong motive for murder—even stronger than Rodian initially realized. Hiding illegal moneylending, along with his scheme upon his wife's inheritance, was certainly motive enough. But Rodian's words washed anxiety from Midton's expression.

"Thank you," the man breathed.

"Call your cook," Rodian commanded. "I will speak to her alone."

Selwyn Midton hurried out the study door.

Rodian already knew the cook would tell him that the master of the house had been home. That left him with one more lead to pursue . . . and he did not wish to.

After a sparse lunch, Wynn shuffled through the guild's inner bailey. She stayed near the wall as she passed through the small arboretum close to the southern tower. Beyond the wall she occasionally heard people come and go. But not many, as the Old Bailey Road wasn't a main thoroughfare.

When the castle's outer bailey wall had been opened long ago, a double-wide cobbled street had been kept clear, running along the outside of the inner bailey's wall. Only the backs of buildings across that road were visible from the keep. All those faced the other way, toward other shops across the next streets and roads. But if one stopped in a quiet garden or copse of the inner bailey, an occasional passerby could be heard beyond the wall.

"Get, you mutt! Stay out of my garbage!"

That angry voice interrupted Wynn's sulking, and she peered up the wall's height, greater than a footman's pike. Some cook in an eatery must have come out back and shooed off a stray dog. Wynn moved on through the remains of a garden.

The tomato bed was barren, its last harvest sun-dried for winter storage. Deflated by Premin Sykion's refusal to let her see the texts or her journals from the Farlands, Wynn contemplated what to do next.

"Why do they deny these crimes have anything to do with the translation work?"

Wynn pulled her cloak tighter as a late-autumn breeze sent aspen leaves raining down around her. She talked to herself too often these days.

High-Tower and Sykion hadn't made her life easy since her return, but they weren't fools. Even if they wouldn't accept what she suspected, that the killer might be an undead, surely they recognized that guild members carrying folios might be in danger.

Half a year of work had passed, and now someone or something was clearly desperate to see material recently touched upon. Whoever it was could read the Begaine syllabary; otherwise the folio pages would be worthless.

But how had anyone outside the guild learned enough about the folios' content to want to see them at all? Most of the guild, besides those involved in translations, knew even less than Wynn did of the content of those old texts. Unless . . .

. . . someone within the guild—at a high level—had already read something of importance.

But what could drive someone to kill for it?

She passed through the narrow space between the wall and the newer southeast dormitory building. Beyond it and the keep's wall was the old barracks and her own room.

Wynn shook her head at the notion that the murder might be someone within the guild. If a vampire was living among them, she should've spotted it long ago. Once, she'd been deceived by Chane, but looking back she remembered all the signs. He'd always visited at night, never ate, and drank only mint tea . . . his pale face . . . and his strange eyes, sometimes brown . . . sometimes almost clear.

Still, there were the moneylender and the young man who'd threatened Elias to consider.

No, the murderer had to be an undead, and one that killed without leaving any marks, and it had to be outside of the guild's population.

She rounded the east tower and peered along the keep's back at the near end of the new library. Every side of the keep but the front had an additional building added on.

Only the spaces around the four towers, as well as the front side, were left open for gardens and other uses.

The two-story library, barely more than two-thirds the keep's height, was tall enough to view the surrounding city from its upper windows. Although its new stone was pleasant compared to the ancient castle's weathered granite, the library contained only the best selected volumes copied for use by the guild at large. Wynn had always been more drawn to the catacombs beneath the castle—the master archives.

She remembered the sight of Jeremy's and Elias's ashen skin and rigid, horrified expressions. They'd died quickly but in terror and agony.

Wynn turned about, heading back toward the keep's front.

Rodian had said that whoever took the folio from Master Shilwise's shop gained entrance and then had to break out. Wynn was sick of every new discovery making no sense.

How and why would a Noble Dead gain unnoticed entrance, and then not be able to slip away just the same? She rounded the southern tower, returning through autumn aspens and fallow gardens, and then heard someone walking outside along the Old Bailey Road.

The steps scraped and clicked, like a small or short-legged person hurrying to keep up with someone else. But she heard no one else.

Beyond the undead that Wynn had seen or learned of, she knew little about the Noble Dead. Called the *Vneshené Zomrelé* in native Belaskian—or *upír*, or even *vampyr* in Droevinkan—the term referred to an undead of the most potent nature. Unlike ghosts or animated corpses, they retained their full presence of *self* from life. They were aware of themselves and their own desires, able to learn and grow as individuals in their immortal existence.

And her peers would think her mad if she said such a thing out loud.

But all this was recorded in her journals. No doubt all involved in the translation project had read them.

As a girl she'd sometimes assisted Domin Tilswith with his research in Numan folklore and legend. She'd enjoyed

her master's dabbling, up to a point. It often left her wondering why he'd become a cathologer, instead of joining
the Order of Metaology, like il'Sänke. Tilswith's fascination
would've been better served that way. She remembered the
day he mentioned an old term—*àrdadesbàrn*.

It meant "dead's child" in one of the pre-Numanese dialects, the child of a living woman and a recently deceased
man. She'd forgotten that bit of nonsense from her days as
an apprentice, until later, when she had met Magiere.

"Ghosts and walking dead   " she muttered, "*àrdadesbàrn*
and dhampirs . . ."

Wynn stepped out of the bailey's south grove, headed
toward the wall's gateway across from the massive gatehouse.

If Domin Tilswith could find references to the *àrdadesbàrn*, what else might be waiting in the catacombs below
the guild, unread and untouched for years? What vampire
could enter a scriptorium covertly, have to leave it by force,
and could feed without leaving a mark?

Her thoughts were interrupted by a skittering outside
the bailey wall.

A memory rose sharply in Wynn's thoughts. She stumbled midstep and froze in place.

Crouched behind a water trough at night, in a small river
town of Magiere's homeland, Wynn had seen everything
before her permeated with the blue-white mist of Spirit.
That first time she'd raised mantic sight by dabbling in
magic, she'd watched a pale undead come up the main road
through the town.

Vordana.

Grayed, emaciated flesh stretched over the bones of his
face and hands, and filthy white hair hung in mats out the
sides of his cowl. His white shirtfront beneath the soiled
umber robe was stained dark by old blood.

And the mist of Spirit in all things seemed to drift toward Vordana.

Beneath his filmy white eyes and pallid skin, Wynn had
seen no translucent blue-white mist. Only darkness, as if
his whole form were a void that no light could penetrate.
Those drifting trails of Spirit within all things were slowly
swallowed into him.

Vordana had fixed upon Leesil.

Leesil buckled to his knees as his life began to drain away into that undead, though Vordana never even touched him.

Wynn snapped to her senses in the castle's inner bailey as a cold gust of wind pulled on her cloak and hood. The clicking outside the wall came and went, again and again, as if someone paced in agitation.

Like paws on stone, claws catching in the cobble.

Wynn stared up wide-eyed to the wall's top. She gasped in a breath and ran for the gateway.

"Chap!" she cried. "Are you there?"

The gates were open, and she raced out into the Old Bailey Road.

There was no one in sight, let alone a dog. She spun about, looking both ways, then ahead down the Old Procession Road. She raced down that main way, skidding into the intersection with Wall Shops Row.

"Chap!"

All around, people went about between the shops. Three finely dressed gentlemen stood talking before a poster board where the day's recent news was nailed up. A city guard atop a black horse leaned slightly aside as he checked in with two local constables. A dowdy woman in drab attire pushed through a small gathering to elbow her way into a confectionery.

A carriage midstreet came on a bit too fast.

Wynn quickly backpedaled before the paired horses ran her down. And her back thumped into someone tall and solid. That someone grabbed her by the shoulders from behind.

"Are you all right, miss?"

She spun about, face-to-face with a tall, clean-shaven young man in a thick wool cap and coat. Through the coat's open front she saw a canvas workman's apron filled with the tools of his trade—a leather crafter. A young woman in a pleated bonnet peered around his side and frowned at Wynn.

Wynn looked about the street, filled with patrons out and about for a noon meal and errands. Something brushed harshly against her leg.

Wynn stumbled again as another clear memory filled her head.

Chap . . .

She saw through his eyes as he ran the dark streets of Venjètz, Leesil's birthplace, but this memory was much hazier than the last. Details of sights and sounds were missing or indistinct. But she could almost feel his rage as he and Leesil hunted . . . a vampire.

Suddenly the undead vanished from Chap's awareness. He'd been hunting on senses alone, and his quarry simply wasn't there anymore.

"Mama, did you see that?"

Wynn shivered as her head cleared.

The young woman in the bonnet sighed. She grabbed the arm of a little boy, who was dressed much like the tall young man. Blueberry stains encircled the boy's mouth, and the remains of a turnover were clutched in one hand. With the other hand the boy pointed down the road.

"It was bigger than me!" he said.

Wynn looked through the people along the street, her heart pounding.

"Miss?" said the young father. "Do you need help?"

Wynn stared blankly up at his worried frown. His wife now tried to get their other two children's sticky hands off the shopwindow. Wynn backed away from the family and peered through the busy street.

She saw no sign of silver gray fur or crystal blue canine eyes. No dogs at all, let alone the one she ached to see.

The young father shook his head and turned to help his wife with the children.

"Chap!" Wynn shouted again, her voice quickly weakening. "Chap . . . please . . . please come."

Wynn felt so suddenly alone on that busy street that she wanted to sink to her knees and weep. By the time she felt tears on her face, other people were looking at her in passing.

If anyone from the guild saw her now, they wouldn't need rumors and spiteful hearsay to think she'd gone well beyond witless. She backed away from hesitant glances and fled back toward the bailey wall's gate.

Why was this happening to her? Why did she hear claw clicks and then wallow in yet more disturbing memories? First of an undead who drew life force from a distance, and then of another event where a vampire seemed to vanish.

Was she going mad? Were High-Tower and Sykion and all the others right about her? Had all she been through in the Farlands driven her into obsession?

In her travels with Magiere, Leesil, and Chap, she'd encountered only one Noble Dead who could drain life without breaking skin—Vordana, also a sorcerer. To Wynn's best knowledge, his rise from death had been unique. Unlike a vampire, he wore a tiny urn that trapped his spirit and kept his corpse animate.

But Vordana had fed upon a defenseless river town merely by being present within it, draining life without touching anyone.

Wynn hurried through the gates and up the stone path.

She wasn't mad.

What she'd lived through in the Farlands was real. And now did some creature like Vordana hunt sages and whatever lay hidden within the texts? If she wasn't allowed to see those ancient works, there was still the wealth of the guild archives in the catacombs.

Wynn stopped before the gatehouse's tunnel, and late autumn's chill sank deep into her body. She turned and gazed back to the busy intersection a block beyond. Those memories, which had risen suddenly, lingered in her mind.

Even before anyone learned how sentient Chap was, what he was, he'd manipulated Magiere and Leesil with his memory play. It was also part of how he communicated with them—and Wynn. At least until a later manifestation of wild magic's taint began to let her hear his mental voice sent into her thoughts.

From anywhere within his line of sight, Chap could call up in someone any memory that he'd dipped at some time before. He could bring it back to their conscious awareness, and he used this to influence people when necessary.

In that second, hazier memory, Wynn had recalled the hunt as if looking through Chap's eyes. But that night Leesil, Magiere, and Chap had left her behind at an inn.

Wynn stared along the bailey wall, wary of claw clicks on cobblestone.

One thing that Chap could never do was send one person's memories to another. He couldn't even send his own to her.

The second memory hadn't been one of Wynn's own, but one of his.

And that was impossible.

Outside the district nearest the sea, Rodian climbed off Snowbird before a beautiful stone mansion. From its uppermost floor one could look over the bay docks to the white-fringed waves rolling into the farther shore. He led his horse to the front walkway and whispered, "Stay."

Snowbird put her head into his back and snorted softly. It was well past noon, and she'd had no breakfast—neither had he.

"Last stop," he said, and walked up the triple steps.

He knocked at the ornate front doors framed on each side by triple columns, and a pretty maid with a lace cap answered shortly.

"Hello, Biddy," he said.

She smiled. "Good afternoon, Captain. The baron wasn't expecting you."

"I know . . . but is he or Master Jason about?"

She shook her head. "They've both gone to temple. The masons are coming to redo stonework on the west side."

Rodian sighed quietly. The last place he wanted to have this conversation was in the temple, but he couldn't put it off.

"Snowbird is out front, and we've had a busy morning. Could you have one of the stable hands find her a stall and bring her some oats and water? I'll walk from here."

"Of course," Biddy answered. "I'll take her myself."

Rodian was well-known at this house—as was Snowbird. He turned and whistled, and the white mare trotted over, empty stirrups bouncing at her sides.

"Go with her," he said, nodding toward Biddy.

Snowbird tossed her head once and blew warm air into

his hand as the maid reached for her bridle. Girl and horse disappeared around the mansion's north side.

Rodian crossed the courtyard, out the tall iron gates, and headed up the street. He barely noticed the surroundings filled with fine townhouses and other mansions, and looked aside only once as he passed an eatery called the Sea Bounty. A bit pricey for a captain's stipend, but occasionally he'd succumbed to the establishment's fine cuisine.

Not much farther on he slowed before a large construction built from hexagonal and triangular granite blocks laced with faint blue flecks. Again, a trio of columns graced both sides of the landing before the large front doors.

Commissioned dwarven masons had built the temple generations past. Each one of its large wall stones fit so well that not a bit of mortar had been used to set them. Climbing roses had been carefully nurtured to twine about the triple columns' bases and ran in trellis hedges along both sides of the path from the street to the entrance. No sign identified this sanctuary, only those trios of columns—a simpler designation of the sacred teachings of this place.

Rodian climbed the three front steps of the temple for the Blessed Trinity of Sentience. Before he took hold of either door latch, voices rose from somewhere around the building's left side. Rounding the corner, he spotted a burly dwarf hefting a granite hexagon for inspection. Baron Âdweard Twynam and his son, Jason, leaned closer.

"Looks fine," the baron said. "I hope these new ones hold up better."

The dwarf huffed disdainfully. "Wind and water always get the best of stone . . . after many years."

As Rodian approached, the mason set down the stone with a thud that shuddered through the ground.

"Siweard," said the baron with a smile. "Good to see you."

Baron Âdweard Twynam was tall and thinned by age, with hair and beard neatly trimmed—both gone steel gray. His polished boots, blue tunic, and lamb's-wool cloak fit him perfectly, and his smile reached all the way to his eyes. His son stood in stark contrast.

Jason was barely a head taller than the dwarven mason, though solid for his size. His thick, dark hair curled to his shoulders, and his skin was dusky like his mother's. He rarely smiled, unless he found himself at an advantage of some kind. His near-black eyes shifted constantly, as if seeking any opportunity to take offense or make a challenge.

Rodian found Âdweard studying him with a serious face.

"What's wrong, my friend?"

"Is anyone else inside?" Rodian asked.

"No ... except Minister Taultian and his two acolytes. We've no meetings or gatherings today. Jason and I just wanted to check on the work."

"Can we speak inside? Something unfortunate has happened."

"Of course." And the baron nodded at the mason. "You have things well in hand, Master Brim-Wright. Send the final bill to the sanctuary, and I'll make certain it's settled directly."

The dwarf nodded curtly and began to direct two men working with him.

The temple's backside faced toward the sea, and though set within the city's wealthy district, storms and salt-laden winds had eroded it as much as any other building. It had been a long while since repairs were needed, and Rodian couldn't spot any place in the wall that showed flaws. But better to replace stones before weathering turned to some more troubling imperfection.

Âdweard gestured to Jason and placed a hand on Rodian's shoulder. "Come. We'll go make tea. My old bones could do with a little extra heat."

The three rounded to the temple's front, passing between the paired triple columns and through the wide double doors. They stepped directly into the main sanctuary room.

Hardwood floors were polished weekly, as were the long tables stretching up both sides of the main chamber to the stagelike altar. But Rodian saw no sign of Minister Taultian or his acolytes. At the room's far end, upon the raised platform's central dais, stood three life-size figures carved from white marble.

A man wearing the clothes of a common laborer stood behind a woman with a book in her arms. Before the pair was a child with long hair, too young to ascertain its gender.

The Toiler, the Maker, and the Dreamer.

Swenen the Father—the Toiler—gathered what had passed and supplied the Mother's needs. Wyrthana the Mother—the Maker—tended and prepared for what was needed at present. Méatenge the Child—the Dreamer—imagined future days and what might be.

This trinity maintained past, present, and future for all sentient beings, and always would. The sages in their scholarly fervor read too much into what they uncovered. Their eager speculations led them astray. Life, as well as sentience, had always been—would always be—ever-growing and continuous from the first spark of sentience itself. There had been no "great war" that covered the world.

Such extreme interpretation of uncovered relics only created fear and interfered with the natural order. The very idea was offensive, as Toiler, Maker, and Dreamer would've never allowed anything so horrible to occur.

Before stepping fully into the sanctuary, all three men paused to whisper in unity.

"By the Toiler . . ." And they raised one hand, fingers up with palm turned sideways.

"By the Maker . . ." And they each closed that hand gently, as if grasping something from the empty air.

"And by the Dreamer . . ." And they pulled their closed hands, thumb side inward, to their foreheads.

"Bless all who turn this way with heart, mind, and eyes open."

Rodian led the way through the sanctuary. They passed around the dais and through a rear door into the minister's office with a small hearth.

It always remained open and accessible to the entire congregation. Furnished with simple chairs with somber-colored cushions, the room also contained a wide ash-wood desk and two smaller matching writing tables. The walls were lined with bookshelves filled with carefully maintained volumes. They held the overview of knowledge and culture of the world, as well as the teachings of the faith.

Knowledge was sacred, and some of these texts contained records of the world's true history, and the manner in which awareness came into being.

Rodian realized he was growing hungry and thirsty. He set a half-full teakettle on a hook over the fire. No one had spoken since their prayer upon entry, and Jason folded his arms. Âdweard cocked his head, studying Rodian with concern.

"I've not seen you this troubled in a long while," he said. "And you missed the last service . . . as well as the social the night before."

Rodian breathed in twice, uncertain where to begin. This would be far different from questioning citizens at large. These two were more than friends—they were brethren. They shared his beliefs that higher thought and its moral processes were the prime virtue that raised humanity to its cultivated state. And knowledge belonged to those who possessed true ability and clarity to use it.

Other members of the order included nobles, politicians, men and women of the legal fields, and even a few prosperous merchants. New members had to be sponsored for a period of two years. Âdweard had sponsored Rodian, with the added advantage of becoming closely connected to elements of the city's elite.

But regardless of discomfort, truth mattered most, even if it meant interrogating two of his own. And if Jason had anything to do with the death of two misguided young sages, then that truth had to be exposed.

Rodian put tea leaves into three cups and poured the softly boiling water.

"I'm conducting an investigation for the sages' guild," he finally said.

Jason's brow wrinkled over a sneer, and even Âdweard couldn't quell the cinch of his brows. The congregation's members viewed the sages as indiscriminate when it came to their choice of initiates, much as they recognized that the guild had also done great good for the people. But they exposed weak-minded initiates to their inflated and imaginative interpretations of history.

"The sages—" Jason began, his voice low and venomous.

"Two journeyors are dead," Rodian cut in, watching him intently. "One was a young man named Elias."

Jason swallowed hard. "Dead? How?"

"Murdered, possibly by poisoning, in an alley near a scriptorium. Do you know a girl named Elvina?"

Rodian fired his final question before Jason responded to anything else. He watched the young man's eyes widen in silence. Jason dropped his arms, turning wary and frightened.

"What is this about?" Âdweard asked sharply.

For the first time Rodian regretted his position. "There is a claim that Jason made threats against Elias . . . because of this girl."

"Who?" Jason demanded. "Who said that?"

"Did you threaten him?"

"He shouldn't have even been speaking to her! A sage . . . not even that, just a journeyor still in—"

"Answer me!" Rodian ordered.

The steel gray of Âdweard's hair echoed suddenly in his hardening gaze, but his son still rambled angrily.

"Someone had to protect her name," Jason growled. "You of all people should know that."

"This is my duty," Rodian returned. "And I am trying to help you. Where were you the night before last?"

Âdweard stared in shock and then ran a hand over his face. "Of course, Siweard, as captain of the guard you must follow this through. Faith as well as duty demand it." He settled slowly into a chair. "Drink your tea. You look tired."

Tension faded as Rodian sat and took a long sip, the liquid's warmth flowing down his throat. He took another sip.

"Jason was with me that night—and Minister Taultian," Âdweard said. "As well as many others here in the temple. We first went to the Sea Bounty for an early supper, and then came here for a social to plan the next gathering. Later we went home."

"How late?"

"Near the mid of night, the fourth bell. Much later than old Taultian could stand. He retired earlier, once ceremonial considerations were in order."

Rodian settled back in his chair and couldn't stop a long exhale of relieved tension.

As with Selwyn Midton, Jason's alibi didn't exonerate him. He could've hired someone else to kill Elias. A father's witness would be suspect, but it was a start. Jason was accused of threatening a young sage, and crimes of passion weren't usually carried out by hired thugs.

"So," Âdweard said, "you now have my word, though you could certainly ask after others of the congregation."

Rodian nodded and waved off the suggestion. Jason was far from a paragon of the congregation, and too sly for his own good. But Rodian didn't believe the son of Baron Twynam capable of such cold-blooded brutality. A petty whelp and a bully, but rarely would that kind go as far as murder.

"I'll need written statements from you both," he said, "and one from Minister Taultian. That should be enough, if any further pursuit of Jason arises. If I can solve this soon, the statements will be filed away without undue attention."

Jason puffed a breath and turned aside, averting his indignant gaze.

"Thank you." Âdweard sighed. "Two young sages murdered. I cannot see why. What do you believe was the true motive?"

"A folio of scribed pages," Rodian answered. "Have you heard anything concerning a translation project at the guild?"

The baron frowned. "Whispers concerning some old find . . . but no more. The royal family has no idea how deluded these sages and their ideas can be. If not for their public schools and pragmatic services, I couldn't see why the king continues to fund them." He shook his head. "If this project is the cause of deaths, perhaps someone in power will put a stop to it."

Rodian blinked and stood up as his thoughts turned inward.

Perhaps the true motive wasn't acquiring the folios but destroying them? This hadn't occurred to him before. He'd considered only greed or desire for secret information.

Âdweard hadn't realized what he suggested and spoke only from an intellectual perspective. On second thought, Rodian considered the motive unlikely. Destroying the transcribed passages still left the originals and the sages' own notes intact at the guild.

"Can we take you to the Sea Bounty for a late lunch?" Âdweard suggested.

"Thank you, no," Rodian replied. "I have other duties at the barracks and should head back. Bring your statements to Lieutenant Garrogh before signing them." He paused and turned. "Jason . . . my apologies, but I am trying to protect you. Stay away from Elvina until all this is over. Remember that, or suffer for it."

For once Jason's sullen demeanor broke, and he nodded. "I was only thinking of Elvina's good name."

Rodian kept his response to himself—*no, you were thinking of yourself*—but he believed Jason innocent of murder.

"I'll see you both at the next service."

He stepped from the office, pausing long enough to pay homage at the altar, then left to find Snowbird. But Âdweard's words echoed in his head.

If this project is the cause of deaths, perhaps someone in power will put a stop to it.

CHAPTER 7

Wynn burst into her room, going straight for her desk table without shutting the door.

But she stopped halfway and glanced at her storage chest. Changing directions, she dropped to her knees and lifted its lid.

Several items from her travels rested inside, but she reached for one in particular: a special quill with a white metal tip. It had been a gift from one of the elven elders during her visit among the an'Cróan, Those of the Blood. Closing her eyes, she could still remember Gleann's kind face as he'd pushed the quill and sheets of parchment at her, so she could keep a record of her experiences and observations.

The notes she recorded had survived a great deal—including a shipwreck and the grueling mountain trek through the Pock Peaks. But since returning home, Wynn hadn't used this quill. With all her journals confiscated, she'd almost felt as if she would betray the memory of Gleann's kindness by using the quill here.

She picked it up now and closed the chest.

Hurrying to her desk, she gathered a bottle of ink and a blank journal. Rubbing her crystal harshly until it glowed, she mounted it in the tin clip holder inside her cold lamp. Arms loaded, she hurried out, the lantern clinking against the door as she shut it.

It had been a long while since she'd been filled with a sense of purpose. She barely noticed Miriam coming up as she hurried down the far stairs.

"Hello, Wynn."

Wynn offered a quick smile and moved on. But when she cracked open the door at the stair's bottom, a double column of ten young initiates marched out of the gatehouse tunnel, straight toward the keep's main door.

Wynn pulled back and closed the door halfway.

A pair of apprentices, one in brown and the other in light blue, walked ahead of the initiates—a rather odd combination. Leading the procession was brown-robed Domin Ginjeriè. She was the youngest domin ever in the Order of Naturology. Obviously she'd taken a band of initiates for a field outing or perhaps some community service.

Right then Wynn had no wish to face anyone.

Thirteen sages passed through the keep's main doors.

And still Wynn waited. Giving them time to clear the entryway, she then raced quickly across the courtyard to the main building. Upon finding no one inside the doors, instead of turning left past the common hall, she went right down a long stone corridor. Passing the hospice, lower seminar chambers, and other rooms, she hooked left at the passage's end, intent upon reaching the spiral stairwell at the base of the east tower. Before she reached the antechamber's door, a smooth voice with a Suman accent floated from out of a seminar room across the passage.

Wynn paused, stepping back to peek through the room's open door.

"The third Element for practical consideration is Air," Domin il'Sänke said.

The domin sat upon a stool before a half circle of small benches filled by a dozen or more young figures in robes. Not all the students were metaologers. Several wore the pale blue of sentiology, and a few others the teal of conamology or the brown of naturology. There were even three initiates, though it wasn't common practice for such to attend seminars on special topics. Wynn knew she shouldn't linger, but she stood fascinated, watching as il'Sänke raised both hands, palms up, and the sleeves of his dark blue robes slipped, exposing his slender wrists.

She'd forgotten that he'd offered to teach during his stay, though she hadn't known he would include seminars for students from any order. Normally metaology seminars were held on the second floor, but it seemed he'd obtained a more commonly used room.

"Many novice practitioners discount Air as a lesser Element," il'Sänke continued, "believing it less useful than Fire or Water . . . or even Earth." He slowly spread his palms, as if moving them consciously through the air.

Some domins and masters could prattle on until their students drooped, half-conscious, but all those here fixed their eyes on the dark-skinned domin. And Wynn noted a particular tall young man in midnight blue sitting far off to the left.

"Dâgmund?" she whispered.

She hadn't seen him in years, and knew him only in passing. He'd made journeyor and left on assignment before she'd even headed to the Farlands with Domin Tilswith. But now he was back? Perhaps he was finished, and returned for a new assignment.

Or was he here to petition for master's status already? It couldn't have been more than three years. And he certainly wouldn't be attending such a general introduction to metaphysical elements.

"Yet Water and Fire, even the dust of Earth, can be carried within Air," il'Sänke continued. "And thus Air could be viewed as most essential among the five Elements, via either conjury or thaumaturgy. It can hold a special place as facilitator when dealing in works of higher complexity."

Wynn sighed. How nice it would be to simply join in, to listen to il'Sänke's teachings. But she didn't have time for such diversions.

Then Dâgmund turned his head, peering toward the door, and Wynn held her place a moment longer.

Stout cheekbones were his most prominent feature beneath pale blue eyes. At first he seemed troubled by the sight of her—or perhaps just confused. Then his high fore-head smoothed. With the barest smile he nodded to her, but it took a moment before she nodded back.

She'd grown so accustomed to disdain, suspicion, and wari-ness cast her way that even a brief friendly acknowledgment was unsettling. Perhaps he hadn't been back long enough to hear about her. She'd barely known him, considering their differing paths, and hadn't seen him since her earliest days as an apprentice.

But she remembered one time in a room like this one.

Some apprentices of cathology wanted to hear a lecture by Premin Hawes on mantic practices of thaumaturgy. It wasn't really of interest to her, but Wynn tagged along any-how. By the time it was over her curiosity had grown, and Dâgmund had been there among a great number of ap-prentices from metaology. She'd asked him a few questions in passing, wanting to read more on the theories and prac-tices of information gathering via the arcane arts. He gave her the title of an obscure text hidden in the archives that covered the basics of rituals in thaumaturgical manticism. Little did she know then how much trouble that would cause her later.

"But what about sorcery?" a small voice peeped up. "That's got none of the Elements in it."

The entire room went quiet. Dâgmund turned sharp eyes of concern on one of the tan-robed initiates sitting in the front row. That word—sorcery—was rarely even spoken.

Domin il'Sänke was still and somber, folding his hands in his lap. How would he answer without squelching simple curiosity?

"Well, it does and it does not," he finally replied. "The Elements are not *in* any magical practice. They metaphori-cally represent the makeup of the universe's greater exis-tence. The fields of magic are not a matter of practice as much as differing ideological approaches ... as related to the Three Aspects of Existence—Spirit, Mind, and Body."

Wynn was dubious, but at least he'd done better than Pre-min Hawes, or especially High-Tower, in dealing with a naïve initiate.

"Each of the five Elements have three forms, according to

the Aspects," he added. "For example, take my own order. Metaology is associated with Spirit among the Elements, but it has three references or representations according to the Aspects: Spirit is, well, the spiritual side, while its intellectual reference is Essence, and its physical symbol is the Tree. Similarly we have Air, Gas, and Wind, and then Fire, Flame or Light, and Energy . . . and so on."

Wynn was familiar with all this, and it seemed the domin was politely diverting from the original question. That same young initiate raised his hand, waving it in the air.

Il'Sänke let out a low chuckle.

"Yes, I know . . . The term Spirit is used for both an Aspect and an Element. But let's leave that puzzle for another day. It is the Aspects, not the Elements, in which we find the grounding for the ideologies of magic. Thaumaturgy is the body, the physical ideology, while conjury is the spiritual or essence-based approach. . . ."

The domin took a deep breath. Perhaps he thought that would be the end of it, but Wynn saw that it wasn't. That persistent little initiate leaned forward expectantly.

"As to sorcery," il'Sänke finally said, "it is little known . . . and no one known to us practices it, even among metaologers. It is . . . severely frowned upon."

Wynn choked—it was more than frowned upon.

Mages and lesser practitioners weren't common, even among the guild. Thaumaturgy was the most accepted, and conjury of limited sorts was tolerated. But sorcery, by whatever term in varied cultures, was feared—hated—and rightly so. The power and skill to apply one's will against the world and other beings had been a death knell as far back as any bits of history uncovered.

And she did know of one such person—Vordana. Fortunately Leesil had sent that one to his final end.

Wynn forced herself to leave the domin's lecture.

Juggling her burdens, she heaved open the antechamber's heavy door. Across that small space she reached one of two doors to be found in either the north tower or the east tower. They were always left unlocked whenever any of the archivists were in the catacombs, and so she pushed this one open.

The cold lamp's crystal illuminated stone steps spiraling downward into the dark. A slight smell of stale dust filled her nose, and she could taste it on her tongue. No candles, torches, or flames of any kind were allowed below. All those entering the catacombs had to acquire a cold lamp from the archivists or bring one of their own. And only those with their own—journeyor status or above—were allowed below without supervision.

How long since she'd been down here? Certainly not since she and Domin Tilswith had left for the Farlands over two years ago. Most texts of general use had been copied and placed in the new upper library. Few of her peers had reason to go digging for anything else.

Gripping the cold lamp's handle with her right hand, she shifted her burdens under that same arm. Tugging up her robe's hem with her left, she descended. Soon a dim light grew from below, and, taking the last step, Wynn emerged into a cavernous main cellar.

In spite of the recent tragedy and frustration, she felt like a scholar again.

Wooden shelves lined the walls, filled with matching bound volumes of dark leather among a few cedar-plank sheaves of loose pages. Several tables filled the space, lit by cold lamps hung at the chamber's four corners. And a withered old man in a gray robe sat hunched over a table, writing rapidly.

"Domin Tärpodious?" she said, stepping closer.

Likely engrossed in recataloguing old volumes, he finally glanced up.

Old Tärpodious squinted milky eyes over a long beaked nose, as if uncertain who had spoken. The expression made him look like an old crow, though his wrinkled skin was the ashen white of someone who rarely ventured out-of-doors. His white hair was thin, and his hands looked brittle, but he rose suddenly with a smile that multiplied the lines in his face threefold. He greeted her with genuine pleasure.

"Young Hygeorht?" the old archivist asked, still squinting. "Is that you?"

Years of working by only a cold lamp's light had limited his eyesight. It happened to all cathologers posted as archivists.

"Yes," Wynn answered. "I've come seeking your help once again."

Flattering Tärpodious's expertise was best, and he rarely received visitors down here.

Archivists were a strange lot altogether, preferring subterranean silence and solitude to even their own quarters above. They spent days and some nights—there was no difference down here—cataloguing, indexing, and organizing centuries of acquisitions held in the guild branch. And any one of them could quickly locate whatever text another sage sought. This was part of what it meant to be a cathologer.

"Has Tilswith returned?" Tärpodious asked, his voice breathy and reedy.

Wynn would have to tread carefully. She could hardly tell him that she suspected the killer of two young sages was undead, not if she wanted his help.

"No," she answered. "He's still in Bela, establishing our new branch in the Farlands."

Tärpodious and Tilswith were old friends whose individual interests so often reached beyond the texts and parchments housed in the new library above. Wynn's former master had spent quite a few evenings down here in the company of the venerable archivist.

"But I'm a journeyor now, and I received a letter from him," she added. "He asked me to come see you. Many outer regions of Belaski are filled with superstitions. And you know how that piques his interest. You once guided him to folklore references . . . especially one about the *àrdadesbàrn*, the 'dead's child.'"

Tärpodious scratched his bony chin. "Truly?"

Wynn held up her journal and shrugged with a forced roll of her eyes. "He wants direct copies of any similar folklore, so I may be down frequently over the next few days. Can you guide me?"

It pained her to lie to the old archivist. Tärpodious lived in such seclusion that he would have no knowledge of—or interest in—the social politics of the guild, and certainly not regarding High-Tower's order that she never mention the undead.

The cavernous chamber, once the keep's main storage room, boasted three archways of large and heavy frame stones. Tärpodious lifted his cold lamp from the table and shuffled toward the east one.

"Tilswith and his superstitions!" He chuckled. "How far he might've gone, if only he'd turned his mind to something real. Come, child."

Swallowing guilt, Wynn followed. She knew how the archives were organized, but it had been a long time since her last visit. And one could quickly get lost in the catacombs.

Hundreds of years past, when the guild took possession of the first castle, they immediately began to excavate with the assistance of dwarven masons and engineers. The work continued over decades. What had once been basic chambers for storage and dungeons were carefully expanded in whatever direction didn't encroach on the city's growing sewer system. There was also a double level of basements below the northeast workshops, where the laboritorium was housed, for the making of cold lamp crystals and other items.

Rooms led into chambers that led through clusters of alcoves . . . which led into more rooms. Faded wooden cubicles and antechambers along the way provided places to sit and peruse texts, for no material could be removed without the archivists' explicit permission—and a very good reason for it.

All spaces and walls along the way were filled with endless rows of shelves, and Wynn soon lost count as everything began to look the same. She blinked once, and the backs of her eyelids projected images of sheaves; bound books, some spineless with only cord stitching showing; and scroll cases everywhere. No cold lamps were placed this far in, and she stayed close on Tärpodious's heels, their two lamps the only illumination to ward off the blackness.

"Here," he said with a sudden stop, fingering a tall set of shelves along a passageway. "Some from the Suman lands, more from our scattered old cultures. A few have been translated into the Begaine syllabary, but not many."

She nodded, peering at the shelves. "I can read some Sumanese."

"Stick to Spirit by Fire, for the general accumulations," Tärpodious added, "or by Air, should you need to branch out into social customs based on old tales."

For an instant the references left Wynn's mind blank. Tärpodious tapped the bookshelf's end, and she saw the faded etchings filled with remnants of paint in the old wood.

Each guild order was symbolically associated with one of the Elements of existence—Spirit, Fire, Air, Water, and Earth. In turn, geometric symbols for such were used to classify, subclassify, and cross-reference subject matter by emphasis and context.

On the bookshelf's vertical end was a circle above a triangle.

Circle—for Spirit and the Order of Metaology, with its study of metaphysics, philosophy, religion, folklore, etc.

Triangle—for Fire and the Order of Cathology, with its devotion to informational and organizational pursuits.

In this section, Wynn would find works cataloguing and organizing collected information on the subject she sought.

"Thank you," she said. "I'd like to get a good start before supper."

Her breath quickened as she scanned faded titles down a few volumes with cracked leather spines. Her gaze paused briefly on one written in Dwarvish. She suddenly longed to be alone, to pore through these volumes in search of answers. But Tärpodious walked farther down the row, his gray robes dragging through the dust.

"These here are the oldest . . . too old to date accurately, some in varied ancient Numanese dialects and a couple in the elven Êdän script. Much of the content is poorly organized and difficult to follow. Not much is of interest anymore, so you wouldn't find it in the upper library."

"Yes, thank you," Wynn repeated anxiously. "I don't wish to keep you from your work."

He squinted again, perhaps hearing her implied intent. "Yes, yes, but don't try to reshelve anything, or it may end up out of place. Be selective, and then leave any works in the alcove. I'll check on you later."

"That would be kind," Wynn said.

Tärpodious shuffled away, only the glow of his lamp marking his passage through the dark. The instant the old domin was out of sight, Wynn backtracked to the nearest antechamber and dropped everything but her lamp on the table. She scurried back to the shelves, and began peering at spines and labels. Finally she pulled two woodbound sheaves, each with no markings or title, and one old book. Clutching the heavy burden, she rushed back to the antechamber.

Wynn paged through the first sheaf of stacked loose sheets and found that it was a collection of various short works divided by hardened parchment separators. Though old and worn, all were in their original languages yet written in ink, which meant these weren't originals but copies, regardless of age.

Texts were often duplicated to keep originals safe in storage. Later, those of greatest importance were transcribed again using the Begaine syllabary, some in their initial language and some translated as well into Numanese—if they were of good general use for the upper library.

Not this sheaf. It remained a hodgepodge, deemed unnecessary for such expense or time. But that didn't mean it held nothing of interest. The first pages were written in Iyindu, a nearly forgotten desert dialect of the Suman Empire.

Wynn grumbled under her breath.

For all her language skills, this was one she barely understood, and her research wouldn't go quickly. She might work her way through dozens of texts before finding a single useful tidbit. She put that first stack aside and paged deeper into the sheaf.

She had no idea what she was looking for, only that she sought an undead, aware and sentient enough to desire the folios—recent ones—and that it could read the Begaine syllabary. And it could drain life without leaving a mark.

Wynn let out a sigh—too many contradictions muddling her thoughts.

The most expedient way to pinpoint a motive would've been through the translation project. Such thoughts—wishes—wouldn't help her now. She didn't even know where the original texts were being kept, let alone where translated portions were being worked on.

Normally translation was done aboveground on the main hall's third floor, close to the offices of the premins. But they and the domins feared anyone outside the project's staff finding out too much. The original texts themselves would be hidden somewhere very secure.

And Premin Sykion and Domin High-Tower would never let her near them.

No, trying to uncover the undead in question was the best she could do for now—better than doing nothing at all.

The next bundle of pages was written in Heiltak, a common enough alphabet used in pre-Numanese languages.

Wynn opened her blank journal, white-tipped quill in hand, and began reading. By the time she neared the bottom of the second stack within the sheaf, piles of sheets were all over the little table.

She barely comprehended a third of what she could actually read, and less than half of one journal page was covered in jotted notes. Not much of it related directly to what she sought. Most were odd terms unconnected to what she would call an undead, let alone a Noble Dead.

Yâkasath—a type of "demon," from Sumanese superstitious references compiled by an earlier scholar. It wasn't even a Sumanese word as far as she could work out. These creatures mimicked the form of a person their victim would recognize and trust.

Had Jeremy and Elias been tricked by someone they thought they recognized?

No, more likely that myth was a variation on the *ghül,* supposedly "living" demons. Banished from their mythological underworld, they were thought to range the barren mountains. *Ghül* had to eat their victims while still alive in order to be nourished.

Wynn shuddered at such a notion, but it was nonsense. As if there would be enough people to feed on in such remote places. And unlike vampires or *yâkasath*, or even the unknown undead hunting the folios, *ghüls* ate flesh. That would certainly leave a mark on a corpse.

She reached the last stack in the second sheaf, and it was

written in Dwarvish. Wynn skimmed the text as she dipped her elven quill into the small ink bottle. She read Dwarvish better than she spoke it, giving her time to work out any older characters. Still, the text was archaic and the syntax difficult to follow, until . . .

Hassäg'kreigi.

Wynn's gaze locked on that one term. She scanned it twice more to be sure she'd read the characters correctly. When those black-armored dwarven warriors had secretly visited High-Tower, and vanished shortly after, the domin had called them by this title.

Stonewalkers.

She jerked the quill back to her journal—and heard something rattle on the tabletop.

Wynn sucked a frantic breath. The little ink bottle teetered and spun amid all the loose sheets. She dropped the quill and grabbed it with both hands, bringing it to sudden stillness. A few black droplets spattered over her thumb.

Wynn broke out in a sweat.

If she blemished even one sheet, Domin Tärpodious might drop dead in his tracks—but not before he took her with him. She slowly released the bottle and carefully lifted her ink-spattered hand away. Ripping a blank page from the journal, she did her best to clean her thumb. Wynn gazed hurriedly across the page of dwarven letters.

There was only one brief mention in a passage about the death of a dwarven female, a thänæ of unknown skills named Tûnbullé—Wave-Striker. That was an odd name, considering dwarves didn't like traveling by sea. Wave-Striker had been "honored" and "taken into stone" by the *Hassäg'kreigi*, the stonewalkers.

Wynn had no idea what this meant. Her thoughts rushed back to what she'd overheard in High-Tower's study.

The two vanishing dwarves were dressed like no others she'd ever seen. It seemed very unlikely that they were masons or sculptors, who carved likenesses of their people's "honored" dead. Nothing more in the text helped her, so she took notes for later use and turned to the book selected along with the two wood-sandwiched sheaves.

Wynn was instantly relieved, for it was written in late-era

Numanese. The book's spine was worn beyond reading, but an inner page carried its title.

Gydes Färleôvan—Tales of Misbelief—was a collection of folktales traced from the various peoples who predated the nations of the Numan Lands. She turned the pages, trying to catch and decipher strange terms.

... *pochel* ... mischievous nature guardians, prone to pranks upon farmers ...

... *géasbäna* ... frail little "demons" who stole people's life essences, turning them into will-less slaves ...

... *wihte* ... creatures or beings created rather than naturally birthed ...

Wynn sat upright at that last term. The coastal country south of Malourné was called Witeny, and its people the Witenon. The similar sound was probably just a coincidence. Then she noticed that the light in the antechamber had grown dim.

Her cold lamp crystal had waned to half strength. How long had she been down here? She took the crystal out, rubbed it back to brilliance, and replaced it.

Wynn lowered her chin on her hands folded atop the open book. She closed her tired eyes for a moment. Her head ached and she'd made no true discoveries. She took a weary breath, straightened up, and read ...

> ... *that* blâch-cheargéa *gripped the young minstrel by the throat* ...

Wynn pulled her hands back and read onward.

> *Try as he might, the minstrel's fists passed through his tormentor as through smoke. He turned pale and dangled dead before the entire village in the grip of* Âthlyensmyotnes. ...

Wynn's thoughts grew still.

Two words in the short tale were unclear, and not part of the narrative's dialect. *Blâch-cheargéa* meant something like "black terror-spirit," but how could a spirit be black, let alone hold up a man in its grip? And the other term didn't make sense.

Âthlyen was a compound word no longer used in Numanese, one that she'd read in accounts of the pre-nation clans that had inhabited this land. It meant ruler by divine or innate right, rather than by bloodline or selection, but the term's latter half wasn't Numanese—not by any dialect that Wynn knew of. She did know a word that sounded similar.

The elven root word *smiot'an* referred to "spirit," as in that of a person and not the Element. The Lhoin'na, the elves of her continent, were the longest-standing culture here—long enough that some of their root words, classified by the guild under the grouping of New Elvish, had been absorbed and transformed in human tongues as pure nouns.

She pulled the book closer, rushing through the text in search of more, but the tale was only half a page long.

A black terror-ghost . . . sovereign of spirits?

It could touch—physically touch. This had to be another superstition. Even if this tale was an account of a true undead, it wouldn't be the first bit of nonsense concerning such.

Leesil and Magiere had tracked and impaled a vampire named Sapphire, only to have the creature vanish when they turned their backs for an instant. Staking a vampire through the heart turned out to be superstition, one that even some vampires believed in. But the tale in the book still left her wondering about Master Shilwise's scribe shop.

Someone had gotten in, without forcing entry, but then had to break out.

Perhaps the creature in this tale was a mage—like Chane or Welstiel—maybe a thaumaturge, working magic of the physical realm. Yes, a vampire mage would have many years to become highly skilled. At a guess, it might learn how to transmute its solid form into a gaseous state at will, and slip through the cracks of a door.

All right, so it was a silly notion for children's ghost tales, but she'd seen stranger things in the last two years. And there was still the puzzle of why whoever had slipped in had to break out.

Wynn took up her quill and turned a fresh page in her journal. She recorded the entire short tale in the Begaine script. For now, her best path was to search Numanese writings for any further mention of the *blâch-cheargéa* and *Äthlyensmyotnes*. Second, she should search any elven works in the archives, considering the strange hybrid title. She stood up, ready to seek out whatever she could.

"Young Hygeorht!"

Wynn jumped in surprise. Domin Tärpodious stood at the antechamber's entrance, his milky eyes wide in horror. At first she wasn't certain why. He shuffled in, disapproval coloring his pale face.

"Surely you didn't need all of these at once for Tilswith's research?"

Wynn glanced about.

Disheveled piles covered the whole table, and a few sheets had slipped off to scatter about the floor.

"Oh . . . oops," she said. "I must've . . . I didn't realize . . ."

With the old master archivist already displeased, she knew better than to offer help in straightening up. She quickly shut the old book.

"Off with you," he huffed, almost to himself. "I should've come sooner and rousted you for supper."

Wynn stared back. "Supper?"

"Cooked, consumed, and cleaned up," he replied gruffly. "An apprentice just brought down my meal. Best get upstairs and find some leftovers."

Wynn hesitated. Now that she had a lead, there was still so much to do.

"Be off!" Tärpodious snapped, already gathering sheets into sheaves.

"Thank you for the help," she said, and retrieved her belongings. "And again, I apologize. I'll be more discerning next time."

Wynn slipped out, turning right down the corridor, her

cold lamp lighting the way between the laden shelves and the catacombs' old stone columns and walls.

"Wynn!"

Tärpodious's sharp call made her whole back cinch tightly. She couldn't help a groan, thinking he'd found some blot of ink she'd missed. She reversed course and peered hesitantly around the edge of the antechamber's opening.

Domin Tärpodious scowled silently at her, and Wynn's stomach sank into her boots.

The old archivist raised a hand, pointing one bony finger toward the passage's other direction.

Wynn flushed, nodded quickly, and hurried off the correct way.

Chane waited in the shadows across the street from the Inkwell scriptorium as two young sages emerged with a folio.

He recognized the pudgy girl in gray. She had occasionally been sent out before. But he had never seen the tall young man in a deep blue robe—too old to be an apprentice but perhaps not old enough for a master or domin. It seemed strange that the guild sent a journeyor of metaology to help retrieve tonight's folio.

Chane pulled farther back out of sight.

As the pair passed by, continuing down the street, the girl clutched the folio to her chest and peered nervously about. When they reached the next intersection, Chane pulled up his cloak's hood and followed from a distance. He had no wish to be seen and remembered.

He kept himself in check rather than close too quickly. But he longed to open the folio and read its contents, and driving desire pressed him forward.

The tall journeyor stopped and turned around.

Other city dwellers moved about in the early evening, and Chane continued walking casually. The blue-robed sage scanned the street, noting a man lighting street lamps, two merchants engaged in conversation, and a flower girl closing her stand . . . and Chane.

"What is it, Dâgmund?" the pudgy girl asked.

"Nothing," the young man answered. He moved on, tugging his shorter companion along.

Chane kept his gait even.

In his time in Bela with Wynn, he had learned enough of the orders to know each branch's general emphasis. To his best knowledge, those in metaology studied metaphysics and lore and related fields. Few if any became practitioners of magic, and those were mostly thaumaturges, working in pragmatic practices of artificing, such as alchemy. Even if this one had gone further, there was still no way he could detect Chane for what he was by spell or device.

Not while Chane wore Welstiel's old "ring of nothing."

This one possession masked his undead presence from anyone with extraordinary awareness or arcane skills of detection. But still, he had been seen, and he could not allow them to realize they were followed.

Chane turned down a side street.

Once beyond sight, he ran for the next intersection. He turned up a street parallel to the sages' route and slowed a bit. He tried to keep a pace even with the messengers'—or just a little ahead of them. And he knew where they would have to turn.

Three cross streets up, he slowed to hover near the corner.

The pair appeared in the intersection down the way, still following their course. As they passed beyond sight, Chane slipped down the side street to follow them directly.

The main street was slightly more populated with shopkeepers and wanderers heading home for the night, and he might blend in more easily. He glanced aside as a man struggled to calm a slender horse pulling a tarp-covered cart. The horse stomped and snorted. But the sages hurried onward, the girl tightly clutching her folio in both arms.

And the sound of screaming cats exploded on Chane's left. He turned on instinct.

Two large felines spun out of an alley, hissing and swiping at each other. The horse behind him screamed.

"Look out!"

Chane dodged at the shout, but as the panicked horse raced by, the cart clipped his side. He spun and stumbled, but didn't fall. Everyone around stopped to gawk.

"Are you all right?" the vegetable man asked, running up.

Chane didn't answer. Both sages had stopped, and the tall male stared straight at him. Recognition dawned on the journeyor's face. Had he been seen back near the Inkwell?

"I am fine," Chane answered in a hoarse whisper. "Go catch your horse."

He slipped back down the side street, cursing himself.

Wynn emerged in the main hall, tired, hungry, and disoriented by how quickly time had passed in the catacombs. Only a few others were still about, talking, reading, or sipping tea at the tables.

Domin il'Sänke sat reading by the fire.

"Wynn?" someone called anxiously from her right.

She turned to find Nikolas awkwardly waving her over. Two covered bowls and slices of buttered bread sat on the table in front of him.

"I waited for you," he said.

Domin il'Sänke glanced up from his book.

Wynn offered him a tired smile and went to join Nikolas. His robe was slightly disheveled, and his straight hair still hung into his eyes, but she couldn't recall the last time someone had waited supper on her.

"I had research to do," she said, her journal, lamp, and quill still in hand. "Keep the bowls covered a little longer. I'll run these things up to my room and be back."

Her answer brought an odd relief to his face. She knew how it felt to be lonely, or just alone, and when company mattered more than food.

"The lentils will keep," he said. "I'll put our bowls by the hearth."

Wynn headed for the hall's main archway. A chill breeze rolled in as she approached, as if someone had opened the keep's doors. She heard someone heave up from a chair too quickly behind her, and she glanced back. Il'Sänke strode straight toward her with a hard gaze, and then Miriam's frightened voice echoed from the entryway.

Wynn hadn't made out the girl's words, and il'Sänke rushed by in a trot, his robes swishing around his feet. She waved to Nikolas, and they hurried after the domin.

Around the corner beyond the main archway, Wynn spotted a panting Miriam standing before il'Sänke halfway down the hall to the front doors. The girl was clutching a folio to her chest, and Dâgmund stood behind her, lowering his cowl.

Miriam's hood was thrown back, and her face glistened as if she'd been running. For once she didn't cringe in il'Sänke's presence.

"Domin . . ." she breathed. "We were followed! Someone followed us!"

Dâgmund looked less frightened than Miriam, but he was clearly troubled.

Wynn pursed her lips. Why had Domin High-Tower sent a journeyor metaologer out with Miriam? A few more initiates and apprentices from the main hall began gathering in the passage behind her.

Il'Sänke turned stern eyes on Dâgmund. "Is this true?"

The young man nodded once. "A tall man in a long dark cloak. I saw him twice. He had to be the one."

Il'Sänke held out his hand. "Give me the folio."

Miriam shoved it at him without hesitation and exhaled loudly in relief.

To Wynn's surprise, il'Sänke stepped past the pair of couriers to the empty entryway. Beyond anyone's reach, he opened the leather flap and pulled out the short stack of pages. The domin scanned their contents once, and then placed them back inside.

Wynn would've given anything to peek over his shoulder.

In that instant il'Sänke glanced at her.

Without a word he strode silently past Miriam and her companion—and Wynn. The cluster of gathered initiates and apprentices scattered to the passage walls to let him through. Wynn quickly followed him back into the common hall, but Domin il'Sänke never paused. He headed straight for the narrow side archway. Wynn sneaked after him, all the way to the turn, and watched him head straight for the door to the north tower—and Domin High-Tower's study.

What had he seen in those pages?

"Come have supper," Nikolas said softly.

Wynn had forgotten about him standing right behind her.

"Put your things away later," he added. "Just come and eat."

She simply nodded and followed him back to the table in the common hall. But Wynn's thoughts were locked on the folio, and the frustration of watching il'Sänke scan those pages right in front of her.

Chane was seething as he stalked back toward the Graylands Empire. He had come so close and then lost the folio through clumsiness. And he was hungry, as if anger made his need that much worse.

In the past, the beast within him had reveled in the hunt, in the smell of fear in his prey, and relished their attempts to fight back. He had fed indiscriminately, taking whoever pleased him in the moment.

Some things had changed since he had last spoken with Wynn.

His choices had become more particular, and the beast within whimpered in suppression or howled in rage at his self-denial. Chane struggled with his longing for the euphoria of a true hunt and a kill.

He had been in Calm Seatt for just over a moon, but he had learned its districts quite well. When he needed—rather than wanted—to feed, he headed into the southern reaches of the Graylands Empire. Tonight he walked shabby and dim byways, listening and watching. Most people here were squalid and wretched, but those were not the criteria of his choices.

An old woman with no teeth shuffled by, muttering to herself, but he ignored her. Finally he passed a shack set between a faded tavern and what might be a candle shop on the corner. Muffled shouting escaped one shutterless window, and Chane slipped into the shadow of the candle shop's awnings.

"You put that back!" a woman shouted. "That's for milk and bread. Wager your boots at dice, if that's all you care about!"

A loud crash followed, and the sound of a woman weeping. The shack's front door burst open as a large man stepped halfway out. He had not shaved in days.

"Leave me be!" he snarled back through the doorway. "I'm going to the Blue Boar to ask about . . . to find some work. I'll get the milk and bread myself, so stop sniveling!"

So obsessed was he with maintaining control, Chane was startled by a familiar, uncomfortable tickle at the back of his mind. And the beast within rumbled in warning, bringing him to awareness.

The man was lying. He turned down the street, leaving the door wide-open.

Chane slipped out to follow. This worthless creature was an acceptable choice—a liar, a wastrel, and a waste of human flesh. He was no loss to this world, just another head in the cattle of humanity. Three streets down, Chane halted short of the next alley's mouth.

"Sir," he rasped in Numanese, knowing that both his voice and his accent might cause suspicion. "I could not help overhearing a mention of dice."

The filthy man stopped and turned, eyes squinting.

For this part of the city, Chane was well dressed in hard boots and a dark wool cloak hiding all but the hilt of a longsword.

The man blinked in indecision. "You lookin' for a game?"

Chane took a step and pulled out his pouch, allowing the coins to clink.

"Depends on the price to get in."

He stepped only as far as the alley mouth's other side, and noted that the closest passerby was two cross streets to the west. The large man's eyes fixed on the pouch, and he smiled, perhaps seeing some witless foreigner to take in among his regular companions. He strolled back toward Chane.

"Isn't no fee to enter," the man said. "And we bet what we please—no holds barred."

The instant he reached the alley's mouth, Chane dropped the pouch.

The man's gaze flicked downward in reflex.

Chane's hand shot out and latched across his mouth and jaw. Spinning, he wrenched the man into the alley's deeper darkness. The man was as strong as he looked and struggled like a bull, and he suddenly rammed an elbow into Chane's ribs.

Chane didn't even flinch. He slammed his victim against the wall and drove his distended fangs into the man's stubble-coated throat. The smell of stale ale and sweat filled his nose, but the beast trapped inside of Chane lunged against its bonds.

Once, he would have played with his victim until fear permeated the air. He loved that sweet, musky smell—or was it the beast within who savored it more?

He bit deeper, gulping like a glutton. Salt warmth flowed into his mouth, and the beast inside grew wild with joy. He drank so fast that the man went into convulsions. The would-be gambler's blood slowed to a trickle before his heart could even stop.

Death was a blink away.

Chane wrenched his head back and released his grip on the man's jaw. He stepped away and watched the body slide down the alley wall, until the corpse sat propped up with throat torn and eyes still wide.

It was over so quickly—too quickly. Even the rush of life making Chane's head swim and his cold flesh tingle with heat brought no pleasure. And the beast inside him whimpered like a dog pulled back before finishing its meal.

Chane had seen his own maker, Toret, and then Welstiel, raise new minions from selected victims. Not all rose from death, which was why careful selection was necessary. But there was still a slim chance that a victim taken too quickly might rise the following night. Toret had believed that for a Noble Dead to make one of its own, it had to feed a victim its own fluids. That was another superstition.

All it took was devouring a life—suddenly, quickly, all at once—and the close contact of a Noble Dead in the instant between life's end and death's coming. Chane had been lucky in the past not to have any of his prey rise.

Or had they? In recollection, aside from his time in Bela with Toret, he had always been on the move with Welstiel. He had never stayed long enough in one place to be certain.

Chane wanted no minions. And certainly not this side of beef sitting limp in the alley. The last trickles of blood ran down the corpse's neck, staining his filthy shirt like black ink in the alley's darkness.

Chane closed his eyes and saw Wynn's pained face staring back at him in accusation.

He opened his eyes, pulled out a fish knife stolen off the docks, and cut the man's throat deeply. When the corpse was found, his death would seem a common murder by some desperate cutpurse. Kneeling down, he searched the man and took every coin he found for his own needs.

Chane stepped from the alley and retrieved his own pouch, adding new coins to old. He began walking "home" toward the inn and never looked back.

CHAPTER 8

Wynn spent the next day in the catacombs with two terms stuck in her head—*Âthlyensmyotnes* and *blâch-cheargéa*.

She searched deep through the archives, even trying to find possible variations on the term "vampire." But her continent's earliest peoples had no such words in any language. The varied ones she'd learned in the Farlands wouldn't be found in this branch of the guild. Several times she got lost in the maze of stone chambers and rooms. All she could do was follow the elemental symbols upon the edges of bookshelves.

Spirit, Fire, Air, Water, and Earth.

Circle, triangle, square, hexagon, and octagon.

The fewer the symbols in a column, the closer she was to the catacomb's front below the keep's rear wall. The most primary and general texts for each field of knowledge, indicated by one lone geometric shape, were closest to Domin Tärpodious's main chamber. Soon enough she found her way back and headed into other reaches of the archives.

Whenever she found a tome, sheaf, book, or scroll of interest, she backtracked to the nearest alcove. There she settled to read, never certain of how long she sat alone in the light of her cold lamp. Again, Wynn gained little more than a head-ache and tired eyes—until sometime close to supper.

> *. . . Master Geidelmon stared at the warth, though he could not make out its face within the cowl. The dark harbinger drifted into the kitchen's dim candlelight, appearing like a tall figure clad in a wafting shroud of black . . .*

That one word—"warth"—wasn't familiar to Wynn, but she quickly turned the page of the old ghost tale.

> *. . . Tall and trim, its stature was much like Geidelmon once had, before he had sunk into years of gluttony. Rapture in food and wine had left him so rotund he could not even rise and flee. And following the por-tentous visitation, the next morning he was found slumped dead upon the table, a joint of mutton still lodged between his teeth.*

The term, and even the whole tale, sounded like some-thing Wynn had read before. But everything was beginning to sound like something she'd read before. She propped her elbows on the table, resting her head in her hands. She'd fi-nally had enough of it.

Just the same, she recorded the term in her journal and then left for the comfort of her own room. But as she emerged into the castle's main floor, she paused.

The new library wasn't far off.

Wynn wove through the passages to its nearest entrance. It had no door, only a tall double-wide archway of finely crafted frame stones. The topmost four were engraved with Begaine symbols, one after the other, for the sages' creed.

> *TRUTH THROUGH KNOWLEDGE . . . KNOWLEDGE THROUGH UNDERSTANDING . . . UNDERSTANDING THROUGH TRUTH . . . WISDOM'S ETERNAL CYCLE.*

Hurrying in, she fingered along a tall bookcase on the main floor, passing over a dozen lexicons, until she found the one she sought on the bottom shelf. Groaning at its bulk, she hefted it up and dropped it on a table. It took time to find any similar term.

>   *waerth, n. [Origin unknown; found in early southern regional dialects, prenationalization of the Numan Lands.] One of several possible alternate spellings for the obscure modern Numanese term wraith [râth].*

Wynn flipped pages to find the referenced entry for "wraith":

>   *a dark or black apparition, sometimes similar to, or in the likeness of, a particular person. Found in folk-lore as an omen of immediate impending demise, though sometimes said to be seen shortly after an individual's death.*

Wynn slammed the thick book shut—portents indeed!

More superstitious nonsense, which brought her no closer to the truth concerning what hunted her people and the folios. She jotted down the new term and definition next to her entry for the warth and left the library, hurrying all the way to her room.

Once inside, with the door tightly shut, Wynn flopped onto her bed. After a while she crawled over to peer out her narrow window. Somewhere in the distance, beyond the keep's walls, she heard eight bells ring out softly.

The last eighth of day, called Geuréleâ—"day's winter"—in the dwarven time system used throughout the Numan Lands. Dusk was coming, and the day's work hardly seemed useful.

Every time she thought of how she'd carried back a wealth of texts written by ancient undead but wasn't even allowed to see them, it left her so angry that her stomach burned. If she could only find some common thread within the folios' contents, she might provide Premin Sykion with a possible motive.

But for this to happen, the Premin Council had to acknowledge that the folios—and the entire project—were connected to the deaths and thefts. Otherwise, even a sound theory of motive would be disdainfully dismissed, like her tales of dhampirs, vampires, ghosts, and . . .

Wynn sighed and dropped back down on the bed. Rubbing her temples, she tried to drive angry obsession from her head. She needed clarity and calm as she went to her table-desk and began reviewing her notes.

Nonsensical accounts of animated corpses feeding on flesh replaced anger's burn with queasiness. She wished Domin il'Sänke would finish the sun crystal. But at least she was shut away in her room once again, where she worked best.

Her possessions were simple: a bed, a table for a desk, her cold lamp, a small chest, and all her journaling equipment. In spite of slight nausea, she was getting a bit hungry, having not eaten since breakfast.

At a knock on her door her heart thumped hard, and she thought, *Please let it be il'Sänke, with the sun crystal finally completed*. She ran for the door and jerked it open.

Nikolas stood outside, his face drawn and pale.

Wynn sagged in disappointment but tried to express concern. "What's wrong?"

He opened his mouth once, then closed it, and Wynn forgot her own worries.

Others called him little Nervous Nikolas, but he wasn't exactly little. He was slender, but not spindly, and of medium height. Perhaps his constant cringing and the twitching worry in his plain brown eyes had led to that nickname. She wondered what in his past had rooted this perpetual anxiety.

"Come in," she said, stepping back, "and tell me what's wrong."

He quickly slipped past her, but not before glancing both ways along the outer passage.

"I'm . . . I'm . . ." he began in a stammer.

Wynn took a deep breath and waited patiently.

"I'm being sent for tonight's folio!" he blurted out. "Me, with Miriam and Dâgmund, and they were followed last night!"

Wynn froze in disbelief.

"Domin il'Sänke must have told Domin High-Tower what happened," he rushed on. "So how could he send more of us out?"

"Nikolas!" Wynn said. "Calm down."

"I don't want to go!" he half shouted, and ended in stuttering whimpers. "But if I refuse I will . . . seem unhelpful."

Pity mixed with Wynn's frustration. The one thing an apprentice never wished to be called was "unhelpful"—a thinly veiled euphemism for "lazy" or "incapable." But in spite of two deaths, a ransacked scriptorium, and an account of two messengers being followed, her superiors remained insistent that these events were unconnected and had nothing to do with the translation project.

Nikolas stared at her expectantly, as if she had the power to save him.

"I cannot change their minds," she said bitterly. "And I can't go with you. They won't allow me anywhere near the translation work."

Nikolas seemed on the verge of tears as his lips began quivering.

"But I can do something," she said, returning to her table.

Wynn tore a blank page from her journal and scribbled a quick note. She held it out for Nikolas to read with her.

> *To Captain Rodian, commander of the Shyld-fälches,*
>
> *Two sage messengers returning last night with a folio believe they were followed. Neither was injured, but three more go now, as of dusk. Please send men to Master Calisus's shop—the Feather & Parchment—and make certain they return safely.*
>
> *With regards,*
> *Wynn Hygeorht, Journeyor*
> *Guild of Sagecraft at Calm Seatt, Malourné*

"I'll have an initiate run this to the captain," she said. "He wants no more trouble over the folios. I'm certain he'll send guards to protect you."

Nikolas's brown eyes flooded with relief. "Thank you, Wynn . . . Wait, what if Domin High-Tower finds out? He's already angry with you over that day you returned home with the captain."

"I don't care," Wynn answered coldly. "All that matters is that the three of you come back."

If her instincts were correct and the killer was a Noble Dead, Rodian's men might not be able to stop it. But it had always struck when no one was watching, perhaps wishing to remain unseen. The sight of a few city guards might give it pause, and any vampire would think twice about engaging multiple armed soldiers.

Nikolas dropped his gaze to the floor. "I should've thought of this myself. Elias would have. He always knew what to do."

Wynn patted his arm. "Go get ready, and I'll find a messenger."

Nikolas nodded quickly, and they both left the room. As he took off across the inner courtyard, Wynn's ire at her superiors sharpened. But so did her concern for any innocent sage caught in harm's way.

The premins and domins were denying the plain facts before their eyes—and it made less sense every night.

Rodian left the barracks that evening with Lieutenant Garrogh. They headed for supper at a favored local inn called Mother's.

Its founder was long dead, and her grandson now ran the establishment. Close by, with modest prices and good basic food, it was popular among the forces of the second castle. Sooner or later most of the city guards and regulars, and even some of the cavalry, stepped across its threshold. Though the barracks boasted a full cooking staff, and the food was healthy and plentiful, sometimes it felt good to eat elsewhere than the meal hall.

Tonight Rodian picked at a bowl of thick seafood stew with his spoon while Garrogh shoveled in mouthfuls. The lieutenant stopped with his spoon halfway to his mouth.

"Don't you like it?"

"It's fine," Rodian answered, glancing idly about.

A group of his city guard sat at a nearby table, though he saw few regular soldiers tonight. The place was packed, just the same. Aside from price and quality, people were more at ease anywhere they saw the city guard—the People's Shield—take their rest. All around, private citizens and red surcoated Shyldfälches ate and drank with boisterous chatter.

The noise was beginning to bother Rodian.

He'd spent a restless day trying to focus on neglected duties. But his thoughts had kept wandering to dead sages, a ransacked scriptorium, the faces of Wynn Hygeorht and Duchess Reine . . . and Domin High-Tower's determined glare. As if the guild's murder investigation were his only duty to attend to.

It wasn't. Aside from reviewing reports filed by his men, he had his own to write for the minister of city affairs. Why did the sages continually impede his investigation? And why were Duchess Reine and the royal family shielding them from his inquiries?

"You're thinking on those sages again," Garrogh said, and took a gulp of ale.

Rodian returned his companion a hard look. He needed no reminder of his continuing failure. He sighed and dropped his spoon, all appetite gone.

"I don't like having my hands tied," he answered.

"I know you don't," Garrogh grumbled under his breath. He leaned over to clean his bowl, and strands of his unwashed hair dangled in the stew's gravy.

Rodian grimaced. Though trustworthy and attentive, Garrogh's personal manners were appalling.

"If you're finished, we should head back," Rodian said. "I still have work to do, and it's getting late."

He dropped several coins on the table, and they exited into the pools of lantern light along the street. They untied their horses, then decided to walk rather than ride. Snowbird didn't need to be led, and followed.

"You're certain nothing but the folio was taken from Shilwise's shop?" Rodian asked.

This time Garrogh shot him a hard look. "You read my report."

"I'm not suggesting . . ." Rodian began, and then faltered. "I'm just trying to decide what to do next."

He'd received written statements from all requested parties regarding the alibis of Selwyn Midton and Jason Twynam on the night of the murders. That left only the razor-thin possibility that one of them had hired an outsider. But in his gut Rodian knew pursuing either of those lines was a waste of time.

He and Garrogh entered the second castle's courtyard, handed off their mounts to the stable warden, and turned toward Rodian's office and room. The only useful option left was to press the sages yet again, but the duchess had publicly asked him not to.

"Captain!"

Rodian turned around as Lúcan, one of his men, jogged across the courtyard.

"What now?"

"Sir, a boy from the guild arrived just before dusk, but you'd already left. He has a message for you, but the little whelp wouldn't give it to me."

"Where is he?"

"He's been waiting outside your office the whole time."

Rodian broke into a trot. He burst through the barracks' side door, looking down the wood-planked corridor. A boy of eleven or twelve in a tan robe fidgeted before the office door. He was clutching a folded scrap of paper in one hand.

"Give me the message!" Rodian called, hand already out as he strode down the corridor.

The boy jumped slightly. "You are Captain Rodian?"

"Of course," Rodian barked. He closed on the initiate with Garrogh right behind him.

The boy swallowed hard and thrust out the folded slip. "Journeyor Hygeorht said I must give this only to you."

Rodian hesitated before snatching the message. Why would Wynn send a note for his eyes only? He snapped the sheet open and scanned the contents—and his half-full stomach rolled.

Last night's folio messengers had been followed, and High-Tower had still sent out more this night.

Rodian whirled about, face-to-face with a puzzled Garrogh.

"Get four men and our horses . . . now!"

Once Nikolas, Miriam, and Dâgmund had left, Wynn couldn't bear waiting in her room. She went and volunteered to help serve supper, hoping time would pass more quickly. No doubt the captain would send someone to protect the messengers. But her thoughts also wandered to the sun crystal.

It might be the only real protection against a Noble Dead hunting sages and folios.

As she served vegetable soup in the common hall, she watched for Domin il'Sänke, but there was no sign of him throughout the evening.

"You missed me," a small voice said.

Wynn looked down. A little initiate in pigtails looked up at her, a mix of hurt and pouting indignation on her freckled face.

"I'm sorry," Wynn said. "Here you are."

As she set a bowl down in front of the girl, Domin High-Tower entered from the narrow side archway. He paused to study her from across the crowded hall.

Wynn had no wish to face the stout domin, but she handed out the last of the bowls on her tray and worked her way through the tables.

"Have you seen Domin il'Sänke?" she asked. "He hasn't come to supper yet."

High-Tower's mouth tightened within his thick beard. "He went out earlier. I haven't seen him since."

"He went out? How long ago?"

The domin's pellet eyes narrowed at her impertinence. "A domin's comings and goings are none of your concern!"

He strode past her toward the hall's hearth, his footfalls vibrating the stone beneath her feet. She didn't even flinch at his admonishment.

Instead Wynn peered toward the main archway. What possible reason could il'Sänke have for going out this night?

* * *

Ghassan il'Sänke lingered around the corner of a dry-goods shop, watching across the vacant street as three young sages approached the Feather & Parchment. The only other living thing he saw was a pony harnessed to a small cart in front of the scribe shop.

"Where are they?" Nikolas said too loudly. "Wynn promised—"

"Enough!" Dâgmund snapped. "We can't stand about waiting for the city guard. The sooner we get back, the better."

Il'Sänke straightened, glancing up and down the street. How had the city guard learned of tonight's folio retrieval? There was no sign of the Shyldfälches, so perhaps Nikolas's expected message had never arrived.

Once again, Nikolas turned hesitantly about, looking back the way they had come.

"Stop doing that!" Miriam squeaked.

"Both of you, be quiet," Dâgmund warned. "Now get inside."

He squeezed the front latch, stepping into the shuttered scriptorium. Nikolas nearly tripped over the front step as he backed up, still watching the street. Miriam shoved past, scurrying through the door an instant before him.

Il'Sänke remained where he was, awaiting their departure.

He did not truly need to hide. They would not have seen him if he stood right before their eyes. No one would have . . . not if he spotted them first. And on their return to the guild, it would be easy enough for him to addle their minds, even incapacitate them if necessary. He would have a peek at this latest folio's contents before anyone else.

And if necessary, no one else would ever see it, leaving only the original texts to be found and dealt with later.

A creak and rattle of wooden wheels carried up the street.

It had not been hard for Ghassan to convince High-Tower of his scheme. He had used the ruse that the messengers were in danger and had to be protected. The old dwarf and Premin Sykion would not risk involving outsiders, such as the inquisitive captain of the city guard. Nor would they send domins or masters to retrieve folios. Such notable messengers would raise general suspicion and interest from any bystanders along the way. The content of the folios was more important—more dangerous—than the guild wanted anyone to know.

They contained more information than the Numan guild members themselves should know, as far as Ghassan was concerned.

A rickety wagon turned the far corner, and a pair of mules hauled it closer under the guidance of a lad at the reins. As one cart wheel hit a deep cleft between cobblestones, the wagon thumped, jostling a shovel and rake in its bed.

Ghassan ignored the refuse wagon. There was nothing along this city block to clean up. He watched the scriptorium's front door, the dull yellow light behind its shutters, and the occasional shadows of people moving about inside.

High-Tower had been dubious of the plan at first, but Ghassan assured the stout domin that he could guard over the messengers this night. For as little as anyone knew of his full abilities, his reputation as a mage of thaumaturgy carried weight.

And someone else in this city sought the folios.

If that someone appeared this night, Ghassan would see tonight's folio first, one way or another. Then he would make certain that his competitor never hunted sages again.

The refuse wagon slowed, as if coming to a halt.

Ghassan's gaze flicked from the scribe shop's door to the driver. He snorted in frustration as the young man looked his way.

His concentration had slipped. The incantation, which had removed his presence from the trio's mental awareness, was no longer in his thoughts, ready to be spread to others.

Ghassan blinked only once. In the dark behind his eyelids, lines of light spread.

Sigils, symbols, and signs burned bright within the border of a doubled square. Within the inner space a triangle appeared, and another inside that, but inverted. He did not utter his incantation. The words sounded with greater speed in his thoughts as . . .

He finished that brief blink. And the glowing pattern overlaid his sight of the young driver, centering upon the lad's face.

The driver blinked as well.

He looked about as if he had seen something, but it was not there anymore. With a shrug he flicked the reins, and the two muscular mules pulled the wagon onward.

Ghassan had not expected any rare passerby to halt and stare. This time he kept the spell's glimmering pattern in focus, ready for use. Once embedded in a target's mind, it would last for a while, depending upon how much will and command he put behind it. His presence would not be remembered with certainty by anyone so touched.

The trio finally exited the scriptorium, with Dâgmund in the lead.

Miriam stepped out next, tightly clutching the folio. Nikolas came last, hesitating in the doorway until Dâgmund reached back and tugged him along. All three turned back the way they had come, hurrying along the empty street.

Ghassan slipped around the shop's corner. He quickly split and tripled the glimmering pattern overlaying his sight.

Three glyph-adorned double squares drifted across his vision, and each centered on one young sage. Three recitations flickered through his thoughts as quick as a finger's tap.

Ghassan hurried to close the distance to the trio.

Not even his footfalls or the rustle of his robe would register in their awareness.

Rodian slackened Snowbird's reins, letting her canter through the streets of the outer merchant district. Even so, the pace was too slow as she dodged carts and citizens making their way home. Garrogh's bay gelding followed behind, and Guardsman Lúcan and three others brought up the rear. Several startled citizens shouted angrily at them, but most rushed aside at the sight of the Shyldfälches' red surcoats.

Taverns and eateries gave way to shops patronized only during daylight. People in the streets grew sparse, and Rodian tightened his legs on Snowbird.

"Go!" he called.

She lunged, her light hooves clattering on cobblestones.

When they neared the next main intersection, Rodian reined her in and turned east toward the Feather & Parchment. A small pony and cart waited out front of the freshly painted shop. Otherwise the dim, narrow street was empty. Snowbird skidded to a stop, and a thin man with a flat nose started in surprise. He nearly dropped a heavy iron key ring before he could lock the shop's door.

"Master Calisus?" Rodian called as he slid from his saddle. "Where are the sages?"

"Pardon me?" the man asked.

"The sages! Have they come and gone?"

The scribe master blinked in confusion and sputtered, "How do you know ... Yes, they just—"

A scream echoed down the empty street.

Ghassan il'Sänke was barely half a block away when he heard horses' hooves and flattened himself against the nearest building. Before the Feather & Parchment were five—no, six—of the Shyldfälches. And that annoying Captain Rodian was badgering the master scribe.

Then Miriam's terrified scream pierced Ghassan's ears.

He glanced the other way, and all three sages were gone.

The young ones were in danger—and the folio as well—but he could not be seen here.

Ghassan ducked low, pulling his cowl forward to hide his face. He turned his eyes upon the city guard and saw Rodian running toward him.

Six at once was not easy.

Each of the three arcane patterns doubled in his vision. Six patterns drifted over his sight, centering on each city guard. All patterns expanded until they overlapped and linked. One recitation of the incantation sped through his mind.

Ghassan bolted onward, racing ahead of the captain as he searched the night for three young sages.

Rodian dropped Snowbird's reins and ran toward the scream as horses' hooves scuffled on cobblestone behind him.

"Captain, wait!" Garrogh shouted.

Then something moved near the base of a building.

Rodian swerved toward the street's center and pulled his sword. The nearest street lantern was too far off to reveal . . .

He looked again, but nothing was there.

Another scream erupted.

He had no time to search the shadows, and ran on. His boot heels ground on cobble as he halted to check a narrow side alley. Halfway down the shadowy path he spotted a light, but it was low to the ground and didn't fill the space between the close buildings.

A black mass stood between the walls, like a piece of slowly shifting night.

Rodian took one quick step, then flinched at a shout reverberating out of the tight space.

"Fire . . . from light!"

Flames erupted across the alley floor.

Rodian stumbled back as flickering orange-red tongues curled up the side walls. A sudden wall of heat rolled out around him. But the darkness remained up the alley's center path, splitting the fire's light—and it moved.

A black mass . . . a tall figure with its back turned . . . stood amid raging flames squirming over its form. Fire crackled but barely illuminated the figure's garments of night-black fabric. A great cloak writhed as if the heat filling the alley made it dance, sending its folds spreading to the alley walls.

Cloying fear crawled over Rodian. He shuddered once and lunged into the alley, raising his longsword as he shouted, "Hold and yield!"

The figure didn't turn—and it lashed sideways at the alley wall.

Rodian thought he saw a robe's sleeve emerge from beneath the billowing cloak. The sleeve slid up an arm wrapped in strips of black cloth. Its like-covered fingers gouged straight into the brick, tearing out a hunk as smaller fragments scattered everywhere.

Rodian raised his free hand, shielding his face from bits of brick.

Before he recovered, the figure whipped its hand, slinging the chunk of wall down the alley beyond it.

A dull impact cut off a shriek, and the fire instantly vanished.

Rodian blinked, blinded for an instant by the sudden loss of light. He cocked his sword and rushed in.

Ghassan faltered at the dark form filling the alley. A wave of fear washed over him—into him—as though northern autumn rain had drenched his clothing. He did not look away from the figure, even as he heard the captain coming up the alley behind him.

The light upon the alley floor was a cold lamp crystal cast there, still glowing brightly. And Ghassan heard a whisper from beyond the tall, black-robed figure.

He would never have recognized those nearly voiceless words, even if he had heard them clearly. But he knew what was happening. All mages found their own utterances, just as their symbols, necessary for their art.

Somewhere down in the alley, Dâgmund was chanting.

Out of all those of Ghassan's order at the guild branch of Calm Seatt, only Dâgmund had shown true aptitude for the deeper skills. Not even Premin Hawes had the boy's instinct for thaumaturgy via spellcraft. This was why Ghassan had chosen the young journeyor to accompany whoever retrieved the folios.

He had tried his best to tutor Dâgmund, sharpening the young man's well-developed skill. But Dâgmund was not a seasoned mage—and thaumaturgy could not create as conjury did. The journeyor was too slow for this moment, even with the speed of a spell.

"Fire . . . from light!" Dâgmund suddenly shouted.

Flames erupted from the alley floor—from the crystal's brilliance—and raging red light silhouetted the tall black cloak and robe.

Ghassan shielded his face from the glare and heat. He knew what Dâgmund had done.

The journeyor had cast his crystal at the figure's feet and used thaumaturgy to transform and magnify its light into fire. An easy change, since Light and Flame were of the same

Element. But Ghassan was still startled by the magnitude of the effect.

Flames licked high around the figure, more so than Ghassan would have expected Dâgmund could call. But not one bit of the night-black fabric even smoldered.

Flickering red-orange tendrils tangled about the writhing cloak, slipping along its curling and rolling surface to splash off like water upon oiled cloth.

"Hold and yield!" Rodian shouted from the alley's entrance.

The last thing Ghassan needed was the captain blundering into his back, and he banished the glimmering patterns held in his sight. They had barely faded when he replaced them with one doubled square framing nested triangles. Fresh glyphs, signs, and sigils ignited in the pattern's spaces as his mental incantation finished. The pattern raced across his sight, centering on the back of the black cowl.

Flecks and chips of brick struck il'Sänke's face as the figure lashed out at the alley wall.

Ghassan lost focus as Dâgmund cried out.

He flinched, growing colder inside as he heard the journeyor's voice cut short.

The fire died instantly.

Ghassan heard a rustle and snap of cloth. His sight adjusted to only the cold lamp crystal's light. He flattened against the alley's wall as the figure turned.

The cloak's wings snaked and twisted up both walls, clutching at the brick surface as if alive. And the creature held the folio in one hand wrapped in shredded strips of black cloth.

Its cowl, that pit of blackness, turned directly on Ghassan.

He instantly released the pattern and symbols, quickly calling others. As they rose in glimmers across his sight, he collapsed them inward around—into—himself, sinking deep into his own mind. Someone shouted, "Sir!" from the alley's open end, and the black-robed figure raised its other hand.

Ghassan threw his will against the ground beneath his feet.

The figure lashed out at him just as Ghassan's body shot upward into the night.

Rodian squinted, trying to make out the dark shape filling the narrow space and blocking out the small light upon the ground. Fear sharpened as he made out layer upon layer of black cloth billowing like a cloak over a dark robe. The cloth lashed the alley walls as if the air were still driven by heat.

And the figure whirled about.

Though it was backlit by the light beyond it, Rodian couldn't make out a face inside the heavy cowl. There was only more darkness in that hollow—but it didn't center on him.

It swung left, and whoever hid within it fixated upon the wall. In its hand was a leather folio.

"Sir!"

At Lúcan's shout of warning, Rodian ducked away as the shadowy thief struck out. Its black hand—or was it covered in cloth?—slammed against the wall.

A sharp crack of splitting brick filled the alley as Rodian twisted away. He heard the chitter of falling fragments beneath the ringing in his ears. The black-robed mass swirled away.

As it fled down the alley, the whipping hem of its cloak passed beyond the light that had been behind it. And the alley brightened.

Rodian froze.

A glowing crystal lay on the alley floor, slightly bigger than the end of his thumb, but bright enough to hurt his eyes. When his sight adjusted, he grew chilled.

Three bodies lay in the alley.

The closest was the pudgy girl who'd taken Snowbird's reins on his first visit to the guild. She was curled on her side, and her limbs were twisted against her torso, as if she'd died in convulsions. Her wide eyes stared blankly from an ashen face disfigured by horror.

Just like before—just like Elias and Jeremy.

Beyond her sprawled a taller companion in midnight blue robes lying on his back. But his face was a crushed and bloodied mess. Past his head lay a heavy chunk of the brick wall. And the third and last down the alley was slender and frail.

A young man in gray robes curled up as if he'd tried to hide within himself as he died. He was pale and sallow, and his eyes were open, like the girl's.

"Maker, Toiler, and Dreamer," Rodian whispered.

All of them were lost.

Ghassan lit upon the rooftop as he heard the dark figure's hand crack against the brick wall. He caught only a glimpse of bodies beyond the black thief.

He saw the one in a midnight blue robe.

Ghassan had only an instant of cold regret at the sight of Dâgmund, and then the figure bolted away.

Ghassan leaped over the alley, thrusting with will as much as his legs. The spell still sunk within his mind helped carry him to the next rooftop. He scrambled along the shakes parallel to the alley, and when he reached the eaves overhanging the next street, he looked about.

There was no one below—and then he spotted it.

Like some giant ebony-draped spider, it clambered up the wall of a building fifty yards down the street. When it reached the roof, a street lantern upon a pole exposed its form against clay tiles.

It still held the folio clutched in one hand.

Ghassan cleared his sight once more, calling yet another pattern of glowing lines. These he sank into himself and reached out toward the distant figure with one hand.

He clenched his fingers closed in the air.

The thief spun upon the distant rooftop. Robe and cloak whipped in the night as its arm and hand holding the folio snapped out toward Ghassan's rooftop. The folio hung in the air, still locked in its grip, and it pulled back.

Ghassan's own arm straightened, and his feet slipped along the shakes. He ground in his heels and tried to pull his clenched hand inward.

The figure stumbled. It reached out and clutched the folio with both hands, continuing to pull. Ghassan did the same, both his hands tearing at the air.

A hissing carried from the distant rooftop.

The night air began to swirl around Ghassan. His robe whipped about him. He bent his knees, trying to sink lower, holding his hands clenched as if he physically gripped the folio so far beyond reach.

A sudden rush of wind struck him.

Breath was punched from his lungs, as if a wall of air slammed against his whole body. His feet slipped from the shakes as he fell and landed on his back.

Ghassan barely had enough awareness to flatten and keep from sliding off the edge. He rolled onto his knees, gasping for air, and stared across the city's rooftops in stunned silence.

The thief on the distant rooftop was gone.

Ghassan remained still, too stunned and shaken. Either thaumaturgy or conjuring could have shaped that wind. It was a mage, and a potent one for such quick and strong force.

The folio was gone. Three young sages lay dead. And all before Ghassan could subdue them himself and see those precious translated pages.

Running feet hammered down the alley.

Ghassan dropped low upon the roof. He had to reach guild grounds before word traveled of what happened here. He did not know how he would explain all this to High-Tower or Sykion, let alone that the city guards would tell a differing tale—one that would not include his presence.

He climbed quietly to the roof's peak and rose to his feet. He took one last look southwest for any sign of his adversary. But halfway through his turn, he stopped.

A shadow raced over the rooftops of the next city block, a dark cloak billowing in its flight.

This new figure came from the north, and no sound rose from its footfalls. When it reached the roof's end of a two-story building, it leaped across the street to the lower building across the way. Midflight, it clutched its flapping hood or cowl with one hand as the intersection's street lantern caught it with light.

No, not a cowl or a hood—but a hat with an extremely wide brim.

Ghassan watched the shadow race south, in the direction that the black-robed figure had vanished.

Someone else had been nearby, hunting the thief. But there was no time left to ponder—and he was too worn and drained. Ghassan stepped quietly along the roof's peak, heading for the next side street and any hidden way to flee.

Rodian leaped over the bodies, running along the alley. He shot out its far end and halted amid an empty street. Pools of wide-spaced lamplight stretched away in both directions. He turned about twice, listening for footfalls, but neither heard nor saw anyone.

Nothing on foot could've vanished so quickly.

"Captain!" Garrogh shouted from back down the alley. "One's still alive!"

Rodian backed up, still scanning the empty street, then spun and ran.

Garrogh knelt over the frail young man in a gray robe. Lúcan stood beyond with the other guardsmen, staring at the other bodies in silence. The younger guardsman finally blinked and crouched down.

He hesitated once as he reached for the brilliant crystal, perhaps fearful of being burned. Rodian knew better, for he'd seen such devices at the guild.

"Give it to me," he ordered.

Lúcan picked up the crystal, eyes widening at finding it held no heat. He handed it to Rodian.

"A faint heartbeat," Garrogh said, his ear pressed to the young sage's chest.

Rodian crouched down with the glowing crystal, and he recognized the boy's face. This one had been sitting with Wynn Hygeorht at breakfast the morning of the robbery. His face was as ashen as the girl's, but he was breathing shallowly.

"What about the girl?" Rodian asked.

Garrogh simply shook his head. "And the folio?"

Rodian didn't answer and put two fingers to the young sage's throat, feeling a faint pulse. "He needs a healer."

"No," Garrogh answered. "Take him to the guild. They'll

know what to do more than some healer at a city ward. Remember my sister's cough? I took her to the sages."

Rodian almost barked a denial. The last thing he wanted was for the sages to hide away the only witness he had. He reached out and closed the young sage's blank eyes so they wouldn't dry out. A life to save mattered more than anything else.

"What's happened?" someone called.

Rodian raised his head and saw Master Calisus with his pony and cart at the alley's mouth.

"Stay there!" he ordered, and then looked to Garrogh. "I'll take this one to the guild. Make certain no one comes into the alley until it's thoroughly searched for any clues. Lúcan, you and the others find a way to take the other bodies back to the barracks."

The young guardsman didn't move or speak. His eyes shifted to the mangled face of the victim in the dark blue robe.

"Now!" Rodian snapped.

Lúcan jolted into motion and ran down the alley.

"Who would do this, and how?" Garrogh whispered softly.

Rodian found his second staring over one shoulder at the dead girl.

"What did . . . ?" Rodian began, and then faltered.

He doubted his own senses and the memory of what he'd seen.

"What did you see?" he finally asked. "When you came in behind me?"

"A man," Garrogh answered, his brows gathering. "A tall man in a black cloak. Why?"

Rodian quickly hefted the surviving young sage. Holding his charge carefully, he strode down the alley toward the cart. His anger flared as he stepped over the girl's body.

The royal family valued its misguided sages. Now two more were dead, and another might soon follow. But no matter who had done this, High-Tower and Sykion were responsible. They'd refused to acknowledge the danger and sent more of their own out in the night.

This time Rodian would drag the truth from them.

*   *   *

Wynn still waited in the common hall, but too much time had passed. Only a few others were still about, either reading or writing or chatting softly. She fretted over some way to look occupied.

If she just sat doing nothing, and Domin High-Tower or Premin Sykion came by, either would surely comment. They never missed an opportunity to note any odd behavior on her part. But she dared not leave even long enough to fetch a journal or book from her room.

Supper was finished, and still the messengers hadn't returned. What was taking them so long?

Wynn's dilemma ended as a slam from the keep's front doors echoed down the outer passage into the common hall. She lunged off the bench, racing to the main archway to meet Nikolas, Miriam, and Dâgmund.

But instead, Domin il'Sänke appeared, pulling back his cowl.

"Wynn," he said, and his slight smile seemed forced. "You look disappointed to see me."

"Where have you been?" she asked bluntly.

His smile faded. "I ate supper early in the kitchens, perhaps too much. At my age, one needs to walk off such a meal before turning to other matters."

"Sorry," she said, feeling foolish for her urgency. "Nikolas, Miriam, and Dâgmund have not returned. After what happened last night . . ."

She trailed off as his expression changed again. His left eye twitched, and he licked his lips.

"The folios are not your concern," he said, barely above a whisper.

Wynn clenched her jaw so tightly her teeth ached. Now il'Sänke reminded her the texts were no longer her business—as if she needed to be told that again. And she'd thought he was her only ally in this place.

"Pardon," he muttered, and his gaze suddenly fixed elsewhere in the hall. "It has been a long day, and I have one more thing to attend to."

Wynn turned her head.

Domin High-Tower stood in the narrower side archway,

not looking at her but beyond her, perhaps at il'Sänke. He seemed expectant, even in his usually dour state, but his expression suddenly changed.

High-Tower's wide features slackened in some shock.

Wynn saw his chest expand in a deep breath and one exhale. Then he sagged. By the time Wynn looked back to il'Sänke, the elder Suman was stone-faced. She was left wondering what had just passed silently between these two, who had always been plain regarding their irritation with each other.

And a thunderous boom echoed down the main passage beyond the archway.

Wynn heard one of the keep's front doors recoil sharply off a wall. She made for the archway to go see who forced such a hurried entrance.

Il'Sänke raised an arm in her way.

She barely glanced up, finding his gaze turned toward the outer passage, and then Captain Rodian came around the turn.

His face tight with anger, he carried the limp form of Nikolas Columsarn.

Rodian's hard gaze settled on il'Sänke as the first sage of rank in his sight.

"Get one of your physicians," he barked over heavy, exhausted breaths.

Il'Sänke was already reaching out. "Here, Captain, let me take him."

The tall Suman lifted Nikolas from the captain's arms and headed for the nearest table.

"Where are Miriam and Dâgmund?" Wynn asked.

Rodian ignored her, looking about the hall. "Where's High-Tower . . . and Sykion?"

As il'Sänke carefully laid Nikolas on a table, others in the hall rose from benches and chairs, drawing nearer.

"Here," High-Tower answered.

His gaze locked on Nikolas as he closed on the table's far side. Il'Sänke put a hand on the young sage's chest and leaned down to listen at Nikolas's slack mouth. He glanced up at High-Tower, nodded once, and the dwarven domin breathed a sigh of relief.

Wynn exhaled, not realizing she'd held her breath in that moment. "Where are Miriam and Dâgmund?" she repeated.

Rodian didn't even look at her. He kept his angry eyes on High-Tower.

"Dead," he said sharply, "in an alley near the Feather and Parchment."

All the warmth drained from Wynn's flesh.

Il'Sänke grabbed the sleeve of a female apprentice in brown. "Get Premin Adlam or Master Bitworth ... or any elder in the hospice. Quickly, girl!"

Rodian kept his eyes on High-Tower. "And your folio is gone as well," he hissed.

High-Tower finally looked up, but he didn't appear surprised.

Wynn went to the table, pushing aside others in her way. Nikolas's eyes were closed, and his skin was pallid. Strands of hair down the left side of his head were grayed. There was not a mark on him that she could see, and she glanced back at Rodian.

"The others," she whispered, "the same, like Jeremy and Elias?"

He closed on the gathering at the table. "Yes ... or one of them."

Wynn hesitated at the answer, looking again at Nikolas's ashen features. If they both died, but only one in this way, then how ... ?

"Someone *is* killing for your folios," Rodian snarled at High-Tower. "And you're going to tell me why." Without looking away from High-Tower, he jabbed a finger at Wynn. "What is in those texts she brought back?"

Wynn flinched as too many eyes turned her way among the initiates and apprentices gathered around. High-Tower's iron-pellet irises fixed on the captain.

"Chlâyard ... do not!" il'Sänke whispered.

For an instant Wynn was lost by that one word, though she knew what it meant—the high tower.

It had been so long since she'd heard anyone utter the domin's name in Dwarvish, and her gaze flickered between

High-Tower and il'Sänke. What was happening between these two?

"What's in those texts?" Rodian shouted, and his voice echoed about the still hall. "Why do you throw away more lives in your denial and ignorance . . . and deceit?"

High-Tower's face flushed within his red beard and hair.

"Captain!"

Wynn turned at the sharp female voice. Duchess Reine and three of the Weardas stood in the main archway.

"I heard—and came straightaway," she said more softly.

She wasn't dressed in her split gown this time. Beneath the sea green cloak of the royal family she wore a leather vest over a stark cotton shirt, and leather breeches tucked into high riding boots. She looked far more like one of her own, the horse people of Faunier, than a member of the Âreskynna family. Her gaze drifted to settle upon Nikolas's frail form.

How had she learned of this tragedy so quickly?

Rodian's jaw tightened, and he looked baffled by the sight of the duchess.

"Highness," he said, with only a curt half bow. "How . . . ?"

Wynn sensed a battle of wills about to smother all else.

"We must get Nikolas to the ward," she urged. "There's no time to waste."

High-Tower's hands were tightened into fists the size of sledgehammers, but he seemed to hear the sense in her words. He quickly dispersed the cluster of apprentices and initiates.

"Get the boy proper help!" Rodian spit. "Then you and I will talk."

High-Tower glared back and took a step around the table's end. Il'Sänke pressed a restraining hand to the dwarf's shoulder, but it didn't slow him. Il'Sänke ended up stumbling aside. In that instant Wynn feared for Rodian's safety.

"Captain," Duchess Reine repeated, and she stepped between the two. "These people have suffered again. Any necessary discussion will wait."

High-Tower held his place with deep, slow breaths and finally turned aside.

"Apologies, my lady," Rodian answered coldly. "But it is a tragedy of their own making . . . and it's time I was given a free hand."

"The king might feel differently," she said softly.

Rodian's angry expression wavered. "Pardon, but feelings have nothing to do with the law."

"The king is offering his assistance," the duchess went on "A royally appointed physician has returned from a journey south. A Suman, one who knows toxins. The king has asked him to visit the barracks tomorrow to . . . examine bodies and provide any information he can for your investigation. For now, leave the sages be."

Rodian breathed in twice and shook his head, and Domin il'Sänke watched him carefully.

Wynn didn't know what to think. Clearly the royals wanted these ugly murders stopped, yet again they shielded the guild from the captain of the city guard.

She should've been relieved—and part of her was. People like Rodian wouldn't understand the breadth and importance of the project. But if he were kept from delving deeper into these horrid events, he might never uncover what she already believed. The killer was unnatural, and sages would keep dying and pages would keep disappearing, unless someone pulled the truth from denial.

The apprentice il'Sänke had sent off came running back with two others dressed in brown robes. They settled a stretcher on the bench beside the table. Premin Adlam entered on their heels. All activity in the room focused on getting Nikolas to the hospice for proper attention.

Nikolas never even moved as High-Tower and Adlam lowered him onto the stretcher and the apprentices rushed him off. But there was nothing to be done for Miriam or Dâgmund.

"As you wish, Highness," Rodian said. Without even a nod to her, he backed toward the hall's main exit.

"Expect the royal physician tomorrow," Duchess Reine told him.

The captain turned and left without another word.

After polite farewells, the duchess and her bodyguards followed. Wynn stood uncomfortably with silent High-Tower and il'Sänke. She wasn't certain whether fear, anxiety, or denial was thickest in the hall.

"I must report to Premin Sykion," High-Tower muttered.

"May I go to Nikolas?" Wynn asked.

"No!" he growled. "Premin Adlam doesn't need you. Return to your room."

Stung, almost hating him, Wynn stalked out and down the passage to the front doors.

Two more of their own were dead! A third barely clung to life, struck down by something no one would admit was real. And she was sick of being treated like some addle-brained mental invalid who should be shut away.

She nearly ran across the courtyard and up to her room, slamming the door behind herself. Sinking onto her bed, she felt her anger drain away, but despair rose in its wake.

She tried not to imagine what had happened to Miriam and Dâgmund, and what it meant when Rodian said only one had died like Elias and Jeremy. Why hadn't the captain sent his guards to protect them? Or had he, and they arrived too late? Had they seen anything to shed light on the murders and who—*what*—kept after the folios?

Wynn sat there, sinking in hopelessness for so long that her cold lamp's crystal nearly winked out.

A soft knock came at her door, but she had no wish to see anyone, except perhaps the captain.

"Who is it?" she called weakly.

"Open up," il'Sänke answered.

Wynn remained where she sat, uncertain whether she even wanted to see the one person who believed any of her "wild tales." She finally rose to let him in.

Domin il'Sänke pushed her back as he entered and turned to close the door. He held something long in his hand, nearly as tall as himself, but it was hidden beneath loose wraps of dull burlap. He glanced toward the dwindling cold lamp on her table.

"Fix that," he said with a curt gesture.

Wynn was staring at the strange long bundle, but she couldn't bring herself to ask about it yet. Hope was something she'd grown wary of, but she went to the table-desk and rubbed the lamp's crystal back to life. As light filled the room, she found il'Sänke standing by her bed, gazing down at the unwrapped item laid there.

Amid the folds of opened cloth lay a polished oak staff. One end was sheathed in a long, loose leather sleeve, held closed around the wood by a drawstring.

"Such an item takes time," il'Sänke said. "And cost, in trial and error as much as resources . . . more for as much as I hurried."

Moons had passed since Wynn had first gone to the domin. To her, that hardly seemed like a hurry. But she now understood what was beneath that leather sheath.

"Finished?" she breathed. "Finally finished?"

"Finished?" He snorted. "Perhaps . . . but there is no more time to test it further."

Wynn swallowed hard. "I'm not complaining, just—"

"Come here," he commanded.

He reached down and gripped the staff's tawny shaft, lifting it. Turning it over, he let it slide through his soft grip until its butt thumped upon the floor. And finally he pulled the sheath off its top end.

Mute glimmers exploded around the room as light struck the sun crystal. Its prisms played multicolored wisps upon the walls. Wynn was so mesmerized, she barely heard the domin's warning.

"Do not judge High-Tower," he said harshly. "He is stricken by Miriam's death . . . as I am by Dâgmund's."

Wynn's gaze shifted to his face, seeing cold anger beneath suppressed grief. She'd had no idea that Dâgmund had any close association to the visiting domin. But her eyes quickly returned to the crystal.

"This will take time and practice to use," he said. "And you will treat this object with great care, as a replacement might not even be possible. Are you prepared for a first lesson?"

Wynn was suddenly hesitant, especially when he looked down at her.

Domin il'Sänke's dark brown eyes held none of their habitual sly humor. They were hard and frightening. But she reached out and grasped the polished staff.

"Yes . . . I've been ready all along."

CHAPTER 9

The following afternoon, Rodian barely listened as Garrogh went over the latest barracks issues to address among their own contingent.

"And some of the men are complaining about the new cook," Garrogh went on. "Lúcan says she drinks. Should I look into it or just have her replaced?"

Rodian glanced up from his desk. After a nearly sleepless night, he hadn't heard most of what Garrogh was saying. He'd spent the day trying to occupy himself while waiting for the appointed royal physician to determine Miriam's official cause of death.

As for the other dead sage found in the alley, a journeyor named Dâgmund, the cause was obvious—head trauma. The young man was barely recognizable, his face caved in by a hunk of brick wall.

Rodian hoped this Suman physician might tell him something of use, at least more than the city ward's healer had concerning Jeremy and Elias. He still remembered the instant that tall black figure had broken a brick wall with only its cloth-wrapped hand. Who—or what—had killed those young sages? And he couldn't stop thinking about the last of the trio, the one named Nikolas Columsarn.

Any living witness was worth more than the word of a dozen Suman physicians, royally appointed or not. But it was too soon to know whether Nikolas would recover enough to answer questions.

"Should we stop for today?" Garrogh asked, dropping the stack of reports on the desk.

Rodian looked up. Two whitish stains stood out on the lieutenant's tunic from last night's seafood stew. He was suddenly disgusted with his second—with the entire lot of sages—but most of all, with the interference of Duchess Reine.

Garrogh must've mistaken his expression for frustration and leaned forward. "They say this Suman knows more about poisons than anyone."

Rodian glared at him. "And who are 'they'?"

His second in command shrugged, clearly having achieved the wrong effect. "A couple of the royal guards . . . just what I've heard."

"You've been talking to the Weardas?"

"A few asked about our progress," Garrogh said. "I wouldn't make much of it. With sages being murdered in alleys, the whole city is starting to talk."

Rodian sighed. Rumors were like a disease upon wisdom. And he would look like a fool for his failure. But if this physician was indeed an expert on toxins, why was he employed by the royal family? The Âreskynna had little to fear of being poisoned. They were beloved by all, with a few exceptions in their ancestry. Perhaps this foreigner had other skills they valued, like that strange and silent elf the duchess kept in her company.

A knock came at the door, and both Rodian and Garrogh sat upright, exchanging expectant glances.

"Come," Rodian called.

Guardsman Lúcan stuck his head in the door. "Captain, are you free? That Suman physician is asking for you."

Rodian ducked around his desk before Garrogh made it off his stool.

"Get a journal," he told his second, "and take notes."

He didn't wish to be distracted by doing so himself. An instant later they were out the door and hurrying down the twisting passageways toward the kitchens. The bodies had been temporarily stored in the cold cellar.

Rodian walked as quickly as he could without appearing anxious, slowing only as he passed through the large kitchens to the scullery beyond. Pulling open the heavy door to the cellar, he was down the stairs, boots clomping on the stone floor, before Garrogh even closed the upper entrance.

The physician stood with his back turned, leaning over a short chopping-block table.

Rodian had met him earlier that morning, but they'd exchanged few words. The man was slender, with dusky skin, dark hair, and a neatly trimmed goatee. He wore clean muslin robes of a sandy color, and a cloth wrap was held about his head by a twined braid of amber cord. He didn't look old enough to be an expert on anything.

Miriam's pallid body was laid out naked upon the chopping-block table, like some unskinned side of pork.

All Rodian could see around the physician's bulky robe were her head and shoulders and her thick calves and feet. Her eyes had been closed, but this did nothing to soften her twisted features locked in horror. Shots of ashen gray ran through the natural brown of her hair.

And then Rodian noticed a bloodied curved knife. It lay near where the Suman leaned a hand upon the table. But Rodian was too eager for answers to give it immediate thought.

"Well?" he demanded without a greeting, for he was tired of remaining polite.

The physician turned, exposing a clear view of the table, and Rodian's mouth went dry.

The girl's torso was split open from her throat to her privates. The skin across her chest and abdomen had been peeled back, exposing internal organs and ribs.

Behind Rodian, Garrogh whispered something under his breath.

"What have you done?" Rodian began, and then he went mute.

The Suman frowned, openly perplexed by his visitors' reactions. "I was told to make a thorough examination."

Rodian found his voice. "Yes, examination . . . not mutilation!"

This young girl had died horribly. She'd been violated enough in that alley. And now he'd unwittingly authorized this butchery.

"Without an internal assessment," the physician said coldly, "I cannot provide any dependable conclusions."

Rodian took three weak breaths, trying to regain his calm.

He was dealing with a Suman—like il'Sänke—who saw no connection between the body and the sentient spirit. Humans of all races, and dwarves and elves, were the highest of living beings in the eyes of Toiler, Maker, and Dreamer. Even the body—the vessel—was sacred. This Suman could never begin to comprehend such truth.

Rodian would have to go to temple and pray for this mistake of oversight.

"What have you learned?" he demanded. "How did she die?"

The physician wiped the girl's gore from his hands with dampened burlap. He stepped to the table's head, scowling down at Miriam's tormented face. About to speak, he stopped and leaned lower, as if inspecting some overlooked detail. Then he shook his head and began again in his thick accent.

"Upon initial examination, I felt certain the cause was poison. You must have noted the grayed flesh and lack of injury?"

Rodian didn't respond. He could only stare at Miriam's split flesh.

"I searched for methods of introduction," the Suman went on, "hoping to lift traces of any substance used. There are quick-acting compounds that can be introduced by breath, contact with the skin, or even through orifices other than the mouth."

"You found something?" Rodian asked, his anxiety building. "You must have."

Some gain had to be achieved for this atrocity.

"No," the physician answered.

Rodian forced his eyes to follow as the man pointed inside the girl's opened torso.

"Her lungs are whole and healthy," the Suman continued, "as is the lining of her throat. There are no signs of chemical or particulate damage to her internal organs. I found nothing in the nostrils or ears or anywhere upon her skin. Anything introduced to the eyes might have thinned in tears but would also have left traces for such a quick death."

The physician shook his head, huffing through his long beak of a nose, and his frown deepened.

"Then what?" Garrogh demanded, the journal and a shaft of writing charcoal in his hand.

"I do not know what killed her and caused such discoloration and discomfort. She simply died suddenly."

Rodian felt his throat closing up.

The girl had been mutilated for nothing, and the sound of Garrogh scribbling notes didn't resume. Rodian whirled for the stairs, hurrying to get out of this cold, dim space.

"Sir," Garrogh called. "Where are you going?"

"The guild. Please see our *guest* back to the royal grounds."

He nearly ran up the stairs, out through the scullery and kitchen, not caring if the staff saw his state. He didn't slow until he reached the courtyard and the stables along the south wall. Breathing fresh air as fast and deep as he could, he strode past the stable warden and saddled Snowbird himself. He patted her when she tried to nuzzle him, but then quickly swung up on her back.

Rodian tried to wipe the image of the cold cellar from his thoughts as he urged Snowbird into a canter down the second castle's gatehouse tunnel. He couldn't get the sight of Miriam out of his head, but he felt equally tangled in the strands of some web. It held him in place, forcing him to do little but watch, like a bound and useless spectator.

How could Duchess Reine, or the rest of the royal family, send him that Suman butcher?

The Numan Lands had seen no war in Rodian's lifetime, but he had seen battle in his younger days. One tour of duty had placed him near, and even beyond, Malourné's far eastern border. Even farther out were the Broken Lands—

wild terrain with little to no civilization, stretching nearly to the eastern coast. Sometimes straggling bands of hulkish little beasts on two legs wandered into the farthest farmlands and forest communities.

He had seen soldiers bashed and torn apart, for those things ate nearly anything digestible. Hence their name—goblins . . . the little "gobblers."

They weren't so little. Ranging up to two-thirds the height of man, they hunted in packs, like wild dogs, and could tear apart a man, hauling his pieces away for their food.

But it wasn't the same as that girl cut open in the cold cellar.

He'd never thought how different these southlanders, the Sumans, were from his people. How could anyone in Calm Seatt expect such foreigners to exhibit decent moral reasoning, let alone ethical behavior?

Rodian tried to call up an image of the Trinity set in white stone upon the temple's dais.

"Forgive me," he kept whispering, "for my ignorance and failing of foresight."

As Snowbird's hooves clopped on cobblestone, Rodian was barely aware enough to steer her course. He tried to clear his thoughts with what few facts he possessed.

The killer knew about the sages' project and could read their symbols. The translation had been ongoing for perhaps half a year. The killer had waited, seeming to know—or guess—which folios to go after.

Was the murderer someone inside the guild?

The killer had torn out a piece of a brick wall with only his hand. And not a stitch of his clothing had succumbed to the sudden fire in the alley.

A mage perhaps?

Rodian knew of few such in the city, let alone elsewhere. Several apothecaries claimed to be alchemists, dabblers in what the guild called thaumaturgy. Dâgmund had clearly possessed such skill. But Rodian didn't know of anyone who worked the other art the sages called conjury.

There were two dwarven "stone-melders" who'd taken up residence in Calm Seatt. They often plied their trade as special masons for those who could afford them. But the figure in the alley had been tall, perhaps even trim beneath that billowing cloak, so certainly no dwarf.

Rodian considered the strange elf he'd seen with members of the royal family.

And then there was the guild—and its Order of Metaology.

It was said that they made the crystals used in the sages' special lamps, and occasionally had a hand in other works of this thaumaturgy. But he'd never heard of any, inside or outside of the guild, who could stand in fire or shatter brick with one hand.

Metaologers wore midnight blue robes.

Rodian closed his eyes and saw swirling black robes that appeared to float over the alley walls. Like Domin il'Sänke's robe, easily mistaken for black in the dark.

What had Wynn said about him? *He is a master of metaology.*

Il'Sänke had no alibi for the night of Elias's and Jeremy's deaths, or not one that weighed much under scrutiny. Rodian knew better than to make a claim against a sage, not until he had sufficient evidence. And the royal family would be deeply disturbed if it turned out to be true.

Or would they?

Il'Sänke wasn't a sage of Calm Seatt. He was from the empire far south beyond the Rädärsherând—the "Sky-Cutter" range separating the north from the vast desert. He was a Suman.

Snowbird slowed as Rodian turned her up Old Procession Road, straight toward the guild's gate. By now, Sykion and the entire Premin Council would know of last night's events. Likely the whole guild would be whipped up in panic.

May the Trinity forgive him, but he hoped so. All the better, all the more pressure when he pressed them for answers, regardless of Duchess Reine's shielding influence.

Where had Domin il'Sänke been last night?

He urged Snowbird through the gatehouse tunnel, not bothering to halt when a slim initiate in tan scurried out for his horse. He rode straight into the courtyard before dismounting.

"Stay," he told Snowbird.

Rodian didn't bother knocking and pushed through the double doors. Several apprentices coming out quickly jumped aside as he turned down the passage toward the common hall.

"Sir! Can we help you?"

He ignored them, though one young man in a teal robe chased after him.

"Please, sir. You cannot just wander about.... Is there someone you wish to see?"

Rodian walked straight through the common hall for the smaller side archway—and the passage to the northern tower. When he climbed the turning stairs to the third level, the door stood open.

Some of Rodian's cold anger drained away as he peered in. High-Tower sat behind his desk with his wide face in his large hands. His gray-laced reddish hair hung in a mess. When he lifted his head, his eyes were blank and bleak.

The young apprentice ran puffing up behind Rodian.

"Domin," he panted. "Apologies ... I know you're busy.... I tried to stop him."

Standing in the doorway, Rodian glanced about the study. Other than stacked texts he'd seen on his last visit, it didn't look like the domin was occupied.

"It is all right," High-Tower mumbled. "Go back to your studies."

The apprentice glared disapprovingly at Rodian, then turned and stomped back down the stairs.

"I was about to send for you," High-Tower said quietly.

Rodian almost asked why. But he waited as the domin folded his massive hands together, lacing his thick, short fingers. High-Tower's gaze hardened, but not at Rodian. Instead the dwarf stared across the room at the wall or out the window beyond the open door.

"I sent out no folio today," High-Tower added. "I cannot risk harm to any more of our own. So our work has come to a halt ... for the moment. You had best come in, Captain. There is much to discuss, but close the door first."

Rodian didn't care for the *feel* of this moment. He'd come for his own reasons, and the dwarf was suddenly far too accommodating. He stepped in, reaching for the open door's handle.

A dark figure stood in the evening shadows, hidden between the obstructing door and the room's deep-set window.

At the sight of a black cloak, Rodian reached for his sword.

The figure tilted its head up.

Beneath a wide-brimmed black hat with a flat top, Pawl a'Seatt fixed glittering brown eyes on Rodian.

"Good evening, Captain," the scribe master said evenly.

Rodian faltered. "Why are you here?"

"I was asked," a'Seatt answered, and his gaze slid smoothly to High-Tower. "Now, perhaps you would shut the door so that we may both be enlightened."

Several days passed without incident, and Wynn had made little headway with her research. Not that there weren't more shelves of texts to go through, or that she'd ever get through all of them, but what little she found added nothing to what she'd gathered.

At times her thoughts drifted to Miriam, Nikolas, and Dâgmund. She alone understood that the killer was unnatural, and that knowledge felt like a curse. It left her wondering what more she could've done to protect the three young sages. The guilt was almost crippling.

But to know the truth was better, no matter how alone and terrified it left her.

Wynn had visited Nikolas several times. He hadn't awoken but was no worse off by Domin Bitworth's estimate, though the master naturologer could offer no guesses as to what ailed the young apprentice. Bitworth seemed quietly disturbed by Nikolas's new gray hairs.

Premin Sykion made it clear that no one was to whisper any wild notions or spread any rumors until Nikolas woke up and gave his own account of what happened. Silently, Wynn believed an undead had somehow tried to feed upon Nikolas so rapidly that it caused effects akin to premature aging. She researched this, but the archives held nothing concerning the myths of vampires found only in the Farlands.

And the days passed so slowly.

She wanted to practice with the sun crystal, as the only means to protect herself and others. But Domin il'Sänke made her swear not to "toy" with the staff outside of his supervision. And he'd been busy, often locked in his chamber or down in the workshops. Hopefully he would come tonight.

So she sat in her room, reorganizing her notes, though soon she should head to the main hall for supper. If she saw il'Sänke, she might corner him and arrange more time for lessons.

Closing the journal, Wynn headed out, but as she neared the stairs at the passage's end, low, rapid voices made her pause. She crept forward just enough to peek around the corner.

On the bottom landing before the door to the courtyard, three apprentices stood chattering in hushed tones. That nasty Regina Melliny was closest, with her back turned to the stairs, but the other two wore the gray of cathologers beneath their heavy cloaks. Wynn had seen them both around the guild but didn't know their names.

"What did High-Tower say?" Regina asked.

"Not a blasted thing!" a young man with sloping eyes replied. "I almost fainted when the old stone-face told me to go fetch a folio tonight."

"Watch your tongue," the other warned. "You mustn't talk like that about our domin."

"I don't care!" the first countered. "I'm just glad we made it home . . . and I wasn't sorry not to carry back a folio. Master a'Seatt can face him for that."

Wynn drew back out of sight.

Not a single folio had been sent out since the night of Miriam's and Dâgmund's deaths. But High-Tower had sent one to the Upright Quill and then sent messengers to retrieve it. What was he thinking?

Wynn tried to lean out again without being seen.

"Well, did Master a'Seatt say anything?" Regina asked—as if it were any business of a naturology student's.

"He just said the work wasn't finished . . . and he wouldn't hand over anything. He sent us off, and I didn't argue. He scares me more than High-Tower."

The three young sages stepped out, likely headed to the main hall for supper. Wynn waited until their chatter grew faint before she descended. But she paused at the door, mulling their words over and over.

If High-Tower risked sending out another folio, its contents must be important to whatever work was still ongoing. Maybe the passages even connected to those taken from Miriam, Dâgmund, and Nikolas. But it didn't make sense that Master a'Seatt hadn't sent the folio back. His shop had never failed to complete work on time.

And yet, a folio was still at the Upright Quill.

This might be her only chance to see just what, among all the texts, was now targeted by an undead.

Wynn rushed back to her room. She grabbed the crystal out of her cold lamp and then paused near the bed.

What would happen if she were discovered? She'd been ordered more than once to keep away from anything to do with the project.

Magiere wouldn't have let anyone stop her, and neither would Leesil. Chap, as well, had always taken his own course.

Wynn couldn't give up her only chance.

CHAPTER 10

Just past dusk, Chane crouched upon the roof of the Upright Quill scriptorium, listening to all that transpired below. One of the scribe masters had sent the guild's messengers away empty-handed, which meant an unfinished folio was still inside the shop. It was a strange twist, but a fortunate one.

Although Chane wasn't fluent in the Begaine syllabary, back in Bela, Wynn and Domin Tilswith had explained how it worked. Not an actual alphabet, it was for rendering word parts or syllables. Based on blending and simplifying the strokes of modern Numanese's thirty-eight letters, and combined with additional special marks, it could be used to transcribe almost any known language. It saved space versus almost any other writing system, and for those who could read it, it was faster to take in what was written.

Chane had a passable grasp of spoken Numanese, but he was not fully proficient at reading or writing it. Even in his own notes, any Numanese terms he used were written with Belaskian letters.

The sages' script would be a struggle, but he had to know what kind of texts Wynn had chosen from the vast library of the ice-trapped castle. Especially—specifically—whether any related to the mysterious blacked-out scroll. He had to see what was in the folio, and he waited long before the shop's front door finally creaked open again.

"Out with you," said someone with a reedy voice. "All of you."

"Do you have the key?" a girl asked.

"No, I left it inside to annoy you . . . Now scoot! Master a'Seatt is waiting."

Chane shifted to the roof's edge and peered over the eave.

A dark-haired man in a charcoal jerkin, carrying a wide-brimmed black hat, stood below on the street. An old, balding short man in spectacles shooed scribes from the shop. A young girl with kinky hair and dark skin followed in the old one's hobbling footsteps as they stepped out.

Chane stiffened under a tingle that made him shudder.

Something about the dark-haired man unsettled him. But his extended awareness as an undead had grown dull from his wearing Welstiel's ring for so long.

A key scraped in the lock. Soon all of the shop's staff strode down the street. And Chane lost any hint of that strange sensation. He turned his attention back to the shop below.

Closing his eyes, he lay down and leaned his head all the way over the eave. In a deep inhale, he tried to drink in the scent from the night air—tried to smell for any living thing still inside.

There was nothing but a lingering after-scent. He listened carefully as well, but the scriptorium seemed empty for the night. He pushed back atop the roof, contemplating the best method of entry.

Breaking through the door or a window was not an option. Someone might see or hear him this early at night. There was only one other way. He roused the bestial part of himself that always hungered for a kill.

Hunger surfaced, hardening his fingernails and filling his cold flesh with strength.

Crawling to the shop's rear, Chane dug his fingernails into the roof's shakes.

He pried up and removed seven as quietly as he could

and found the underplanking was solid and sound—troublesome but expected. Rising slightly, he scanned the street once for anyone in sight, and then punched through the planks. He kept at it, clearing a hole large enough to pass through.

As he dropped lightly into the shop's rearmost room, he fully widened his sight. The scribe's workroom was so sealed off from outside light that even he had difficulty. He barely made out worktables, chairs, and the lighter tone of piled parchment and paper.

He felt his way about, recognizing objects clearly only when he was close enough. At the back shelves he found a lantern and an old tin cup full of crude wooden matches. He lit the lantern, turning its knob until only dim illumination filled the space. Leaving the lantern in place, he turned to scan the room.

Where would a master scribe or proprietor secure the folio?

And there it was. A leather folio lay on a short side table beside the largest desk just two steps away.

Chane took those two steps and then hesitated.

Why was it out in plain sight? This seemed too unprofessional. Perhaps the scribes had worked late, being too far behind in their efforts, and the folio had not been properly stored away. But even that did not seem plausible.

Chane picked up the folio.

By its thickness and heft, all the guild notes and excerpts were still inside. He glanced across the near desk and quickly at the others in the room. All were cleared and orderly. No transcription work appeared to be left lying about, so perhaps that had been stored away.

He pulled the folio's leather lace and opened its flap.

At the sight of the sheets, all scribbled upon in ink and charcoal strokes, his shoulders sagged in relief. But he could not linger here, nor turn up the lamp and risk its light being spotted through even the crack of a shutter. He turned down the lamp until its flame snuffed out and quietly hurried out to the shop's front room.

Carefully cracking open a window, enough to do the same with its outer shutter, Chane held the stack of pages close. He angled them until weak light from a street lantern fell upon the top sheet.

This time he sagged in frustration.

Aside from his limited understanding of the Begaine syllabary, some of these sages had terrible handwriting. To make matters worse, the notes were written with sharpened charcoal sticks. Cheaper and more convenient than quill and ink, they often left characters blurred. Even though some notes were not written in Begaine symbols, he could not sound out all of them. Many appeared to be copied in their original languages, which Chane could not even identify.

He turned a few more sheets and finally gave up, realizing he needed more time to decipher the folio's contents—and for that he could not remain in this shop.

A tingle crawled over his skin.

The beast chained within him growled in warning.

Chane pulled the window closed, latched it, and stepped back, watching the street outside through the narrow space of the ajar shutter. A soft shift of shadow flickered to his left.

Beyond the shop's door, the front wall's far side wavered. Wood appeared to bulge inward like an ocean swell, and then settled flat around a tall shape emerging.

A black figure stepped straight through the wall into the shop's front. But it looked as solid as anything else in the room.

Garbed in a flowing robe and cloak, the latter's folds shifting and swaying, the figure paused in stillness. A voluminous hood covered its head and face, and even Chane's undead eyes couldn't penetrate the dark within that opening.

He stared as his senses fully awakened.

He had not felt it coming. Not even a tingle, until it had pushed through the wall like water or vapor. Before he could utter a demand or warning threat, the figure raised a hand toward him.

Its sleeve slipped down, exposing forearm, hand, and fingers—all wrapped in strips of black cloth. A soft hissing rose around it, as it slid forward across the floor.

Chane shoved the pages into the folio and backed against the side wall beyond the window. And still it came at him. He vaulted the front counter on his free hand and retreated toward the open doorway to the back room.

The only way out was through the hole in the workroom's roof, or to shatter his way through the rear door. Either path meant turning his back on this thing that had just walked straight through a wall.

Chane jerked out his longsword.

"Do not be closed . . . *do not be closed*," Wynn muttered over and over as she ran through the streets toward the Upright Quill.

If Master Teagan were still there, she might bluff her way in to retrieve the folio. Perhaps a threat that Premin Sykion insisted on its return might do the trick, regardless that the work was incomplete. Wynn could simply promise to have it back first thing in the morning—and hope that later she wouldn't be cast out of the guild for interference.

One way or another, she was going to get into serious trouble. But a look at the folio was all that mattered.

"Please be open," she whispered again, and then halted, her mouth dangling open.

The Upright Quill was as quiet and dark as any other shop on the street.

"*Valhachkasej'â!*" she hissed—and then bit her tongue.

Swearing in Old Elvish was a bad habit she'd picked up from Leesil. A few profane expressions were about all the half elf could pronounce correctly in his mother's language. Wynn took a long breath, shuffling toward the shop's door. Now what?

One window shutter was slightly cracked open, and she hurried over.

Swinging the shutter wide, she flinched when it creaked too loudly. She craned up on tiptoe to peer through the panes.

Light from the nearest street lantern wasn't enough to fill the shop's front room, but perhaps someone was still working in the back. She would have to knock at the door after all. Then two closely spaced footfalls pounded inside the shop. It sounded like someone stomping.

Wynn grabbed the sill with both hands, pulling herself up with her face close to the panes. But she saw nothing.

An indistinct form shifted in the dark, near the door to the back workroom.

Wynn's nose squashed against the pane.

A tall, broad-shouldered man in a dark cloak stood beyond the front counter. His hood was down, and he held a leather folio in his hand.

Wynn's stomach hardened.

Someone had beaten her here and gotten in, and she tried to make out his face. Besides Master a'Seatt, she'd never seen anyone of such stature here. In the dark, his skin was so light she began to make out a narrow face, straight nose, and red-brown hair, and maybe . . .

Sparkling eyes looked about the shop's front room.

Wynn stopped breathing . . . and stared at Chane.

The last time she'd seen him was south of the Farlands in the company of Welstiel, Magiere's undead half brother. Half a world away atop the Pock Peaks, in the library of Li'kän's castle, he'd promised never to follow her.

He'd promised—yet here he was, holding a folio.

Confusion scrambled Wynn's thoughts.

It wasn't possible, not for the way all the victims had died. Except that Chane had kept company with Welstiel for a long while. And Welstiel had been trained by his father's retainer—Ubâd, that decrepit necromancer and the architect of Magiere's unnatural birth.

Welstiel was a conjuror. As a Noble Dead he'd had many years to refine his skills. And what might Chane, a conjuror himself, have learned under that madman's tutelage?

Everything kept racing along twisted paths in Wynn's mind, and they all led to Chane.

She remembered spirits, walking corpses, and dismembered body parts floating in milky fluids within Ubâd's hideaway. Chane had been there as well, trying to save her, but looking back . . .

Wynn's chill faded, and bile burned in the back of her throat.

It was him. Chane was murdering sages . . . her own kind.

He suddenly shoved the folio under one arm, and a long line of silver appeared before him in the dark shop.

Wynn quickly realized it was his sword—but why was he drawing a weapon? He wasn't looking her way but off toward the shop front's far side. She tried to shift left along the window and glimpse the room's far right side.

A black form floated across the floor into sight.

Wynn's eyes widened as she followed it—and then she flinched back.

Chane was looking right at her. His eyes widened as well, but he quickly returned his attention to the black mass.

She thought she saw the shape of a black hood and cloak upon a tall form—just before a shout filled the night street.

"Move in!"

A strong arm latched around Wynn from behind and heaved her off the ground.

Chane heard a male voice shouting outside, and then Wynn cried out.

He glanced toward the window, but the shutter's narrow space was empty. And the wafting black figure rushed him—straight through the counter.

Chane didn't even think to swing his sword. He twisted sideways into the doorframe, blade out, but he still couldn't make out a face within the hood.

The figure hesitated. Was it looking at the sword? Then it surged forward, and Chane slashed.

The blade's tip passed through the figure's midsection.

The steel didn't even drag, as if cutting only air. Lack of resistance took him by surprise, and he lost the sword's balance. It jarred against the doorframe, and the figure's cloth-wrapped fingers shot out at him. On instinct Chane jerked the sword's hilt upward, blade tilted to block.

The black hand glided straight through the steel and sank into his chest.

Agonizing cold spread through him before he could shut out the pain. The frigid cold in his chest was so harsh it felt as if he burned. Something seemed to gnaw at him from within.

Chane's knees buckled in weakness. Then a hollow moan filled the shop. It rose to a shriek, piercing his ears with equal pain.

The black figure jerked its hand from Chane's chest. It held up shivering fingers, as if it had suddenly succumbed to the same searing cold.

Chane wobbled, and his shoulder struck the doorframe before he could catch himself.

A hiss grew inside the shop.

The sound seemed to rise all around as the figure's pit of a hood turned to its own raised hand wrapped in shreds of black cloth. Its fingers twitched in convulsions as it retreated through the counter. And the hood's opening turned once more toward Chane.

He felt the cold fade within him and his strength returned.

He had no notion of what had just happened, but it had not been what his attacker expected. Once its hand jerked from his body, the sudden weakness simply faded. As if it tried to drain his strength and failed.

And Chane had felt something else in that painful contact—empty of life.

He righted himself in panic. This thing that walked through solid walls was undead, but unlike any he had ever seen or heard of. Chane quickly glanced to the rear door and then up to the hole in the roof.

He had to escape, and Wynn was still out front. But he would never gain the roof quickly enough, nor have time to get past the rear door's inner bar. Not before . . .

He glanced back again. The rear door's brackets were empty, and the bar leaned against the wall beside it. The door might still contain a basic lock, but why had it not been barred when the staff left the shop?

The robed form curled its fingers into hooks and slid through the counter again.

Chane dodged out the doorway and behind the counter. The back room was too tight and cluttered for fighting. At best, he would have to break through a front window and run. Then the folio was jerked from under his arm.

"No!" he rasped.

He snatched hold of the leather case with his free hand and spun about, swinging his sword back in reflex.

Chane watched his blade pass through a black-wrapped forearm and hit the countertop. The figure's fingers still clutched the folio's other end. Chane barely blinked as something struck the side of his head.

He felt the figure's other hand driving his head sideways and down. He thought he smelled spices—perhaps cinnamon—and dust. Then his skull smashed against the counter's edge, hammering the side of his jaw.

Darkness swallowed Chane's sight as he felt the folio ripped from his hand.

Wynn struggled, kicking back at her captor, until she heard him shout, "Move, all of you!"

The voice behind her head was deafening, but she recognized it. Captain Rodian held her off the ground with one arm.

"Take the back door first," he called.

Three red-surcoated Shyldfälches ran into sight with swords drawn. One took position at the shop's front door while the other two watched the front windows. Wynn heard more running feet and the sound of battering and breaking wood from somewhere at the shop's rear.

A grating hiss rose into a hollow wail inside the shop.

Wynn shivered inside, wanting to cover her ears.

"Move, all of you!"

Chane barely heard the shout through the ache in his head. He tried to push himself up, but gouged his hand on a piece of broken wood. His balance failed, and he toppled against the second door behind the counter. He had no idea what was happening, but he heard that voice again outside the shop.

"Take the back first!"

Chane crawled to his knees and peered into the rear workroom. The back door bucked and crackled as something heavy struck it from the outside. It had been locked but not barred, which would slow any escape but still make it possible to force entry from the outside. Chane grabbed his sword off the floor and struggled to his feet.

The figure stood just beyond the counter.

Its cloak and robe were quiet and still, and the folio remained gripped in its hand. Its hood turned slowly, as if whoever hid within it looked from one front window to the door.

How could this thing be solid and then not, at the same time? Yet it never showed a sign of that change.

Finally it fixed upon the other window—the one where Chane had seen Wynn—and it stopped.

Another slam hit the rear door, and Chane heard wood splintering sharply. Someone had set a trap here—but to catch him or this thing? He threw himself over the countertop's remains, rolling to the far side. As he lunged for the folio, the figure slipped beyond reach. It flew straight at the window like whipping cloth driven on a windstorm—and passed straight through.

No glass shattered; no wallboards broke. Not even the shutters beyond the panes swung in its passing. Then the folio in its grip hit against glass—and did not pass through.

The black figure might be noncorporeal, but the folio was solid.

Chane lunged for it.

An angry wailing shriek echoed outside, and the window shattered outward.

The shop filled with the sound of breaking glass. Then the noise of breaking wood and shouts carried from the rear workroom.

Chane bolted for the broken window as a scream erupted outside the shop.

Rodian watched something blacker than night bleed through the shop's front wall. He still held on to Wynn, but the sage had ceased struggling.

The blot spread quickly over the shop's wood planks, blocking out one window. Then it bulged like a shroud cloth in a gale. It took shape in something he'd seen once before.

The black-cloaked and -robed figure halted, one arm

stretched out behind it. Its hand was still beyond one pane of the window. And Rodian saw what it held in its trailing grip.

It held a folio, still stuck behind the window, inside the shop.

The pane creaked and began to crack.

Rodian dropped Wynn and shoved her out of the way, and the window exploded outward.

He raised his sword arm before his face. Glass fragments tinkled off steel and across his glove. A wailing scream rose before his sight line cleared.

Then Wynn cried out, "Captain!"

He'd kept three guardsmen with him out front: Shâth, Ecgbryht, and Ruben.

And Shâth was rushing toward the black figure.

"Stay back!" Rodian ordered, raising his sword.

The figure stood before the shop, folio in one hand, as its cloak writhed around its robed form. But its other hand . . .

Black fingers lanced through Shâth's chest and out his back, like barbs of shadow emerging from the guardsman's body. The rest of its hand followed instantly as Ruben and Ecgbryht closed in. Shâth hung impaled and shuddering as the figure's hand clenched into a fist.

Mute crackling rose as Shâth choked, but he never screamed. A dark stain spread across the back of his tabard around the figure's protruding wrist. The robed figure wrenched its arm back.

Shâth arched as the black fist ripped back through his torso.

Blood spattered over Ecgbryht as Shâth collapsed. His body hit the street hard, with his face frozen into a gaping mouth and eyes.

The front of his tabard and hauberk were torn around a mangled hole.

It happened so fast.

A low hiss rose all around in the street. The dark space of the figure's wide hood turned toward Rodian—no, beyond him, toward Wynn. And it rushed her like some coal-colored ghost, solid and real and yet not.

Rodian dodged in, uncertain what he could do against this thing. Ecgbryht was closer, and swung hard at the figure as Wynn scrambled back across the cobblestones. Rodian stepped in front of her.

"Wynn . . . stay away! Do not let it touch you!"

Those rasping words came like a shout. Rodian didn't know who'd given this warning, but then he saw someone crouched upon the shattered window's sill.

The man wore a long dark cloak with its hood thrown back. His face was pale and narrow, and there was something wrong with his eyes. Two killers emerged from the scribe shop—but why had the second one warned Wynn off?

"Stay behind me!" Rodian shouted at her. He swung, aiming for the black figure's wrist just above the clutched folio.

Too much happened at once.

The black figure swung its free hand and latched it solidly around Ecgbryht's throat. Rodian's blade passed through the figure's wrist with no resistance, and its tip clanged off a street stone.

Garrogh bolted out of the shop's front door with two guards, Lúcan and Taméne, running behind him . . . just as Ruben charged the figure, trying to force it off Ecgbryht.

The second killer upon the sill, sword in one hand, reached out and grabbed the folio.

All this passed by the time Rodian righted his sword.

Locked in the figure's grip, Ecgbryht drew short, rapid breaths. His features twisted and paled. The robed one released him, and he crumpled instantly. It tried to pull the folio back, and the second killer slipped off the sill to the street. Garrogh closed on the other would-be thief clinging to his end of the folio.

"Get back!" Rodian shouted at his men. "It's a mage!"

The robed one turned its hood toward Wynn.

"No!" the other thief hissed. "You will leave her alone!"

He jerked hard on the folio, and Rodian faltered.

The two caught in his trap were at odds, but not just over the folio. Another conflict existed between them over the journeyor. Rodian set himself against either coming at Wynn.

And then a snarl trailed into a howl somewhere in the open street. He heard rapid claws on cobblestone and had to turn his head.

A tall, dark-coated dog charged along buildings in the thicker shadows beneath their eaves. Or was it a wolf?

Rodian thought he saw a streetlight catch upon its eyes, which glittered like pale blue gems.

Wynn barely spotted Chane before Rodian stepped in her way. All she saw around the captain was the robed figure. When she stared into its hood, the pitch-black within it seemed to bleed over everything in her sight. She couldn't look at anything else.

Then she heard a distant snarl.

It seemed so far away, but so did every other noise around her. Then it trailed into a familiar wailing howl. She'd heard it so many times she knew it like the voice of an old friend in her head.

Chap was here, and he was hunting!

She wasn't mad, delusional, like everyone whispered. This thing killing her people was an undead. No other reason would cause Chap to howl like that.

For an instant his face rose in her thoughts—fur so silver it might tint blue in moonlight, and eyes like crystals catching an afternoon sky.

A hissing shriek rang in her ears as she heard claws scrabbling on cobblestones. Another deep snarl sounded as a dark gray form rushed past her. It spun and circled before her on four long legs ending in large paws, and its head swung briefly toward her.

Wynn saw the outline of tall peaked ears over a long muzzle—and pale blue eyes gazed at her. Then the dog wheeled, facing the robed undead beyond the captain. She reached out, screaming his name.

"Chap!"

Rodian sucked a breath. He'd lost all control here. Everything splintered into chaos.

Garrogh grabbed the pale-faced man by his cloak, jerking him back. The man lost his grip on the folio but ducked around the lieutenant and took a swing. His fist landed hard, and Garrogh twisted away under the impact, slamming against the shop's front.

"Don't let him escape!" Rodian shouted.

Lúcan rushed the pale man, while Ruben swung his sword at the robed figure's back.

A hissing shriek broke over the noise and shouts.

Rodian lurched sideways as the robed figure recoiled. Only then did Ruben's sword connect and pass straight through, not even ruffling robe or cloak. The figure's hood remained fixed on Wynn somewhere behind Rodian. He glanced back.

Her eyes were wide yet vacant as she stared up and beyond Rodian, as if locking her gaze with whoever hid inside the robe's large cowl.

And the wolf rushed in between him and Wynn.

Rodian instinctively turned his sword point toward the animal, but it didn't go for the sage. It circled her quickly, coming around between her and everyone else. Its charcoal fur was nearly as dark as the robed thief, but strange shimmers showed wherever muscles rolled beneath its coat. It was taller than any wolf that Rodian had seen, and its eyes scintillated blue in the dark.

The animal glanced once at Wynn and then rushed at Rodian, snapping its jaws.

Rodian lunged aside, raising his sword.

"Chap!"

He flinched at Wynn's voice and saw her reaching out after the wolf, and the animal raced by him. Jaws clacking beneath snarls, it went straight for the robed figure.

The murderous, faceless mage cowered back—and then bolted, folio still clutched in its hand. Ruben was behind it, and Taméne was the only guard still standing in its path. The figure struck him across the face. Rodian heard bones crack as Taméne went down limp and flopping.

And the wolf ran after the figure. An eerie baying rose in its wake.

Rodian was stunned. But Ruben and Lúcan both instantly spread wide to either side, boxing the pale man against the shop's front. Garrogh climbed to his feet, blinking as he shook his head once. The lieutenant spun about and lifted his sword.

Rodian regained his wits, pointing at the pale man. "Put *him* down, if you have to," he barked at Ruben and Lúcan. "But don't let him get away."

With a quick wave for Garrogh to follow, Rodian rushed after the fading howls of the wolf.

Chane locked eyes on Wynn, but she did not look at him. She looked down the way, where the officer had vanished.

"Chap?" she whispered weakly.

She teetered around, and at the sight of him, Chane heard breath rush between her clenched teeth. The fear in her eyes was nothing compared to the hate that followed, spreading quickly over her face.

He had fallen so far from what she had once thought of him.

He had given her up that night in the ice-bound castle. With all the time that had passed, it should not still hurt this much. But after all she had been through, and seeing him in Welstiel's company, what else could he expect from her now?

"Drop your weapon!" one guard barked.

Chane let the sword sag in his hand and could not take his gaze from Wynn's hate-filled brown eyes.

Wynn's head ached. She had to find Chap, but here was Chane, staring at her. How could his gaze hold even a hint of remorse after all he had done?

"Drop your weapon!" one guardsman ordered.

Chane sagged, but he never looked at the pair of guardsmen ringing him in. He looked only at her, eyelids drooping, and his sword tip dipped toward the paving stones.

And Wynn faltered.

Three city guards lay in the street, the first still staring up at the night sky with a mangled hole in his chest. Chane hadn't done that, and *something* else had come for the folio as well.

"I said drop it!" the guard shouted again.

Wynn looked from the dead man to Chane. His eyes were fully open again as he studied that same lifeless body.

The guards inched in on him, yet he neither released nor raised his sword. He turned his eyes on her, nearly colorless in the dark, and slowly shook his head.

"Not me," he rasped.

He spoke in Numanese, her language. How had he learned it so quickly? When his gaze returned briefly to the mangled body, it suddenly hardened. He shook his head again.

"It was not me!" he snapped hoarsely.

"Shut your mouth and do as you're told!" the second guard demanded.

Doubt crept in upon Wynn.

She knew nothing of how he was involved here, but she might never learn if he were arrested. Not that two living men had a fair chance of containing an armed undead. There was only an impulse to guide her.

"Run!" she called.

One guard turned wide eyes on her. The other cursed under his breath and charged.

Only then did Wynn go chill inside, realizing what she'd just done.

Chane whirled.

He caught the charging guard with an elbow in the man's chest and slashed at the other with his sword. The blade's tip clipped the second guard's shoulder as the first one buckled with a gasp. Both toppled as Chane bolted up the street, disappearing beyond sight.

Wynn turned all the way around.

She searched the night, listening for Chap's voice. But all was silent save for the curses and muffled groans of the guards. Alone with the wounded and the dead, Wynn went numb.

Somewhere ahead, the wolf's howls ceased.

"Where are they?" Rodian shouted. "Do you see them?"

"There!" Garrogh panted, and he pointed west down a side street. "Down there, I think."

His expression was furious as they ran on, and Rodian felt the same. Their own trap had turned against them.

They burst out of the side street into a wide main way,

but it was empty. Rodian saw no dark wolf or black-robed fugitive. Frustration choked him.

He'd had the killer in sight, cornered by his men, and then the second one appeared. Worse still, they had seemed at odds with each other. Just how many thieves and killers was he trying to catch? How many unknown individuals found some gain or threat in whatever the sages were doing with Wynn's texts?

"Garrogh, do you hear anything?"

His second cocked his head for a long moment, and then his expression fell into a weary scowl.

"No . . . nothing."

"Damn it!" Rodian struck the street with his sword. A quick, sharp scrape mingled with a steel clang rolling along the vacant avenue.

"Wait," Garrogh whispered, and then pointed. "There!"

In the edge of a pool of lantern light lay a leather folio upon the cobblestones.

Rodian ran for it and snatched it up. The leather lace was broken, snapped rather than untied, and he flipped the folio open.

All the pages were still inside, but it didn't matter. They were fakes, arranged by High-Tower and a'Seatt in this effort to lure and trap the killer.

Rodian raised his eyes, looking through the dark broken pools of lantern light.

Had their quarry—at least the one who'd gotten away—realized the pages were a ruse? How could anyone have even glanced inside the folio during flight?

"Ruben and Lúcan should have the other in custody," Garrogh said. "We'll get some answers out of that one!"

Rodian simply nodded. Turning, he headed back at a trot, all the way to the Upright Quill. But upon drawing closer to the scriptorium, he slowed in caution.

Four of his men lay in the street.

Only Lúcan was on his feet, hovering with sword in hand over Wynn, as the sage tended Ruben's bleeding shoulder.

Shâth lay with limbs askew where he'd fallen in a bloody mess.

Far to the shop's right lay Ecgbryht's limp form, his

head cocked up against the shop's wall. Nearly all color had faded from his rough face, making the stubble of his blond beard stand out. His features were frozen in shock beneath tangled strands of gray-streaked hair. Taméne lay where the figure had struck him . . . his eyes open, his neck broken.

And the pale-faced man was nowhere in sight.

"Where is he?" Rodian snarled. "Where's the other one?"

"Ask her!" Lúcan snapped, nudging the sage with his boot's toe.

Wynn held a torn wad of tabard against Ruben's bleeding shoulder. She didn't even look up.

"What have you done now?" Rodian demanded.

Her shoulders curled forward as if she might collapse in exhaustion. Then she squeezed her eyes closed in a pained cringe.

"Gods damn you!" Rodian snapped, not caring what anyone thought. "*You* are under arrest."

Wynn tucked the makeshift bandage inside Ruben's split tabard, closing the edges over it. She rose up to lock eyes with Rodian, and then movement in the corner of Rodian's sight made him jerk around.

A shadow-cloaked figure approached along the deeper darkness of the next shop's awning. Rodian raised his sword, inching toward the silhouette draped in a black cloak and . . . a hat?

Pawl a'Seatt stepped out, wearing a black cloak over his matching vestment and a pressed white shirt.

Upon his head was the flat-topped hat of black felt with a brim almost wide enough to shield his shoulders. He swept his gaze over the scene, pausing briefly on the shattered window of his shop.

"What are you doing here?" Rodian demanded. "You and yours were to keep away until I told you otherwise."

Master a'Seatt didn't answer.

"Did you find the dog?" Wynn whispered.

Rodian glanced back in disbelief. Wynn gazed down the empty street like a child who'd wandered off and only just realized she was lost. Rodian didn't care.

After all the careful setup and planning, he'd failed. There had been not one but two perpetrators here this night, and both had escaped. Three of his men were dead and another injured—and he had nothing to show for it. And it was all wrapped around one meddling little sage.

"Garrogh, see to the men," Rodian growled, and he snatched Wynn by the arm, dragging her down the street.

CHAPTER 11

Wynn sat alone on her cell's bunk within the military's castle, staring at a heavy wooden door with no inner handle. On top of everything else that her superiors held against her, being arrested was going to destroy any grain of credibility she had left. She took a deep breath, trying to calm thoughts spinning out of control, but the effort failed.

A shrouded black figure, who could walk through walls, had stolen a folio and killed three of the Shyldfälches. The city guards had barely slowed it down. This only strengthened Wynn's belief that it was an undead as well as a powerful mage.

And Chane had appeared in the company of this monster, just as he had with Welstiel.

Then Chap had bolted out of the dark to protect her—only to vanish in pursuit of the black-robed undead.

It was too much to hold all at once in her head.

If Chap was here, then where were Magiere and Leesil? Though she ached to find Chap, to learn why he'd come, her jumbled thoughts kept turning back to Chane.

Once a minor noble in life, he was a scholar and sometime warrior who'd stood between her and death more than once. He was also another monster, a killer who fed on the living and had ended or ruined many lives. She'd tried to shut him out, to make him leave her once and for all in that forgotten castle of the Farlands' highest peaks. Yet here he was again—always again and again.

Wynn slumped, elbows on knees, and buried her face in her hands. Why had she believed his denial in the street?

She'd been disoriented by that thing coming out of the wall and the sudden appearance of Chane ... and then Chap. Too much had happened in those panicked moments. Yet, even if Chane was a Noble Dead, he'd always revered the guild.

In Bela, across the eastern ocean, before anyone knew what he was, he'd often come at night to sit with her and pore over historical texts. Not once had he shown the slightest threat to her, Domin Tilswith, or the others trying to establish the bare beginning of a new guild branch.

So how and why was he involved with the missing folios? And what had happened inside the Upright Quill that led to a conflict between him and the cowled figure? Perhaps Chane was more interested in the work of sages than she'd ever guessed.

She stiffened at a metal jangle outside her cell door. The heavy lock clacked, and the door opened partway.

Rodian hung in the opening, staring at her.

What could she say that would matter at all to him?

Oh, don't worry. The wolf was actually an elven dog, a kind you don't know about. And along with a woman you've never met—a half undead, half something you don't believe in—and a half elf you've never heard of, they hunt undeads, and ...

Oh, yes, that would fix everything. They wouldn't lock her up for interfering with the city guard. No, they'd just stick her in a room in the city ward until she was cured of madness.

When the captain finally stepped in, Wynn could tell he was calmer than when he'd nearly thrown her into the cell. But his neatly bearded face was drawn tight, and dark rings surrounded his eyes. His jaw muscles bulged slightly as he ground his teeth.

"You set a trap," she said.

Rodian paced before the door, taking only four short steps to cross the cell before turning back the other way.

"Domin High-Tower must have helped, if he sent out that folio," she went on, "and Master a'Seatt."

The captain stopped, and the lack of his boots' rhythmic scrape made Wynn tense in the silence.

"What were you doing there?" he asked flatly.

For an instant Wynn considered telling him the truth. That the texts he'd been denied had been penned by ancient vampires. And that she was trying to learn which pages were being stolen and why.

"Answer me!" he snapped. "You're already complicit in three guardsmen's deaths . . . though after the fact."

Wynn almost shouted a denial. She swallowed immediately, studying his face.

Yes, she'd told Chane to run, but Rodian wouldn't care about her side. His only interest lay in stopping these murders, giving the royals a rational and satisfactory answer—and in so doing, advancing himself. He had no interest in the truth, and he certainly had no intention of reporting anything from her that might get him laughed out of his position. As things stood, he would have a hard enough time explaining a culprit emerging through a shopfront.

No, he could handle only pieces of the truth.

"I overheard messengers returning from the Upright Quill," she began. "After what happened at Master Shilwise's shop, I feared the worst. So I ran, hoping to find someone still at Master a'Seatt's scriptorium and check on the folio, perhaps bring it back. That's why you caught me peeking in a window."

His expression never wavered. "You knew the second man."

Wynn panicked, ready to deny this as well.

"Don't bother lying," Rodian said. "He knew your name."

"Since returning from the Farlands," she answered, "many people I've never met seem to know my name."

She expected him to press further, as her answer was hardly satisfactory.

Instead he asked, "Did you get a clear look at the man who took the folio?"

"Man?" Wynn repeated.

"The mage in black robes." He paused and squinted at her. "What did you see?"

Wynn settled farther back on the bunk. The captain didn't want to know what she saw—or rather what she knew. He'd already convinced himself otherwise.

A mage, perhaps—but an undead as well—though one thing didn't quite fit: Its body passed right through a wall, yet it was unable to make the folio follow. It had to break the window to get the folio out.

"You saw it shatter the window . . ." Wynn said, then wavered, anxious at his darkening expression.

"Was il'Sänke at the guild before you left?" he asked.

The venom in his voice startled her. "I don't know . . . I was coming out of my room when I heard about the folio, so—"

"Why would a mage be working with a wolf?" Rodian demanded.

Wynn lost her temper in the jarring shift of questions. "The *dog* wasn't working with that *thing*!"

"And how would you know?" Rodian asked quickly. "The wolf, or dog, jumped out into the street when the thief ran, and it followed. They both fled together."

For all the captain's acclaimed cleverness, he was the half-wit, not her. Even he should've seen that Chap had chased off the undead.

"Why ask me?" she shot back. "When it doesn't matter what I say?"

Rodian ran a hand through his hair and fell silent.

"How long will you keep me here?" she asked. "If I'm to be charged, then get on with it."

He hesitated, and Wynn waited.

She had shouted at Chane to run and interfered with an attempt to catch a murderer. Even if a charge of complicity were dismissed, fouling the captain's investigation wouldn't be taken lightly. The high advocate of the people wouldn't have much trouble proving her guilt.

"Your superiors are waiting," Rodian said, and the words seemed to stick in his throat. "I'm releasing you to them."

He pushed open the cell door. It banged against the outer wall, and he just stood there, waiting.

Wynn rose slowly off the bunk, watching him in bafflement, even as she stepped into the dim corridor with its line of other heavy cell doors, all closed and silent. Rodian followed and led the way to the far stairwell in silence. Wynn kept quiet as well.

They climbed to where two regular soldiers stood in the alcove at the top. One unlocked the outer door as they approached. Wynn stepped out with the captain and followed closely as they crossed the paved courtyard to an old two-level barracks. They entered through a side door at the near end.

"My office," he said quietly, pointing.

Down the corridor, Wynn walked into a large room furnished with little more than a desk and two chairs. Premin Sykion and Domin High-Tower were waiting inside.

The latter ceased his heavy pacing, and his thudding footsteps were nothing compared to the weight of his glower.

"My dear," Premin Sykion said, closing on Wynn. "We are thankful you are unharmed. You must not go wandering off without telling someone."

The premin placed her slender, wrinkled hand on Wynn's shoulder, patting it twice before turning to Rodian.

"Thank you for looking after her, Captain."

Wynn's heart sank. Wandering off? Looking after? They painted her as a half-wit again, so no one might give her any credence.

"I'm sorry tonight's endeavor was not successful," Sykion went on to Rodian, but she cast a dark glance at High-Tower.

Wynn realized the premin hadn't known of the scheme hatched between the domin, the captain, and Master a'Seatt.

Rodian only looked at Sykion with a hint of distaste. Then he glanced sidelong down at Wynn, not even bothering to face her directly.

"You are free to go," he said.

Just like that. First he arrested her, locked her up, and questioned her concerning mostly obvious answers he never let her finish—almost none of which had anything to do with what mattered. And with a few condescending words from Sykion, she was being sent home to bed.

Wynn suddenly wondered what Magiere might say in this moment. Probably nothing, but both the captain and the premin would be bleeding by now. Magiere never backed down from anything. Beneath her derisive uninterest, always wishing to be left alone, she was furious when something got in her way or threatened those she cared for. And Leesil could be coldly vicious beneath his outer warmth and wit when it came to protecting his own. And Chap . . .

He'd always been manipulative, though usually for the best of reasons. He wasn't above putting people in a hard place to save them from themselves.

Wynn began to see that a bit of all of her wayward friends' attributes would be necessary here. She straightened.

"I apologize if I sound dense," she said. "But are we still embroiled in a murder investigation?"

"That was never your concern," High-Tower warned.

Premin Sykion reached for Wynn's arm. "Come, dear. You've been through enough, and none of us wishes you burdened any further."

Wynn pulled away, backing toward the office door.

"The captain failed tonight, and more people are dead . . . over the contents of a folio. I want access to the translation work, to see which passages are being sought."

"Not this again!" High-Tower growled in disbelief. "You have mucked things up enough!"

Wynn dropped her own voice to a low threat. "Perhaps you can't stomach that a mere journeyor discovered a treasure of history on her own. Are seven lives worth a little damage to your pride?"

Premin Sykion went pale, losing any crafted display of sympathy, and High-Tower flushed with rage.

But Rodian watched this exchange intently, his eyes shifting quickly among them.

"Wynn!" High-Tower rumbled. "This is no time or place

for your nonsense. Tighten up your cloak. We are going home."

"Yes, my dear," Sykion added. "It is time to leave."

Wynn didn't budge. She'd heard all this before, and she no longer cared if they thought her addle-minded or even mad. There was only one option left, though it could end in her permanent dismissal from the guild.

"I want my journals from the Farlands returned," she said, not even acknowledging their evasions. "I want my property back ... *now*."

No one said a word. Even High-Tower's blusters faltered, but Premin Sykion's expression grew sterner than Wynn thought possible.

Rodian turned his eyes on Wynn, but he wasn't glaring or scowling anymore.

"You are a cathologer of the guild—" Sykion began, and the edge in her voice belied her dignified manner.

"Very well," Wynn interrupted, "then I'll file legal claim to have the texts returned to me. I found them. I brought them halfway across the world. I *allowed* the guild access to them ... but they are *mine*, by right of discovery."

"Discoveries made in service!" High-Tower snarled, finally regaining his voice. "All you are, you are because of sagecraft ... and thereby the texts belong to the guild by law."

"I know of no such law," Rodian said quietly.

Sykion turned her stricken expression toward the captain, and another dead silence followed. But Wynn found Rodian studying her with cold interest. Whether from duty or ambition or anger at his being stonewalled thus far, her gamble's hope was reflected in his intense eyes.

"Do I have a legitimate claim?" she asked him.

"Certainly not!" High-Tower cut in.

Rodian raised a hand for silence. "If a journeyman smith or leatherworker finds a new technique or technology, does it belong to the master to whom the journeyman has contracted? Or if he or she develops or obtains new knowledge in the craft, is it the master who takes credit?"

High-Tower took a heavy step toward the captain, his

gaping mouth working hard. But he couldn't get out one word.

"Not by law," Rodian said, supplying the answer.

"This is different," Sykion countered.

"Wynn," High-Tower rasped. "You would not do this to—"

"Give me access," Wynn demanded. "Or I will go to the high advocate—and take the texts from you! And whether my claim against your unlawful seizure is upheld or not . . . the texts will still be revealed for the judgment."

This time outrage flushed High Premin Sykion's face. It quickly faded, as fear overwhelmed the head of Wynn's order and the guild branch as a whole.

The following morning Rodian paced around a lavish sitting room in the royal castle overlooking the bay. He'd received a summons at the barracks and was now uncertain what to expect. Perhaps the royals wished for a personal report on his progress—or rather, his failure.

Three of his men were dead. The costs of repairs to a'Seatt's shop were growing, for apparently the roof and front counter had been damaged as well. A member of the royals' favored Guild of Sagecraft had been caught in his trap, but not the perpetrators. And all he had to add to this, concerning the actual investigation, was that at least one of the suspects possessed a mage's skills the like of which he'd never thought possible.

Rodian halted in place.

He had to plan out the most logical and succinct account of events. Certainly the royal family couldn't hold him accountable for facing down someone with rare arcane skill. He could redirect his account to restore confidence in his ability. And now he had a new chance to learn what all of this was about—the texts of the guild's translation project.

Wynn Hygeorht, troublesome as she was, had given him that much.

After he'd released her last night, the trio of sages went off together, none of them speaking to one another. He'd suffered a short sleepless night wondering what might come of Wynn's demand. Would Sykion, as head of the Premin Council, legally challenge Wynn's claim? Would the journeyor back down if the premin refused to concede?

More than anything else, Rodian hated uncertainty. Wynn's determined, angry face kept slipping into his thoughts, and he pushed it aside. He still had this meeting with the royal family to get through, and he began pacing again.

He barely noticed the thick carpets and deeply polished furnishings tended with great care. Some had likely been in the Äreskynna family for generations. Couches of walnut were upholstered in silks, refined or raw, mostly dyed in shimmering sea greens and cyans, and embroidered in variegated patterns. The plastered walls were painted a rich shade of cream offset by golden yellow curtains and draperies around the entrance. The double doors were carved with the large crest of the royal family—an upright longsword upon a wide square sail over a troubled sea.

This was a world far removed from the eastern grasslands and farms of his youth, and he'd clawed his way to his current position on ability and merit. He wasn't about to fall because of some mage murdering sages over bundles of old texts.

The ornate doors opened wide.

Rodian stared into the large amber eyes of an old elf in a white robe with poorly disguised contempt on his tan face. More than the elf's age, the robe bothered him. It was cut much like that of the sages, but white wasn't a color of any of the five orders.

"Princess Âthelthryth Âreskynna and Duchess Reine Faunier-Âreskynna," the elf announced, stepping in and to the side.

Rodian breathed quickly through his nose.

From the outer crossing passage, Duchess Reine rounded through the entrance first.

Her chestnut hair hung loose, pushed back above each ear with a mother-of-pearl comb shaped like a foaming sea wave. She wasn't wearing a frontal-split gown, only her people's preferred riding boots and breeches along with a matching vestment over a white shirt of shimmering fabric. And a rider's saber hung upon her left hip from a white satin sash lashed about her waist. The effect made her look almost roguish and younger than her years.

"Captain," she greeted him. "Are you all right? You were not injured last night?"

"No, I'm well, Highness," he answered carefully, still wondering why he was here. "But I cannot say as much for my men."

Princess Âthelthryth glided in next, a sharp contrast to her sister-in-law.

Rodian had seen her only a few times in his life. Nearly as tall as him, she was as slender and upright as a young aspen tree. She shared the wheat gold hair of the royal bloodline, as well as their aquamarine eyes, narrow features, and a blade-thin nose stretching down to a pale pink and thin-lipped mouth. Her pastel teal gown was simple and long-sleeved, but no one would ever mistake her for a minor noble. Where Reine always exuded an aura of quiet inner strength edging upon wildness, Âthelthryth filled any room with somber, intense reserve and detached awareness of everything.

Rodian dropped to one knee, bowing his head, and waited to be acknowledged.

"Captain," the princess said quietly, and he raised his head just enough to see the subtle tilt of her head.

"Come and sit," the duchess added. "We require a service from you."

Rodian rose as the duchess settled on a couch, pointing to another across from her. Then she stretched a hand up to the princess.

"Come, sister."

The royals and highest nobles always referred to the wives or husbands of brothers and sisters in this manner. It upheld the impression of unity before the people, a politically sound presence for the rulers of a nation. But as Âthelthryth approached, she lightly grasped and squeezed Reine's hand once, then took position standing behind the duchess like one of her family's Weardas, the Sentinels.

There was more than solidarity here. Rodian could see

that the Âreskynna shared genuine affection with Reine. He settled on the couch across from them.

The tall elf closed the doors and took a place a few steps off from the two ladies of the royal house.

"We received a distressing report," the duchess began. "A young guild journeyor was involved in last night's tragedy."

Rodian blinked. What report, and from whom?

"Not involved," he corrected. "She'd heard a folio was not returned and went to check on its safety, not knowing of my arrangements with Domin High-Tower and the master of the shop. Her presence was unfortunate but happenstance."

Princess Âthelthryth frowned. It startled him to see any expression whatsoever break her serene exterior.

"You are certain?" she asked without emotion. "She bears no guilt in these events?"

Rodian grew wary.

The royal family defended their precious sages to a frustrating degree. Yet now the princess seemed almost to insinuate culpability upon a young journeyor of the guild.

Indeed, Wynn was somehow connected to one of the murdering thieves. But she wasn't directly involved in the thefts, not that Rodian could see. He'd released her to Sykion and High-Tower in the hope that he might still learn more through her.

But if the royals had already heard of Wynn's involvement, had they also heard of her claim upon the texts? Were they looking to discredit her, one of their sages, and keep the texts in hiding?

"She bears no guilt that I'm aware of," he answered carefully.

Reine sighed softly, but Âthelthryth's slight frown returned.

"We have heard this journeyor is making a personal claim," the duchess continued, "upon the texts she brought to the guild ... even to taking it before the people's court. This would halt the guild's work on translation."

Rodian kept his expression placid. Only two of the guild knew of Wynn's claim—High-Tower and Sykion. And only the latter had direct contact with the royal family—"Lady" Tärtgyth Sykion, the duchess had called her.

Rodian's frustration began to mount.

"We have spoken with the high advocate," Princess Âthelthryth added. "It appears that Journeyor Hygeorht may have a legitimate claim. But if she takes full possession of these texts, there is no telling what might become of them . . . who might gain access to the contents. We are told the material is of a sensitive nature."

It took all of Rodian's effort to remain calm. What was the royal family fighting to protect—or at least keep hidden—to a degree that they would let their sages be murdered in the dark?

"The project must continue," the duchess said, leaning forward, "and thereby the texts must remain in guild hands. We wish you to go to Premin Sykion, as an unofficial arbiter, and seek a compromise."

"A compromise?" he repeated.

Âthelthryth took up where Reine left off. "We wish you to ask Premin Sykion to grant Journeyor Hygeorht access to all completed work—pages that have already been translated but under controlled circumstances that will keep the texts protected from the public. If the journeyor will agree not to pursue full possession, she may see all translations since her return from the Farlands."

"Siweard . . ." the duchess began anxiously, dropping any pretense of formality, "do you think this will appease the young sage?"

The princess glanced down at the duchess's familiar use of his given name. Then she, too, turned expectant eyes on Rodian.

"Perhaps," he answered shortly.

Wynn had expressed interest in seeing which folios were being targeted. She knew there was something specific being sought in those pages. The culprit—one who could apparently walk through solid walls—hadn't tried to gain the original works, or at least not as far as anyone knew. But higher-ranking sages had shown nothing but contempt for Rodian's demands.

"Why me?" he asked. "Surely Sykion would be more amenable if she heard this from you, Duchess?"

Reine shook her head slowly. "It would not look well if the royal family intervened in this case. It might draw undue attention to the guild's sensitive work. It might even be seen as royal interference with the law, and push Journeyor Hygeorht to rash action. You have always shown good judgment and discretion ... both in upholding the peace and in serving your people's best interest."

Rodian studied her. Did she expect him to use the power of his office if Sykion refused?

"Do you have any leads on who escaped last night?" Âthelthryth asked abruptly.

The change of focus caught him off guard, and he hesitated. The black-robed figure appeared taller than Ghassan il'Sänke, but the Suman sage had something of a reputation as a true mage within his own guild.

"One," he answered. "But I won't name a suspect without more concrete evidence."

The princess's frown vanished. As her features settled to their ever-placid state, Rodian caught an instant of relief in her aquamarine eyes.

"We desire you to stop these murders," she said, "but keep the guild's project protected at the same time. If you can do this, we would be grateful ... most grateful, Captain."

Rodian thought his heart stilled as he held his breath.

Her words were as close to an open admission as he might ever hear. The royal family wanted him to keep Wynn's ancient texts buried in secret. This veiled request left him caught between duty, faith, and ambition.

He knew lives depended upon him as the highest officer of the Shyldfälches, even the lives of these well-intended, if deluded, sages. But he also knew the rewards of royal gratitude.

Rodian took a slow breath. "I will not fail."

By late morning Wynn still lay in bed. Drained by last night's turmoil, she'd drifted in and out, but true sleep never came. Finally she swung her legs over the bedside, her small feet settling on the cold stone floor.

What had she done with her meddling and threats?

Certainly she'd jeopardized her place in the guild. Neither Sykion nor High-Tower spoke a word to her on the walk home. Since returning from the Farlands she hadn't been happy here, but life as a sage was all she knew. What would she do if she were dismissed and cast out?

Still, the thought of lives lost, the persistent denials of her superiors, and what her wayward friends might've done in her place convinced her there was no other choice than the one she'd made.

But at a soft knock on her door, Wynn shrank in apprehension. She had to force herself up to go crack open the door.

Domin il'Sänke stood in the outer passage. The wrinkle of his dark brow might've been worry—or scorn, if he'd already heard what she'd done.

"Get dressed," he said. "The Premin Council has called a general assembly."

Wynn's throat tightened. Was she to be cast out in front of everyone?

It didn't matter. She would still go after the texts by whatever means necessary.

Il'Sänke shook his head once. "I do not believe this concerns you," he said, perhaps reading the worry on her face.

Wynn realized she was standing there in her night shift—not that he seemed to notice. She held up a finger, telling him to wait, and closed the door to dress. Without bothering to brush or tie back her hair, she hurried out to join him. She found him staring intently down the hall.

Wynn glanced along his sight line. The passage was empty all the way to the landing above the stairs to the courtyard door.

"I'm ready," she said.

Il'Sänke started like someone interrupted from listening closely to a nearby conversation. He nodded, and she followed him to the stairs. When they finally reached the common hall, a surprising sight awaited Wynn.

The place was nearly bursting at the seams.

Every initiate, apprentice, journeyor, master, and domin in residence had been summoned. All five premins of the orders stood before the massive hearth, facing the gathered assembly. But more puzzling was the presence of scribe masters or shop owners from every scriptorium hired within the past half year—the Gild and Ink, the Inkwell, the Feather & Parchment, and Four Scribes in House. They all stood closest among the crowd before the council, all except for those of the Upright Quill.

Masters Pawl a'Seatt and Teagan stood off at the hearth's left end.

Wynn continued scanning. Anyone not a robed sage stood out in the mass. Captain Rodian stood near the hall's back, close to the wide entrance archway. As she crept in beside il'Sänke, the captain turned, arms crossed over his red surcoat, and his gaze briefly met hers. Then it locked on il'Sänke, and his expression hardened.

Last night in the cell the captain had specifically asked about il'Sänke's whereabouts. But why hadn't Rodian asked about anyone else?

Premin Sykion raised her hands to quell the buzz in the hall from too many speculating discussions. She stepped up on the hearth's frontal ledge. Domin High-Tower stood nearby, below on her right.

"After much consideration," she began in a clear voice, "regarding recent events, the council is forced to make changes that will affect those involved in the translation project . . . and indeed everyone residing at the guild."

She paused and looked around the quiet hall.

"We wish no speculation to cloud our intent, so we have called this gathering. It has been decided that no further folios, nor any work related to the project, will leave these grounds for any reason. Therefore, we will engage scribes from only one shop to come each day to accomplish their contracted work . . . here within our walls."

Soft whispers grew to murmurs among the crowd, until Wynn couldn't hear the hearth fire's crackle. Relief showed on many faces, but a rumble among the scribe masters began to rise above the noise.

"Which shop?" demanded Master Calisus of the Feather & Parchment.

Premin Sykion cleared her throat. "We have engaged

Master a'Seatt's staff of the Upright Quill. In a recent attempt to assist the city guard his shop was damaged, and we feel partially responsible."

"My shop was ransacked before his!" shouted Master Shilwise of the Gild and Ink. "And far worse, from what I've heard. But I don't see the guild offering me compensation."

"All scriptoriums have done worthy service for the guild," Sykion returned, "but Master a'Seatt's kept the best schedule and often provided additional assistance . . . beyond the commonly shared high standards you have all shown."

"Standards be damned!" Shilwise snapped, and even discontented Calisus appeared startled by his vehemence. "I've put aside too much other work trying to meet the guild's requirements and schedules—and you still have a contract with my shop! I won't be pushed out like this. My scribes should be brought in as well."

At this, Calisus and the other two scribe masters chimed in with a cacophony of demands and accusations. Sykion put narrow fingers to her temple and had to shout over them.

"All scriptoriums have performed well in their task. We intend no slight by this decision, and you will be compensated for the sudden change."

"Not good enough!" Shilwise returned. "There's more than just coin involved—my shop's reputation is at stake."

"Your reputation is why you were originally chosen," Sykion responded.

"We've put other customers' needs second to the guild's," Shilwise shouted back. "On top of that, what happens when word gets out that a'Seatt is your favorite? I demand you fulfill your contract . . . or I'll see you in court, Sykion!"

Several of the premins pushed in around Sykion, all whispering to her. Sykion tried to wave them off and fixed her full attention on Master Shilwise. Her voice shocked the hall's air, startlingly loud for her tactful nature and frail stature.

"Compensation will be offered as promised. The matter is closed!"

At this, the master of Four Scribes in House tried to pull

Shilwise back. But Shilwise shoved the stout man off, casting a seething glare to the hearth's far left end.

Pawl a'Seatt stood silent and unaffected, his heavy cloak and wide-brimmed hat in hand. Stooped old Master Teagan pushed round spectacles up his beaked nose, and he wrinkled that nose at Shilwise. But then he glanced nervously up at his employer.

Shilwise shoved through his competitors and strode out between the crowded tables and bystanders. He headed straight for the hall's main archway.

As he passed, Wynn saw his glistening face.

Master Shilwise had broken out in a sudden sweat. The owner of the Gild and Ink seemed more panicked than outraged as he rushed out. Wynn turned back but stopped halfway, her awareness catching on Domin il'Sänke.

His head was half bowed, as if he'd lost interest in the events. Instead he focused completely on Rodian.

The captain stood partly twisted around, staring after Shilwise, clearly as perplexed as Wynn by the scriptorium owner—not because of the man's outrage, but the extreme nature of it, and the strange change that came over Shilwise as he fled. Instead of turning back to the proceedings, Rodian's gaze dropped to Wynn. Only after a discontented breath through his nose did he turn away.

Wynn heard a sharp sigh—from il'Sänke—and she quickly looked up.

The tall domin's brow wrinkled under the barest shake of his head before he turned his own attention back across the hall.

Wynn kept looking about, from the captain to the domin to the archway where Shilwise had vanished. And she started to feel dizzy.

What had just happened? Why was Rodian even here? And was il'Sänke aware of the captain's suspicions?

"There is more," Sykion called out, pulling Wynn's attention. "Until further notice, all members—from initiates to premins—will remain within guild grounds between dusk and dawn. Those with family or homes elsewhere in the city shall also remain here. There will be no exceptions. Thank you, that is all."

Premin Sykion stepped down from the hearth's ledge, gathering with the other council members to speak in soft tones. The murmur in the hall grew as people began to rise, joining into small groups or drifting toward either exit.

The audience was over, but Rodian remained. Sages young and old passed around him, but he only watched the council before the hearth. With nothing further to hear, Wynn turned to leave.

"Wynn!" a deep voice called, and she whipped around.

Domin High-Tower stood near the hall's center. This was the first he'd spoken to her since Rodian's office the night before. She glanced up at Domin il'Sänke.

"You had best go," he said.

Wynn took one more worried look at High-Tower before she pushed forward against the current of others leaving the hall. High-Tower was already heading for the narrow side archway. At his gesture, she followed him.

He said nothing more, leading her all the way to the north tower and his study. Wynn steeled herself, and any relief at not facing dismissal before the entire guild was gone. It would be no better in the private chamber of Domin High-Tower. But when they entered, he didn't sit down. He stood before one narrow inset window, looking outside along the keep's old battlements.

"Premin Sykion . . ." he began, and then faltered. "We have decided you may have access to pages translated so far, but not the original texts . . . and only on the condition that you give up this treacherous notion of a claim."

Wynn held her breath, caught somewhere between relief and frustration.

A claim in the people's court before the high advocate concerning all the texts could take moons to settle. There were precedents regarding the rights of anyone working in any form of guild, and in the end she might still lose. For now she needed to see only the translations, to try to learn what the black-robed figure was after.

And she wasn't being cast out.

But Wynn was not about to let High-Tower hear her wild relief.

"And the codex," she said, not a quaver in her voice. "I

need the codex as well to know which pieces of finished work are related to or from the same source. Too many pages and drafts have been lost so far."

He would already know this. She would need to see every stage of the translation to truly understand what the murderer sought.

High-Tower never turned from the window as he nodded curtly.

"How soon?" she asked.

"Tomorrow," he replied. "Preparations will be made for you."

A moment's frustration passed over the prospect of another delay, but Wynn didn't argue. If no more folios were carried back and forth, tomorrow would be soon enough.

And still, Domin High-Tower wouldn't look at her.

In his profile she could see that he thought her ungrateful and disloyal—or certainly above herself. But all that mattered was that an undead was hunting sages, maybe even hunting High-Tower, eventually. And no one but her seemed willing to acknowledge the truth or follow a proper course of action.

"Agreed," she said, and turned for the door.

"What has happened to you, Wynn?"

She froze with her hand on the latch. He sounded sad, almost defeated. She jerked the door open, stepping out into the tower's spiral stairway.

"I grew up," she answered.

She didn't look back as she shut the door.

CHAPTER 12

Just past dusk, Chane paced about his shabby attic room. Wynn had seen him—and knew he had broken into a scriptorium to steal a folio.

He stopped and settled slowly on the bed's edge, looking around at the faded four walls and slanted ceiling. Events seemed to be hurtling forward without direction, without his control. How had he come to this state?

He pushed his red-brown hair from his forehead, thinking back, remembering what had driven him from Bela all the way to this continent....

After learning that Wynn had returned to the Numan Lands, he seemed merely to exist, passing from night to night in Bela with little purpose and no future.

In desperation he often worked on furthering his grasp of Welstiel's arcane objects or deciphering bits from the man's two journals. Little came from great effort, but he uncovered one mystery, seemingly unrelated to Welstiel's conjury.

The oldest of the journals had a parchment covering folded over it. The covering was annoying in handling the book, so Chane took it off. And there on the left of its inner surface was a list. Though most were common herbs, one was written in Belaskian among the other Numanese terms.

Dyvjàka Svonchek—"Boar's Bell."

Chane knew it, also called by other folk names such as Flooding Dusk, Nightmare's Breath, and Blackbane. Its yellow bell-shaped flowers faded to dark plum at the edges. Toxic and deadly to the living, its mere odor could also cause delirium. He knew its fishy scent in two ways. One from dried petals left on a table in the back room of the healer-monks' hidden mountain monastery. And the other . . .

Chane fished deep in Welstiel's belongings.

He pulled out a long and shallow box, bound in black leather and wrapped in indigo felt. Inside were six vials in felt padding, each with a silver screw-top cap. But only one and a half held any of the strange liquid. The unwary might have thought it watery violet ink.

Chane carefully sniffed at the full one without even opening it. His head filled with its fishy sweet odor, and he quickly pulled the vial from his face.

He looked back to the parchment cover's inner surface. On the right half was a diagram with symbols, most of which he didn't know. Perhaps it was a formula of some kind.

All the vials had been full when he and Welstiel had left the monastery—in company with six monks raised as feral undeads. Somewhere along the journey to the Pock Peaks and the castle of that ancient white female vampire, the rest of the vials had been used. What purpose had Welstiel's concoction served? And how was it made, let alone used?

All Chane knew was that during the journey, Welstiel continued to grow more agitated and more obsessed with getting his "orb." That and when Chane slipped into dormancy each night, Welstiel was still up and alert. When Chane arose the next dawn, Welstiel was already up and about, perhaps for a long while.

Chane had no doubt the list of ingredients was for this deadly liquid, and only the flower would be difficult to find. Some claimed it had healing properties, but he did not think so. Chane rewrapped the vial case, stored it in the pack, and refitted the parchment cover on the journal.

On a few nights his frustration at too little progress began to mount, and he would return to Bela's great docks. Or he would wander to the city's southern edge and stand upon the shore, staring out over the Inner Bay and ocean beyond. He did take the time to seek an apothecary, who reluctantly admitted that he carried Boar's Bell in secret, for sale to select customers. Chane paid heavily for a small amount, not having the time or opportunity to search for the flower in the wilderness.

Sometimes he hunted, turning more often to the lowly districts.

His existence became more and more pointless, until one night he caught a flash of dark fur near a loading platform on the southernmost pier.

He ignored it at first. Dogs often roamed the city's quarters, scavenging for a quick meal. But the animal's movement pulled his attention back.

The dog hung its head over the dock's upper level and watched the men below.

On the lower level of that nearest dock, three men busily loaded cargo into a wide flat-bottomed skiff. Even under the dock's hanging lanterns, they couldn't see as well as Chane in darkness. He stepped close to the dock's land-bound end, having nothing better to occupy him.

The dog was taller than he had first thought, perhaps the height of a timber wolf, but with long legs and muzzle, and taller ears. Charcoal-colored, its coat seemed to shimmer faintly in the lantern's light.

"I'm sick of all the rush," said one sailor below. "When are we going to take time for some eats?"

"Get on with it!" another snapped. "We're outbound by dawn, and we're short on cargo for the crossing. So much for profit shares at the journey's end."

"We'll fix that once we hit the far coast," the third replied.

The dog lifted its head and looked out toward a three-masted vessel in the harbor, almost as if it knew what the men spoke of.

Chane saw its blue crystalline eyes catch the lantern light.

The animal slunk silently to a side-hanging walkway and padded softly down the ramp to the dock's lower level. For a moment, Chane thought he was looking at Chap.

But this dog was much darker, more slender in build, and a younger animal, perhaps not yet having gained its full weight. Chap was unique, a hunter of undead, yet the animal was certainly of the same breed. Chane moved quietly out to peer over the dock's side.

The dog crept around a massive, slightly dented trunk waiting to be loaded. The sailors were busy grumbling and wrestling with cargo and never noticed as the dog parted the trunk's lid with its nose. It squirmed inside amid piles of folded cloth.

Chane watched in fascination before he called out, "You, there . . . where is that ship headed?"

One sailor straightened up, wiping his sweating brow with a sleeve.

"Langinied, at first light," he replied, "if we can get her loaded in time. We've cargo going straight across; then we're south for the long haul to the eastern Suman coast."

Chane lifted his eyes to the vessel out in the bay. He knew of Langinied, a large island off the coast across the ocean. It was supposed to be one of the few civilized places this side of that continent—Wynn's continent. There was a long land journey beyond that to reach the far west coast and her homeland.

Two sailors picked up the old trunk and hefted it atop the crates already overburdening the skiff.

A strange dog stowed away on a ship bound for Wynn's continent. The only other of its breed that Chane had ever seen was a close companion to Wynn.

"Is it still possible to buy passage?" he asked.

"What?" the third sailor called back, steadying the skiff as his mates loaded a rope-bound bale. Perhaps he could not catch Chane's words in his voiceless rasp.

"Passage!" he called again.

The man huffed at him. "All passengers are supposed to be onboard already. You'll have to speak to the purser . . . over there."

The sailor pointed along the pier's lower level. Chane

spotted a gaunt man directing others in loading water casks onto another skiff.

Before long Chane had arranged passage, and the price took nearly all the money he possessed. He ran inland, and was well beyond the port before finding a coach to hurry him the rest of the way out of the city to his inn. By the time the coach returned him to the docks, the eastern skyline was just barely lightening. The purser was waiting impatiently by an empty skiff.

The moment Chane boarded the ship, he hurried below, but not to his cramped quarters. He crept into the cargo hold, searching among lashed crates, barrels, and bundles for that one old trunk.

If the dog were truly like Chap, it could sense an undead, let alone anyone else's approach. But this did not concern Chane—he wore Welstiel's ring of nothing. More than once the ring had hidden Welstiel and himself from Chap's and Magiere's unnatural awareness. And Chane needed to learn why this animal appeared to be heading in Wynn's direction.

He found the trunk, its straps still unbuckled, but he hesitated at flipping it open. Though the ring hid his nature, startling the dog could ignite an assault. He lifted the trunk's lid half a handbreadth, but it was too dark in the hold for even his eyes to see into the hidden space. Finally he had to open it wide.

The trunk was empty but for the bolts of cloth.

Chane glanced about the hold. There was no sign of the dog, nor could he smell it. He finally turned away, heading back for his small cabin.

At least the animal was not trapped, would not starve to death on the voyage. Beyond that he wanted nothing to do with it, other than to learn why it was here—and if it was truly headed toward Wynn.

In the long voyage, he took only two victims: one penny-poor passenger, lodged in steerage, and one sailor. But only during rough weather at night, when he could dump the bodies overboard, as if they had been lost at sea. Otherwise he held himself in check, trying not to exert himself and force further feeding.

Not once did he see the dog, and he wondered if it lived on vermin in the hold or had somehow settled in with the crew. Perhaps it had even been taken in by one of the officers in the fore or aftcastle quarters.

To his relief, the ship reached the free port of Langinied, the long island off the coast of the middle continent—and it docked at night. He insisted on leaving immediately, though the purser was put off at arranging oarsmen and a skiff before dawn.

Though the city sprawled over a large rocky area in both directions beyond sight, it was far from an actual nation or even a city-state, more like a chaotic growth of trade operations and other businesses with residents needed to support them. Langinied had spawned long ago from the needs of whatever ships came up the coast from the Suman Empire before making the difficult run across to what the sages called the Farlands. Added to this, some caravans braved what he learned were called the Broken Lands. A wild, uncivilized territory spanned the continent from this eastern coast to nearly the edge of the Numan Lands on the western side.

Chane stayed in Langinied, watching the ship as much as he could, until it left port on the fifth dusk. He never saw the dog again. Without its lead he was left adrift, once more questioning his actions. He had sworn to Wynn that he would never reenter her life—but he eventually set out for Calm Seatt on his own.

The journey across land made the sea voyage seem short.

Little along the way came to bother an undead. At times he lingered in places past dusk, trying to decipher more of Welstiel's writings. Or he paged through the varied texts taken from the healer-monks' monastery. Every ink mark made with quill, no matter what it said, reminded him of Wynn ... sitting in a room by the light of her cold lamp, perhaps doing likewise with the ancient texts she had recovered.

Chane hunted wildlife along the way to sustain himself, though it fed him poorly compared to longer-lived humans. Among wolves, wild dogs, bears, and a ranging mountain lion, which he gave a wide berth, only once did he ever see anything on two legs.

It was neither human nor elf.

He emerged early one night from the tarp used to protect himself from the sun, and felt something watching him.

The only item of Welstiel's he had learned a little of was the steel hoop that conjured fire within itself. Without looking about and letting the hidden watcher know he was aware of it, he laid out the hoop.

Its circumference was slightly less than a dinner plate, and its black thread-thin etched lines and marks smelled faintly of charcoal. With a hoarse hiss—which was the most Chane could manage for the necessary chant—he traced a finger around the hoop's circumference. Then he snatched his hand back; he still did not know how Welstiel had handled the hoop while hot without being scorched.

Red pinprick sparks appeared in the hoop's markings and quickly spread along all the dark swirls, until the hoop's etchings became fiery and hard to look upon. It provided little light in the growing dark, but enough for Chane's undead sight. He glanced sidelong without moving his head.

Beyond a far tree in a sparse copse of firs and pines, two eyes reflected the hoop's glow. But they were yellow, not red.

The creature was hard to see at first, peeking around one tree, but the position of its eyes marked it as roughly two-thirds of a man's height. Finally it leaned out just a little, peering intently at Chane.

Wildly spotted fur covered its hulkish body, thinning across its face—if one could call it that. Longer bristles sprouted about its head, so caninelike, though its muzzle was short by comparison. It snorted, grunted, and perhaps sniffed hard, which wrinkled its muzzle, exposing oversize canine teeth.

Chane finally turned his head, staring it down.

The creature leaped sideways into open view. Sickening yellow irises glared unblinking at Chane.

He had read of apes in the books of his father's library. Many kinds were known in the southernmost parts of the Suman Empire and the jungles beyond that. This thing seemed much like those descriptions, though shaped disturbingly more like a small, grotesquely overmuscled and furred man—except for its head and face, like some abhorrent breed of wild dog had bred with ... what was it called? ... a mandrill?

The result was far larger and more monstrous than either. In place of nails it had claws at the end of each thick finger. But more startling was the rusted and rent chain vest on its torso. And it gripped a thick cudgel made from a gnarled tree root.

The beast grunted in a staccato rhythm and raised the club in the air.

Chane dropped a hand to his longsword's hilt. The thought of feeding on something with more life than a deer made the beast inside him thrash against its confinement.

The creature shrieked and pounded the earth with its crude weapon. It sniffed and snorted sharply. With huffing grunts it backed away.

Chane stood instantly, but it spun, flinging forest mulch in the air, and fled through the trees. It ran on three limbs, hauling its crude weapon over one bulging shoulder with the fourth. Chane dashed after it.

Before he passed half a dozen trees, he lost the sound of it. He crouched, checking for its trail, and found prints. A few were distinct among others in the torn earth, and their shape was like nothing he had ever seen. Claws had torn the ground in front of its toes, and the tracks were a bizarre mishmash between those of a beast and a wide-footed man.

Chane crouched lower and sniffed. No, not male but female, and in heat, but its overall scent was unfamiliar to him. Then he spotted more tracks.

At least six other trails led away into the dark, parallel to the creature's own. All the foot-paw prints were like the creature's, matched with the imprint of wide knuckles or claw gouges where they ran on three or four limbs.

Chane listened in the dark but heard nothing. He was not about to face a half dozen of these unknown beasts in the wilderness. He could only guess why they had run off. Since Langinied, he had not seen a need to wear Welstiel's ring. Perhaps the female "scout" had sensed what he was and warned off the others. Some animals grew nervous in the presence of an undead.

He returned to camp, gathered his belongings, and continued the long walk westward. Until one night he finally entered widespread farmlands dotted sparsely with small towns. He skirted any military outpost but used the main roads to lead him onward. More nights passed, and then he saw the scattered lights of Calm Seatt in the distance.

Somewhere therein was Wynn's home, the founding branch of the Guild of Sagecraft.

How he longed to walk among its library shelves.

And now, sitting in his attic room, Chane knew the torment of watching paradise from outside its walls. Ever the outsider—and a beast—he would never enter Wynn's world. But he pulled the scroll case's pewter cap and gently slid out its contents.

Rolling it open, he stared for the thousandth time at its black-coated surface.

"Wynn," he whispered. "What texts did you bring back? Could you find any hint to this secret?"

And last night he had seen the dog again outside the Upright Quill. She had grown and filled out, but it was the same animal he had followed across the western ocean.

And Wynn had seen him inside the scriptorium trying to steal a folio.

What would she deduce, though she had told him to run? She had also seen the *thing* that attacked him, solid before his eyes and yet nothing he could touch.

Chane knew he had to do something, no matter how risky. In truth, he had little left to risk. Wynn knew he was in her city, and at this point a straightforward course was best.

Ripping a blank page from a freshly acquired journal, he penned a quick note.

Then he went downstairs, found the grease-stained proprietor, and handed over his message for delivery.

Before supper Wynn stopped at the hospice to visit Nikolas. He lay on a narrow cot, his condition unchanged. Though he continued to live and breathe, and she saw the barest hint of color returning to his features, he was still curled up, fetal. Half-opened eyes stared at nothing and never seemed to blink. Even when his lids opened fully for brief periods, he remained as if lost in mind-dead sleep.

She had overheard Domin Bitworth, a master of naturology, tell High-Tower they had to use rather unpleasant means for getting Nikolas to swallow broth and water. Wynn wondered what those "means" might be, but if anyone could keep Nikolas alive, Bitworth or Premin Adlam could.

"Come back soon," she whispered in Nikolas's ear, stroking one gray streak in his hair.

She left the hospice, heading for the common hall, and wondered how she would be received. The instant she stepped through the archway, a few people looked up.

Whispers spread quickly, causing other heads to turn, until every eye glanced at least briefly her way. Word of her threatened claim must have spread like winter sniffles through the initiates' dormitory. Perhaps Premin Sykion had even leaked the story herself. Wynn tried to wet her dry mouth and looked about for the emptiest table, hoping to be left alone.

In recent days she'd found the company of Miriam and Nikolas a welcome change. Now Miriam was dead, and Nikolas was lost in a seemingly endless inner terror—all because her superiors refused to accept the truth.

The hall was quite full, considering the curfew. No one would leave the guild tonight, not even for a change of meal at a local inn or tavern.

Wynn finally spotted a nearly empty table in the right corner, farthest from the hearth. She ladled a bowl of brown bean soup from a crock on a central table and went off to settle in private. And not surprisingly, everyone sitting at that table's other end was suddenly finished with their meal.

Keeping her eyes on her supper, Wynn tried to ignore the whispers. Once she made the mistake of glancing up.

Regina Melliny sat with a small huddle of apprentices from different orders, all speaking in quiet but rapid voices.

Wynn heard the word "traitor," and Regina lifted her head, peering over with a rude wrinkle of her nose.

It was too much.

Wynn grasped her bowl and stood up. At least she could be alone in her room and not feel like an outcast yet to be formally cast out. As she was about to leave, an apprentice in a sienna robe entered through the main archway, looking about.

"Journeyor Hygeorht?"

Wynn sighed and briefly closed her eyes. By the time she opened them, he was standing before her.

Judging by the set of his mouth, he wasn't thrilled to speak to her. "There is a boy with a note at the front gate. He is asking for you."

Wynn set the bowl down. Most likely it was from Captain Rodian, though she wondered why he'd sent a message. He probably knew about the offer High-Tower had made to her, concerning the translation project. Rodian would be all too eager to know whatever she discovered of the folios' contents.

"Thank you . . ." she began, then realized she had no idea what the apprentice's name might be. It didn't matter, as he'd already hurried off.

Wynn left the common hall, heading out the double doors to the courtyard, but a startling sight met her as she approached the gatehouse tunnel.

The old outer portcullis had been lowered—and she'd never seen it closed in all her days.

Beyond its stout crisscross of iron bars as thick as her forearm stood a small boy, too young to be out alone at night. Dressed in tattered clothes, he wiped his nose with the back of his hand. Then he spotted her coming closer.

"You Wynn?" he asked.

What was Rodian thinking, sending such a child?

"Yes," she answered, wondering if she should find someone to walk him home, as she was trapped on guild grounds. "You have a note for me?"

He poked his little hand through the portcullis, holding out a folded bit of paper with a torn edge. The outside wasn't addressed in any manner.

Wynn hesitated. Rodian wouldn't send a message like this. Proper and elitist, he would've used quality paper, perhaps an envelope, and addressed it specifically. Appearances mattered greatly to him.

She fished in her pocket, but all she had on her was two silver groats. Even one was more than the rate for a messenger.

"Thank you for your trouble," she said, and gave him one coin just the same. "Be sure to go straight home. It's getting late."

The boy grunted and was off down the path toward the bailey gate.

Wynn waited until he was out of sight before returning to the courtyard. She lingered beneath one of the gatehouse's inner braziers and unfolded the paper, reading . . .

Meet me behind the stables south of the guild's grounds.
I need to speak with you.

The ragged note wasn't signed, and it was written in Belaskian, not Numanese. Even so, she would've known the handwriting anywhere.

Chane.

Wynn didn't blame herself, but she knew she had to be part of the reason he'd traveled here. Even after all this time, she found her feelings toward him were conflicted. She just stood breathing for a few moments, rereading his brief note.

Of course she would go—if only to find out why he had come all this way and broken his promise to leave her alone. And she had to know of his involvement in the deaths and thefts, and what he'd been doing in Master a'Seatt's scriptorium, holding that folio.

Wynn looked up as two apprentices walked out the main doors and headed across to the southside barracks, where her own room was located. She couldn't get out the front gate, and she still needed a few things before she faced Chane.

She waited long enough for the pair to reach their own quarters, then hurried inside and upstairs. Reaching her room, she closed the door and leaned against it. Reading the note again, she remembered the first time Chane had come to the guild in Bela—the handsome young scholar. And then the night he'd appeared in Apudâlsat's dank forest, and she watched in horror as Magiere cleaved his head from his neck. And last, atop the Pock Peaks inside Li'kän's library, his features taut and rigid as he promised . . .

I will not follow you anymore. You will not see me again.

Those words had brought pain—and relief. His reappearance rekindled both.

Wynn took the crystal from her cold lamp and pocketed it before opening her small trunk to retrieve a warm cloak. Climbing to her feet, she spotted something else.

The staff leaned in a corner, the sun crystal atop it covered in the protective leather sheath.

Under Domin il'Sänke's tutelage, she had tried to ignite it only once. The best she got from it was a soft glimmer, and that had cost her. When it winked out, she felt as if she'd been hauling some heavy burden for ten leagues without water. And the next day she had been so tired that she could barely get up to eat.

Magic, even artificed permanently into an object, was no wonder to idly enact with quaint words and a flourish of fancy gestures. It was dangerous, taxing, and costly. She knew as much from the plague of her mantic sight. But still, even a glimmer of light with the nature of the sun might be enough if Chane could no longer be trusted.

She stared at the staff for a long moment of indecision, then grabbed it and headed out. In the outer passage she paused in frustration.

How could she get out of the keep, let alone unseen? There was only one possibility, and it was risky. Sighing, she headed for the stairs and out to the courtyard.

She tried to keep the staff close, wrapping the folds of her cloak around it, and hoped she didn't run into il'Sänke. He always seemed to *know* too much about what she was thinking. When she entered the main building, she took the long way around to avoid passing near the common hall. She reached the keep's back at another entrance into the library and peered carefully around the archway's side.

No one was in sight among the nearest tables or tall bookcases, but that might not hold once the evening meal ended. She hurried for the central stairs up to the top floor.

She'd spent little time in this building since her return. It was well organized and a welcome place for study and research. But it didn't hold the wealth of knowledge to be found in the archives. Generations of sages would enjoy the wide library's open design, with windows allowing in natural light during the day, so unlike the excavated catacombs below the guild. Premin Sykion constantly sought to improve it.

Long rows of oak shelves, attached stoutly to the ceiling, stretched out before Wynn. Specially designed cold lamps were mounted in the stone walls on small iron bases shaped like the bottoms of oil lanterns. Within those bases, the guild metaologers replenished treated fluids that generated a low heat. This fed the lamps' crystals, so there would always be light here.

Wynn heard soft voices several shelves off and headed quickly to the library's back wall. She reached the nearest window and peered out the finest panes the dwarves could make.

The new library was constructed behind the main keep at the back of the inner bailey. It filled the space all the way to the bailey wall. Wynn could see that the drop down to the wall's top would be easy, but the rest of her plan might prove more difficult.

She tucked the staff under one arm and propped the window open as quietly as she could. Climbing upon the sill, she clung to the window's frame for an instant before she hopped outward. Her knees buckled as she dropped atop the bailey wall's walkway; it was a little farther down than it looked. With one backward glance, she hurried along the old battlements.

Wynn rounded the eastern tower and headed onward, taking the chipped and faded stone steps below the southern tower into the orchard of bare-limbed maple trees. She crept through the barren gardens toward the bailey gate before the gatehouse tunnel.

In getting this far, she'd successfully bypassed the closed

outer portcullis. All that remained was to open the bailey gate. None of her peers or superiors would be outside, so she should be able to slip away without being seen. Slowly she crept to the edge of the nearest barbican framing the gate and peered out.

"Ah, no," she whispered.

Two of the Shyldfälches stood just outside the portcullis. She hadn't heard of Rodian placing guards to watch over the guild, and she backed into hiding. Chane was waiting, but she had no idea how to get out unseen.

Ghassan il'Sänke stepped to the library's window and watched as Wynn sped off along the wall. His grip tightened on the sill when he saw the staff in her hand. He shook his head and waited until she rounded the wall's turn beyond the eastern tower.

He had followed her, apprehensive of what she was up to and where she was going. In his long life, very little surprised him anymore. But earlier today he had been shocked upon learning that she had been granted access to the translated pages and the codex. She was neither mature nor experienced enough in the dangers of knowledge for such a thing. Then again, neither were some of the domins and masters of this branch.

Ghassan had seen the few ancient Sumanese passages he had been asked to help translate. That information alone had to be kept hidden at all cost. Still, he wondered what was in the rest of those folios, and perhaps even envied Wynn's special indulgence. Somehow it must have been facilitated by the meddlesome captain of the city guard.

What would happen if this knowledge, this Forgotten History, became known to the common people? So many ideologies and beliefs had eradicated what little was known of civilization's birth—and death—in the world. Or rather its fragile rebirth since that long-forgotten war few believed had ever happened at all. It was best left that way, even for what might lie ahead.

After supper he had planned to write another letter to his comrades at the Suman branch. Then he overheard someone mention a private message delivered for Wynn.

He shadowed her, removing his presence from her mind, all the way from her room and through the library.

Ghassan briefly closed his eyes. Glimmering strokes and marks took form in patterns across the backs of his eyelids.

As an incantation slipped through his thoughts, he stepped off the windowsill, floated down to the wall's top, and walked quickly off after Wynn. He caught sight of her as she rounded the southern tower and headed along the keep's front.

But then she stopped, hiding near the closer barbican of the gate—for two of Rodian's men had been posted before the gatehouse. Ghassan watched her go back into hiding, and he frowned in indecision.

Perhaps he should just leave her with no way out. Let her abandon this covert journey and go back to her room. But then he would never learn what she was up to. Touching her thoughts might suffice, but her erratic mind often required wading and waiting for things to become clear.

Ghassan rubbed his eyes. He would have to get her off guild grounds himself. Closing his eyes again, he altered the patterns, lines, and sigils in his thoughts and then focused on the two city guards . . . on their senses . . . their hearing. . . .

"What was that?" one asked suddenly, and looked northward along the inner bailey. But the other was already running, and the first took off behind him.

Wynn peeked out at the voices. She stepped into the open and stared to where the men disappeared beyond the western orchard and tower. She just stood there.

"Oh, please! Just go!" Ghassan whispered.

Finally she rushed out and slipped through the bailey gate.

Ghassan gave her a moment, watching her over the wall as she headed south. Then he descended directly into Old Bailey Road and followed.

CHAPTER 13

Chane crouched at the stable's rear corner, uncertain what he would say to Wynn. And the smells of dung, old leather, and straw rose around him.

The horses inside had already been fed and settled for the night. No one would come out back after dusk. This was the nearest and safest place he knew of for a private word without having Wynn walk too far at night. Something . . . someone besides him was after the folios—and it had fixed upon Wynn outside the scribe shop.

Chane had brushed out his cloak and combed his red-brown hair, which had once hung to his shoulders. More than a year ago, in Venjètz, Welstiel had cut it jaggedly to disguise Chane for a ruse played on Magiere. The hair would never grow back. He pushed a loose strand behind his ear, closing his eyes briefly.

Wynn would come, but how could he explain his actions, driven by obsessions that he did not fully understand?

He watched the street from along the stable's side. Across the way he could just make out the tops of the guild's keep towers above shops, inns, and one eatery across the street. Then movement pulled his gaze back down.

Wynn stepped into sight on the street, wearing a brown cloak over her gray robe.

She gripped a walking staff taller than herself, and the two hands' length above her head was sheathed in leather. She halted, reached into her pocket, and pulled something out. When she flattened her hand against her wool robe and rubbed brusquely, Chane knew it was her cold lamp crystal. Faint illumination filtered through her fingers, and he stepped quickly along the stable's side to its front corner.

Wynn halted midstreet, staring at him. Faint lines of concentration creased her forehead.

An ache swelled in Chane's chest at the sight of her oval face within her robe's raised cowl. Wynn embodied what little he held worthwhile in this world—all the things he could never have. She finally came toward him, stopping a few paces off, well beyond his reach.

Something about her face was different, not in her features but in her expression. She seemed older, too serious, and poignant. All Wynn's youthful curiosity, her wonder and innocent passion . . . it all seemed gone from her soft brown eyes.

But so long as he saw no fear, he could bear anything else.

"I did not kill them," he rasped in Belaskian. "Any of them! I would never harm a sage."

Watching her flinch made him hate the sound of his maimed voice more than ever before. But her reaction to his words was far more important.

"I believe you," she whispered, yet as her gaze searched his face, he still saw doubt. "Why did you send for me?"

Blunt and to the point, but she certainly had many other questions. Why was he here, halfway across the world, and how was he involved with the folios' thefts? But she had not asked him any of this. She treated him like a stranger, and the ache in his chest became a pain.

Chane reached into his cloak and drew out the aged tin scroll case.

"Did you ever see this . . . while in the castle of the Pock Peaks?" he asked.

He had found it on the floor as he fled that place, not knowing who had dropped it there.

For a moment Wynn looked at the case in puzzlement. Then her eyes widened, staring with intensity—and recognition. She opened her hand slightly, allowing more of the crystal's light to escape.

"Where . . . How did you get that?" she whispered, taking two steps closer.

Chane saw the Wynn of past days as she looked up at him with that old curious astonishment.

"Near the passage out of the library," he answered. "I actually kicked it as I left. I still do not know why I picked it up."

Wynn reached out hesitantly toward the scroll case. "Li'kän took it from the library shelves."

"Li'kän?" Chane asked. "Do you mean the white undead?"

Wynn did not seem to hear him. She was fixated on the scroll case, shaking her head slightly.

"She went right to it . . . never touched anything else," Wynn whispered. "She wanted me to read it to her."

Chane hesitated before saying, "That is not possible."

Wynn's brow crinkled again. Before she could ask, he pulled off the case's pewter cap. Scholarly wonder always got the better of her, and Chane was more than willing to distract her from the harder questions concerning him. He slid out the leather scroll and opened it.

"You could not have read this to her," he said.

Wynn stepped all the way to him and held the crystal closer. It was instantly clear what he meant when she saw the ink coating.

"I don't understand," she said, her small fingers lightly touching the blackened surface.

"There is something hidden beneath it," he added. "Something marked in the fluids of a Noble Dead."

Her gaze flicked up, and he could swear her face paled.

"How do you know that?" she asked.

"I can smell it."

Doubt and suspicion returned to Wynn's eyes. "It's too old.

No scent would last that long. No one, even something . . . someone like you, could catch it."

Chane tried not to flinch: some . . . *thing* . . . like him—an undead with senses to match any feral beast's.

"I did not smell it until I had nearly finished restoring the scroll's leather. The scent was faint but exactly the same as freshly spilled fluids from one of my kind."

"Like the writing on the castle's inner walls," she whispered, gazing again at the scroll.

Chane remembered the vague, thin smell inside the white undead's fortress.

"This is why I want to see the folios," he said carefully. "From those texts, from that same library, I had hoped to learn what it is, if not what it contains. I could not risk stripping the coating to see what was hidden. Then I heard . . . saw how the works that you brought back had placed you and the guild in danger."

"Why?" she demanded. "Do you know what is hunting us?"

Sharp as it was, her earnest question held no accusation toward him. The pain in his chest lessened a bit.

"I do not," he answered. "At first I assumed the texts you chose were ones clearest to read. But with your project still ongoing, that must not be the case for all of them."

"I selected a range of works from the library," she explained, "based on what was oldest but still sound enough to transport . . . and what I—or others skilled in old tongues—might have a chance at translating."

"Yet the work continues," he said.

Wynn shrugged weakly. "Yes, the translation has been . . . seems more difficult than I guessed."

"Someone hid whatever is in this scroll," he added with his own emphasis, "either the author or someone else, in place of simply destroying it. I believe it is of importance. More so now, as your Li'kän wished you to see it, knowing there was nothing here you could read. Perhaps it might be a key to uncovering other secrets in your texts. . . . Why else would that black figure be shadowing the folios and killing for them? I think it, too, is having difficulty in finding what it seeks."

Chane held out the scroll to Wynn.

She took it and stepped around him along the side of the stable. Leaning her staff against the wall, she dropped cross-legged on the ground and opened the scroll upon her lap. Holding the crystal above it, she touched its black surface.

"This is why you came to Calm Seatt," she said, not even looking up. "Why you came after me again."

Chane crouched beside her but thought better of mentioning the dog like Chap that he had followed at first.

"Domin Tilswith and other sages in Bela would have never trusted me long enough to ask anything."

"May I keep it, for now?" she asked. "I need to take it back for further study. There may still be one or two people willing to help me."

A flash of anxiety overwhelmed Chane at relinquishing the scroll. But more than one phrase from Wynn's lips left him wondering. What did "further study" actually mean, since there was nothing in the scroll that could be studied? And her last words implied that she, too, now had few people to trust in the world, even among her own kind, it seemed.

What had happened to her in the guild branch of her homeland?

But he trusted her above all others, and he could only cling to the belief that she trusted him a little.

"Of course," he answered, handing over the case and cap.

Wynn carefully rolled the scroll and slipped it back into its protection. Then it struck Chane that he could not— could never—go back to the guild with her, as one more she could rely on in deciphering this new mystery.

"I should get back," she said, rising. "Where are you staying?"

Clearly she wanted to be away from him. Chane would never blame her for that.

"Better you do not know," he answered. "I will send word soon, when and where we should meet again."

He stepped into the street, heading away from her.

"Do you still . . . kill to survive?" she whispered, a little too loudly.

Chane did not let those words make him falter, not until he rounded the nearest turn.

He stopped there, half collapsing against a shop's side wall. Peering back around the corner, he watched Wynn until she slipped beyond his sight.

Wynn's heart pounded so hard that her ribs ached. She forced herself to walk calmly without looking back. She'd almost forgotten the long, clean lines of his face.

Chane was part of a past she had given up. Once she'd heard Leesil mutter to himself, "One should never walk backward through one's own life." It was trite, of course, but a sound thought nonetheless.

Yet, how long had it been since she'd spent even moments with someone who actually cared for her—who *knew* her? Someone who not only believed her accounts of undead, but who knew more of them than she did.

He was one of them—akin to that robed monster murdering her people—and yet he'd come across the world to seek help and to help her. She needed help from someone, anyone, who fully realized what her guild faced.

Part of her longed to linger in his company, but he hadn't answered her last question. His omission spoke volumes— like any accounting of all his victims.

Wynn slipped the scroll case and her crystal inside her cloak.

As she walked, she kept the staff from striking the cobblestones and making any sound that would attract attention. In spite of her warring emotions over accepting Chane's assistance, a flicker of hope seeded in her thoughts.

Her superiors had finally granted her access to translated passages and the codex. Now Chane had provided her with Li'kän's chosen scroll. The combination might lead to answers—if she could find a way to uncover what was hidden beneath a coating of old ink, written in the dried fluids of an ancient undead. She tried not to think about such impossibilities, or her seeds of hope might be ground to dust. She turned down Leaful Street, headed toward the Old Bailey Road.

Two patrolling men in red surcoats stepped out from the intersection's left side.

Wynn quickly scurried over against a shop's front wall. She held her breath beneath the awning's deeper night shadows.

She'd seen only two of Rodian's men when she'd slipped out of the keep. It never occurred to her that he would've put even more on patrol around the whole grounds along the loop of the Old Bailey Road. She listened as their boots clomped slowly along.

How was she going to reach the gate, let alone get past the pair stationed before the gatehouse? How many guards had Rodian sent out here?

She'd been gone only a short while, but if she didn't hurry back, someone might miss her—especially if il'Sänke turned up at her room. She had certainly badgered him enough about learning to use the staff.

Wynn swallowed hard.

If she were caught outside, in defiance of Premin Sykion's mandate, it would most certainly weigh against her. It might even cost her access to the translations.

Wynn crept along the shops and peeked around the corner.

The guards were still too close to the intersection for her to slip past behind them. Her hand clenched the staff, and she turned back down Leaful Street.

With a frustrated exhale, she cut into the next street paralleling the southeast side of Old Bailey Road. She stuck close to the buildings until she spotted a narrow walkway that would take her back to the loop around the keep. When she ducked in, she could just make out the alley's far end. Beyond, she spotted part of the wall across Old Bailey Road. She needed a vantage point farther behind the patrolling guards to check for any others circuiting the guild. And as yet, she still had no idea how to get past the two at the gatehouse.

Wynn padded along the narrow space and suddenly came upon a widened area midway. It opened on her left, and for an instant the change confused her in the dark.

A quick staccato of scratches filled the space. Wynn backed against the alley's opposing wall.

Digging in her pocket, she was already scanning the dark area as she pulled out her crystal. Light washed over a wide alcove behind the building.

Tall, narrow barrels and a few crates were stacked around three worn wooden steps leading to a rear door. A tawny rat darted across the alcove's floor stones into hiding beneath those stairs.

Wynn took several slow breaths. Her nerves were so on edge that now she was startled by vermin. Wouldn't that have given Leesil something to gibe her about, after all the dangers they'd faced in their journeys?

Fearful of revealing her presence, she stuffed the crystal back in her pocket and turned toward the alley's far end.

There was only darkness ahead. No faintly lighter space showed where the alley opened into Old Bailey Road. Only impossibly deep black filled the narrow alley.

Wynn backed up.

The dark began moving. Flowing up the alley, it seemed to eat what little light came from the street beyond.

Chane turned down the street's gradual arc. He knew he should stay away from Wynn for her own good. Yet she had asked him questions laced with eagerness for his help, and hints concerning her life at the guild left him wondering.

Was she lonely among her own kind? Enough that even the sight of a familiar monster was welcome? Or was it just that he wished it so? He could not let himself wallow in false hopes, and he headed off toward the Graylands Empire and his small attic room.

The beast inside him rumbled in agitation.

Chane's fingernails instinctively hardened as he halted. He spun sharply around in the empty street. Barely an itch inside him, but still, something pulled at the edge of his awareness.

Since entering this city he had taken to wearing Welstiel's ring of nothing at all times. The longer he wore it, the duller his awareness became. But he felt something *wrong,* something that made the feral beast within him rise in warning.

Chane looked down the dark street as his senses fully widened—and panic crept in.

After his botched attempt to seize the folio, that black figure, so physical to his eyes and yet not, had fixed upon Wynn. If it still watched for her, and she now carried the scroll from the same source as the texts . . .

He had been so relieved at her acceptance of him, that he had not thought of the further danger in which he had placed her. He had not even thought to trail her home in secret.

"Fool!" Chane hissed at himself, and bolted back up the street.

Blackness vanished suddenly from the alley.

Wynn saw the dim outline of the exit reappear. Still, she took another step back.

Had she seen that pure darkness at all? Or had she grown so paranoid that her mind played upon her fears?

Down the alley she clearly saw the tall bailey wall and the keep's southern tower above it. Both remained plainly visible. In a slow, angry breath, she gripped the staff with both hands.

"So . . . paranoid it is," she grumbled to herself and stepped forward.

Reaching the alley's far end, she carefully peeked around the left side.

The guild's southern corner hid the front gate and gatehouse from sight, but she didn't spy any patrolling guards. A quick glance right found that way empty as well. Wynn stepped out, prepared to dash for the wall and follow it around to the castle's front.

A black column stood twenty paces off in the middle of the road.

Pieces of it began to waft, like night-colored sails unfurling under a rising breeze.

Wynn glanced quickly up at the keep's southern tower.

As during her escape, all its windowed archer's slits were dark. No one was there to see her. When her gaze dropped she lurched backward.

The figure stood no more than five paces off.

Folds of its heavy black cowl sagged across its cloak's shoulders. And the cloak's layers over its long black robe floated on a wind that touched nothing else in sight. Wynn gripped the staff in both hands, glancing frantically about.

She wasn't skilled enough with the staff's crystal for this rushed moment—she wasn't really skilled with it at all. She couldn't outrun this thing in the open, but fleeing into the alley was foolish. All the murdered sages had been caught and trapped in tight spaces. As much as her own safety or life, she didn't want the scroll to fall into this thing's possession.

Should she scream out, call to any guards who might hear?

Wynn whirled to run the other way, hoping to catch the patrol she'd evaded, and a chill wind swirled up around her. It tore at her cloak and robe until her hood ripped back and her hair whipped across her face. She slapped the tendrils out of her eyes.

There it was again.

The black figure loomed in front of her. She stumbled back and it rushed her. A hand wrapped in shreds of black cloth reached out.

Wynn twisted away in the only direction it hadn't appeared. She ran straight into the alley.

Her robe's skirt slapped against her legs. Any instant she expected to see the figure appear before her, but she didn't look back. She reached the alley's far end, skidded into the next open street, and wildly searched for anyplace to hide.

No open inns or eateries lay in sight with any lighted windows or people about, just dark buildings, one with storage bins out front and marked with the sign of a dry-goods shop. She looked back to the alley.

Darkness rolled toward her, swallowing any scant light upon the brick walls. The figure slid into the open without the sound of a footfall.

Wynn choked once as the air turned frigid around her. Sucking in a freezing breath, she retreated toward the street's far side. As numbing cold spread through her, a savage howl erupted along the street. Wynn turned her head as a dark form rushed forward.

A charcoal-colored wolf wove and twisted, snarling before the robed figure. Its ears flattened as its jowls pulled back, exposing fangs and teeth glistening with spittle.

Wynn blinked as the black figure shrank away one pace, and the wolf, so tall—too tall—spun to one side.

She saw its pointed ears and long muzzle. And its glittering eyes, like pale and faceted sapphires . . . like Chap's eyes.

It was a majay-hì, but it wasn't Chap.

A hiss of unintelligible whispers filled the street in answer to the animal's threat. The dog lunged in.

"No!" Wynn breathed. "Don't!"

The air's chill waned as the figure pulled farther back.

Wynn stared at the snarling dog.

How could it be here, and why? Chap was the only majay-hì that she knew of beyond the bounds of the elven lands. Unlike his silvery gray, this one's charcoal-colored fur was almost inky, though faint shimmers rose within its coat.

As much as for herself, Wynn feared for this animal so far from its native land. And all she had for defense was the sun crystal staff. She'd brought that more for show, in case she needed to threaten Chane. She'd promised il'Sänke never to attempt to use it without his guidance. And honestly, she wasn't even sure if she could.

The black figure slid sideways, trying to get around the dog, and the pure silence of its movement terrified Wynn. The majay-hì darted quickly to cut it off, and the figure swung one hand down at the dog's head.

"No!" Wynn shouted, though it came out voiceless and strangled.

She'd seen this creature kill three city guards with little effort.

The dog twisted its head clear of the strike and whipped back with a snap. Its jaws bit into—through—those wrapped fingers. The majay-hì's teeth clacked, as if they'd closed on nothing at all.

The figure snatched its hand back, fingers quivering as if in pain.

An eerie, hollow screech erupted around Wynn. And the dog's yelp rose over that. The majay-hì backed toward her, shaking its head in whimpers.

Wynn was so startled that she forgot about the staff and crystal.

An undead mage, with the skill to become incorporeal, and yet the snap of a Fay-descended majay-hì had hurt it in turn. Both dog and figure recovered quickly and fixed upon each other with caution. Wynn tried to block out the threatening snarls and hissing.

She ripped the sheath off the sun crystal.

Letting it drop, she gripped the staff with both hands and shut her eyes, trying to remember what little Domin il'Sänke had taught her.

Not a spell, but more a series of thoughts—symbols— matched with plain words so that her voice reinforced her intent. She leaned the staff's head out and concentrated, seeing the long crystal's shape in her thoughts.

"From Spirit . . ." she whispered, and a circle surrounded the crystal in her mind's eye. "To Fire . . ." And she added a triangle within the circle. "For its light"—and another inverted triangle appeared within the first—"of life!"

A final circle filled the inner space of the pattern, overlaying the crystal's image. Wynn held her focus, keeping the pattern alive in her mind.

A soft warmth spread upon her face.

The insides of her eyelids brightened slightly—as if a candle had been lit before them. Clinging to the mental pattern, Wynn turned her face aside.

"Wynn!"

She snapped her eyes open at the rasping voice.

Only the barest light showed around her. Horror flooded Wynn at the sight of Chane running toward her, his sword drawn—and the pattern vanished from her thoughts.

Light, like a noon sun, ignited before Wynn's face.

Three sounds struck her ears amid sudden blindness— a dog's startled yelp, a hiss rising to a wail, and Chane's grating shout of agony. Everything washed white, erasing Chane from Wynn's sight.

And a last sound smothered the other three.

A shriek filled Wynn's skull, riding on the searing light's

pain lancing through her eyes. She felt herself hit the cobblestones.

That last sound had torn from her own throat.

Ghassan il'Sänke heard a howl and followed the sound, half leaping and half floating from rooftop to rooftop. When he reached the next street, Wynn stood with a dark wolf between her and the tall black-robed figure.

A cloaked man was running toward her, gripping a sword. "Wynn!" he cried in a rasping voice.

Then a glimmer rose in the long crystal of Wynn's staff.

"No!" Ghassan growled, and extended his hand in the air, aimed toward the staff. Not one symbol or shape came quickly enough into his mind.

Yellow-white light erupted, turning night into instant day, and Ghassan ducked, raising a sleeve before his eyes. He heard a hissing wail, a yelp, and a rasping shout. Wynn's shriek smothered all three.

Daylight winked out.

Caught half-blind between colored blotches over his sight and the sudden return of darkness, Ghassan dropped quickly over the eave's edge. But when he landed upon the street, still blinking and squinting, the black-robed figure was nowhere in sight, and neither was Wynn's armed protector. Both had fled in the crystal's flash—but not the wolf.

It shook its head, whimpering, and Ghassan ran to kneel where Wynn lay.

Curled upon the cobblestones with her eyes shut, she shuddered in a growing sweat with the staff still clutched in one hand. He jerked it from her grip, but when he tried to touch her damp brow, the lanky wolf charged at him.

Ghassan slapped his robe's skirt aside and spun away on his knees with the staff in hand. The wolf hopped straight over Wynn's quivering form to block him from reaching her.

He raised a hand, symbols and shapes forming in his vision, and prepared to cast the animal aside as easily as he lifted himself to the rooftops. The wolf pulled up short, head low and jaws parted in a snarl, but it didn't advance.

Ghassan paused and studied this aberrant animal.

It stood its ground, directly between him and Wynn, as if guarding her. And the more he saw of it, the more it seemed too oddly formed. Wolves were not found in his homeland, but its legs, ears, and snout seemed exaggerated, from what little he knew of them. And its eyes . . . glittering crystal blue eyes . . .

There was something familiar about this beast.

Ghassan had little time left if he were to free Wynn from the effects of a failed attempt with the staff. He turned his gesture from the wolf to her, closed his fingers tightly, and jerked his fist back.

Wynn's curled form slid sharply across the cobblestones—right into the wolf's legs. The animal toppled in surprise, tumbling over her. Wynn came to a stop in front of Ghassan.

He pointed the staff's crystal outward as the wolf thrashed to its feet. It hopped aside, trying to get around, but Ghassan already had his free hand on Wynn's fevered brow.

He sank into her thoughts—and erased the lingering trace of the patterned shapes submerged in her mind.

Wynn went limp and still, moaning softly as she tried to roll over. Ghassan already felt excessive heat fading from her forehead.

"The dog . . ." she whispered weakly. "Bring . . ."

She fell unconscious, and the wolf ceased rumbling, staring at her as its ears rose. Then it turned its eyes on Ghassan.

Its jowls curled, exposing teeth, as if warning him away from Wynn.

When he set the staff down, prepared to lift Wynn, the dog lunged at him and snapped.

Ghassan froze as his brow wrinkled in impatience. Wynn needed more care, and his first instinct was to just slap this animal aside—or perhaps he should kill it. Tonight had already been filled with enough nonsense.

Some form of nonsense always circled around Wynn.

But the wolf, or dog, puzzled him, as much for its sudden appearance as for its strange form. And when the black-robed mage had come after Wynn, this wild beast had tried to defend her.

He gripped the staff with his right hand, rose slowly to his feet, and swept his left hand across his sight of the wolf. More symbols formed in his mind.

"Halt," he murmured, reaching for the animal's simple thoughts.

It stopped cold, as if bound where it stood.

Ghassan gestured in the air over Wynn, and her body rose off the street. When she reached his waist, he cradled her in his arms, still gripping the sun crystal's staff.

The wolf went into a snarling frenzy.

"Silence!" Ghassan snapped, and reached deeper into the animal's limited mind.

Something in there slapped his mental intrusion aside, as surely as if it had slapped his face. He nearly lost hold of Wynn.

The wolf lurched forward, one slow paw at a time, and Ghassan stared in surprise.

A simple beast should not have resisted his command so easily, let alone felt—or responded—when he entered its thoughts. He turned away, heading down the road toward the guild. He had no time to deal with getting some strange wolf onto the grounds, even if Wynn wanted it.

The animal's snarls intensified, and he paused, glancing over his shoulder.

It had not kept up, but it still made headway against his will.

Ghassan sighed. In a quick flash of symbols and a silent chant, he ripped the command from the wolf's mind.

It lunged forward and circled him.

Ghassan hissed back at it, hurrying on, and the wolf hopped aside before it got caught by his boots.

Chane lay on the far side of a leather shop, gritting his teeth in pain. Thin trails of smoke rose from his charred face and hands. It took effort not to whimper and betray his presence as he climbed to his feet and peered around the shop's side.

A tall sage with dusky skin and dark hair knelt beside

Wynn's curled form. He was older and wore the midnight blue of a metaologer. Chane remembered him from the night the first two sages were found murdered in an alley.

At least the black figure was gone, and in the company of one of her own, Wynn might be safe for the moment.

The dark-skinned sage picked up the crystal-adorned staff, but when he tried to touch Wynn's forehead the dog lunged at him. What followed cut through Chane's suffering as he watched, to the instant Wynn floated up into the sage's arms.

This man was more than a sage. Chane's amazement succumbed to pain as Wynn's savior headed off, carrying her in his arms. And the dog followed, still snarling and circling.

Chane barely fumbled his sword back into its sheath. He was almost grateful for the Suman's arrival, as he certainly could not carry Wynn anywhere in his present state. He needed to feed, and soon, and he didn't care whom he found. Almost anyone would do, but he continued to watch the retreating deep blue robe.

Chane knew conjury, though he was less skilled than a true mage. Nothing in that art could have raised Wynn from the ground without a telltale sign—perhaps a geyser of conjured air. He had felt no wind, let alone one powerful and controlled enough to lift her small body from the street.

Thaumaturgy's manipulation of the physical world had better possibilities, but he had never heard nor read of a thaumaturge who could turn a breeze into wind so precisely shaped and with such strength.

This sage had appeared suddenly, in just the right place and moment, barely an instant after the black figure had vanished.

Chane grew anxious—and frustrated with his own weakness—for there was nothing he could do. Had he left Wynn in the hands of some new and unknown threat living within the walls of her own guild?

CHAPTER 14

Wynn groaned as she opened her eyes. She found herself in her own bed, in her own room.

She felt as if she had both a fever and a sunburn, and her right hand tingled uncomfortably. When she raised it, her hand and forearm were their normal tone. She remembered falling in the street, burning inside, as if the crystal's light had sunk within. . . .

Wynn sat up too quickly.

Colored blotches spun over her sight, and she blinked against dizziness. How had she ended up in her room, and where was the inky-colored majay-hì? And what had become of Chane after the crystal ignited?

She remembered him rushing toward her, but no more, and she had no way to find him. At a grunt and a whine from the room's far corner, her mouth dropped open.

The majay-hì lay curled on the floor near her desk. The tip of its bushy tail covered its nose, and its crystal blue eyes stared back at her.

"How did you get in here?" Wynn breathed in wonder.

The dog's tall ears pricked at the sound of her voice. But when she swung her legs over the bedside, trying and failing to stand up, the majay-hì lifted its head with a rumble.

Wynn sat perfectly still. "It's all right," she whispered.

Then she realized she wore only her shift.

She scanned the room in panic for her cloak and spotted it draped over the desk's wooden chair. The majay-hì rumbled again as she wobbled to her feet. She stumbled over and dug into the cloak's inner pocket. At the feel of old tin, Wynn exhaled and pulled out the scroll case.

It looked the same as when Chane had offered it to her—safe and sound. She tucked it back into the cloak and turned about.

The majay-hì watched her intently, ears slightly flattened at her close proximity.

A pitcher of water and a clay mug rested on her bedside table. Ignoring the mug, Wynn retrieved the washbowl atop her chest and filled it from the pitcher. But when she tried to step back across the little room, she made it only halfway.

The majay-hì let out a sharper rumble.

Wynn set the bowl down in the room's center. Even as she backed to the bed, the animal didn't move. Its gaze shifted only once to the bowl.

"It's all right," she repeated, but the words made no difference.

Finally the majay-hì rose.

Holding its place for a moment, it then padded one careful step at a time to the bowl. Lowering its muzzle to lap the water, it never took its eyes off Wynn. A wave of sadness washed through Wynn as she thought of Chap—and the majay-hì's ears rose up.

She couldn't help a stab of regret that this four-footed stranger wasn't him—not by its color, let alone that it was obviously female. She remembered the pack that had helped her and Chap find Leesil's mother in the an'Cróan's Elven Territories. A yearling majay-hì had run among them.

This charcoal-colored female looked about the same age, if Wynn guessed right. But then, she didn't know the life span of the majay-hì. Its color was almost as dark as that of the grizzled pack elder. By contrast, Wynn remembered Lily, Chap's beautiful white companion with yellow-flecked blue eyes that looked green from afar. Lily's strange attributes were rare for the wild protectors of those faraway elven lands.

The strange female stopped drinking and lifted her head.

Wynn couldn't fathom how this young one, maybe only a yearling, had traveled so far from home. And why had the dog come to her, let alone at the moment the black figure appeared? She crouched to the dog's level and hesitantly stretched out her hand, palm up.

"It's all right," she said again.

The majay-hì shrank away with a twitch of jowl—but she cocked her long head as well.

And a moment passed.

The dog stretched her neck just a little, reaching out her nose, though she remained well beyond Wynn's reach. The majay-hì sniffed at Wynn, and then shook herself all over, and those pale blue eyes gazed intently into Wynn's.

The same way Chap had sometimes studied her. And the way Lily had looked her over when they first met.

The young female huffed suddenly and took a step.

Wynn remained still, with her hand extended, but the female paused as if waiting for something. The dog finally backed up. That brief instant of near acceptance—and its sudden passing—frustrated Wynn.

The majay-hì pack had also had a hard time accepting her. The grizzled black elder had barely tolerated her at all. Lily was the first to allow Wynn close.

The young female's ears pricked up again.

Even Lily wouldn't have let Wynn touch her without Chap present. How was she going to establish trust with this lost sentient being—without getting bitten? Wynn leaned forward with her hand still outstretched, until she had to brace her other hand on the floor. She hesitated every inch for fear of startling the anxious female.

The majay-hì finally extended her head in like manner, until her cold, wet nose touched the tip of Wynn's middle finger.

A barrage of memories erupted in Wynn's mind. Wobbling under the onslaught, she barely caught a glimpse of one before it washed away under the next.

Chap, his silver-gray fur glinting in shafts of sunlight lancing through the forest canopy . . .

Lily running somewhere nearby, more brilliant white where the light touched her coat . . .

Violet-tinged ferns in the underbrush whipping across them within the vast Elven Territories . . .

Wynn snatched her hand back with a gasp and dropped sharply on her rump.

Hazy and blurry as they were, there was something very wrong about these memories. She'd never run with Chap and Lily—not in such a moment as she'd just remembered.

The young female cocked her head and huffed once.

Even with lingering fever's heat, Wynn sat shivering on the cold stone floor.

Chap could evoke anyone's memories that he'd seen in them once before. He played upon people who were completely unaware of what he did. But he'd left the Elven Territories nearly two years ago.

And those memories had come to Wynn at a touch.

Only the majay-hì could do this. They communicated among their own kind through "memory-speak." But this wasn't possible for Wynn—or anyone. Resting one night among the pack, she'd tried to "listen" in among them, but nothing came to her.

Wynn had remembered Chap and Lily in the forest, as if running with them, but that blurred imperfect memory wasn't her own. And it couldn't have been passed to her, a human, from a majay-hì. Nor could one so young have known Chap.

What had just happened?

In shallow breaths, Wynn lurched forward onto her knees. The female didn't shy away and stepped two paces closer. Wynn reached out slowly, touching the soft fur between the dog's ears. The female raised her head, forcing Wynn's hand to slip down along her neck.

As Wynn's fingers combed through thick fur, separating the hairs, she saw an almost cream undercoat beneath the outer dark charcoal. She lowered her gaze, meeting the animal's own.

Wynn stared into crystalline blue irises . . . with the faintest flecks of yellow.

Another image of Lily surfaced in Wynn's thoughts, as if from nowhere.

This time the recollection was clearly Wynn's own. It came from when she'd first been allowed to stroke Lily's head. The sudden unsought flash felt familiar. Like when Chap intentionally called up one of Wynn's own memories. And more images flooded her mind....

Four pups nestled around a creamy white mother with yellow-flecked eyes, each with its own varied shade of coat. Two males of silver-gray, and one more steely in tone, but the last little female was charcoal gray.

Moments and flashes came and went....

Four cubs wrestled and tumbled over a downed tree coated in moss and lichen....

Little furred bodies, grown stronger, ran with their white mother in the forest....

In hunts for wild hares, or strangely colored wrens, or the chocolate-toned squirrels, their legs had grown faster than their bodies. One of them took a horrible spill down a steep incline as it tripped over its own paws....

Each moment that came to Wynn stepped across moons of time. The little ones grew from adolescents into young adults, until finally Wynn saw the charcoal female touch heads with her white mother. The two lay alone beneath a wide fir tree, speaking in memories of their own. In that dim space, hidden from sunlight, the young female's coat appeared inky black, and the white mother was like the shadow of a ghost.

A hazy image of Chap suddenly overlaid that moment, as if the memory of him wasn't quite perfect and didn't belong to the female.

And then Wynn saw an image of herself.

She wore elven clothing, as she had during her time in that land—then suddenly her garb changed to the gray robe of her guild.

Both these last images of Chap and herself were not as clear and crisp as the ones of the pups' lives. Perhaps these were secondhand, passed from mother to child. Wynn ached inside at the memory of Chap, and how much he'd hurt upon leaving Lily behind.

She couldn't help the tears.

Wynn pulled her hand from the charcoal female's neck and looked down in astonishment into those lightly yellow-flecked eyes.

The eyes of Chap and Lily's daughter, sent from half a world away.

Wynn knew Chap feared for her safety since the night his kin, the Fay, had caught her listening in while he communed with them. They'd turned on her, tried to kill her, and might have succeeded if not for him and the pack. And Wynn understood.

Lily had been pregnant when Chap left the Elven Territories. He must've arranged all this through her.

In leaving to guide Magiere and Leesil onward, Chap hadn't wanted Wynn left unattended for so long. But how had his daughter managed to find her?

Wynn wasn't certain she liked the idea. This animal was so young.

The majay-hì whined, sounding almost frustrated. Wynn wasn't adept at memory-speak, let alone that it was impossible for a human. Although . . .

Chap could speak his thoughts directly to her—another aberration of the taint left in her by dabbling with a mantic ritual. Perhaps as his daughter, this young one shared some manifestation of her father's singular qualities. He was Fay, who'd chosen to be born into one of the Fay-descended majay-hì.

Too many complications and guesses, yet it was the only explanation Wynn could think of. Chap, and now his daughter, were unique in this world, each in their own way, it seemed. And Wynn recalled the evening when she'd heard something outside the bailey wall, like claws on cobblestone.

A memory of the hunt for the undead sorcerer, Vordana, had suddenly entered her head. She'd run into a crowded street, searching for Chap, and something had brushed her leg. Another memory had come, as if she were looking through his eyes. But the first unsought recollection hadn't come from any contact.

Confused, Wynn backed away. The female huffed, her

brief growl turning into a whine, and she took a step to follow. But Wynn held her hand up out of reach.

She had to try something that might gain her more answers. Could Chap's daughter communicate with her from afar, without touch, as her father did?

The recollection of hunting Vordana stuck in her mind. In the river town plagued by that sorcerous undead, Wynn had encountered another dog, not nearly so lovely as a majay-hì. She willfully focused on the memory of an old wire-haired wolfhound named Shade.

The young majay-hì stared at her without moving. And with a sigh, Wynn gave up.

Obviously she couldn't transmit a memory to this one any more than she could speak back to Chap through thought. That left only one other thing to try, and she scooted forward on her knees. She moved oh so slowly as she placed her hands upon the sides of the female's face. Using touch, she tried again.

She recalled the memory of the wolfhound standing beside Chap in the courtyard of the manor house outside of the river town.

The female's ears pricked up—and the memory echoed back to Wynn. She quickly tried one more.

She hadn't been there when Shade had roused Chap from a phantasm cast by Vordana. But Wynn did her best to imagine it—to envision it—from Chap's later description.

The female remained silent and still, poised in waiting.

Wynn frowned. Constructed thoughts weren't enough. It seemed only those experiences seated into her memory would work. But the way that memory of the wolfhound and Chap had repeated gave Wynn another notion.

She recalled the female's own recollection of playing in the forest with her siblings.

The female sniffed wildly at her. A maelstrom of like images, sounds, and scents whirled up in Wynn's mind. And Wynn's mild hunger knotted into nausea.

"Wait—not so much!" she squeaked, and jerked her hands from the dog's face.

She clamped a hand over her mouth and buckled as her head finally emptied of memories.

Wynn took several hard breaths until her stomach settled. The female cocked her head in silent puzzlement, and
Wynn scowled at her. They could communicate, to a point,
but only with memories shared by touch, or by Wynn's own
called up by the female.

A knock came at the door, sounding too loud in Wynn's
quiet little room.

The female snarled, turning toward the door.

Wynn clambered to her feet in dread. However she'd gotten back in her room, no doubt others knew she'd broken
curfew. Either Sykion or High-Tower now came for her, or
a messenger sent to summon her before the council. She
was in deep trouble, enough to ruin any chance of seeing
the translations. And how could she ever explain a "wolf"
in her room?

"You are finally awake," someone called from outside.

The familiar voice was far less than patient. Wynn knew
it was Domin il'Sänke even before she squeezed the latch.

The instant the door cracked open, il'Sänke pushed it
wide, not waiting to be invited. Shooing Wynn back with a
flick of his hand, he stepped in and closed the door. He was
carrying the staff with its crystal now sheathed.

Wynn shrank a little inside.

Entranced by the majay-hì, she'd forgotten even to check
for the staff. And if il'Sänke had it . . .

"Yes, I found you," he said coldly.

Wynn backed away from his glare.

"Before someone . . . or something else did," he added.
"Not that I should have had to."

The dog watched him carefully, her jowls twitching, but
she didn't growl. Her yellow-flecked eyes locked on the
staff he carried.

"You were not to use this without my supervision,"
il'Sänke snapped, and then softened only a bit. "Though I
suppose you had little choice, amid your foolish outing."

Wynn braced for an onslaught. What was she doing alone
outside the guild at night? Why would the black-robed murderer be hunting her if she carried no folio? Where had this
wolf come from, and why had she come to protect Wynn?

To her surprise, il'Sänke walked over and leaned the staff in the corner by her desk.

"You might have died," he whispered, his back still to her.

For an instant, Wynn was struck mute by his concern.

"I'm all right," she managed to say. "That thing never touched me, so I'm—"

"You lost your focus!" he hissed, and then whirled around.

Wynn flinched away from the fury tightening all of il'Sänke's features.

"You are not an adept, let alone a mage," he continued. "Though it was neither spell nor ritual that you toyed with, it is still thaumaturgy imbued in the crystal . . . as well as a trigger of my own devising."

Wynn was tired, feverish, and overwhelmed. The last thing she needed was another lecture from a superior.

"Then why make it so hard to use?" she asked angrily.

"To keep it from those wise but malicious," he nearly snarled, "as well as the witless! And I did not *make* it difficult. Magic *is* difficult—and dangerous . . . even when embedded in an object through artificing!"

The domin slid forward, too much like that black assailant in the night.

Wynn backed up at his threatening tone, until her legs bumped against the bedside. Even Chap's daughter circled away to the room's far corner, though she growled.

Anger's flush further darkened il'Sänke's complexion, until his face appeared to sink deep within the shadow of his cowl. Before Wynn could muster another retort, his voice lashed at her again.

"No created artifact is used by brandishing it with arrogance, or waving it about while babbling some poetically arcane phrase. Such nonsense is for children's fables and peasant lore! A thaumaturge feels the inherent connections of the five Elements within the physical world. But he detaches himself in manipulating them, holds himself outside the web of things . . . or succumbs to the very effects that he—"

"You told me already," Wynn warned, as anger got the better of her fright.

"Then remember it!" il'Sänke whispered loudly. "Unless you enjoy the feel of elemental Fire cooking your insides! Disobey again, and I am done with you!"

Wynn remained quiet. Il'Sänke's ire was born of fearful concern as much as disapproval. But another rumble rose in the room.

The female majay-hì paced warily around the domin along the door's wall and crossed over to join Wynn.

"I see." Il'Sänke sighed, frowning tiredly at the animal. "One of your elven dogs."

Wynn glanced up at him. How did he know that?

He seemed to feel her eyes on him and straightened, still studying the female.

"Like any who have worked on the translations," he said, "I have read some of your journals."

Wynn was almost relieved. She didn't care for any more mysteries at the moment. Not that she would ever see her journals again, after last night.

"Now sit," il'Sänke commanded.

The young majay-hì remained on all fours.

"I meant you," he added, looking at Wynn.

She settled on the bed's edge. He came to her, laying his tanned palm upon her forehead as he closed his eyes. In that moment of silence, more questions popped into Wynn's head.

She wasn't the only one who'd broken Sykion's curfew. What was *he* doing outside the guild last night? And for that matter, how had he managed to come upon her? Had he seen Chane?

Domin il'Sänke opened his eyes with a muffled grunt. "You are well enough. The remaining backwash you suffer should fade in a day or two."

Wynn studied his dark brown eyes. Well enough for what? His right eyebrow arched as he watched her in turn.

"Yes?" he asked.

"You saw it," she said, challenging him to deny this. "The black-robed figure in the street, so silent in movement. I'm not losing my wits!"

"I never said you were." Il'Sänke's mouth tightened, and he nodded with an answer. "Only for an instant, before the crystal flashed."

"Do you know what it is?" she blurted out. "Rodian insists it is some malevolent mage, after seeing it walk through the scriptorium's wall. Maybe it is, but it's more than that. He is just seeking a rational explanation for the royals."

The domin turned away, gazing at the floor, and laced his fingers together in his lap.

"I am not certain. Its abilities are a serious concern, and in that, the captain may be partially correct, but that does not account for the way in which our young ones have died."

Wynn's mind reeled. Not only was he admitting that the killer could be unnatural, but it seemed he knew more than he said.

"Even in folktales, I've never heard of any mage who could walk through walls," she rushed on. "Let alone one that could let a sword pass through him and then tear out a man's chest."

"Yes, yes." And il'Sänke held up a hand before she continued. "Such skill seems difficult to accept, but I will not make conjectures based on a few moments of what anyone has seen."

He paused, and his expression hardened.

"And not a word of this to anyone, Wynn. No more wild rumors without substantiation. It might yet cut you off from what you have been waiting to see."

Wynn tensed, afraid to grow hopeful.

"And I trust," il'Sänke went on, rising and heading for the door, "that you will use equal discretion regarding anything you find? This knowledge must be protected. Now get dressed. I will wait outside."

He grabbed the latch and opened the door, but Wynn couldn't budge.

"Well?" he said. "Are you coming or not? Your precious translations and codex will not sprout legs and come to you."

"But . . ." she started.

Domin il'Sänke turned halfway, with the barest hint of a smile beneath his sly eyes.

"No one knows either of us was out. Now put some clothes on!"

The door thumped shut. Wynn didn't care how he'd done this. She snatched up her robe, struggling to get it on in a hurry. As the robe's neck finally cleared her head, she found the majay-hì standing before her.

The young female tilted her head with only one ear raised. She stared with wide unblinking eyes, as if trying to figure out what Wynn was doing.

The dog—the female , , , the charcoal-colored majay-hì . . . Chap's daughter. None of these seemed right for a being that Wynn knew was as sentient as herself in its own way.

The an'Cróan elves of the Farlands had an aversion to forcing a name upon another sentient being. Even their children eventually went before their ancestral spirits for what they called "name-taking." By whatever vision was gained there, they chose a name of their own in place of the one given at birth. And still . . .

"What am I going to call you?" Wynn asked, though she wouldn't get an answer.

As she gathered her elven quill, a bottle of ink, and a journal, stuffing these in a satchel, she thought of other dogs she'd known, aside from Chap or Lily. She slung the satchel's strap over her shoulder, but when she reached for the door's latch, a cascade of images flickered through her mind.

Chap alone—then with Lily, their heads touching—and finally a hazy secondhand memory of the old wolfhound.

"I know who your parents are," she said. "It doesn't help."

She wasn't certain what those raised memories truly meant. When she opened the door, the majay-hì trotted out before Wynn could stop her.

"Wynn . . . what are you doing?" il'Sänke asked, an edge of warning in his voice as he glared at Chap's daughter.

"She stays with me," Wynn answered.

"And how will you explain a wolf's sudden company amid curfew?" he asked. "Do you want your outing to be discovered?"

Yes, that was another matter, as well as how il'Sänke had managed to conceal it.

She stepped off down the passage with the female close behind, not giving the domin further opportunity to argue. Chap and Lily had sent their daughter. Much as Wynn questioned that decision, she would keep this young female as close as she'd once kept Chap.

Il'Sänke remained silent as he followed.

Wynn knew she should thank him for saving her, but he hadn't been the only one there. She dropped her hand, uncertain of how much Chap's daughter had become accustomed to her in so short a time.

Wynn's hand suddenly lifted and dragged across furred ears, as the female pushed under her palm.

Chane had been there, too. She longed to ask il'Sänke about him, but she held her tongue. As she opened the door to the courtyard, she glanced over her shoulder.

"How did you get us back?" she asked, and her gaze dropped to the majay-hì as they approached the main keep's double doors. "How did you get her to come?"

"She was persistent," he answered. "And I was too burdened carrying you to get rid of her. My first thought was to bring you to the hospice, but you didn't seem in serious danger. Taking you both to your room was best, before anyone learned you were gone."

Yes, but how did he get past the guards? He hadn't offered that, so she suspected he wouldn't answer.

Wynn opened one of the double doors and stepped into the main building's entryway. Amid the rush of others coming and going, she reached the common hall. As expected, the sight of her with a tall wolf brought a sea of stunned stares and frantic whispers.

"You and your dramatics!" il'Sänke grumbled.

Wynn forced an outward show of calm, but inside she was thankful not to spot Domin High-Tower among the forest of faces. He would've confronted her directly for an explanation. Then a less than proper notion popped up into her head, and she stroked the head of Chap's daughter.

"Perhaps I should introduce you to Regina Melliny and her pack of gossips," she whispered.

The female rumbled, and a quiver ran through the dog's back under Wynn's hand.

Wynn glanced down to find the dog looking about nervously.

Wynn's small room had been hard enough on the female—a strange and alien place for a majay-hì, who'd known only the forest wilds and perhaps the elves' tree enclaves before arriving in this city. But this enormous half-filled hall of humans must be nearly overwhelming. Wynn stepped quickly to the nearest table.

"Wynn?" il'Sänke called in warning.

She leaned between a pair of initiates and grabbed two bowls of vegetable stew and a doughy wheat roll.

"What do you think you're doing?" someone hissed.

"You lunatic!" another growled. "Get that thing out of here!"

Before Wynn spotted either source, the young initiate to her right screeched.

The boy nearly threw himself into the lap of a willowy apprentice in pale blue next in line on the bench. He stared off behind Wynn as his startled savior glared first the same way, and then at Wynn.

"Haven't you caused enough trouble?" the apprentice demanded.

Suddenly the boy's breathing turned to rapid whimpers as others around the table lunged away in all directions. A rumble rose directly behind Wynn.

"Wynn, move on! Now!" il'Sänke snapped at her.

She glanced back.

The majay-hì crept in with a soft snarl, but the dog was shaking almost as much as the boy. Who feared whom more?

"She won't hurt you," Wynn quickly tried to assure the boy.

She reached for his small hand, and the apprentice holding him slapped her hand away.

Chap's daughter snarled as Wynn quickly swung her arm back to block the dog. She'd made another terrible mistake.

Her brethren saw only an overly tall and ominously dark wolf—not a majay-hì.

The very term meant "hound of the elementals" or "Fay dog," something she'd learned in scant writings and the mentions of Domin Tilswith. It was a quaint fable for a young girl not even an initiate at the time. Even others who might've heard of these beings in the deep forests of Lhoin'na to the south probably never saw one. No one had, not even Wynn, until she'd met Chap. But she'd recognized him—or at least guessed in wonder at what he was that first time some two years ago.

But Chap's daughter looked nothing like him, and she wasn't like him. She'd been born wild, for all her sentience, in a far-off land, where humans were an enemy to be guarded against. How many ways could Wynn alienate herself inside her own guild?

"Get going!" il'Sänke growled, his voice directly behind her.

Wynn pushed the majay-hì along and headed straight for the narrow side archway. Wide-eyed initiates and apprentices glowered at her until she slipped from sight into the outer passage. All the way to the heavy stairway door leading to the catacombs, she heard Domin il'Sänke muttering behind her. And they descended into the shadowy spiraling stairwell.

Although Wynn would've never agreed, it seemed strange that il'Sänke hadn't demanded that she get rid of the dog. Her life in the guild was going to get more complicated than before. As they emerged into the catacombs' cavernous entry room, Master Tärpodious sat at the back table, scribbling rapidly with a quill. But he looked up.

"Ah, young Hygeorht," the old archivist began, his tone chill.

He scowled over the bowls and bread clutched in her hands. Food wasn't allowed in the archives. Then his gaze shifted to the female with a harsh squint.

"What . . . is . . . *that*?" he sputtered. "I was asked to prepare space for reviewing the codex, and assist you as needed. What is that beast doing in my archive?"

Assist indeed—more likely keep an eye on her. High-Tower or Sykion must've gotten to him, and she'd lost another friendly acquaintance.

"She must remain with me," Wynn answered without apology, and kept a hand on the female's back. "She won't even nudge the shelves, I promise, but it's my duty to watch over her."

"Not in here!" Tärpodious croaked, and heaved himself up with wrinkled hands.

Domin il'Sänke slipped around Wynn, straight at the old man, and began whispering. The old archivist sneered in a twist of astonishment.

"That is nonsense!" he hissed. "I've never heard of anyone even seeing one ... let alone the notion of it outside Lhoin'na lands!"

Wynn's gaze narrowed on il'Sänke, still whispering in Tärpodious's ear. If the Suman had read her journals, others involved in translation had done so, High-Tower especially. Yet they still refused to believe her recordings any more than her verbal claims concerning more deadly matters than a majay-hì.

"Fine, if she's that far gone," Tärpodious grumbled. "But you're responsible, Ghassan, if that animal causes damage."

Wynn also hoped Chap's daughter would behave, but she didn't like the hint of how il'Sänke had gained the elder sage's agreement. Tärpodious hunched where he braced upon the table's edge and eyed Wynn like a vulture waiting for her to drop dead.

"But no food inside!" he warned. "You may finish it here or leave it behind."

Domin il'Sänke ushered Wynn to a table farthest from the archivist.

"What did you just tell him?" she demanded in a whisper.

"If you are thought a madwoman—or act like one—at least take advantage of it ... and anything that seemingly soothes your addled mind."

She glanced down at Chap's daughter.

"I'm not mad!" Wynn hissed. "And you of all people know it."

"Not by that nonsense in the common hall," il'Sänke returned. "Keep your new companion away from the populace. Now finish your meal, and Tärpodious will show you to your place."

With that he turned and left, and Wynn settled at the table, unshouldering her satchel. She set one bowl of stew on the floor for her "companion." The female sniffed it uncertainly, but finally began lapping at her stew, finishing off the gravy but not touching the vegetables.

Wynn sighed. "We'll find you something better tonight."

She quickly ate her own meal, pocketing the roll for later, and shouldered her satchel once more.

"Where am I to study the translations?" she asked.

Tärpodious grunted and gestured to the archway behind himself. "In there."

Wynn walked over to peer inside.

There were few shelves in the small antechamber. It was probably an old storage room turned into a temporary holding place for material waiting to be reshelved. Dust trails on the floor suggested the shelves had been recently moved. The room now contained a table for her *special* workspace. The table had been placed in a direct sight line with the room's doorless opening.

Tärpodious had been told to watch over her.

Why did Sykion and High-Tower always have to paint her as untrustworthy? But the arrangement was better than none—and all she planned to do was read and take notes.

"Thank you," she said politely, and stepped into her prepared space.

Four heavy stacks of scribed sheets lay upon the table, some bound and some not. Beside them rested a large makeshift book, laced together with temporary waxed string—the codex. Forgetting hurt pride, Wynn motioned to the dog.

"Come."

Whether Chap's daughter understood or not, she trotted in, sniffing the floor and scanning the strange surroundings.

"Stay in here with me," Wynn said softly, "and do not knock anything over."

The female cocked her head, whined once, and went back to sniffing about.

"Come here," Wynn insisted, settling into her chair.

The majay-hì didn't look at her.

Master Tärpodious glanced over his shoulder, watching with his lips pressed tightly together in disapproval. Wynn pretended not to notice him.

Chap's young daughter hadn't traveled as her father had. Likely she didn't understand spoken words, let alone human tongues. But perhaps she'd heard a little of the an'Cróan dialect, enough to understand a few basic words—if she chose to.

Wynn pointed at the floor beside her chair. "*A'Shiuvalh, so-äiche!* Walk . . . come, here!"

The female craned her head around, and then sneezed. Snorting to clear her nose of dust, she wandered about the room, but finally settled beside the chair.

With a long exhale, Wynn turned to the materials before her, suddenly daunted. She'd waited so long for this, but now where to start?

Some sheets were bound in thin volumes of hardened cloth covers. It was easy to discern that these were complete sections, perhaps whole chapters, kept together because they related to a particular text. But others were merely neat, loose collections awaiting further translation or transcribed passages. Wynn closed her eyes, gathering her thoughts.

Translation had been ongoing for half a year. A good deal of work had been accomplished from the look of things, but Wynn knew better. She'd brought back two large bundles and one ironbound sheaf of hardened leather sheets. The inked content here was written with compact Begaine symbols but with extra space between lines for further notes and corrections. At a guess, less than a fifth of what she had brought had even been touched. But the murders and thefts had only recently begun, so she knew she shouldn't spend much time on the pages completed earlier.

But which ones were they?

And more important, she had to be able to cross-reference which pages existed in the codex but weren't present on the table—as the murderer had taken them.

These would be the pages she needed to examine, and she wouldn't receive an ounce of guidance from her superiors.

She opened the codex, flipped to its rearmost pages, and breathed in relief. The record of scheduled work had been kept intact, all the way to the project's beginning. At least she could roughly determine which pages were most recently translated. She took a moment to scan the names of those who'd been involved.

Cathology was the second smallest of the orders, next to metaology. Of course High-Tower's name appeared time and again, as well as two others. But there were also domins and masters from the other orders, as needed. Ghassan il'Sänke appeared infrequently. It seemed even he, as an outsider, had seen only a minimum of the work.

Wynn picked up a thin, bound volume and looked at the opening page—volume seven, section two. But which text did this refer to? Most of the texts she'd selected hadn't had any titling on their crude bindings.

She didn't know how her superiors had tabulated the originals, so she checked the reference against the codex's schedule of completed work. This thin volume had its last addition made on the fourth of Billiagyth—Leaf's Shower—the last third of autumn by the elven calendar used throughout the region. And that was within the present moon.

Taking up loose pages, Wynn prepared to read, but she stopped upon seeing two running columns of text on each page.

Both were scripted in the Begaine syllabary, but the left column represented the original language, while the right was a translation into Numanese. Her estimate of how much work had been completed had just been cut in half again.

Many passages didn't make sense, for only bits and pieces had been finished. In some she found strings of dots between the syllabic symbols, which indicated the number of words that remained unreadable or untranslatable from the original. There were also long strokes across entire columns for anyplace in a text that was too faded or worn to count words. And there were margin notes wherever a readable word or phrase had defied translation so far.

Yet the passages before her clearly held information regarding a war—or rather, battles fought in locations she'd never heard of. She struggled through broken terminology and gained a sense that different sections, further separated by blank lines, were written from the perspective of differing authors. But one dimension of content remained constant.

Details, such as numbers of combatants lost or territory taken or estimation of enemy forces slaughtered, were related as cold facts in past tense. As if death and suffering were irrelevant to those who recorded it long ago. The countless dead were of no more consequence than an itemized account of possessions, of no personal value in being lost.

Taken as a whole, in quick estimate, the numbers were staggering . . . unbelievable.

Wynn guessed at the original text these passages had come from, as she and Chap had looked for books that might contain references to the Forgotten History. One in particular had seemed to contain an accounting of past events, like some general's tactical campaign history. Chap advised her to take it for the sheer weight of concise information.

How had her superiors decided which pages to translate first? By sampled content topic? By estimated order in which they'd been written?

She picked up another collection of pages, looking for translator's notes on the text's internal chronology. But even strange dates mentioned were noted as vague or approximate and without correlation. In most cases a time reference wasn't present at all, leaving only a guess concerning the chronology of how one text might fit among the others.

Wynn rubbed her eyes. The elven calendar, based on the seasons, each divided into named thirds, had been taken on 483 years ago, when King Hräthgar had first united territorial clans in the beginnings of Malourné. From that time forward was now known as the Common Era. But how many years, centuries, or more came before that, since the lost time of the Forgotten History? No one knew, not even the elves, the Lhoin'na . . . supposedly.

Any dates mentioned by the ancient authors of these texts would be of little use. There was no point of reference to compare a long-lost calendar system used at that time with the one now part of life in the Numan Lands.

Domin Tilswith, Wynn's old master, believed the war had taken place well over a thousand years ago. No one was certain of this, even among the guild, and the large gap in time made determination of long-past events unverifiable.

And Wynn realized part of why the guild was being so secretive.

Without proof, including time frame, these writings could be dismissed as speculation or a mere collection of accounts from differing periods as well as places. And not from the same war that had devastated the known world.

Varied ideologies and religions, including the major four of the Numan Lands, believed the war never took place. Or if it had, that it wasn't nearly as far-reaching as the catastrophe suggested by the guild. Wynn knew the royal family would take great pains to avoid anything that might cause unrest or discord—or open outrage and conflict. Even if solid proof were established, what could be more threatening than having one's beliefs shown to be in error?

If anyone learned what Wynn believed—what Most Aged Father believed—that the Enemy was returning, even those convinced of the war's magnitude might turn on those who didn't, and in more than just heated disagreement. Fear would spread, and those who clung to unfounded beliefs or even incorrectly reasoned conclusions would in turn look upon others as the carriers of an incurable disease.

Wynn quieted her wandering thoughts. Was this what the undead killer searched for—proof that the enemy was returning? But to what end? She put aside any conclusions. At least now she understood part of High-Tower's and Sykion's fears—as well as il'Sänke's warning.

She began trying to determine which pages or volumes listed in the codex weren't present—the ones stolen by the black figure. She scanned section after section of the codex, taking notes on the breadth of the project. She turned to organizing and checking off volumes and pages of completed work, searching for what was missing.

Within the catacombs, without a window or the sound of city bells, she had no idea how long the task took—but long enough that the twin columns on the pages began to blur before her eyes. She took a pause before continuing.

Of course, she couldn't guess what was in those missing folios, but she could look at adjacent pages and sections that she did find. Perhaps therein was a clue to what the black figure had sought and stolen. She returned to inspecting more pages—and she found a gap.

There were pages listed in the codex as worked upon that weren't in the loose stack in her hands. She flipped back to the last present page before the gap.

She came upon something that made her cold inside.

The page was covered in dots, much of the original being unreadable, though the words could be counted. There were also blanks in the right column for equivalent parts in the left one, indicating a section of text that had so far defied translation. From what Wynn could tell, the original had been written in one or more lost dialects of Sumanese. Of what had been translated, one term appeared a number of times.

in'Ahtäben—the Children.

What children? Whose children? And why the emphasis, as if it were a title? Baffled, she scanned the three pages that followed what was missing and then stopped. Her eyes fixed on another strange phrase within an incomplete sentence.

> *. . . the Night Voice . . . . Beloved . . . of the Children.*

Wynn shifted to the left column of original text rendered in Begaine symbols.

> *. . . . in'Sa'umar . . . . Hkàbêv . . . myi in'Ahtäben. . . .*

At first it didn't seem like the same phrase, but she was reading ancient Sumanese. She'd heard one of the Ancient

Enemy's names spoken in more current Sumanese, as repeated by Magiere and Chap, and its translation had been the same: *il'Samar—the Night Voice . . . in'Sa'umar—the Night Voice.*

By the similar prefix on *in'Ahtäben*, that also had to be a title—the Children. And here was one more title for the Enemy: *Hkàbêv*—Beloved.

Wynn wasn't reading about actual children—they were some group who'd served the Enemy of many names. She began searching for other names or anything concerning who these Children might be. On the very same page, in the left column, she sounded out two Begaine symbols for a name she would never forget.

Li'kän.

The white undead had selected a tin scroll case from her castle's library—the same one that Chane had brought to Wynn. And Wynn found two more names near Li'kän's.

Volyno and Häs'saun.

She didn't know her hands shook until the sheets' upper corners began to shiver. She'd seen these names written on castle walls in the faded black fluids of Li'kän. Three guardian undead had once inhabited that place, but Li'kän was alone when Wynn and her companions had reached the castle.

Wynn read further and came upon a reflexive proper noun. Volyno had written this passage. When she turned to the next sheet, the page's numbering jumped by three.

She stopped, quickly checking her notes, and then scanned the codex for any date on which missing pages or selected passages had been sent out for transcription. When she found it, finally realizing the time frame, Wynn sank into depression.

It was the night Jeremy and Elias had died.

Whatever was missing had been in that stolen folio, and the black figure had willingly killed for it. Wynn returned to the loose stack, reading onward, and found two more strange titles aside from the Children.

The Reverent and the Eaters of Silence.

Upon her return home with the texts, Domin il'Sänke had been asked to extend his visit and assist with any ancient Sumanese dialects found therein. Likely he'd worked on these terms. Unable to stop, she read on and found more proper names scattered throughout the pages.

Jeyretan, Fäzabid, Memaneh, Creif, Uhmgadâ, Sau'ilahk, and more . . .

In places, she could tell where another person was referred to, but next to these were only a blank space or a margin note—"marks or letter system unknown" or "symbol or ideogram unknown." She counted these anyway, making note in her journal. It was impossible to tell if any name belonged to any particular group or none of them at all. But she found two closely positioned near another mention of Li'kän.

Vespana and Ga'hetman.

She didn't like the implication.

In the very next sentence—or fragments of it—the white undead was referred to as "daughter of Beloved."

Wynn froze.

Daughter, as in a child—Li'kän was one of the Children. Vespana and Ga'hetman were mentioned with her as well. And Volyno and Häs'saun had been with her at one time in that ice-bound castle.

The Children—like Li'kän—were all ancient Noble Dead.

"Valhachkasej'â!" Wynn swore in a whisper, more from fright than anger.

Vampires from a thousand or more years ago had served their "Beloved" in a war that erased the world's history. There were five, not one, not Li'kän alone, and that one had survived for so long. . . .

Wynn didn't want to finish that thought.

How many of the other four still walked the world to this day?

A vampire versed in one of the three magics, who had existed for a thousand years, might develop power beyond what any mage could hope for in one lifetime. Perhaps even the power to walk through walls, to become incorporeal at will, and yet physically tear out a city guard's chest.

Was Rodian half-right concerning the black figure? She had even seriously entertained his notion. Was it a mage as well as a vampire—like Chane?

Was it one of the other four among the Children?

Wynn flipped to a blank page in her journal and began writing every name she could find.

She marked the names of five of the Children. The rest remained to be identified as either the Reverent or the Eaters of Silence, or someone separate altogether. She scanned onward, reaching a place where the original text had decayed too much. Only fragments of Volyno's entry remained.

> ... through victory sweet [unknown symbols/letters] .... world in tatters still and .... great numbers of the obedient chattel ..... western force was destroyed. Beloved took refuge ..... the Children divided.

Wynn paused with her quill hanging motionless above her journal.

The Children, the five, divided—what did that mean? Did they become at odds with one another? And why had the Beloved taken refuge, and from what?

Volyno and Häs'saun had gone with Li'kän and the orb into the Pock Peaks, where the castle had been built by minions in that high frozen waste. Wynn knew too well what had become of those "obedient chattel." Magiere had seen hundreds of ancient skeletons, only some of them human, left crouched and curled in obeisance within small stone cubbies—left to starve in the cavern below the castle. The sanctuary they had built housed the orb that Magiere, Leesil, and Chap now attempted to hide somewhere in safety.

But what had happened to Volyno and Häs'saun?

It was hard to imagine that they'd simply left, since Li'kän seemed trapped there. Every time the white undead had tried to do anything, something unknown and unseen had reined her in. In over a thousand years she'd never left that place. Alone for so long, and sinking into her madness, Li'kän had even forgotten the sound of spoken words. It seemed likely that for whatever reason, Volyno and Häs'saun were no more.

And if "divided" did mean "separated," there was still the

question of where Vespana and Ga'hetman had gone. And why decrease their strength in numbers, as well as abandon their master? Three had gone with the orb, so what had the other two done?

And most of all, where had their Beloved gone?

Perhaps these answers were what the black-robed undead was searching for—other ancient servants of the Enemy. Wynn reached a disconnected phrase so puzzling it knocked out all other questions.

. . . . *the anchors of creation* . . .

She checked the left column. Its translated part sounded like some kind of Sumanese, possibly Iyindu, but the rest was missing. If Domin il'Sänke had translated this, she would have to ask him. But when she scanned the rest of the column and looked to the codex for any further reference, she found nothing more. Surely if il'Sänke had any notion of its possible meaning, he would've noted it for others working on translations. With no other texts as old as these ever found, internal referencing was what would be leaned upon most.

Volyno's writing grew more and more sketchy, more broken by untranslated or unreadable pieces. Soon Wynn found it difficult to distinguish between a possible name and just indefinable proper nouns. She did come across a word translated as "priests" near another reference to "those of the Beloved."

She remembered the calcified remains Magiere had spoken of along the curving tunnels and cavern of the orb. Li'kän had walked between those long-dead worshipers in utter disregard. Again Wynn found herself understanding—sharing—the fear that drove Sykion and High-Tower to deception and subterfuge.

Had a dark religion existed behind the force that sought the end to all sentient life?

Wynn didn't care to think how people like Rodian would take that, coupled with an ancient history they denied. Had the Children also been a religious order?

No, not with other groups mentioned. Those ancient

Noble Dead might have been seen as holy, but by mere title, the more likely "priests" were the Reverent. So which of the other names belonged to the third group—the Eaters of Silence? And who or what had they been?

Wynn bit her lower lip in frustration and turned the page. It was the last one in the stack.

She dug through the piles, checking volume numbers for any section that followed, but she never found one. Further work on volume seven hadn't been completed yet.

In the end, she had a list of seventeen names and nine blanks as possible names where the writing systems were unknown to the translators. Of the former, five were the Children of the Beloved—Li'kän, Volyno, Häs'saun, Vespana, and Ga'hetman.

Wynn swallowed hard and then started at a grumbling whine.

"Young Hygeorht!" Tärpodious croaked from the outer room. "If that animal has an accident in my archives, you'll answer for it! It is late for supper already."

Had an entire day slipped by again? Wynn glanced down.

The female looked up, not even raising her head from her paws, and a wave of guilt hit Wynn. Her new companion hadn't gone outside all day.

She restacked all the pages as best she could and gathered her things. About to close her journal, she glanced once more over the names there. The majay-hì finally raised her head and sat up, peering over the tabletop.

"Names and more names." Wynn sighed, carefully stroking the female's head, remembering the day she'd haphazardly named Lily. "And I still don't know what to call you."

A quick chain of images shuffled through her thoughts—Chap alone, then with Lily, their heads touching, and finally the old wolfhound.

Wynn groaned. "Stop that. It doesn't mean anything to me."

But it didn't stop. The images merely slowed in repetition.

She saw Chap leaning into Lily, slowly sliding his head

along hers, as the majay-hì did in memory-speak. This time, when the wolfhound's image rose in Wynn's mind, it flickered with the image of a charcoal-colored pup tussling with her siblings.

Again, and again, until the image of Chap speaking to Lily faded into the mother's memory of a dark-coated daughter—now sitting beside Wynn. That last memory wasn't Wynn's own.

Wynn slipped from the chair, kneeling before Chap's daughter. She had no experience in memory-speak, so it had taken time for the meaning to finally sink in. Another instant of looking into the female's yellow-flecked eyes finally brought clarity.

Wynn didn't need to find a name.

Chap had already supplied one, taught to Lily, and through her to their daughter, in a way without words. A name called from his own memory of an aging wolfhound, honoring a simple animal who'd once saved him.

Wynn carefully put her hands around the face of Chap's daughter.

"Shade," she whispered.

The dog didn't respond in any way. Wynn relaxed all conscious thought to let her own memory of the wolfhound rise. As an answer, she received a warm, wet lap of tongue across her face.

It was going to take time and effort before they understood each other better.

With that, she gathered her things to leave, and Shade followed her into the outer chamber.

"Master Tärpodious, will everything be kept as I've arranged it? I didn't know if the materials would be secured for the night or left out for me."

For a moment his wrinkled face softened, perhaps at the concern and diligence of her studies. He was an archivist, after all, dedicating his life to the catalogues of knowledge. Then he scowled at the "wolf's" presence.

"I'll return it myself . . . to its safe place," he said. "But I'll pay heed to your arrangements when it is brought back out tomorrow."

"Thank you," Wynn said, but she wondered where the translations were being kept.

"Come, Shade," she said. "We'll have to hurry if you're going out to the gardens before the portcullis closes for the night. I don't think anyone would appreciate your relieving yourself in the courtyard."

She hurried for the stairs, and Shade trotted beside her without being urged. As they neared the side arch of the common hall, Wynn began to fret. Better to take the main passage around to the front than go through there again. Before she even passed the entrance, Domin High-Tower came thumping down the passage from the other way.

"Oh, perfect," Wynn grumbled, quickly grabbing Shade's scruff.

No doubt the domin had heard about her new companion and came to put an end to such nonsense. But High-Tower barely glanced at Shade. His brow wrinkled, and he seemed agitated.

"What?" she asked.

"Nikolas is awake and . . ." High-Tower didn't finish, and his frown turned to a frustrated glower. "Captain Rodian has arrived . . . but Nikolas is asking for you."

CHAPTER 15

Rodian followed a brown-robed apprentice through the guild. As they reached the hospice ward, he spotted High-Tower and Wynn hurrying down the corridor behind him. High-Tower only nodded in greeting, but Rodian barely noticed. He was staring at the tall, leggy wolf beside Wynn.

It looked exactly like the one from the fiasco outside the Upright Quill.

"Back to your studies," High-Tower told Rodian's escort, and the apprentice scurried off.

Rodian turned his attention to Wynn. "You are a never-ending source of complications."

"I'll explain later," she said quickly. "I'm here to see Nikolas first."

Wynn pushed through the door before he could object, and the wolf stayed at her side.

Rodian followed. Indeed, Wynn would do a great amount of explaining at the earliest opportunity.

High-Tower was last to enter the long room with four narrow beds. A small table stood pushed against the back wall, with shelves above filled with glass vessels of herbs, powders, and other concoctions. Nikolas was in the first bed, and an aged man with bony features and a brown robe leaned over him. But the attendant straightened when he saw the visitors.

His astonished gaze fixed on the wolf, but at a shake of High-Tower's head, the other sage said nothing.

"Captain," Wynn said politely, "this is Domin Bitworth. He has been caring for Nikolas."

Rodian merely nodded and looked down at the young man lying on the cot, conscious at last.

Nikolas's hair was slightly laced with gray strands, but some color had returned to his face. He looked thin and haggard. Wynn settled on the bed's edge.

"I'm glad to see you awake."

The wolf paced over beside her, sniffing the blanket. To Rodian's surprise, no one stopped it. But Nikolas's eyes widened in fright. He weakly pulled up his legs beneath the blankets, shrinking back against the short headboard.

"It's all right," Wynn assured him, placing a hand on his arm. "This is Shade. She's a majay-hì, not a wolf."

Rodian didn't know what she was talking about, but he noted Domin Bitworth's stunned side glance at High-Tower. Typically, the dwarf just scowled and sighed.

Nikolas remained in retreat, but panic faded from his sickly expression.

With that, Wynn placed her hands beside the wolf's face and gazed into its eyes. The animal froze and then turned its head toward Nikolas.

Terror returned to Nikolas's expression as he noticed everyone in the room, particularly Rodian.

"They won't tell me anything," he said to Wynn. "Where are Miriam and Dâgmund?"

Color drained from Wynn's face as she glanced at High-Tower and Bitworth. High-Tower swallowed with difficulty, and Wynn finally looked to Rodian.

"I'm sorry," Rodian said to Nikolas. "I couldn't reach them in time."

Nikolas stared up, expressionless. He doubled over, sickened again, as if whatever had taken his strength in the alley assaulted him once more.

Rodian felt responsible.

No matter what the premins and domins had done—or not done—it was his duty, as captain of the Shyldfälches, to keep the citizens of the king's city from harm. And he could have, if the sages had informed him that they'd sent out another folio.

"The captain brought you to us as quickly as he could," Wynn added.

"Enough," Bitworth warned, stepping closer.

The wolf shifted away from him toward the bed's head with a growl.

"He has only just awakened, and you'll wear him out," Bitworth warned.

"Yes, yes," High-Tower intervened, and looked down at Nikolas. "Are you up to talking a little? The captain needs to know what you remember from that night."

Nikolas was still shaken by the loss of his companions. His brown eyes shifted so erratically that Rodian couldn't tell what the young man was looking at or for. Domin Bitworth gently waved High-Tower aside and stepped around the bed. He helped Nikolas take a sip of water from a mug.

"Anything might help," Rodian urged, feeling harsh for doing this so abruptly, but the sooner the better.

"Tall . . . big . . . so black," Nikolas whispered, and his haunted eyes looked only at Wynn. "A cowled robe . . . and a cloak that . . . moved . . . climbing the walls. It chased us into the alley . . . then Miriam started screaming . . . like Sherie."

"Sherie?" Wynn whispered.

Nikolas didn't seem to hear her. He trembled, staring blankly at nothing. Suddenly the frail apprentice cowered and pressed his hands over his ears, trying to block out a sound no one else could hear.

"Who is Sherie?" Rodian asked quietly.

Wynn shook her head slowly, still watching Nikolas in wary puzzlement. When Rodian looked to High-Tower, the domin shook his head as well. Bitworth knelt beside the bed.

"Nikolas," he whispered, "try to focus on the alley, nothing else."

The young man's eyes wandered. "I tried to keep her in front of me as we ran away, but it . . . he . . . was everywhere . . . in front . . . behind . . . everywhere in the *forest*."

Bitworth sighed. "He is slipping again. Some other memory keeps intruding."

Rodian only half understood. Ignoring mention of a forest, he kept his voice calm but firm.

"Nikolas, you weren't far from the scribe shop when I found you. When did you first notice the black-robed figure following you? Did it say anything?"

Nikolas blinked, awareness perhaps sharpening again. "We were walking, and it was just there in front of us, in the street . . . not moving, not a sound. We turned back, and it was there again, but closer. It reached for Miriam. Dâgmund jerked me back and shoved me into the alley. . . . I ran . . . and heard Sherie scream."

Again, some other name in the place of Miriam's.

"It got so cold . . . between the trees," Nikolas whispered. "And the black . . . it grabbed Sherie, and she stopped screaming. Karl tried to reach her . . . but his father grabbed the folio. That hand . . . fingers all wrapped in black cloth . . . it went straight through her and closed on the folio."

Rodian exhaled in exhaustion. Unknown names kept bouncing around in Nikolas's head in place of Miriam and Dâgmund, along with someone's father cast as the black figure.

Bitworth rose and stepped to the bed's foot.

"I've heard pieces of this before," the healer whispered, "when Nikolas rambled in his sleep. It happens sometimes when the mind suffers a severe trauma. Some other overwhelming past event can become mixed with the more recent one. Until Nikolas regains his will and full awareness, he cannot separate the cause of one trauma from another of the past."

Rodian rubbed his forehead. The splinter of a headache felt like it would cleave his skull in half. Wynn looked at Nikolas in sympathy, with her hand on the wolf's head, and Rodian stepped back.

He needed information to catch a murderer—or murderers—and all he'd gotten was more senseless confusion.

Sykion and High-Tower wouldn't face up to what was happening, or they tried to get around him in their own scheming. Bitworth's assessment of Nikolas was no help.

And now Wynn brought a wild animal into the guild, and no one seemed to object.

Rodian pulled his hand down his face. May the Blessed Trinity of Sentience preserve him, for he was standing in a madhouse.

He couldn't go to the royals with more nonsense, but when he looked down, Wynn was glaring at him. The anger in her face sparked his own resentment.

She couldn't possibly expect him to believe there was anything of note in Nikolas's rambling. High-Tower appeared just as uncomfortable with Nikolas's account as he was.

"Did Domin il'Sänke leave the guild at all that night?" Rodian asked.

High-Tower lifted his head, puzzlement disturbing his scowl, but Wynn cut in first.

"Why do you keep asking that?"

"Was he here the whole time?" Rodian demanded, ignoring her, and High-Tower hesitated. The pause was the only confirmation he needed, but the dwarf finally answered.

"Domin il'Sänke was handling a private task for me that night. It has nothing to do with what happened, but I can attest that he was engaged in guild business."

Rodian clenched his jaw—more evasions. He would get no rational help from these sages, even to save them from themselves. He started for the door but halted at another sharp rumble from the wolf.

Pawl a'Seatt stood in the hospice's doorway. Small Imaret peeked around his side, bearing an ink smudge on her brown cheek. Master a'Seatt's expression was flat and cool, but he was intently fixed upon either Wynn or Nikolas.

"Forgive us," the scribe master said. "Imaret wished to see how Nikolas fared."

The wolf's rumble shifted into an open growl, and Rodian glanced back.

Wynn reached for the animal. "Stop that," she said to it. "These are friends."

But the wolf remained tensely focused on the doorway, still growling.

Rodian followed its gaze back to Pawl a'Seatt, who now watched the wolf in turn.

High-Tower cocked his large head, and Bitworth's face filled with alarm. Even Wynn grew concerned. She raised a hand before the wolf's face, perhaps commanding it to stay. The animal held its place, its noise lowering to a rumble.

Pawl a'Seatt's brow wrinkled only slightly.

"What are you doing here?" Rodian asked bluntly. The shop's scribes had been laboring all day inside the guild, but masters didn't engage in the general work.

"I came to check on my staff," Pawl answered calmly. "And to see them safely home."

"I've already assigned men for that," Rodian replied.

"Forgive me, but your guards have not always been effective."

Rodian's throat tightened. He couldn't argue with that, though he failed to see how a scribe master could do better. Something else was wrong here. If a'Seatt overheard any of Nikolas's jumbled recollections, what had caught him so much that he'd stood silent in the doorway without announcing himself?

"Come, Imaret," Pawl a'Seatt said. "We must gather the others. Perhaps your friend will be better tomorrow."

Rodian almost stopped the scribe master, but he could think of nothing specific to ask. And would he receive an honest answer? Hardly. Truth had become as intangible as the black figure murdering sages for folios.

"That is enough for today," Bitworth said. "Everyone out. Nikolas needs rest."

High-Tower nodded agreement and gestured toward the door. Rodian shook his head in frustration and stepped out. But he had one other matter to address.

Wynn must have seen her coveted translations by now.

"Walk me out," he said as she stepped into the passage, and his tone implied that it wasn't a request.

"She's not had supper," High-Tower growled.

Rodian wasn't deceived by false concern. The domin simply wanted to keep Wynn away from him. He didn't care.

"I'll return directly," Wynn said, and then glanced back through the door at Bitworth. "Thank you for caring for Nikolas."

The wolf stalked out behind her, passing High-Tower with a quick snort. The dwarf rolled his eyes, grumbling under his breath as he stomped away. Rodian gestured down the hall as he stepped onward.

"How did you come by that animal?"

Wynn fell into step beside him. "She found me," she answered, as if she'd told him all that was necessary.

There had to be more, but at the moment he had other pressing concerns to address. She looked a little weary, with ink stains on her right thumb and forefinger. Did these sages do nothing but study and write? No wonder they were so misguided.

No, that wasn't fair, for he knew what she'd been doing all day. He'd had a hand in her gaining access to the translations—and he expected to be compensated.

And Rodian's attention drifted to the wolf or . . . what had she called it?

It was taller than any he'd seen during his military assignment in the eastern reaches. Packs sometimes raided farm livestock in deep winter, but this one . . .

The animal's head reached Wynn's hip, and it walked with her in some tame mockery of its true wild nature. How— why—was this beast even tolerated by her superiors?

When they finally reached the courtyard, Snowbird saw him from the front gates and whinnied. The wolf stopped, ears pricking up, and Rodian eyed it warily, ready to cut it down if it went for his horse. But the beast remained quietly at Wynn's side.

"What did you learn today?" he asked. "Anything rational that might help?"

Wynn just stood there, gazing across the courtyard and down the gatehouse tunnel at Snowbird. Rodian's anger got the better of him.

"Someone wants something here badly enough to kill for it," he nearly shouted. "And you saw that black-robed man outside of a'Seatt's shop. Whoever it is has knowledge of the folios' movements . . . and can read your sages' script. How many people does that leave, Wynn? Not many, from my count."

"You're not hunting a living man!" she responded harshly. "And you'll never stop it through your usual means. If you truly wish to protect your people and the sages, then you'd best alter both your strategy and thought ... immediately."

Angry as he was, Rodian was still taken aback. Wynn breathed hard and calmed slightly.

"Talk to Nikolas again," she said, "when he is more himself. Talk to il'Sänke—he has knowledge that you don't. Talk to *me* ... when you're actually ready to listen."

He stood dumbfounded at her outburst. Of all the things he'd expected, a torrent of evasive nonsense wasn't among them. She now sounded like one of her superiors.

"What is in those texts?" he demanded.

Wynn shut her eyes tightly for an instant, as if the answer wasn't something she wanted to think on. Rodian almost faltered at whatever weight seemed to press her down.

"More things you wouldn't believe," she whispered, "especially from me."

Rodian's anger hardened like ice. He'd thought her sensible, possibly his only ally within the guild, but they'd gotten to her—High-Tower, Sykion, possibly even il'Sänke. What had they demanded in exchange for placating her desire for the texts and avoiding her claim in court? Or perhaps they were right, and she was so addle-minded that she couldn't see he needed her help.

"Faith that denies fact isn't faith," she whispered suddenly. "It's only fanaticism. Even if I could tell you, I won't batter myself against that wall inside your head. Tear it down yourself, if you've any real interest in the truth."

Wynn walked away with the wolf toward the keep's main doors, leaving Rodian standing alone.

Anger spent, Wynn felt numb as she shoved through the main doors. Rodian wasn't going to acknowledge the truth.

When she reached the common hall's main archway, she held out one hand, palm open, trying to make Shade wait.

"I'll be right back with dinner."

She backed away into the hall as Shade watched her, but

the dog did stay. Wynn hurried to ladle a bowl of soup, and then plopped a joint of roasted mutton on a spare wooden plate. A warm fire blazed in the hearth, and there were few people left in the hall. Wynn suddenly didn't want to sit locked in her own room.

And then Shade appeared at her side.

Either ignoring or not understanding that she shouldn't come in, the dog looked up at Wynn, then raised her nose, sniffing at the plate.

Heads turned their way, and Wynn almost fled the hall. But Shade kept poking at her arm and huffing. Wynn took a long breath. Trying not to meet any eyes, she strode toward the hearth. She settled at its right end upon the ledge, far from where most people sat at the tables.

Wynn set the wooden plate on the floor, and Shade began chomping on mutton. She set aside her bowl and stepped over to retrieve a water pitcher from the nearest table, along with an empty mug and bowl. Three initiates were still cleaning up, but none came to clear the tables nearest Wynn. She heard frantic whispering that grew louder as she headed back to the hearth.

"There's no such thing! It's just a wolf."

"Kyne, don't get stupid!"

"Let go!"

"That thing could eat your whole head."

"Oh yeah, well . . . you're just a big, ignorant coward. . . . Let go of me!"

Wynn kept her head down, focusing on her bowl as she ate.

"Is she really . . . a majay-hì?"

Wynn flinched at the surprisingly close voice and looked up straight into an ivory face covered in freckles.

The girl in an initiate's tan robe and smudged apron couldn't have been more than thirteen. Her wonder-struck eyes peered cautiously at Shade, now with the mutton pulled off the plate and trapped between teeth and forepaws.

Wynn swallowed a piece of carrot. "How do you know that word?"

"Reading," the girl answered, still staring at Shade.

Wynn almost smiled. Now, here was a cathologer in the making standing before her.

"Can I pet her?" the girl asked.

Wynn glanced down. Shade had stopped chewing, her unblinking eyes locked on the girl. Wynn didn't know if Shade would ever submit to being touched by anyone else, but she preferred not to hurt the girl's feelings.

"She's still getting used to things here," Wynn answered. "Maybe later."

The girl's expression fell, as overcome fear washed away in disappointment. She backed up and scurried off.

Looking down into her spoon, Wynn grimaced at the irony of worrying about a young initiate's feelings. Sages were dying over the ancient texts she'd brought here, but she still thought upon the wonder of one small girl. Had she ever been so naïve herself?

Probably.

Shade renewed chewing her mutton, all the way down to the bone, and then rose on all fours to lap water from the bowl.

Wynn's dinner became as tasteless as sawdust. Reaching out, she touched Shade's back, allowing a memory to surface of them sitting on the floor of her room that morning.

Shade raised her head with pricked ears and whined. Perhaps privacy seemed welcome to her as well.

Wynn picked up the bowl and plate and left them on a nearby table. Shade slipped ahead of her, straight toward the main archway, and Wynn hurried to catch up. Out in the courtyard the dog appeared to remember the way perfectly, heading for the south dormitory's door. But on the way up the stairs, Shade startled several apprentices. They all flattened against the upper landing's walls.

Shade padded past, giving them no notice, and Wynn followed quickly, not looking at them either.

She breathed a sigh as she reached her room. But when she slipped inside and Shade pushed in around her robe's skirt, Wynn kicked a folded slip of paper lying on the floor. Her name was written on its outer fold.

Someone had pushed it under her door—a common

practice when a message was clearly addressed and the re-
cipient couldn't be found. Leaning down, she picked it up
and unfolded it. Her breath caught when she saw the handwriting and the message written in Belaskian.

> *I need to know you are all right. I am at an inn called
> Nattie's House, at the corner of Starling and Twine streets
> on the outskirts of the Graylands Empire. Come, if you
> can, and bring me a cloak. If not, send me word now.*

Wynn held on to the paper as her concern grew. What
was Chane thinking? If anyone had sneaked a peek at the
note . . .

She didn't want to think of what might've happened
from that. At least he hadn't been badly injured or was well
enough to write. Yet he'd told her where he was, after insist-
ing it was better she didn't know.

What had she done to him with the sun crystal?

"Shade," she called. "We must go out."

The dog poked her head out from beneath the table-desk.
For an instant Wynn considered showing her a memory of
Chane—and then quickly thought better of it.

What might Shade sense—or see—in such a memory?
Somehow the majay-hì hadn't picked up Chane's undead
nature last night. Strange as that was, Wynn had no wish to
give this natural hunter of the undead any more knowledge
of Chane than was necessary. Not yet.

But she couldn't leave Shade locked in her room. If the
majay-hì became agitated, and someone came at any sound
of commotion, it would just cause more trouble. She would
have to figure out how to keep Shade away from Chane
when the time came.

Wynn grabbed her cloak and pulled the scroll case from
its deep inner pocket. She still didn't know if the black
figure had come after it or her last night. But leaving the
scroll behind seemed a wiser choice. She stuffed the case
deep under her mattress, bracing it against one of the bed's
support boards, and then grabbed the staff from the corner
beyond her desk.

She paused, staring at the leather sheath protecting the crystal.

If Domin il'Sänke found out, after her renewed promise, she might never learn how to use it correctly. But what else could she do? She couldn't go out without some means of defense. Though she still didn't know for certain what the black figure was, it had vanished after the crystal flashed. Sunlight drove all vampires into hiding.

One more thought occurred to her.

She dashed to her trunk, pulling out a tiny jar of healing salve. Would it even work on Chane? Either way, it wouldn't hurt to try. Then she spotted Magiere's old dagger tucked in the chest's side—given to Wynn as a gift.

Wynn stared at it. She'd used it more than once, even against the undead, and sometimes with disastrous results. Still, she couldn't ignore anything that might help keep her alive, and she picked it up.

Shade slipped under Wynn's arm and clamped her jaws over the dagger's sheath. At the brush of the dog's muzzle against Wynn's hand, an image erupted in her head and consumed her.

She saw the black figure.

Like a cloth-draped column of solidified night, it slipped straight through a building's back wall.

Wynn was disoriented in fright, and had no idea where she was in that memory. She seemed to be looking down an alley behind that place, but from a lower height, as if she knelt upon the filthy cobblestones. The noise of wood cracking, glass breaking, and other racket erupted from within the building.

And then everything in the alley suddenly raced by. She bolted, swift and low, along the alley floor, charging by the building and out the alley's far end. Swerving through the empty street, she rounded the city block to its front side. There she slowed, creeping along the buildings, finally coming to a stop. Above the peeling door of a garish and weathered shop, Wynn saw a worn painted sign.

Shilwise's Gild and Ink—the scriptorium where a folio had been left overnight and stolen.

She was crouched two shops down from it, but the scribe shop was now silent.

Until the weathered front door exploded outward in the night.

Shattered wood shards scattered over the porch and street as Wynn cowered back. The black figure slid out through the opening, a leather folio clutched in its cloth-wrapped hand.

It didn't waver in Wynn's sight. This was Shade's own memory.

The figure looked as solid and real as anything along the street. But when it turned, gliding along the buildings, it passed straight through a lantern post, as if the stout iron pole wasn't even there.

The memory's intensity softened.

Wynn stared at Shade, eye-to-eye, with the sheathed blade still in the dog's jaws. Had Shade been hunting the black figure, as well as watching over her all this time?

And on the night Rodian had sprung his trap, the figure had slid out through the front wall of the Upright Quill—but pulled the folio through a window. Perhaps, by whatever magic, it couldn't pass the folio through something solid.

But why destroy the front door of the Gild and Ink? With no one about, it could've simply slipped through the wall and pulled the folio through an easily breakable window. Or better yet, it could've found some less telltale way to get out, with no one around to see it.

No one but Shade, that was.

Wynn was at a loss for what any of this meant, nor why Shade had shown her this now. It had been a clear image of the undead breaking out of a shop, appearing solid, yet it had walked through an iron pole.

This attempt to talk in memories was frustrating, but it was all Wynn had. Shade was trying to tell her something about the black figure. How many Noble Dead, or even other undead, had Wynn known of since she first met Magiere, Leesil, and Chap? She had to at least eliminate the obvious, and put her hand on the side of Shade's neck.

Wynn relaxed her mind, letting memories rise, but careful not to let any of Chane come clearly to mind. There was Vordana, Welstiel, and the memory of Magiere speaking of her undead father, Brien Massing. The first two were mages as well as Noble Dead.

Shade growled and looked away with a huff.

Wynn exhaled sharply. Shade's reaction wasn't like Chap's clear usage of two barks for "no," but it was plain enough. So now what? The only other undead that Wynn had encountered were Ubâd's animated corpses and enslaved spirits.

Shade dropped the blade and grabbed Wynn's wrist in her jaws. Rapidly alternating memories filled Wynn's head—her own memories. . . .

The ghost of a murdered girl who served the necromancer . . .

Then the black figure on the night Shade had come to Wynn's aid . . .

Black figure and ghost child alternated over and over.

Wynn didn't like what this implied.

"A spirit?" she whispered, remembering the ghost child who'd once spoken with that vile necromancer's own voice.

Shade gently tightened her grip on Wynn's wrist.

Wynn looked at the dog and suddenly wished she still had her doubts. It would've been far less unsettling to cling to her notion of an ancient Noble Dead mage grown powerful over a thousand years.

How could a spirit, as much as it might pass through a wall, pick up a folio in its hand, rip out a city guard's chest, and look as solid and real as a cloaked man? And why hadn't Shade simply shown her ghosts in the first place?

The latter answer came quickly. Because Shade had never seen a ghost, until that memory rose in Wynn's mind when she'd thought of other forms of undead.

Shade couldn't dig for memories but only recall ones she'd seen surface in someone else's thoughts. And she'd never seen a ghost herself, because the undead couldn't enter the an'Cróan's elven homeland—Shade's homeland.

Wynn glanced at Magiere's useless dagger lying on the

floor between her and Shade. And again she wished Shade was wrong.

This black spirit took lives, fed upon the living. Only Noble Dead did this to maintain their fully sentient existence, versus ghosts, mindless corpses, and such lesser undead.

Wynn felt even worse.

Was this thing—spirit—a new form of a Noble Dead? Vampires were Noble Dead, the terms merely interchangeable.

With no more time to ponder the rest of what Shade had shown her, Wynn dropped Magiere's blade into the chest; then she hesitated again. Rodian still had men outside the portcullis. Could she be lucky enough to slip by them again, this time with a large wolf? And she saw her old clothing—elven clothing, weathered and travel-worn—in the bottom of the chest.

At the very least, it was better not to be spotted beyond the guild grounds in a sage's robe. She quickly changed clothing and pulled on her old cloak.

Wynn peeked into the passage outside her room. Spotting no one, she slipped out with Shade. She checked again before they stepped into the courtyard and then hurried across—not to the keep's main doors, but to the building on the northern side, where supplies and kitchen stores were kept.

She carefully opened a door there and, finding the storeroom dark, slipped out her cold lamp crystal. With one quick stroke along her tunic's front, the crystal glowed no more than a low candle. Rows of barrels, crates, and sacks of dried goods filled the space, but she urged Shade in and turned immediately to the right. Through another door she entered the back scullery behind the kitchen.

Stacked, emptied crates and bottles waited to be taken away. And there also, spare cloaks hung on wall pegs, for anyone who had to take milk bottles or refuse out. She grabbed the largest one and pulled it on over her own. Although it was too big for her, this was easier than carrying it, and the extra bulk might further disguise her. When she reached the courtyard again, still trying to think of some way to get Shade out through the library, another notion came to her.

Pawl a'Seatt had come to escort his staff home from working all day in the guild. But had they already left, or were they still inside? Either way, what Wynn had in mind was a gamble. She hoped none of the guards outside had ever seen her before.

Wynn pocketed the crystal, smothering its light, and crouched before Shade.

She didn't know how to explain with memories that Shade needed to keep quiet. She reached out carefully for Shade's nose—again hoping she didn't get bitten—and clamped her hand over the dog's muzzle. She quickly covered her own mouth in like fashion.

Shade let out a brief grumble and fell silent. Wynn hoped that meant the dog understood.

She headed down the gatehouse tunnel with Shade padding behind her. Before she was close enough to touch the closed portcullis, someone shifted beyond it.

In the light of the outer torches, a bearded face leaned close between the stout bars. He wore the red tabard of Rodian's men and held the shaft of a polearm in one hand.

"What's this?" the man demanded. "It's after dark ... orders are that no one goes out."

"Do I look like a sage?" Wynn answered, trying to sound indignant. "I'm with Master a'Seatt, from the Upright Quill."

The man lifted his head, looking away, and Wynn lost sight of his face.

"He already left," another voice outside answered.

The first guard peered in again. "Where were you?"

"Domin High-Tower had a fit about some mislaid notes," Wynn answered, and sighed as deeply as she could. "I got stuck finding them for him."

The bearded guard scowled, but he appeared more annoyed than suspicious.

"Open the damn gate!" Wynn snapped.

His eyes widened. "Girl, you'd better—"

"Come on!" Wynn cut in. "I'm tired, I haven't had supper, and I've been dealing with stuffy, petty little scholars all day. Or do you want to tell my employer—and your captain—why I was stuck in here all night?"

The guard let out a long hissing breath and vanished from the space in the portcullis.

Wynn's stomach clenched. She was stuck. They were just going to ignore her.

"Take it up!" someone shouted.

The gatehouse tunnel filled with the racket of chains and gears as the portcullis began to rise. Wynn tried to remain still and not duck under and bolt out. She stepped onward only when the way was fully open.

"What is that?" one guard barked.

She was only three steps down the outer path to the bailey gate when she had to stop and look back. Both guards had their long halberds lowered, the wide head blades aimed at Shade.

"A wolf?" one guard uttered.

The only thing Wynn could think of was another insult.

"Oh, good, you've got eyes ... very useful, since you're standing watch."

"Watch your little tongue!" the second guard warned. "What's a wolf doing inside the guild?"

"Domin Parisean said it was supposed to walk with me," Wynn countered, "since I missed my escort."

"A wolf? What do you take me for?"

"What do you expect?" Wynn snarled back. "All the nonsense in there, you wouldn't believe it ... I don't! But you think I'm gonna argue?"

With that she turned away, walking steadily down the path as Shade trotted out ahead. But Wynn didn't feel steady.

She was shaking, waiting to be grabbed from behind. She was still shaking when she reached the gate and stepped out onto the Old Bailey Road.

And no one followed.

Wynn ran a hand over Shade's silky ears as they set out for the Graylands Empire. How she would get both of them back inside the guild was something she didn't care to think about just yet.

*   *   *

Cringing in bed, Chane cursed his weakness, and another wave of anxiety choked him.

Pain had beaten him down, and he could not banish it. He had finally succumbed and sent a message to Wynn.

Slipping it along with two silver pennies under the inn-keeper's door, he had then rushed back to his room before he was seen. Not long after, the reality of what he had done caught up to him. And fear became companion to the pain.

How could he have drawn Wynn out alone into the night? Or would she just send a reply? No, she would come.

"You coward!" he hissed at himself.

If he sent another message telling her not to come, it might not reach her in time. And he needed to know if she had recovered from whatever had made her collapse. There were also questions about the Suman who had appeared from nowhere to carry her off.

Chane sat up, groaned, and struck the sulfur stick on the stool to light his one candle.

He had fed on a blacksmith working late the night before, but that one fresh life had not been enough to fully heal him. The burns on his hands were still severe, though he had carefully peeled away flecks of charred skin. The ones on his face felt worse. If not for the cloak's hood shielding his hair, he would have lost some of that as well.

His shirtsleeves and one side of his cloak had caught fire from his own flesh. Tearing charred cloth from his forearms had been excruciating. He had an extra shirt, though he was not wearing it. The touch of the cloth on his wounds was too much. But he possessed no other cloak. Without one he could not hunt effectively, as the sight of him would shock his prey into flight and cries before he could close for a kill.

Chane had never been in such a state, never needed help like this—and he had no one to trust except Wynn.

A soft knock sounded at his door.

Chane could not separate shame, relief, and fear.

"Wynn?" he whispered.

"Yes. The innkeeper sent me up."

Shame and fear grew—one for calling her here and the

other at the thought of her looking upon him. But he was no longer alone in his suffering.

He lunged for the door and whimpered as he gripped the handle with his burned hand. When he cracked the door, he saw the charcoal-colored majay-hì.

Wynn pushed in past him, and the dog followed. Chane quickly shut the door, retreating to the wall beyond it and lowering his head. The one candle barely lit the room from the other end near the bed. It was enough for Chane to see, with his sight opened wide, but he cowered back as far as he could from its light.

Wynn whipped off one cloak and tossed it on the bed, along with a staff, its upper end covered in a leather sheath. She glanced at him, about to untie a second cloak beneath the first, but her fingers stopped with the strings pulled out straight.

A shudder ran through her when she peered at him.

"Oh," she whispered. "I . . . ah, no!"

He must look worse than he realized.

"It will pass," he rasped, and then cringed. He had become accustomed to the sound of his maimed voice, but hearing it when he spoke to her made him hate it more.

"I should not have asked you to come," he whispered.

The majay-hì began sniffing sharply, watching him. Its jowls curled.

"Stop it," Wynn said, sweeping a hand before the dog's nose.

When she looked back to Chane, her mouth opened. A frown passed briefly over her face, and her lips closed, possibly in some abandoned question she decided not to ask.

She pointed to the bed. "Sit down."

Chane stepped closer, and the dog did growl. Wynn flinched at a clearer sight of him, and a flicker of fright rose as her gaze shifted rapidly between him and the dog. He settled on the bed's edge, loathing himself for the relief her presence brought him.

Wynn gasped softly. "Your back! Did that happen last night?"

It took an instant before he understood. She had never

seen him without a shirt, and his back was covered in white scars.

"No, those are old," he said. "From . . . before."

This was not the time or place to tell her of his life before death, or about his father. Changing the subject, he gestured at the staff lying behind him on the bed.

"Is that what you carried last night?"

Wynn remained silent too long. When Chane finally glanced up, she averted her eyes. She began digging in the pocket of her yellow tunic.

"Without Magiere or Chap," she said, "I needed my own defense."

So it was the same staff—and under the leather sheath was the searing crystal.

"Where did you get it?"

"Our guild alchemists make certain things, such as the cold lamp crystals," she answered, her tone careful and matter-of-fact. It was obvious she did not want to say much about it. "I'm still learning to use it properly," she added.

Chane considered himself intelligent, though only moderately skilled in conjury, but to create or even conceive of a crystal that carried light that burned like the sun . . .

There were moments when Wynn still astonished him. What the making of the crystal had taken was beyond what he could imagine—much like most of Welstiel's items.

She drew a small ceramic jar from inside her pocket. "A healing salve," she explained.

"That will not help . . . me."

"You're suffering," she said bluntly, and knelt down. "It may still numb the pain."

Chane kept quiet, fearing she might vanish. It was hard to believe she was here, tending to his comfort. Only the pain seemed truly real. The rest felt as though one of his fantasies harbored over the last year had suddenly swelled into a full delusion.

Her light brown hair hung in loose wisps, sticking to one olive cheek at the corner of her small mouth. Candlelight warmed her brown eyes as she reached for his right hand resting on his knee. Her eyes flickered briefly to his bare chest, and he wished he had donned his spare shirt. Wynn's fingers hung for a moment above his hand.

"This may hurt," she said. "I didn't mean to injure you. I was trying to drive off that . . . thing, just before Domin il'Sänke appeared."

Wynn slowly applied salve to Chane's right hand. Discomfort heightened under the delicate pressure, but he did not care.

"Il'Sänke?" he echoed. "The one who carried you off?"

"Yes, and—"

"And he's a mage."

Wynn glanced up. "Yes."

"Perhaps the one who created your crystal?"

Wynn frowned. "He's the only one who believes that we're dealing with an undead, besides you . . . and Shade."

The dog behind Wynn, so akin to Chap, sniffed at him. Her ears flattened as her jowls twitched.

It would sense nothing of his nature—not while he wore the ring. Likely the female smelled that he was not *right*, or at least was not like other people. Chane wanted to ask Wynn about the animal, but the mention of the Suman brought back images of the night before.

The black figure attacking Wynn, the dog trying to protect her, the flash of the crystal's light.

Chane flinched. Wynn jerked her fingers from a spot of raw skin on his wrist, where he had ripped away a charred sleeve.

"Sorry," she whispered.

But her voice sounded distant, as if he were some stranger she tended to. She leaned back to dip her fingers in the salve jar on the floor and looked about his small attic room.

The shabby walls, the slanting ceiling below the roof, the stool for a table, and the dusty, chipped water basin . . .

Chane was not accustomed to embarrassment. The son of a nobleman in life, he had lived in a lavish manor, worn fine clothes, and had even educated himself beyond what most would gain—beyond what most gentry thought was worthwhile. Now he lived—existed—in squalor, with little more than his studies to distract him.

For once he had no one else to blame, not even Welstiel.

Wynn began gently reapplying salve, working around the brass ring on his left hand without seeming to notice it. Then he realized the sting in his right hand was beginning to dull. The ointment might not heal him, but something in it still affected his dead flesh. He loosely closed his right hand, and the pain barely increased.

"Have you learned anything about the scroll?" he asked.

Wynn's expression shifted with a hint of interest. "No, I haven't had time. I was in the catacombs, studying translated portions of the texts. By evening I began to figure out which sections of the translations had been stolen."

He froze, for her words confused him on several levels.

"You have had no access before? You brought those texts back—they are yours."

Wynn sighed. Picking up the salve jar, she stood and began dabbing at his face.

"It's complicated . . . but no, not until today. Only masters and domins working on the project are allowed access. There is precedence for this decision."

She sounded defensive, even resentful. This was a sensitive subject, so he did not press for more.

"Do you have any idea what is in the missing pages?" he asked.

She stopped dabbing, and her eyes drifted.

"Li'kän's wall writings mentioned two companions—Volyno and Häs'saun. I don't know what became of them, but I read some translations that came just before one set of missing pages. . . ."

She told him of ancient undead, like the white woman with strangely shaped eyes in the castle of the Pock Peaks. And of something called "Beloved," among other names, that might have been what had been whispered to Welstiel and sent Magiere her dreams of that castle. And also of how those undead had "divided."

Chane wondered at those other names Wynn mentioned. Did others like the white woman still roam free in the world after centuries?

Wynn paused, lost in thought, and then looked intently down at Chane.

"Did Welstiel ever speak to you about his patron . . . the thing in his dreams? Magiere suspected something was guiding him."

Chane shook his head. "I know only that someone whispered to him in dormancy, perhaps telling him where to go. But in the way we wandered, I believe he was not told much. He was obsessed with herding Magiere ahead of him, as if he needed her. When you and yours entered elven land, I think he tried to turn to finding his artifact on his own."

Even speaking Magiere's name made Chane's insides heat up. He thought he saw Wynn's eyes flicker once, perhaps glancing at the scar around his neck.

"Some of what Welstiel was told in dormancy turned out to be false," Chane went on. "When did Magiere start having these dreams?"

"When we reached the northern bay of the Elven Territories," Wynn answered. "We were promised a ship to take us south."

Chane shook his head. He had wandered the Crown Range with Welstiel for so long it was impossible to match the time frames.

"The night we found the monastery, Welstiel began shouting at the night sky. He must have believed he was being led to the castle, but that was not what we found. I think he broke with his . . . 'patron' . . . that night, after being tricked too many times. Whatever spoke to him, perhaps it decided to let Magiere find the orb without him. And she shares the nature of the Noble Dead."

Wynn studied him, perhaps wondering if he told the full truth. Chane's thoughts slipped back to the names she had spoken—and the black-robed figure hunting sages, folios, and her.

"Do you think one of these other old undead is the black-robed mage?" he asked. "Some ancient vampire, grown powerful over so much time?"

Wynn started slightly. "It's not a mage, but it is a Noble Dead."

"No . . . vampires are Noble Dead."

Wynn tiredly closed her eyes. "Not only vampires. There is something else . . . a wraith."

Before he could ask, she shook her head.

"It's the word I use for it, among older ones, though none of them may be accurate. Just something mentioned in old Numan folklore."

"Then it is not—"

"It feeds, Chane. It has to feed on life. And it is fully aware. Shade is convinced the black figure is a form of spirit."

Chane stared at the majay-hì, not quite grasping what she meant. By Wynn's words, this animal shared Chap's antagonism toward the undead. Much as that might add weight to Wynn's conclusion, it was not enough. How had she learned this from a dog?

"She's been hunting it, as much as watching over me," Wynn continued. "I don't understand everything yet, but on the way here I kept thinking of something I overheard in one of il'Sänke's seminars. Like the five Elements, the sages also divide all things in existence by the three Aspects—physical, mental, and spiritual."

Chane knew this concept by different terms, but it still did not explain her assumptions.

"A vampire is distinguished in nature from a mere raised corpse," she went on, "or anything in between those extremes . . . but they all are physical. So what is the difference? We both know from experience that ghosts exist, as well as other less-than-corporeal forms of the undead. But nonetheless, we've seen the dead come back . . . in spirit, as well as body."

Right then he wanted to deny her, for where she headed with her reasoning was too harsh and dangerous—especially for her well-being.

"It's fully aware and reasons," she whispered. "Even if it's a mage as well, then it has grown within its sense of self, as if it were still alive. And it has to feed . . . what else is that but a Noble Dead?"

Chane had no response, but this was not good at all. Uncertain as he was, he still trusted her intellect, as well educated as his own and then some. Caught between doubt and faith in her, which should he choose to follow?

And if she was right, how could he protect her from something he could not fight?

They still had no concrete idea what this creature—this wraith—was truly after, and they had not yet unlocked the secret of the scroll. Chane was not fanciful, but he could not help believing that the scroll had come into his possession for a reason. That the white undead had tried to show it to Wynn confirmed that instinct.

Whatever was hidden beneath the black coating might shape dangerous days ahead, and the future. At present he had no future.

"You said Li'kän wanted you to read the scroll to her," Chane began, "or perhaps just to read it yourself. I do not see why this forgotten Enemy would want or allow that, so our next step should be to solve its mystery."

Wynn looked at the floor. "I've been thinking the same thing."

"So how?"

Wynn hesitated a long while. "I might have a chance."

He stiffened. "You?"

"Do you remember when you found me at the smithy of Pudúrlatsat? You protected me from Vordana, and I was . . . in a state."

Yes, she had been sick, and, strangely, she could barely see.

"Just before, I attempted to give myself mantic sight via a thaumaturgical ritual—the ability to see elemental Spirit in all things."

Chane had never heard this before. "*That* was foolish!"

Wynn stiffened. "Magiere needed to locate Vordana quickly—who, as you well know, was a sentient undead."

He fell silent.

"But my attempt went wrong," Wynn whispered.

"You failed?"

"No." She took a long breath. "I couldn't end it afterward. Chap had to do it for me, and that turned out to be temporary."

Chane shook his head. "How would seeing Spirit let you read the scroll's content?"

Wynn studied him for a moment. "Because with mantic sight, I also see the absence of Spirit in a Noble Dead. Spirit as in the Element, not the Aspect."

Again, Chane disliked where this was headed. He had suffered mishaps in his youth when first attempting conjury on his own with no tutor. One had left him bedridden for many days. The physician called by his mother had no idea what was wrong with him, nor why he had succumbed to a sudden burning fever that made his body seem to dry out and left him with an insatiable thirst.

"I not only see where Spirit is strong or weak," Wynn explained, "but where it is lacking or where something other than life draws it in. The scroll and even the painted ink on top may hold a residue of elemental Spirit, but—"

"The writing in undead's fluids would not," Chane finished.

"Side effects of the sight," Wynn went on, "have been with me ever since my mistake. But I can call it up at times, and I might be able to read what is beneath the scroll's coating."

"No!" Chane hissed, standing up.

And the dog—Shade—rose on all fours, growling.

"Chap is not here," he said. "If you cannot stop this *sight* on your own, then we will find another way."

"There's no time," Wynn returned. "And I've been experimenting since returning home. Domin il'Sänke has helped tutor me."

"You trust him?" he asked harshly. "Enough to let him know about the scroll?"

Her lips pursed in indecision. "I trust him more than my own superiors . . . though sometimes I think he has his own agenda."

"Then do not trust him further."

The room fell silent except for Shade's rumble.

"I have to try," Wynn said quietly. "It's all we have, at present."

Chane's first urge was to hold her in this room until she swore not to do this. Not even if it meant never learning the scroll's secret and why it had come to him.

"Do you have it with you?" he asked.

"No, it's hidden in my room. I was afraid the wraith might try to take it if I had it with me."

Chane pulled on his spare shirt, wincing slightly, and

then snatched up the second overcloak she had brought. "You cannot walk back alone—and you will not attempt this alone. I am coming with you."

"Inside the guild?" Wynn countered loudly. "Absolutely not!"

"We do not know what is in that scroll! Nor what will happen to you if you cannot end your *sight*."

He had placed her in enough danger already with his obsession, and her stubbornness could lead to worse. Donning the cloak, he pulled the hood forward as far as it would go.

"And what about Captain Rodian?" she demanded. "What if he is there? He saw you, as did some of his men, and he has stationed guards around the guild's grounds."

Chane scowled. "I have no concern over city guards."

"You can barely close your hand," she said. "And would you shed blood at the guild?"

He flinched, ashamed at his lack of thought. Wynn was still an innocent in many ways, no matter what the last two years had shown her. And the two of them had grown far apart from the time she had first learned who—what—he was.

"Is the captain expected tonight?" he asked.

"No, but he shows up unexpectedly, whenever he wants."

"Then we will be cautious—but I am coming with you!"

"I don't even know how to get back in myself," she said. "There is a curfew in place at the guild, which is why the city guard is there, to protect us from this killer. I had to bluff my way out, and I can't get back in the same way, let alone bring you."

"And the other night, when you met me at the stable?"

Wynn scowled, growing visibly tired of this debate. Chane hoped she would simply give up altogether.

"I crawled out of the new library and along the inner bailey wall," she said. "Then down the old stairs near the south corner. But I still had to go out the bailey gate, in front of the gatehouse, and the wall is too sheer and tall to climb from the outside."

"Too tall for the living," Chane corrected.

Wynn narrowed her eyes at him.

Despite the risk, Chane could not help a rising excitement.

It had been a hopeless dream until now, and though this was not the way he would have wished for it, tonight he would step inside the guild and Wynn's world.

CHAPTER 16

Wynn turned the final corner, heading toward Old Bailey Road. She knew bringing Chane was wrong.

He was a killer, regardless that he had nothing to do with the deaths surrounding the lost folios. Turning him over to Captain Rodian would've been the rational choice, but she couldn't. Rodian would never solve the murders and thefts. Monster that he was, Chane at least tried to uncover the truth, to help her find out what this "wraith" wanted and why. Besides Shade, who else did she have?

Her whole world had shifted in two days, from her being nearly alone to having two companions, each carefully watching along the dimly lit streets. She felt almost as she had in company with Magiere, Leesil, and Chap—almost.

As she slipped across Old Bailey Road to the wall, she glanced both ways for any sign of patrolling city guards. The road was empty, so she urged Chane left along the wall toward the bailey gate, keeping herself between him and Shade.

At least bluffing her way out of the keep provided one advantage: The guards at the portcullis didn't know who was a real sage or not. A fictitious domin named Parisean sending a "wolf" to escort a delayed scribe meant Shade might get back in on her own. If the dog pestered the guards enough, they would simply open the portcullis and let her in. Once Wynn was inside—if Chane could get her inside—she could go to the courtyard and bring Shade into the dormitory.

Shade trotted close, brushing against her leg, and a memory appeared in Wynn's thoughts.

She saw through Shade's eyes and found herself peering across a large dark room filled with barrels and bundles lashed to the floor and walls. No, not a room, but the belly of a ship. And she saw Chane on the hold's far side. He opened an old chest, glanced inside, then looked about as if something were missing therein.

Another memory came of Shade watching Chane from the shadows as he moved about the ship at night.

"You were both on the same ship?" Wynn whispered.

Chane glanced back at her.

"Shade says you were both on the same ship."

"How...?" And he glanced warily at the majay-hì. "I will tell you everything later. First we must get inside and out of sight."

But those flashes from Shade left Wynn wondering more about her disparate pair of companions.

"Why doesn't Shade sense what you are?" she whispered. "She is like Chap, and her kind hunts yours."

Chane didn't answer at first. It still struck Wynn as odd that Shade hadn't turned on him the night they both came to her aid against the wraith. Since taking Shade in, Wynn constantly monitored her own thoughts—or rather her memories. The majay-hì's dependence upon memory-speak meant there was no way of telling when or if Shade might dip into her mind for rising memories. Wynn didn't want Shade to learn the truth about Chane at the wrong moment.

Chane stopped and held up his left hand, spreading his fingers, but Wynn still didn't understand.

"The ring," he whispered. "Welstiel made it long ago ... called it the 'ring of nothing.' I took it before Magiere finished him. It seemed to protect him from Magiere's and Chap's awareness. He was also able to shield those he touched, perhaps expand its influence further through his skills."

Wynn swallowed hard and quickly suppressed rising images of Magiere speaking of Chane's actions within the orb's cavern. He'd used his sword to slice off several of Welstiel's fingers. In the aftermath, Wynn had wanted to believe Chane was trying to help Magiere. She hadn't truly believed it even then, and now . . .

Disgust must have surfaced in her expression.

"I could not have escaped the castle without it," he said defensively. "You asked, and I told you—far more than you have said concerning your staff and its crystal. I assume you went to great lengths to acquire it—yes?"

Wynn mutely pushed him onward.

They came within yards of the bailey gate, framed by its two small barbicans. It was shut tight, and Wynn flattened against the wall.

She couldn't step out and open it to let Shade through—not in plain sight of the portcullis guards. Shade would have to draw one of them down. Wynn couldn't think how to explain this with memories.

Then Shade ducked around her and headed out.

"What is that animal doing?" Chane hissed.

Shade paused before the gate, looking back, and a memory rose in Wynn's head . . . her own memory of running the other way along the inner bailey wall.

"Come on," Wynn whispered, and pulled on Chane's arm. "She knows what to do."

When Wynn reached the bailey wall's southern turn, Shade's first barks filled the quiet night. The dog was drawing attention to herself. Hopefully one of the guards would let her back inside.

Chane stalled and looked back along the wall. A strange, wary tension flooded his features at the dog's noise.

Wynn jerked him onward. Creeping around the wall's bend, she watched for city guards in the open road.

"So . . . what do you have in mind for us?" she asked.

"To scale the wall," he answered, and before she blurted out disbelief, he pointed along the wall's southeastern side.

"Get to the corner where that jutting barbican joins the wall."

Wynn looked ahead. A shallow inward corner existed where the bailey wall bulged outward in a wide half-round shape, like a small tower. In older days, when the royals' ancestors lived here, soldiers and archers could've stood atop that open barbican and fired along the wall's outside. Should enemy forces have breached the original outer bailey wall, now broken into remnants, this would be the last line of defense against a direct assault upon the keep.

Wynn scurried along the wall's base and ducked in beside the barbican's outward surge. As Chane joined her, she tilted her head back and peered upward.

The tops of the wall and barbican were beyond the height of a footman's pike, as any sensible fortification should be. She could still hear Shade barking in the distance.

"Now we climb," Chane said, and unshouldered his pack. "You first."

Wynn glowered at him. "No one can climb this."

He withdrew a coil of narrow rope from his pack, but there was no weight or hook on either end. Obviously it was just something he still carried from his travels rather than part of any carefully considered plan. He began making a large loop in one end, and Wynn couldn't believe they were going to try this.

Chane collected rope coils with the loop. He glanced both ways along the road, stepped away from the wall, and flung the gathered rope upward.

The rope uncoiled, but its end barely cleared the barbican's wall through a space between two rising ramparts. Chane huffed in irritation. Wynn didn't know why until he pulled on the rope, and it all came tumbling down. She realized that he was trying to loop one of the ramparts.

"Did you even think this through?" she whispered.

"I do not recall you offering a plan of your own."

She wasn't sure what angered her more—his half-witted scheme, or that she couldn't think of a better one.

Chane crouched against the wall and drew his sword. Before she could berate him again, he pulled off his cloak. He wrapped it around the blade and cinched the material tight by knotting the rope around the sword's midpoint. Wynn watched as Chane flung his muffled makeshift anchor, and then flinched at the dull thump somewhere above.

And that was all she heard.

Wynn straightened, looking off toward the rounding of the wall's southern corner. Shade had stopped barking.

Chane stood with the rope's end in hand and looked off the same way.

"Is she in?" he whispered.

"I don't know. Maybe," she answered, and Chane scowled at her. "I think she needs a line of sight to . . . Oh, never mind, just hurry up!"

Chane pulled on the rope, and it drew taut this time.

Wynn crept along the barbican curve but didn't make it far enough to peer around. The soft clomp of boots on cobblestone carried along the street. She quickly sidled back along the wall, waved at Chane, and jabbed a finger back the other way.

Chane glanced once and crouched low. He hooked a thumb in the air over his shoulder, pointing toward his own back. Wynn went wide-eyed and glanced up the wall.

Get on . . . now! he mouthed.

It was one thing to be caught breaking curfew. It was entirely another to be found breaking in by the city guard.

Wynn gave Chane a scathing look, but she climbed upon him, trying to grip his shoulder with her right hand. She placed her staff crosswise between her chest and his back, and then wrapped her arms around his neck. Chane lurched to his feet, hoisting her off the ground.

With one boot braced against the wall stones, he pulled hard on the rope.

Wynn lost track of footfalls on the road as Chane hauled both of them up the wall as quickly as if he were walking on flat ground. He stopped just before a space between two barbican ramparts and whispered, "Climb over."

Wynn pulled one arm from his neck and grabbed her staff. She slid it over the wall's top, and then felt Chane's hand cup under her left foot. That he managed to hold them both up with his one-handed grip surprised her.

She quickly clambered over him through the rampart's space.

His cloak-wrapped sword was anchored across the opening, but when she turned back to help him, he was already up. He pushed her down, crouched beside her, and began hauling up the rope as fast as he could.

Wynn heard the footsteps again.

They came from right below in the street as the rope's trailing end flopped onto the barbican's platform. She and Chane remained still, waiting for the steps to pass by.

Then silence—the footfalls stopped altogether.

Wynn's stomach knotted.

It was far too long before the footfalls resumed, moving onward until they grew faint somewhere off toward the bailey wall's southern corner. Chane rose just enough to peer through the rampart space. He nodded to her.

Wynn glanced down at his sword. "You need to do something about that. Sages do not carry such weapons."

He nodded. "I will hide it better once we are inside."

Wynn wanted to kick herself. No matter what Chane did, he would never pass for a sage. And even without current circumstances, visitors weren't commonly allowed after dusk. What would anyone say or do if they caught her sneaking an unknown man into the guild grounds? Especially one so burned.

Wynn frowned. They wouldn't say anything at first, because they'd be wondering how she'd sneaked out.

She led the way along the wall's ramparts and kept glancing up. But she never saw even a flicker of light in any of the tower windows.

When they reached the library on the northeastern side, Chane boosted her by one foot. She peeked through the nearest window, but by the light of wall-mounted cold lamps she saw no one along the nearest shelves facing the windows. When they climbed inside, Wynn peered around the casement's end. The next row and the cubby beyond it were empty as well. When she turned back for Chane, she found him scanning the texts upon the shelves.

Some hint of pain filled his pale features beneath a gaze filled with awe. Or was it longing?

She couldn't help wondering what he'd been like in his living days. A scholar or just another spoiled, useless noble? Perhaps both. Few times had they ever spoken of his past—before or after she'd learned what he was.

"This way," she whispered.

He blinked as if waking from some dream, and the wonder faded from his eyes. But that hint of pain took an instant longer to follow. He nodded. They sneaked along the library's southern end and down the side staircase.

At every turn, archway, or door along the way, he waited behind as she stepped out to see if all was clear. Not that she wouldn't look suspicious in her old elven clothing, but everyone here already thought she was odd. The last path to the keep's double doors was the worst.

The entryway was empty, but she heard voices carry from the common hall. She cracked the left door and peered into the courtyard. It was empty as well, but this wasn't a welcome sight.

Where was Shade? Had she failed to get in?

Wynn began frantically trying to think of some way to find Shade and bring her in. Then a shadow moved at the courtyard's far left corner. Wynn tightened her grip on the crystal's staff.

The shadow shifted around the cistern beyond the dormitory's end. Two crystal blue eyes sparked in the light of the iron-bracketed torches burning upon the gatehouse's inner wall.

Shade stepped a little way out into sight. Her ears rose as she peered back across the courtyard, and Wynn started breathing again.

She stepped back to wave Chane forward, and they both ducked out, cloak hoods pulled up. They sneaked around the courtyard, rushing quickly as they passed the line of sight with the gatehouse tunnel. Shade was already waiting at the dormitory door. Once Wynn was certain the stairs and upper passage were clear, all three of them hurried to her room.

Closing the door tightly, Wynn leaned against it, took a deep breath, and dug for her cold lamp crystal. When she rubbed it hard, its light exposed Chane standing before her desk, glancing at her mess of quills, journals, and paper. She still couldn't believe that Shade and Chane had somehow traveled here together. He had a lot to explain.

"I must be mad," she said. "The premins and domins already think so ... for all my warnings about undead. Now I've got one into my room."

Chane glanced over. He didn't even scowl at such a bad joke. He only shook his head.

"They are the mad ones ... in discounting your greater experience in these matters. At least you think for yourself. I would have thought better of your elders here. Tilswith had a far more agile mind."

"I miss him," Wynn said.

Chane fingered a blank sheet on the desk. "So do I, at times."

She stood straighter, watching him roll a quill shaft with his pale fingertip. He was such a mass of confusing contradictions. Shade hopped up on the bed and settled. Everything else in Wynn's room looked the same.

Only a vampire and a majay-hì were new additions.

No, there was also the scroll.

Wynn stripped away her cloak as she leaned the staff in the corner. "My journal notes from today are on the desk. See what you make of them while I prepare."

"My grasp of the Begaine syllabary is not good," he said, picking up the journal.

"Some of it is in plain Numanese letters. Can you read those?"

"A little, from what Tilswith taught me. Welstiel tutored me in speaking while we traveled. I learned more from my time in this city."

Wynn's education in languages was more extensive, required by her vocation as a cataloger. But Chane's intellect was impressive. Domin Tilswith had commented on his natural gift for picking up bits and pieces so quickly. At that time her old master hadn't known Chane's true nature. Perhaps Chane's ability was more than natural, but it was impossible to say, since she'd never known him in his mortal life.

She knelt down and reached under her bed, pulling on

the scroll case pinned against a support board. She popped
its pewter cap and slid out the scroll; then her gaze fell on
Shade's long charcoal-colored face peering over the bed's
edge.

How nice to be so naturally camouflaged for night. Wynn
leaned in and lightly stroked Shade's cheek.

"You clever girl."

Shade sprang up to all fours and snarled at her, sniffing
wildly, and Wynn lurched back as she heard Chane rushing
toward her.

Shade dropped her head low, her sniffing nose extended,
and Wynn looked down at the scroll in her hand.

"What is wrong with her?" Chane rasped.

Wynn unrolled the scroll, studying its faded black coating. "It seems you're not the only one who can smell what's
hidden here." Very slowly she touched the top of Shade's
muzzle. "Enough . . . it's all right."

She spun about on her knees, facing the open floor of her
small room. Chane dropped the journal on the bed.

"How does this work?" he asked.

She handed him the empty scroll case. He was no stranger
to the arcane, but the taint of mantic sight wasn't something
controlled just by learned skill. Since her first so-called successful attempt, traces of the sight had never left her, and
summoning it had never worked out well.

"It's not like what you do," she said. "More just intent,
wishing, and focus . . . It's hard to explain."

And she didn't care to, especially not with how she used
the memory of Chap as a means to summon her sight. When
she lifted her head, Chane stood over her, arms crossed.

"No more arguments," she warned.

He stepped back, giving her space to lay out the scroll
upon the floor.

Wynn pushed all thoughts from her mind. Domin il'Sänke
had taught her tricks as well—not true ritual or spellcraft
but some of their trappings. But even that hadn't been any
use in ending the sight once it came. With her right first
finger, Wynn traced a sign for elemental Spirit on the floor
and then encircled it.

At each gesture she envisioned the pattern in her mind,

as if actually drawn upon the stone. She scooted forward, kneeling upon the imagined symbol and circle, and then traced a wider circumference around herself. A simple pattern, but it helped bring her into focus and shut out the world for a needed moment.

Remaining still, Wynn closed her eyes.

She focused upon letting the world fill her with its presence and tried to feel for a trace of Spirit in all things, starting first with herself. Then she imagined breathing it in from the air, feeling it flow upward from the floor's stone. In her darkened sight, she held on to the first simple pattern stroked upon the floor.

Wynn called up—constructed—an image of Chap, just as she'd once seen him in her mantic sight, his fur shimmering as if made of a million silk threads. His whole body was encased in white vapors that rose like flame from his form.

Moments stretched on tediously, one after another.

An ache in her knees threatened her concentration.

She tried hard to hold on to Chap's image ... to hold him there behind the envisioned circle around the symbol of Spirit. Until vertigo came—and nausea—in the dark behind her closed eyes.

"Wynn?"

She felt as if she were falling and threw out her hands.

They slapped hard against cold stone, jarring her shoulders, but she stopped herself from slamming face-first into the floor. In fright, Wynn opened her eyes too quickly.

Nausea lurched up her throat, and she gagged.

A translucent mist of white, just shy of blue, permeated every dimly lit object in the room. It covered everything in a second view of the world overlaying her normal sight ... smothering her normal sight.

"Wynn!"

She raised a hand, weakly waving Chane off, but she didn't dare look up at him. She didn't want to see him with mantic sight. Turning her head the other way, a beacon of bluish light atop the bed nearly blinded her.

Beneath that brilliance was Shade's own shape and dark color. Her Fay-imbued body glowed more powerfully than anything around Wynn. But where Shade's father had been a blaze of fiery silken threads for fur, Shade was a wolf of night overlaid with a burning aura that hurt Wynn's eyes.

Shade lowered her head, her eyes like blue gemstones held before the sun, and her wet nose touched Wynn's cheek. So close to Wynn's face, Shade's light grew too intense, and Wynn flinched her head the other way.

Chane filled up her sight.

Wynn recoiled from him and then stared in shock.

Back when she'd first summoned mantic sight in Pudúr-latsat, she'd seen shadows. Small ribbons of black had flowed through Magiere's living flesh. And Vordana, the walking corpse of a sorcerer, had been pure blackness within. All the mists of Spirit had drifted toward him like an ebbing tide to be swallowed within his inner black silhouette.

And Chane . . .

He'd come for her when Vordana had cornered her in the town's smithy. She hadn't seen whether the mists were swallowed into him as well. But he'd been so black within, so devoid of elemental Spirit, that she could barely make him out in the forge's darkness.

But now he was just Chane.

There was no darkness, no shadow copy of his flesh—and no ghostly duplicate of blue-white mist permeating him, either. He looked exactly as he had before she began straining to call up mantic sight.

"Are you all right?" he demanded, crouching low to study her face, her eyes. "Did it work?"

His appearance, so untouched by Spirit, worried Wynn. She glanced at his left hand braced upon the floor.

The ring was gone.

She didn't remember seeing him take it off, and he wouldn't have, if it hid him from Shade's awareness. Nausea rolled through Wynn's stomach, and she clutched her mouth.

"Yes . . . it worked," she managed to get out.

Her doubled view of the world made her so dizzy and sickened. She wondered if she would be able to see anything in this state as she panned her gaze to the scroll.

It was not completely black anymore.

The coating of old ink, spread nearly to the scroll's edges, had lightened with a thin inner trace of blue-white. Whatever covered the words had been made from a natural substance, and even after ages it still retained a trace of elemental Spirit.

Within that space pure black marks appeared, devoid of any Spirit at all.

"I can see them," she whispered.

"What is there?" Chane asked.

"It's Sumanese," she breathed out, trying not to gag. "Old Sumanese . . . I think."

But those swirling, elaborately stroked characters weren't written as in the other texts. Short lines began evenly along a wide right-side margin. Written from right to left, they ended erratically shy of the page's left side. The lines of text appeared to be broken into stanzas of differing length.

"It looks like a poem," she whispered. "But the dialect . . . I can't make out what it says."

She tried, but only a few words seemed vaguely familiar compared to what little she knew of contemporary Sumanese.

"Children . . . twenty and six steps . . . to hide . . . five corners?" Wynn mumbled. "To anchor amid . . . the void."

She skimmed down the page, at a loss over how little she could translate. Those black characters blurred for an instant under her shifted gaze.

"Consumes its own . . . of the mountain under . . . the chair of a lord's song?"

The dark marks blurred again, though she hadn't moved her eyes. Wynn's stomach convulsed.

"My journal," she moaned, buckling forward. "Get me something to write on. Quickly!"

Three labored breaths passed before she felt Chane lift her hand and fit a quill between her fingers. She raised her head as he slid a blank sheet in next to the scroll. Wynn began to write, not even trying to read anymore, and Chane guided her hand each time she tried to re-ink the quill's head. She had to keep her sight clear and be certain of each blindly copied stroke.

The "Children" had to be the same as those she'd read

of in the translations, but what of "twenty-six steps," "hide," and "five corners"? The only thing she remembered was that Beloved—il'Samar, the Night Voice—had sought refuge when its Children "divided." And she had no idea what "the chair of a lord's song" meant. And how could a "mountain" be under a chair?

Häs'saun was a Sumanese name, and as one of Li'kän's companions perhaps he had written this cryptic work. But why had he hidden it under the ink? Or had someone else done so later? Why hadn't it been destroyed instead of being painted over so that no one could read it?

Nausea sharpened again, and Wynn choked as Chane grabbed her arm.

"Enough," he said. "Whatever you have so far is enough!"

No, it wasn't. She had to get it all, or she might never learn to understand its hidden meaning.

"Wynn, look away!" Chane rasped. "Now!"

She looked up.

He was the same as he had been before her sight came. No white mist or black void overlaid him, and her nausea weakened.

"Twenty and six steps . . . five corners," she mumbled.

A low growl rose behind her, and Wynn glanced over her shoulder.

Shade's bright form stood upon the bed, but she now faced the other way, toward the wall and its one narrow window. Her snarls kept growing.

"What is wrong with her?" Chane asked.

Shade cut loose an eerie wail.

Wynn had heard that before. There was no other sound quite like it in the world. And it had poured from Chap's jaws—whenever he picked up the presence of an undead.

But Shade was wailing inside Wynn's room, inside the guild.

"No!" Wynn moaned.

Shade spun and leaped off the bed, straight over to Wynn.

The stone wall around the window blackened as it bulged inward.

*　　*　　*

Chane jerked on Wynn's arm, heaving her across the floor toward the door.

"Run!" he rasped.

Searing pain ignited in his hand as he jerked out his sword.

The majay-hì's yowling snarls battered at his ears as the animal spun about before him to face the bed.

The black figure—the wraith—slid through the wall.

It stood *in* the bed, as if it were not truly there. As if it were real and the bed was not. Chane looked into its voluminous cowl but saw no face within the black pit of cloth. Then the cowl turned downward, its opening fixing upon Wynn.

Chane raised and leveled his blade, knowing it would have little effect. All he wanted was to catch this thing's attention and distract it long enough for Wynn to get out.

The hood snapped up, and its black-filled opening turned on him. It remained where it stood, the lower half of its robe and cloak penetrating the narrow bed.

Perhaps after their last encounter, it did not wish to touch him again. He could use that. But the dog's noise must have awakened everyone in the building, if not elsewhere on guild grounds.

The figure hung there as if studying him. Beneath the dog's wailing and snarls, a low hiss rose, like whispers too hard to hear. It seemed to come from everywhere in the room.

Chane heard startled voices in the passage outside the room's door.

Short-lived relief at the wraith's hesitation washed away in panic. What would this thing do if startled sages came running in? Not only did he have to get Wynn out of its reach—he had to draw it away before more sages died.

Snarling and snapping, Shade wove across the floor before Chane. The wraith drew back and lashed down at the dog with one cloth-wrapped hand. Chane quickly swiped his blade at the hood.

The sword's tip passed through, not even ruffling fabric. Shade yelped as the wraith's fingers grazed her shoulder.

She stumbled away toward the desk, pulling up her left foreleg.

Wynn rose up onto her knees, scrambled to the corner by the door, and latched both hands around the staff.

Chane stiffened. Surely she wouldn't use it while he was still in the room?

A shout rose in the passage beyond the door.

"All of you, back to your rooms and stay there!"

Chane's panic grew. Someone of authority had been alerted and was already outside. At any moment that person would reach the door.

The wraith spun away from the dog at Wynn's movement and fixed upon her.

Chane shifted quickly into its way, but there was only one thing he could do.

And it was going to hurt—more than the burns on his hands.

Shade regained her feet and darted in, snapping at the shadow creature, trying to drive it back through the wall.

"Chane, get out!" Wynn shouted.

The wraith's hood twisted sharply toward the dog, and Chane lunged.

He thrust out with his empty hand.

At the scriptorium, he and the wraith had had a moment of contact, which neither of them had cared for. Chane heard Wynn whispering as his hand passed straight through the figure's forearm.

A shock of cold raced through his arm.

His burned hand felt as if he had thrust it into fire. When the frigid cold reached his shoulder, he could not help crying out. He let anger bring hunger to eat that pain, but he could not smother the fresh searing in his hand.

Chane snatched his hand back, curling it against his chest as the hissing whispers in the room rose to a screech. The wraith whipped its arm away, sliding rapidly back through the bed toward the wall. And Wynn's crystal atop the staff leaned out into the side of Chane's view.

He hated any thought of abandoning Wynn, and even so, he would never make it out of here in time. Not with whoever was outside the door.

"Get down!" Wynn whispered. "Cover up!"

Chane wavered briefly. He crumpled and flattened upon the floor. But as he jerked his cloak's hood forward, pressing his face to the stone floor, the door burst open and bashed hard against the wall.

"Wynn, stop!" a deep voice ordered, and the door slammed shut.

But she didn't. She barely recognized il'Sänke's voice, and tried to keep her focus amid the sickening vertigo of mantic sight.

The wraith was inside the guild—inside the dormitory. There were too many apprentices and initiates close by. She held the crystal's triggering pattern in her mind but kept her eyes upon the wraith, hesitant and writhing before the window.

And for an instant she saw it—*him*—within the cloak and heavy robe.

Blue-white mists permeating the room began to shift, drifting slowly toward this thing. Wherever they touched the figure they were swallowed by it. The traces where they vanished formed outlines. Wynn saw shapes beneath the figure's black garments and the cloth strips wrapped about its body.

A skull faced her within the cowl.

Consumed mists marked its outline like glistening moisture upon bones as black as coal beneath the wraps of its skeleton form. Then a wisp of another image overlaid this as well.

She saw a face.

Not like Chane or any other undead she had seen, retaining their appearance from the moment they were killed. Aged, emaciated, and sunken features suddenly covered the skull in another layer. As if this thing—man—had died of old age before he rose again.

She couldn't be certain, with no complexion to gauge, but the prominent cheekbones, nose, and chin made him appear Suman, like il'Sänke. His eyebrows had grown long and unkempt, and the straggles of a remaining beard hung in wisps along his jawline.

His eyes weren't clear to her, as if the open sockets were only glaring wells of obsidian. She was nothing more than a small thing in his way.

A hand clamped over Wynn's eyes, blocking everything out.

Vertigo vanished, leaving only nausea in her gut. She lost the pattern in her mind as her head was jerked back against someone's chest.

The staff bucked in her hands under someone's grip.

"No, not yet!" she shouted, and then she heard il'Sänke murmuring near her ear.

Chane was still in the room, but was he fully covered?

A last raging howl from Shade hit Wynn's ears. Then a burning flash of light filtered suddenly through il'Sänke's hand, turned red-orange by his flesh.

"No!" she screamed.

Il'Sänke's voice faded as darkness winked in behind Wynn's closed eyes. When his hand lifted from her face, she thrashed free, searching for Chane. The wraith was gone, and the room was no longer filled by the blue-white of Spirit. Il'Sänke had taken away her mantic sight again. Chane was hunched on the floor, cloak hood pulled over his head.

For an instant she thought she saw thin trails like morning mist rising from his hunkered form, and then they were gone. He glanced up around the edge of his hood.

"Do not move!" il'Sänke hissed.

Wynn whipped around in fright.

Domin il'Sänke stood with one hand latched around the staff, just above her own grip. She knew only by the downward tilt of his head that he watched Chane—because she couldn't see his eyes.

He was wearing spectacles with a heavy pewter frame.

In place of clear lenses, these were so dark they hid his eyes. The lenses began to change, growing clearer, finally revealing his unblinking gaze locked on Chane.

Wynn rarely saw Domin il'Sänke truly angry. Even through lingering nausea, she winced at the cold expression on his face. Pounding ceased at the door, and Premin Sykion's voice rose from the other side.

"Quickly! We must break it down."

Wynn tensed with dread at the thought of anyone else entering her room. Then puzzlement followed. The door didn't have a lock, so why would they need to break in? Il'Sänke had entered easily enough, so . . .

Wynn looked at the tall domin.

Il'Sänke quickly gestured for Chane to move up against the wall behind the door. Chane glanced once at Wynn.

She had to trust in whatever the domin was up to, or be left to explain Chane's presence.

"Do it!" she whispered.

Chane spun onto his knees and stood up, flattening against the wall.

Il'Sänke released the staff and pulled the strange spectacles from his face. As he tucked them in his robe, he passed his other hand in an arc before the door, never actually touching it. Then he opened it partway, holding it in place so that no one could step in.

"It is nothing," il'Sänke said through the door's space, shaking his head with a half smile. "A large cat got into the courtyard and began to mewl. It set the majay-hì off. In our efforts to quiet her, Wynn and I made quite a racket. I do apologize."

Wynn couldn't see Premin Sykion outside, but she heard the head of the guild let out an impatient exhale.

"We shall speak further of this tomorrow." Her tone was both annoyed and relieved.

"I will make certain everything is quiet," il'Sänke assured her. "You can send everyone back to bed, or we will all be useless in the morning."

Il'Sänke closed the door. His false smile vanished as he turned toward Chane.

Always before, in any conflict involving Chane, Wynn feared for the safety of others. Watching il'Sänke, she suddenly felt the opposite.

"Do not hurt him. I . . . We need him," she whispered to the domin, still fearing that anyone outside might hear.

"I assumed this was not some lovers' tryst," il'Sänke answered disdainfully. "And do not think I have forgotten him from your previous outing! I waited to see what you both might do . . . though this hardly meets my better expectations."

Chane just stood tense and silent.

"Toying with the staff—and your sight, at the same time!" il'Sänke snapped. "The growth of your stupidity is astounding."

He shook his head slowly, and then snatched the staff from Wynn's hand.

"What drew that thing in here?" he demanded. "Did you sneak any translations back to your room?"

"No," Wynn answered. Just what was he implying? Before she could stop herself, she glanced down without thinking.

Her open journal and quill had been kicked against the wall on the door's other side—and the scroll as well. Fortunately no one had stepped on it amid the conflict. She went cold at the sight of ink all over the floor stones, for her small bottle had been kicked under the bed. But the splash of black hadn't traveled to the other items.

By the time Wynn looked up, in no more than a blink, il'Sänke had already followed her gaze. He leaned down and picked up the scroll, frowning suspiciously at its blackened surface.

"Is this what it came for?" he whispered.

"It is mine," Chane rasped, reaching out. "I will take it and go."

"I do not recall dismissing you," il'Sänke replied, though he didn't even look at Wynn's secret guest.

Wynn silently shook her head at Chane, and he held his place. She glanced down at his hand. The ring was there again on his left hand—it hadn't been when she'd looked for it with mantic sight. And she couldn't remember seeing him put it back on, let alone having taken it off.

Il'Sänke's gaze shifted to the journal and quill. He picked up the former, holding it open atop the scroll, and then his scrutiny returned to Chane.

That intense gaze made Chane fidget, and Wynn almost lunged when his grip tightened on his sword.

Il'Sänke cocked his head and frowned.

A strange instant of wary uncertainty washed over his

dark features, as if he'd tried to read something in Chane's face and couldn't.

"We need him," Wynn repeated. "That *thing* came inside the guild. Maybe it has done so before . . . since no one could've stopped it. The three of us are the only ones who even believe it exists. We can't afford to turn on one another if we're to seek the truth and a way to destroy it."

"You are leaping to conclusions," il'Sänke said. "After last night it could have simply been attacking you, as obviously this scroll is unreadable, except . . ."

He bent his head, peering down at the journal.

"What is this?" he asked—like a parent's accusation, who already knew what trouble a child had gotten into.

"A copy," Wynn answered. "But only what I could make out from the scroll—"

"—with your sight," he finished for her, and then he turned to Chane. "So . . . bearer, where did you get this scroll?"

Cold mistrust showed on Chane's burned features.

"From the same library where I found the ancient texts," Wynn answered.

"Wynn!" Chane hissed.

"We cannot solve this alone!" she hissed back. "He needs to know everything."

And she turned back to il'Sänke.

"There is a poem under the coating, penned by one of the ancient undead among the trio who wrote the texts I brought back. I haven't been sure who to trust in this—but we must protect the guild and the texts. If I tell you everything we have learned, will you help us?"

Il'Sänke remained expressionless, but he tilted the staff's crystal toward Chane.

Chane instinctively flinched away.

"Who is he?" the domin asked.

"I've known Chane for some time," she answered. "He often came to our little branch in Bela, studying with myself and Domin Tilswith. He reads several languages from his region and has an interest in history. He . . . he knows a good deal about the undead."

"I can imagine," il'Sänke said drily.

Wynn's heart began hammering. How much had Domin il'Sänke already guessed concerning Chane? And the way the domin had tilted that staff suggested much.

"I should not stay," Chane said. "There will be questions if I am discovered. I came only to ensure Wynn's safety."

Domin il'Sänke snorted once and spoke only to Wynn. "He is correct about questions—but *you* cannot stay here alone. Both of you will come with me—now. I will take him out the library window, atop the wall."

Wynn gaped. He knew how she'd been getting out. But they would be seen if il'Sänke took Chane through the keep.

"No one will see us," he said. "I'm sure I can be quite as sneaky as you. But I will keep the scroll for now."

"No!" Chane rasped, raising his sword.

As Shade snarled, Wynn rushed in and grabbed Chane's forearm. She didn't fully understand why, but it was clear how much the scroll meant to him. Yet il'Sänke might be the only one who could read the ancient Sumanese that she'd blindly copied from the scroll.

"Let him keep it," she told Chane. "He's not like the other domins here. He won't lay claim to it. And even you shouldn't walk alone tonight while carrying it."

"Especially since you already look rather a mess," il'Sänke added.

Chane glanced down at Wynn. With a glower he reluctantly let her pull his sword arm down.

"And you had best take these," il'Sänke said to Wynn, taking out the strange glasses he'd been wearing. "At least until you learn to control the crystal's intensity. Your mantic sight will be all you have left . . . if you stupidly blind yourself."

Wynn snatched the glasses from him, feeling less than grateful. "What was I supposed to do? You weren't here."

"I am not the one drawing so much attention to myself," he countered, and turned for the door.

With a quick glance in the outer passage, Domin il'Sänke ushered them all out. Wynn went last, with Shade beside her. They paused at the door to the courtyard. When il'Sänke nodded that all was clear, they slipped across to the main doors and back inside the keep, heading for the library. He led them the same way by which they'd come in, yet another disturbing coincidence that bothered Wynn.

When they reached the library's first floor, il'Sänke had them wait while he scouted ahead. By the glow of perpetual cold lamps, Chane turned to Wynn, and the burns on his cheek looked orange in the soft light.

"I will help," he said. "I want to protect . . . the guild."

"I know," she answered, but she wouldn't give him more encouragement than this. She could never let him hope for anything beyond ending the current crisis.

Domin il'Sänke reappeared and took Chane upstairs.

Wynn dropped on a bench near a study table, wondering how il'Sänke would get Chane out without being seen by Rodian's men. Or perhaps Chane would simply scale down the wall with his rope.

She badly wanted to pet Shade, seeking comfort in a companion still so new to her, but her thoughts kept turning to Chane. She had to be careful. Any memories picked up by Shade might make it impossible for the dog to fight alongside him again. And she needed them both for now.

After trotting some distance along the wall's top, Ghassan led the way down the stairs into the fallow orchard below the southern tower. He paused there, holding back a hand to keep Wynn's "savior" from stepping past him.

Chane was in no condition to be scaling walls or possibly calling attention to himself if he fell. It was simple enough to fill the guards' minds with the notion of something skulking near the keep's northern tower. Yet even as they took off on an erroneous search, Ghassan was still disturbed.

Not by the strange marred and burned appearance of this one called Chane. More than that, he had not caught the slightest conscious thought in the man's head. He had tried in Wynn's room.

Unlike during the duchess's visit with her entourage, when he had picked up only something akin to a voice muffled inside a closed room, he could not find Chane's thoughts at all. As if the man were not there.

When the guards were gone he waved Chane on. He

received not a word in response as the man jogged off
through the gate.

Il'Sänke returned to the library's first floor and found
Wynn slouched upon a bench with the majay-hì at her feet.
On spotting him, she straightened and stood up.

"Come, you will sleep in the northwest building," he
said, "in the study outside my guest quarters. It is more . . .
protected."

She frowned, then nodded, as perhaps the prospect of
sleeping alone in her room did seem unappealing. He led
the way back through to the main doors and, once outside,
cut across the courtyard. Entering through the storage
building, they headed along a hallway that passed through
the keep's outer wall and into the newer building beyond.
On the ground floor they passed the area where he spent
time among this branch's metaologers. When he glanced
over his shoulder, Wynn was peering through a wide archway on the left. He knew what she saw inside.

Dimly lit colored glass tubes, mortars and pestles, small
burners, and tin plates covered tables made of stone resistant to dangerous substances. Aging books lined high
shelves about the workbenches running along both side
walls. Perhaps she spotted the stairs to the sublevels, where
the alchemical furnace sat, built like a massive barrel of
charred steel mounted to turn and spin as needed. Plates
of thick crystal were embedded in its walls, allowing a view
of the interior to monitor any work in progress.

"I haven't come this way in a long time," Wynn said.

Shade, on the other hand, drew nervously closer to Wynn
as they traveled up a switchback staircase at the passage's
end.

Il'Sänke stopped before a door on the second level. He
preferred to keep this locked the old-fashioned way—to
avoid questions—and took a key from around his neck.

"What's in the lenses of these glasses?" Wynn asked suddenly. "What makes them darken?"

"The glass was infused with a thaumaturgical ink while
still molten," he replied. "Nothing complicated, and not the
best lenses to look through. I later discovered that they

react to sharp changes in heat as well as light. Keep aware of this unexpected side effect."

He opened the door and let Wynn and Shade inside.

Only once they were alone in his study did he feel at ease. A faded wooden couch with cushions was pushed against one wall. On the other side, his desk was a mess of parchments and quills and charcoal sticks. The floor was dusty around the edges where no one walked, and two walls were lined with half-filled shelves. He had brought only a few of the texts from home. The rest were either there when he arrived or had been borrowed from the library. Another door at the back led into the guest bedchamber he used during his stay.

Wynn glanced over the desk, the spectacles still in her hand. Her expression filled with disappointment. "It's so—"

"Ordinary?" he finished for her.

He was in no mood to discuss the state of his quarters. Anything he did not wish others to see was always kept locked away—one way or another.

"Many things that appear ordinary are not," he added. "Your tall friend, for instance, is one of your walking dead."

Wynn stiffened, and Ghassan tried not to smile or laugh.

He could count off the notions running through her head—without even trying to touch her thoughts. First denial, then came reticence to confirm his statement, to be followed finally by resignation.

Wynn flinched, but Ghassan felt no pity. He had picked up nothing, not even stray thoughts in Chane, which seemed impossible. Then again, he had never had a chance before to try such on an undead.

"Yes," she finally answered. "A Noble Dead . . . a vampire . . . but he would never harm a sage."

"And why is that?"

He already guessed, but the longer he prodded her guilt, making her feel as if she had betrayed his confidence, the better it served him.

"I just know," she said tiredly. "What else do you wish me to tell you?"

"My interest lies most in what you might tell others. Much in the texts implies warnings, maybe even predictions, though I have seen little of the material. Knowledge of their content can never leave these protected walls—not in any form. Can you grasp that much?"

Her young eyes seemed so weary as she nodded. "Yes, I think I can."

"Then sit," he commanded, pointing to the old couch, "and start from the beginning. Tell me everything concerning this lost library of an ancient undead. Tell me what you found today in the translations . . . and in the scroll."

As a last emphasis, he held up her journal, taken from the floor of her room, and slapped it down upon his desk as he sat.

Shade hopped up beside Wynn, curling up on the couch and taking most of its space.

Wynn's tired brown eyes fixed on the journal, as if it were the end of a long tale unto itself. She began, softly and slowly at first, telling him what she'd learned in the Elven Territories concerning Most Aged Father, the Anmaglâhk, and fear of a returning Ancient Enemy.

She told him of the long sea journey down the elven coast, and another by land into the rugged Pock Peaks. And then of the nearly mute white undead called Li'kän, who could no longer remember the sound of any voice or her own name. Wynn had found no clues to whatever became of the white one's missing companions, Volyno and Häs'saun.

She told him of events in a cavern below the castle, either ones she had witnessed or those later learned from her companions. He heard of the hundreds of calcified remains of servants, not all human, like statues kneeling with heads bowed for eternity in their burial pockets of stone. And he learned of something called an "orb," and the chaos in a hot and humid cavern when it had been accidentally "opened." She told him how she and Chap, a Fay-born canine like Shade, had chosen the texts she brought back.

But when she came to the translations seen this day,

there was little he did not know already. At her mention of the Eaters of Silence, as opposed to the Children or the Reverent ones, he kept silent, though at that mention, his grip tightened on the chair's arm.

Much of what she had read contained passages he had worked on. She had few conclusions that he had not guessed at as well. When she wound down, all her words spent, they sat in silence for a while. She glanced at him now and then, expecting him to say something—anything—though not about a "wraith."

Yes, he had caught that term from her very thoughts. Along with her deep fear that it would be far worse to deal with than the vampires, the ones she had thought were the only Noble Dead. Now one of them, Chane, and a wayward majay-hì had come to her.

Ghassan had his own concerns about this black-robed undead mage. He was uncertain that even he could deal with it on his own. And for this alone, he could not harm Wynn just yet. Not because of growing fondness for her; that was irrelevant.

She knew much of what he had already suspected was the truth—too much. And he knew she had to be silenced for the safety of the world.

One life for thousands—tens of thousands—was a sacrifice he could live with.

Except for this thing she called a "wraith."

Wynn finally yawned, shyly covering her mouth, as if she worried about disturbing his silence. He got up, taking a heavy cloak from a hook near the door.

"Lie down," he told her. "Sleep. You are safe here."

"We can't let the wraith get more folios," she whispered, but her eyelids were already closing. "And tonight it came inside the guild."

"I know."

"Rodian tried to set a trap for it, but he failed," she murmured.

"I know."

Ghassan glanced at Shade, snapped his fingers, and pointed at the floor. The majay-hì leered at him but jumped down, and Ghassan pushed Wynn sideways by the shoulder. She flopped upon the couch, and he pulled the cloak over her.

"Tomorrow night," he said, "we will set a trap of our own."

Until then, he still saw a need for her.

As she settled into sleep, Ghassan slipped into his bedchamber and closed the door.

CHAPTER 17

The following night, Wynn crouched in the side street near the Upright Quill, the one that led to the same alley where Elias and Jeremy had died. She was waiting for a signal from Domin il'Sänke.

"We should not have agreed to this," Chane whispered.

Shade whined as if seconding that opinion.

"I don't like it either," Wynn answered, "but I can't think of anything better. Can you?"

The light of street lanterns didn't quite reach them, but Wynn still saw Chane frown. More disturbing, the burns on his hands and face had nearly faded. She didn't want to think about how. Even if the salve she'd applied had worked on him, it couldn't have worked so quickly.

"We have to follow the plan," she stated flatly, "and keep our wits."

"Can the Suman do what he claims?"

Wynn hesitated, watching the empty street. "I can't believe he would risk our lives, or the guild, by exaggerating. We may be its only hope for real protection."

This answer didn't sound convincing, even to her.

"But if the Premin Council learns what we did here, I'll certainly be dismissed. And Domin il'Sänke will be sent back to his branch in disgrace, at the very least. He's risking more than his life, so we must trust each other, or we'll fail."

The day's preparations for il'Sänke's trap had been exhausting. The Upright Quill was the only scriptorium to which the wraith had come more than once. After too much speculation concerning how it was tracking folios, this one scriptorium seemed the only choice.

Wynn had gone over and over the details with il'Sänke and spent half the day in further tutelage with the sun crystal. She was more than thankful for the spectacles he'd made. But throughout the preparations her thoughts kept turning over those brief cryptic phrases she'd read in the scroll. More than once il'Sänke had snapped at her, sensing that her attention wandered.

"I do not like him using you—or the scroll—as bait!" Chane rasped.

Wynn didn't care for that either. "It's the best chance for this to work."

For Chane to be effective, he had to keep his ring on. With it, he could mask Shade's presence as well, though it had taken great fuss to get Shade to let him touch her. The dog disliked contact with anyone but Wynn. Il'Sänke assured Wynn that he had his own way to "befuddle" the wraith's awareness of him—whatever that meant.

Wynn was the only one left without protection. And she was the only one who could carry the scroll and be recognized by the wraith. She slipped a hand inside her cloak, checking on the scroll case tucked into her tunic's belt.

"I won't be hurt, or lose the scroll, if you wait long enough," she said. "Stay focused. You and Shade have to come at the right moment."

The plan was straightforward but depended on dangerously close timing.

For now, il'Sänke carried the sun crystal staff. Once he was in place across the street, he would whistle softly from whatever vantage point he found. Then Wynn would head up the street past the Upright Quill. With everyone else's presence masked, she would appear to be alone and defenseless. They still didn't know if this shadow creature was after her or the scroll, but it wouldn't matter if she was carrying it. If the wraith sought both, so much the better to attract its attention.

The main catch in their plan was Shade.

For the last part of the day, Wynn had tried to teach the young majay-hì the most basic words in Numanese. She passed memory after memory of Chap waiting on command during any fight when Leesil had shouted, "Hold!" Chap had known not to close on an opponent if either Leesil or Magiere was engaged with a weapon that required room to wield.

Each time Wynn passed a memory, she'd held out her palm and spoke words like "hold" or "come" or "attack." She had cautiously passed Shade a memory of Chane fighting the wraith the night before, keeping her thoughts locked only on that moment. Hopefully Shade would understand when the time came. By dusk Shade simply lay down and ignored her, either bored or annoyed with all Wynn's nonsense. But Wynn believed—hoped—that Shade understood.

"Don't close too quickly," Wynn whispered to Chane, "or il'Sänke won't have time to pull the wraith's—"

"Yes, you said this before," he rasped. "As has the Suman."

"Sorry."

"But if you are in trouble," he said flatly, "the Suman can fend for himself."

"Stop calling him that! He has a name."

"There is something wrong about him," Chane hissed. "I can nearly *smell* it!"

Wynn was too anxious to argue anymore.

When—if—the wraith took the bait, she was to run in the direction from which il'Sänke had whistled. Chane and Shade would wait as long as possible, until il'Sänke appeared to engage the wraith. Shade would charge out next, suddenly filling the wraith's awareness, as she slipped from the protection of Chane's ring. Then Chane, still shielded by the ring, could surprise the wraith. Hopefully this would give il'Sänke time to take advantage—and get the staff to Wynn as well.

But Wynn was still worried about what harm that *thing* might inflict on Chane or Shade in a prolonged fight. They would have to end this encounter quickly. Il'Sänke claimed he could hold the wraith in place, keeping it from escaping. Chane would dive for cover, and Wynn would ignite the staff's sun crystal.

Step by step, the plan was straightforward ... in theory.

"It will work," she repeated.

Chane sighed.

"How did you and Shade and this domin leave the guild after dark?"

"Out the front gates," she said. "The city guards weren't there ... or maybe they were late."

A long, low whistle pierced the air, cutting off any more questions. It took Wynn by surprise, and she couldn't tell where it came from.

"He is ready," Chane whispered, and pointed toward a small shop half a block beyond the Upright Quill and on the street's far side.

Wynn crept around Chane. Holding her palm before Shade's nose and pointing to Chane, she whispered, "Hold ... Attack with him."

Shade merely rumbled and pushed Wynn's hand away with her nose. Wynn pushed on Shade's snout, and the dog held her place.

Chane gazed across the night street over Wynn's shoulder. "No matter what happens, do not trust everything il'Sänke says. I do not think ... feel ... that he speaks the full truth."

Wynn glanced back. "What do you mean?"

Chane's expression appeared to change, though it was hard to be certain in the dark. Whatever faint color remained in his eyes suddenly drained away. Only the crystalline irises of an undead stared out into the night ... toward the place from which il'Sänke had whistled.

Wynn shivered, but not from the chill air.

In that instant Chane looked like the mad feral monks who had come with him and Welstiel to Li'kän's ice-bound castle.

"Omission can hide the truth ... or a lie," Chane added.

*   *   *

Rodian took supper alone in his office, not caring for even Garrogh's company. He wanted solitude and time to think.

The pieces of this tangled intrigue were disintegrating, and he saw no way to keep them whole. Il'Sänke was the murderer—of that much he *felt* certain. The domin was the only one who fit all the criteria of ability and inside knowledge. But Rodian had no proof.

What was that man after in the translated pages? What was his motive?

Suddenly Rodian regretted his poor treatment of Wynn, regardless of her naïve outburst. Clearly that had been brought on by Nikolas's delusional account of events.

Rodian looked down at his half-eaten beef, potatoes, onions, and carrots, then lifted his gaze to the growing pile of reports on his desk. Petty thefts, one other yet-to-be-solved murder, and a handful of social disputes required his attention. He'd let everything sit while trying to solve these guild murders and thefts. And with royals and sages standing in his way at every turn, all he had left were his other poorly attended duties—and his failure. Still, he couldn't let it go.

He knew exactly who the killer was, but where could he find proof?

There was only one answer—Wynn Hygeorht.

She'd been studying the translations for two days. She must have learned something, at least a hint of what had been stolen. If so, how could he get her to tell him even that little?

He wouldn't pretend to understand this odd and troublesome little journeyor, but she seemed genuinely driven to protect her guild. Perhaps, like her superiors, she was taking matters too secretly into her own hands. Would she still do so if she uncovered something concerning il'Sänke?

Would she give up her juvenile notions of ghosts and the undead?

Rodian got up and strode for the door. Pulling it open, he lifted his sword hanging upon a coat peg.

"Lúcan!" he shouted into the passageway.

But it was Garrogh who finally ducked around the door.

"Sorry, sir. I've got Lúcan watching the guild's gatehouse tonight."

Rodian nodded. So far the only report was of Wynn's strange wolf coming back after dark—after escorting one of Pawl a'Seatt's scribes who'd worked too late. Otherwise none of his men had seen anyone come or go past dusk.

He grasped his cloak. "Have these dishes removed and get Snowbird saddled."

"Where are you off to?" Garrogh asked bluntly.

"The guild," he answered.

"I'm coming with you."

Rodian stiffened. "Pardon?"

"You're not yourself," Garrogh said, crossing his arms. "This sage nonsense has you turned around like a dog that won't stop biting its tail. The men want their captain back, so I'm coming with you, before you bite your tail straight off . . . sir."

Rodian was struck mute. He heated up, ready to put Garrogh in his place. Then he remembered the stacks of reports lying upon his desk and suddenly felt weary. Duty wasn't the only thing he'd ignored, if his second now openly faced him down.

"All right," he agreed. "But when we get there, wait for me in the courtyard. I need to talk to that journeyor again. She's . . . odd, and might speak only to me."

"Of course, sir."

Together they headed for the stables, saddled their horses themselves, and rode out.

As always, Garrogh's big bay protested at being forced out into the cold. The horse clomped angrily, throwing his head and grinding his bit.

"Next time you requisition a horse, I'll pick it for you," Rodian chided.

"Just 'cause you like them dainty doesn't mean I do," Garrogh returned.

"She could run yours into the ground."

Garrogh's brush with near-insubordination had roused Rodian. Along with other matters, he'd forgotten how sensible and aware his lieutenant truly was. And it felt better to do anything but sit and stew. Perhaps Wynn had discovered something that would help him prove the truth, so long as she spoke no more of her deluded beliefs. This murderer was not some undead of folk superstition. Then he might gain legitimate means to get a grip on il'Sänke. Not even the royal family would be able to deny him.

Soon Rodian and Garrogh approached the guild's half-open bailey gate. It was never bolted and barred, but it still bothered him that it stood ajar. He looked up the path to the gatehouse's closed portcullis.

There was no one out front on post.

"Where's Lúcan?" Rodian growled. "And who is on watch with him?"

Garrogh looked about. "I don't know ... Ulwald was paired with him. I've got two other pairs walking circuit around the place. Two more are off duty in the gatehouse above, waiting to rotate with others throughout the night."

Rodian urged Snowbird into a trot all the way to the portcullis.

"Open it up!" he shouted.

One of his men shouted acknowledgment from above, and the portcullis began to rise. Rodian ducked, prepared to ride under before it was fully raised.

"Captain?"

He sat back up, reining in Snowbird. Lúcan and Ulwald came at a trot through the inner bailey.

"What are you doing off post?" Garrogh barked.

Lúcan halted, eyes shifting between the lieutenant and Rodian.

"We heard something in the trees, around the west tower," Ulwald answered.

"You heard something?" Rodian mimicked. "What?"

"Not sure, sir," Lúcan answered. "Something large breaking through the brush and branches."

At Rodian's shifted glance, Ulwald nodded agreement.

"Then one of you goes alone!" Rodian shouted. "Or you get whoever's off duty above to watch while you both check."

"You had to have heard it, Captain," Lúcan exclaimed. "Others have. Gael heard something the other night and—"

"No post is left unwatched!"

Both men stiffened, whether in resentment or fear at the rebuke, it wasn't clear.

"Yes, Captain," they answered, but Lúcan glanced toward Garrogh.

"I'll handle this," Garrogh said. "You go on . . . find that nosy little sage."

Rodian took a slow breath. He wasn't the only one under pressure—or had he passed on his own duress to his men? They wouldn't have left their post together without some real concern. He dismounted, handed Snowbird off to Garrogh, and walked the rest of the way in.

When he reached the main doors, he knocked and waited this time, though his patience had worn paper-thin. The young apprentice who'd led him to the hospice yesterday peered out.

"Ah, sir, it's you." The young man opened the door wide. "Should I announce you? Do you need to see Domin High-Tower?"

"No, I'm here to see Journeyor Hygeorht," Rodian said, and stepped inside. As yet, he wasn't certain where they might talk, but she would probably have an idea.

The apprentice blinked in brief uncertainty. "A moment, sir. I'll see if she is available."

The boy was well-spoken, with a slight accent. Rodian wondered which province he came from, perhaps as far south as Witeny. He nodded, and the apprentice stepped out, hurrying off toward the dormitory on the courtyard's southeastern side.

Rodian paced the entryway for what felt like too long. A few young sages passed on their way elsewhere, but none were anyone he knew. The apprentice came running back in.

"She's not in her room," the boy said. "I'll see if she's at the common hall . . . or if anyone knows her whereabouts."

Rodian nodded and waited again. More time passed, and his patience was all but gone. Finally the apprentice came trotting back down the passage.

"I am sorry, sir, but Journeyor Hygeorht cannot be found. Domin High-Tower was just informed, but—"

"Not again!" Rodian hissed.

He brushed past the boy, striding toward the common hall, and as he rounded through the main archway, he nearly collided with High-Tower. The hall was filled with sages eating, talking, or just milling about.

"Where is she?" Rodian demanded.

High-Tower's red hair and beard looked huge, strands rising in the hall's warmth, but his features seemed even redder, and his dark pellet eyes were wild.

"You have no jurisdiction here!" the domin snarled back. "I thought that much was clear by now!"

But the dwarf looked around nervously, as if Rodian's arrival were an unwanted interruption of something else.

"Where is she?" Rodian repeated more calmly. "And where is il'Sänke?"

High-Tower huffed loudly, but indignation faded from his face. "I do not know . . . nor do I see your point."

Rodian forced himself to calm again and called out loudly, "Has anyone here seen Journeyor Hygeorht or Domin il'Sänke since this afternoon?"

The buzz in the hall diminished, and someone with a nasally voice called out, "I have."

A young woman in brown stood up. She was thin to the point of being bony, and even from a distance her nose was too long for her face.

High-Tower grumbled through gritted teeth and hurried toward her. His wide girth and vibrating steps sent apprentices and initiates shuffling out of his way. Rodian followed on the domin's heels.

"Regina," High-Tower puffed. "Who did you see?"

"All three of them," she answered, her lip curling into a sneer. "Wynn, the domin . . . and that supposed majay-hì. I was helping in the kitchen when they came through from the storage building. They went straight to the other side, to the rear hallway leading to the north tower. But when I peeked out . . ."

High-Tower rumbled as he glared at the girl.

"When I peeked out," Regina repeated, "they weren't there. They were gone, and too quickly to be heading into the keep or even the tower . . . for whatever reason."

Rodian knew of only one destination in the tower—High-Tower's study.

"Where were you about that time?" he asked the dwarf.

"In my study, of course," High-Tower replied. "The door was open, since I was available to students and apprentices. I saw or heard no one."

"There's always the back door," Regina piped up. "It opens on the back of the keep ... right across from the kitchen."

This spiteful pole of a girl glanced up at Rodian, adding, "None of us are supposed to go out at night."

Rodian ignored this thinly veiled accusation, and turned on High-Tower. "If they're here, I want them found. Either you do it, or my men will, and I'm not waiting for permission from your premin."

What followed, after the seething dwarf headed off, were long moments of Rodian pacing before the hall's main arch. Too many curious glances turned his way, not to mention a pack of whispering young sages who gathered around Regina as she smugly returned to her table. And when High-Tower reappeared dourly at the hall's narrow side arch, Rodian knew the domin had found nothing.

Right then he thought of putting Lúcan and Ulwald on night patrol, walking the Graylands Empire for the next moon.

High-Tower waded through the hall, his hands folded behind his back. But Rodian wasn't thinking of Wynn at that moment. There was only one possible way the errant trio had gotten out: Someone had somehow tricked Lúcan and Ulwald.

Ghassan il'Sänke.

Rodian almost demanded whether High-Tower knew how the Suman had done this. But if il'Sänke had such tricks, whatever they were, it seemed unlikely that a murderer would share such with anyone.

"Where would they have gone?" he asked instead.

The dwarf appeared lost for what to say. "I do not know why they would leave, let alone to where. Il'Sänke isn't fool enough to do this without telling someone what he was up to."

Once again, High-Tower provided a less than worthless answer.

"Thank you for your help," Rodian said coldly.

He strode out of the keep and ran down the gatehouse tunnel. Garrogh was waiting there with the horses.

"She's gone again!" Rodian spit, losing hold of his anger. "And so is that Suman sage! No one knows how or why, but they are out in the city somewhere."

He swung up on Snowbird and urged her out, but where could he even begin looking?

"She's alone with the killer," he said, wiping a hand across his face. "Where would she go?"

He wasn't really speaking to Garrogh, but his lieutenant replied, "Both times she's disappeared, she ended up at a'Seatt's shop."

Rodian's eyes flew to Garrogh's face. The first night, when he'd caught Wynn inside the shop, she'd been quite friendly with Imaret. And Rodian still believed that Pawl a'Seatt was hiding something.

"Yes," he agreed, for at least it was somewhere to start.

But what would il'Sänke do if Rodian found them and tried to take Wynn away? The mage had some motive for taking her off alone—and so recently after she'd gained access to the translations.

Rodian pulled up outside the bailey gate. Garrogh's horse skidded to a stop beside him. There was no time to send for more men, regardless that he was about to countermand his own snarling outburst. He needed at least one more of his guards.

"Lúcan! Where's your horse?"

The guardsman looked confused and pointed off along the bailey. "We tied ours off in there, sir."

"Get yours! And come with us."

CHAPTER 18

Wynn strolled up the street past the Upright Quill as if engaged in some halfhearted errand. She kept a lethargic pace, fearing to get too far, too fast. If she traveled more than a block past the scriptorium, then Chane and Shade might grow anxious and try to shadow her through the alley behind the shops. She would be out of their sight line for too long.

The street was still empty as she passed the silversmith's fine establishment and then the perfumery. When she finally reached the far intersection, she stopped near the candle maker's shop.

"Bother!" she whispered loudly, feigning forgetfulness, and turned to head back the other way.

In spite of an outward semblance of being put upon in her late task, Wynn was tense inside. Domin il'Sänke had her sun crystal, and she was completely defenseless. In her mind's eye she couldn't stop picturing the wraith as it had appeared in her room last night. Wraps of black shroud cloth—its burial raiment—covered its shriveled form beneath the robe and cloak.

An undead, but far different from those she'd come to think of as the Noble Dead. It could kill with a touch—could feed upon her with great speed—and nothing seemed able to harm it but another undead or a majay-hì. In comparison, a vampire seemed far less of a threat.

Some of them had unique abilities, aside from knowledge and skills carried over from life. But Leesil, Chap, and Magiere had destroyed such, and Wynn had even helped a few times. Decapitation and incineration were effective in finishing them off, but these were worthless upon a creature with no true physical form. What powers did it possess aside from mimicking physical presence at need? Worse, what if it was still a mage as well?

Forcing calm, Wynn hummed a low tunc she'd learned from Leesil on the voyage from the Farlands. A terrifying truth had been forming in the back of her mind.

The wraith seemed to *know* too many things about the guild's project and the comings and goings of the folios. Tonight's ploy to lure it out depended upon its somehow learning where she was. And no one at the guild knew of this plan.

The wraith had entered the guild last night. Had it done so in the past, perhaps tracking those involved in the project? Obviously literate, since it sought folios, if it had once been Suman, then it could read its native language. Even il'Sänke could read some of the ancient dialects of his own tongue, but only if given enough time.

So why had the wraith been stealing translated passages, instead of going after the original texts?

It could walk through walls, and since Wynn's return surely it could have searched every corner of the guild's keep and catacombs.

Wynn slowed a little too much in her walk.

Any search of guild grounds, for a creature that could go anywhere, would have succeeded . . . unless the texts were stored somewhere else.

Wynn picked up her pace again. This wasn't the time to get distracted by more puzzles.

As she passed the perfumery once more, she slowed to glance at its front windows. The inner shutters were closed and barred, hiding displays of handblown glass and porcelain bottles filled with heady fragrances. With nothing to look at she moved on—and then stopped completely.

A column of night stood ahead in the middle of the street.

Wynn flinched, even though she was prepared for this.

Appearing solid and real, its cloak corners began to lift on their own around the black robe. Unlike what she'd seen with mantic sight, the hollow of its hood held only darkness. So alien—like spotting a black spider running up her arm. Wynn began to shudder.

It just waited, not even coming for her. Was it playing with her? Did it want her to smother in her own fear and run?

"What are you after?" she said, and her voice turned shrill. "What is worth murder?"

Not even an echoing hiss rose around her in response.

Where was il'Sänke? He had to see it. It was standing right there in the open.

The night's chill deepened around Wynn, biting at her exposed face and hands.

The wraith slid forward across the cobblestones, its speed increasing.

Wynn turned and ran.

Chane tensed to keep from charging out, his left hand with the ring still resting on Shade's back.

Wynn raced down the street, toward his hiding place.

There was no sign of il'Sänke, and Chane forced himself to wait. But the wraith was closing too fast. He held back until Wynn blurred past him—and still no sign of il'Sänke.

"Now!" he rasped, and lifted his hand from Shade's back.

The dog cut loose a wail as she lunged into the street, and the sound made Chane quiver. He pulled his longsword, counted off two forced breaths, and bolted out after Wynn.

The blade would not affect the wraith, but his task was to do anything to divert it once it faltered amid too many adversaries appearing. He had to focus on that one purpose alone.

But it did not falter—not even as Shade charged after it, snapping and snarling. It reached out with its cloth-wrapped hand, until its fingers stretched to within a hand's length of Wynn's back.

And Chane was still too far off. But Shade closed the distance.

She leaped, arcing straight at the black figure—and it vanished. Shade landed with a frustrated growl and whirled about.

Chane did the same, quickly searching the street. Like some mockery of light, a black flash caught in the left side of his vision, and he saw Wynn stumble to a halt.

The wraith stood ahead of her, down the street.

Chane veered as Wynn backpedaled and began digging into her robe's outer pocket.

One thing was clear: This creature didn't want the majay-hì to touch it. That gave Chane an advantage. As he rushed at it, he shouted, "Shade!"

The wraith slid sharply to the right, trying to get out of his way as Shade's howl erupted again.

Chane thrust out with his empty hand, driving it toward the black figure. Part of him suddenly hoped the wraith would vanish to escape.

For an instant he thought he saw a darkened shop wall through its form. Momentum speared his hand through the black robe's chest.

A shock of cold stiffened his fingers. It shot up his arm as a brief screech surrounded him. Both the sound and the black figure vanished—but not the pain in his arm. Chane slammed into the shop wall beyond.

His numbed fingers rammed wood planking. He thought he heard one finger crack as his shoulder hit the planks. He rolled along the wall, looking frantically about as a thousand icy needles seemed to slide through his hand, arm, and shoulder.

Shade raced by, snarling like a rabid dog.

He never had a chance to look for Wynn. Coiling wisps like soot-laced smoke gathered into a column in the majay-hì's path.

But it was slower this time, not like the last. For an instant, the thin transparency Chane had glimpsed remained. Then it grew solid black as a screeching hiss exploded, filling the street along with its returning form.

The wraith's ability to vanish and reappear wasn't as

quick as Chane had thought, and now it seemed to struggle even more to become real. And he had hurt it as well. But his fingers barely moved and his arm was nearly limp at his side. He would have to throw aside his sword to try again with his other hand.

Before Shade could leap, the wraith rushed forward and swiped down with its hand.

Shade ducked away, but one forepaw slipped. She fell sideways, quickly rolled over, and her rump hit a shop porch before she could scramble up. Chane lurched off the shop wall as the wraith circled wide around Shade.

Then it jerked to a dead stop.

The hiss grew again in the street, like water pattering upon a hot stove. It whipped about, facing toward Chane.

"Throw it . . . now!"

Chane glanced back.

There was Wynn, fumbling to pull the arms of the spectacles over her ears.

The instant the wraith appeared, Ghassan dropped to the street with the staff in hand—but not from where he had whistled to the others.

While waiting, he had wondered how this thing had learned so much about the folios. If it had skills as a mage of any kind, he did not want it locating him. And when it appeared, he would not have time to obscure his presence from its awareness. If it learned of Chane and Shade's location, that simply served as a further distraction.

In the last instant Ghassan slowed his descent and settled silently behind the robed undead. It seemed utterly unaware of him, remaining still and silent, watching Wynn.

Ghassan fixed upon its exposed back.

Before he even wiped away the spell's remains to call another, the wraith rushed forward down the street, and Wynn took off running.

Ghassan did not know how long Chane and Shade could keep this thing distracted, and Wynn was defenseless. He could not allow it to touch her, or this would all end too quickly with nothing gained.

As Shade charged out, Ghassan lifted to the rooftops again.

Half hopping and half floating over the shakes, he raced along above the street. Before he could halt and focus upon the figure, Chane emerged and the dog leaped at the wraith.

It vanished.

In one blink, it materialized beyond Wynn. She skidded to a halt as Chane rushed by her. And Wynn's pale companion rammed his hand through the black robe. The wraith vanished again as Chane collided into a shop.

Black wisps swirled in the street ten paces beyond as Shade charged past Chane.

Ghassan rushed across another two rooftops and dropped to the street behind those swirls.

He needed only to mask the wraith's sense of place and bind it in confusion. As it struggled to reappear, he banished the spell that let his will lift him and began building walls in his own thoughts.

The wraith swung down at the majay-hì as Ghassan closed his eyes.

The pattern of a new spell appeared behind his eyelids. He began to chant, murmuring audibly, so the sound of his own voice in his ears reinforced his intent. He opened his eyes and reached for the thing's thoughts —if it had any.

The wraith swiveled around.

Ghassan stared into the pitch-black hollow of its cowl— and choked for air.

Something twisted about in his mind.

Like worms trying to bore their way out of his head, they ate at his thoughts as they writhed and turned. Pieces of his spell's shapes and sigils rotted before his sight. The glimmering lines lost all color and decayed to dust.

Worms of rage and hate ate at him from within.

He had connected to this thing, found his target with his own thoughts—but he sensed nothing there, only the worms and their bitter hunger.

The street's lantern light began to darken before Ghassan's eyes.

Somewhere distant from his awareness, he felt the air turn cold. Chill seeped inward until it sank into his mind. Nothing he had ever touched by will or his arts could do this.

Ghassan retreated deep inside himself, behind the walls made of his own thoughts.

He let go of any reach for this undead. He used all that was left of his will and shored up the walls in his mind, until the worms' gnawing grew faint—like scales upon those worms scraping upon stone.

A voice cried out, "Throw it . . . now!"

Ghassan's sight cleared a little, as if called back, and the wraith slid toward him. Wynn trotted up behind Chane, trying to pull on the spectacles.

The staff—all he had to do was ignite the crystal. That thought made his will slip.

The night nearly swallowed him as the scaled worms cracked through stone inside his mind. He found himself staring into the dark space within the black figure's hood.

Ghassan hurled the staff—and the wraith froze, raising its cowl as the staff arced overhead.

"No," Wynn whispered.

The staff was coming down short.

The wraith twisted about, raising its cowl skyward, and it thrust a cloth-wrapped hand into the air.

Wynn's fright spiked as Chane threw himself into the wraith—and passed straight through it. His scream came on the tail of a rising screech that filled the street, seeming to come from everywhere around.

Wynn bolted forward, her eyes locked on the falling staff.

She couldn't look for Chane, Shade, or il'Sänke, not even to see if the wraith still stalled. She couldn't let the crystal hit the street's stones.

The spectacles jostled on the bridge of her small nose as the staff landed in her palms. She closed her grip tightly, too frightened to feel relief.

Then she saw the wraith . . . or through it.

It wavered, more shadow than illusory solid black. Its enveloping shriek still tore at Wynn's ears. Beyond it—through it—Chane was trying to rise off the cobblestones. Il'Sänke straightened himself, stumbling as he shifted around the wraith's left side. He was shaking, his lips parted over clenched teeth. Chane hobbled the other way, until he thumped into a shop's porch pillar.

Something had happened to il'Sänke, and Chane was still too close, but if she didn't ignite the crystal now . . .

The wraith solidified and fixed upon her—upon the staff's crystal.

"Do it!" il'Sänke shouted weakly.

The screech faded to a hiss, and the black undead lunged at her.

Wynn dodged away to the street's center, and Shade charged in, snarling. The wraith faltered and swung at the dog. Shade was too slow in trying to reverse.

The cloth-wrapped hand didn't go through this time.

Shade yelped as the blow struck solidly against her head. She went tumbling across the cobblestones as if she weighed nothing.

Wynn had no chance even to cry out as the wraith turned on her again. She tried scurrying out of reach to get even one instant to ignite the staff's crystal.

The wraith jerked to a halt. The hand that had struck Shade now trailed behind it. Its arm was pulled back taut, as if something unseen had taken hold of its wrist. Wynn heard a thrumming utterance coming from il'Sänke.

"Chane, get out of here!" she screamed.

She didn't dare look away to see if he'd listened. She kept her eyes on the wraith as she envisioned the circle and nested triangles, all wrapped around a final circle. Wynn thrust the staff's crystal out to rest it in the pattern centered on the wraith.

The black figure flickered, briefly transparent.

The last thing il'Sänke taught her was to speak her focus phrases in Sumanese, hoping a familiar tongue might startle this monster.

From Spirit to Fire.

"*Mên Rúhk el-När . . .*" she whispered.

Whatever hold il'Sänke had on its arm broke as it thrashed free.

. . . for its light of . . .

"*. . . mênajil Núr'u . . . mênajil—*"

"No one move!" someone shouted. "Keep your place. All of you!"

Wynn never finished the last word as a clatter of hooves broke her focus.

Three horses charged up the street, with Rodian in the lead on his white mare. He rode straight at il'Sänke with his sword drawn.

The pattern vanished from Wynn's sight as she shouted, "No, not him!"

Rodian heard howling from several blocks away and drove Snowbird through the streets until he burst upon a startling scene.

Il'Sänke stood closest, his back turned. Another man holding a longsword stumbled along the shops at the street's left side. And Wynn's wolf righted itself near a porch up the way.

"No one move!" he ordered, jerking his sword from its sheath. "Keep your place. All of you!"

Then Rodian spotted Wynn.

She held out a staff with a long piece of prismatic glass fixed atop it. Strange glasses with large lenses covered her eyes. Her lips stopped moving as her head turned toward him; then her face filled with panic.

What was she doing here with the Suman and these others?

Il'Sänke remained where he was. Rodian couldn't be certain whether the man was looking at Wynn or . . . ?

Rodian spotted the black-robed figure. He hadn't seen it at first in the dimly lit street with so many others scattered about. Only the figure's hood pivoted toward him.

It was here—but so was il'Sänke. They weren't the same person, but the Suman still muttered a chant.

Rodian flipped his sword tip up and nudged with his heels. Snowbird closed on il'Sänke's back at a fast canter. He would bring an end to this chain of deaths.

"No, not him!" Wynn shouted.

Rodian hammered his sword hilt down on il'Sänke's head, and Snowbird skidded to a halt as the domin crumpled.

CHAPTER 19

Chane stumbled into a narrow path between two buildings, fearing the crystal might flash at any moment. But the burning light never came.

He flattened against one shop's dingy side as shouts and the sound of pounding horses' hooves grew in the street. The sting like iced needles still filled his body, but shock overcame suffering when he peered into the street.

Shade was on her feet, rumbling instead of howling, and she limped sideways toward Wynn.

Wynn stood in confusion, holding the crystal's staff out. But she turned her widening eyes, behind the strange spectacles, toward the first horseman.

The man she called Captain Rodian—the same one who had set the trap at the scriptorium—sat on a fidgeting white mare, his sword in hand. And the Suman lay in a limp mass, clearly unconscious.

Amid all this, the wraith remained still, turning only its hood toward the captain, as two other city guards kicked their mounts, charging at it.

Everything had turned to a fool's chaos. There was nothing left but to get Wynn out of the middle.

Chane willed down pain, letting hunger rise to eat it, and he ducked out, bolting straight at Wynn.

Rodian looked up from il'Sänke's crumpled form as Garrogh charged with Lúcan flanking him. The two raced toward the black-robed man.

"Hold!" Garrogh shouted. "Keep your hands where I can see them!"

"Keep away!" Wynn shouted back.

Rodian wasn't certain whom she shouted at. The wolf hobbled quickly in front of her, but the black-robed figure slid straight into the path of Garrogh's bay gelding.

Garrogh's horse reared with a sudden scream, and the figure thrust out his hand.

His fingers pierced the gelding's chest, and then he slipped aside. As the gelding's foreleg came down, the horse collapsed.

"Garrogh!" Rodian yelled.

His lieutenant was tossed forward, slamming against the cobble and skidding along the street. Lúcan swerved his mount around the downed horse and charged at the black figure.

"Lúcan, no!" Rodian called.

The robed man swung with his hand, striking the head of the guardsman's horse.

The animal never made a sound as it skidded on its folded forelegs. Rodian jumped off Snowbird as Lúcan fought to pull his mount up. But the horse collapsed sideways, and the young guard cried out as his left leg was pinned.

Rodian ran for his men. The black-robed man closed on Lúcan, struggling beneath his mount.

Lúcan tried to pull his sword. The dark man slapped his face—and the guardsman screamed. Garrogh rolled over on the street and lunged up, drawing his blade as he turned on the robed one's back.

"Get away from him!" he shouted.

Rodian's mind went numb. He'd thought il'Sänke was the cause of all this, and that the black-robed man would surrender once his accomplice was put down. Wynn's earlier words echoed in his head as he ran to aid his men.

You're not hunting a living man! And you'll never stop it through your usual means.

Garrogh swung as Rodian tried to get in front of the black mage.

The figure reached back and caught Garrogh's blade. The sword halted instantly, as if no more than a child's stick. Garrogh's eyes widened as Rodian swung at the figure's front.

His longsword passed straight through the cloak and robe. Meeting no resistance at all, Rodian almost lost his balance.

In that brief instant the black one twisted. His other hand struck Garrogh's face . . . and passed straight through.

Horror closed Rodian's throat.

Garrogh's grip released his sword's hilt, and he crumpled.

The lieutenant's face turned ashen in the pattern of a hand overlying his slack features. When his knees hit the cobblestones his legs folded, and he fell backward with his eyes locked open.

The black figure finished its full turn back to Rodian with Garrogh's blade still in its grip.

Rodian backed up a step.

"Don't let it touch you!" Wynn cried, but her voice now came from behind him.

He retreated another step as the figure opened its hand. The blade didn't slide along the cloth-wrapped palm. Garrogh's sword dropped straight down, right through the hand, and clanged upon the street.

Rodian heard a loud snort and hammering hooves. Snowbird was coming. She would kill—or die—for him, but he couldn't afford to look back for her.

"No!" he shouted. "Snowbird, stay!"

Still he heard her hooves.

"Shade, go!" Wynn cried.

Rodian quickly glanced sideways.

Wynn's wolf bolted past him at the black mage, still limping on one foreleg, and began snarling and snapping. Rodian snatched Snowbird's reins as she tried to follow the wolf. He jerked her away and turned around. Wasted moments werc foolish, but he couldn't let her be hurt.

Wynn's wolf harried the black-robed man, yet seemed

hesitant to stay close for too long. It hopped about, staying out of reach, but in turn the black figure flinched each time the wolf made a lunge.

Rodian jerked Snowbird's head aside and shoved on her neck.

"Back!" he commanded. Then he turned and closed behind the wolf.

He had no idea how to fight this man if his sword couldn't connect. Instead of swinging, he feinted and jabbed. His blade tip slipped through the figure's whipping cloak, and whoever hid within the cowl never took notice. When the blade came out, there wasn't even a tear in the fabric.

The figure lashed out at him.

Rodian saw the hand of wrapped black cloth coming for his face and jerked his head aside.

Searing cold spread instantly through his shoulder.

He cried out as if frostbite had erupted inside his muscles. Searing cold strangled a cry in his throat as pain ran down his arm and up his neck. Fear struck him as hard as the cobblestones when he toppled.

Rodian vaguely heard the wolf's snarl, its claws scrabbling on the street, but he couldn't lift his head. He was going to die, and all he could do was lie there, waiting to see the empty cowl appear above him.

Someone leaped over him from behind. He caught only the sight of a whipping brown cloak.

"Shade, hold!" someone rasped, as if too hoarse to speak clearly.

Rodian struggled, curling up to pull his knees under himself. A tall man with jagged red-brown hair, wielding a longsword, held out his free hand toward the snarling wolf. He and the wolf shifted about, keeping the black figure between them. Of all strange things, the figure remained stuck there, hesitant to turn its back on either of them.

Something about the pale-faced man was familiar, and he appeared to have no fear of getting near the robed one.

What was happening here?

Rodian's pale protector lifted his booted foot and kicked Rodian in the chest. As he tumbled across the street, he heard someone whispering, and then . . .

"Chane, run!" Wynn shouted.

The man in the brown cloak glanced once to wherever Wynn called from. His face filled with alarm. With effort Rodian rolled the other way, lifting his head.

Wynn was supporting il'Sänke with her shoulder and gripped the staff in her other hand. A trickle of blood ran out of the Suman's hair and down his forehead, but he stayed on his feet.

The Suman sage was chanting in a breathy whisper.

Rodian heard an angry snort. Despair took him as Snowbird began to charge again.

Ghassan pulled away from Wynn. He summoned a pattern before his sight and focused on the white horse. He could not allow the animal to break his sight line to the wraith. He filled the horse's sight with the image of a stone wall ahead of it.

The mare's hooves tapped a staccato as she halted frantically, whinnying and thrashing her head about.

Chane had served his purpose, but Ghassan could not wait for Wynn's companion to find cover. Weak, injured, and shaken, he fixed upon the wraith.

He had to destroy this thing and keep its truth from surfacing.

Its power was greater than his, and he had not been able to find or touch a mind within it. But how much did it depend upon feeding to sustain its presence? How much of its power had it used up? Perhaps centuries had passed since this thing last faced open opposition.

And since the city guards had assaulted it, the wraith had not blinked away again.

It *was* weakened. Perhaps it feared it might not be able to remanifest if it faded. It was fighting to remain within reach of Wynn.

Ghassan had to hold it long enough for Wynn to ignite the crystal and burn the figure out of existence.

Wynn tried to shut out the sight of bodies and dead horses and il'Sänke's battered and bleeding state. Time was running out, but Chane was in her way, and she couldn't light the crystal with him standing there.

Il'Sänke's chant grew from a whisper to a weak murmur.

Rodian's horse suddenly pulled up short from its charge, but did il'Sänke have the wraith bound at all? And how long could he hold it?

Wynn caught sight of the Upright Quill across the street. Its window hadn't been repaired from the night that the wraith had wrenched a folio through the glass. But the shutters were closed. Were they clasped or barred from the inside?

Chane shifted around the wraith, both of them taking furtive swings as the other flinched away. Shade always whipped around behind the thing, harrying it from the opposite side.

"Chane!" Wynn shouted. "The scribe shop . . . the window . . . go!"

Wynn didn't know if he'd seen il'Sänke or the crystal or her. But his face, normally a shade too pale, looked sickly gray under the street lanterns.

"Go!" she shouted again, and gripped the staff with both hands.

She leaned the crystal out into her sight line upon the wraith. Chane turned and ran for the scriptorium.

The pattern's first lines appeared in Wynn's sight as she heard the domin's murmur falter. The wraith swung away from Shade, and its hood turned straight toward Wynn.

She began to whisper, hearing wood splinter and break at the scriptorium, as the wraith rushed at her.

"Mên Rúhk el-När . . . mênajil il'Núr'u mên'Hkâ'ät!"
From Spirit to Fire . . . for the Light of Life!

The wraith jerked to a halt, as a spark filled the crystal's heart.

The long six-sided prism flashed like an instant sunrise.

Wynn forgot to shut her eyes as the world was smothered in blinding light.

She heard Shade's sharp yelp as everything turned black in her sight.

A screech filled the street, nearly deafening her, and she took a few steps backward.

Even in the dark she held on to the pattern needed to keep

the crystal ignited. Then she noticed that the darkness was only ahead of her, like a circle of black. At its center she saw the long crystal, aglow but muted. Everything at the sides of her vision was as brilliant as daylight, or even brighter.

Wynn remembered she was wearing the spectacles.

They'd darkened so suddenly, shielding her sight, and slowly they lightened only a bit—until she made out a wavering black form.

Il'Sänke was somehow holding it in place! Keeping it from vanishing again.

Wynn had never taken pleasure in the death of anything. But for the first time she might have felt what Magiere had when a murdering undead's body burned to ash.

The shadow shape in her spectacles' dark circle began to fragment. Pieces of it spread like smoke in a whirlwind. Its illusory body began to break up as its scream continued to tear at her ears.

A black flash erupted before Wynn. The wraith appeared to burst apart in the night.

All sound ceased, and the sudden silence made her flinch.

It was gone. All she saw through her shielded sight was the crystal, almost too bright to look upon, even wearing the spectacles.

Wynn wiped the pattern from her mind—and the crystal winked out.

Pure blackness came. She couldn't wait for the spectacles to readjust, and she clawed them off her face, keeping her gaze fixed ahead.

There was nothing where the wraith had stood.

Farther out, Shade groveled on the cobblestones, rubbing her eyes with her forepaws. Rodian's horse backed away, thrashing her head, and her rump hit a shop's porch post. She was snorting in panic, her eyes blinking and wild.

Wynn turned around in time to see il'Sänke collapse.

Rodian gasped for air and couldn't see clearly. His sight was washed with colored blotches left by the sudden light from the crystal atop Wynn's staff. When his vision began to clear, he saw her.

But the black-robed mage was gone.

Rodian began to remember what Wynn and Nikolas had spoken of. That the murderer was . . .

What—some malignant ghost? How could he accept that?

He gasped for air again and could only watch as Wynn ran for the scriptorium. The wolf limped after her, weaving as it shook its head.

Rodian's shoulder burned and yet felt icy within. The figure had barely touched him, but he felt so weak he couldn't even try to stand. A scraping sound caught his attention.

Il'Sänke dragged himself up. The Suman looked terrible, pale even for his dark skin, and he glistened with sweat in the street's dim light.

"It is all right, Captain," il'Sänke said weakly. "It is over."

The sage had been working with Wynn—not with the black figure—but it didn't matter.

Nothing was all right.

Garrogh was dead, and Rodian didn't know if Lúcan had survived. And he still had to explain everything to the city minister and the royals of Malourné.

He had to explain it to himself—and he didn't want to.

What could he possibly say?

Something solid bumped his shoulder with a snort. Rodian was still looking at the haggard Suman as he gripped Snowbird's halter, needing something solid and real to hang on to.

Wynn rushed the scriptorium window, staff in hand, and grabbed the sill. She stood on tiptoe to see through the broken shutters.

"Chane!" she called.

The scriptorium's front room was too dark, or perhaps her eyes had suffered too many sudden changes of light. Either way, she barely made out the counter's dull shape and the darker hollow of the workroom's open door.

Had Chane taken cover in time—or had she burned him again?

A whine made her look down.

Shade hopped closer, limping as if her right shoulder hurt. Wynn dropped down, holding on to the dog. For such a young majay-hì, Shade had done so well—like her father, Chap.

"Here," a hoarse voice rasped.

At the sound of Chane's voice, Wynn ran for the shop's front door. It was unlocked, but as she stepped in with Shade hobbling behind, Chane had already retreated to the counter and slumped against it to the floor.

Wynn hurried over and knelt beside him. Only a bit of light from the street reached through the open door, and his face wasn't clear to see.

"Are you hurt?" she asked. "Were you burned?"

Chane groaned as he pushed back the cloak's hood. "No, not burned."

The earlier burns on his face were almost healed, but he didn't seem well at all—weaker than she'd ever seen him.

"The wraith?" he asked.

"Gone. Domin il'Sänke held it somehow. Its form broke apart . . . dissipating in the light. It was fully gone when I put the sun crystal out."

He only nodded with effort.

"The guild is safe," she added, expecting some response. "And so are the texts."

Chane said nothing to this.

Wynn guessed the pain in his eyes had little to do with his injuries, visible or otherwise. His hand with the ring was braced flat on the floor no more than an inch from hers, but she didn't reach for it.

What would become of him now?

He was a killer, a monster—aside from a wishful, would-be scholar—and one of the few here whom she could trust with her life.

"Chane, I've been thinking . . . about the scroll's poem . . . and about—"

"Journeyor Hygeorht . . ."

Wynn raised her head at a masculine, hollow voice beyond the counter.

"Move away from *him*!" the voice added in a slow, even demand.

She scrambled to her feet, disoriented, and Shade began to growl.

Someone stood in the doorway to the scriptorium's back workroom.

His head was covered by a large round object that seemed darker than the room, and his form was draped in black cloth.

"No!" Wynn breathed, pointing the staff's dormant crystal at it. "You . . . you're gone! You were burned to nothing!"

The dark figure stepped forward. Heavy boots clomped against the shop's wood floor.

A ribbon of dim street light slipped sideways across his head as he neared the countertop's flipped-open section.

Master Pawl a'Seatt gazed at Wynn from beneath a wide-brimmed hat.

Shade's growl was tinged with a pealing tone, as if she might howl again, but wasn't certain whether she should. It was the same confused tone Wynn had heard in the guild hospice as she sat with Nikolas—as Pawl a'Seatt had appeared there with Imaret.

The scribe master pushed aside his cloak's edge and braced his left hand on the counter's edge. The wood creaked under his grip.

Chane struggled up, dragging his sword in one hand. As he stumbled back toward the open door, he grabbed Wynn's shoulder and jerked her along.

"Get out!" he rasped.

Pawl a'Seatt flipped the cloak's other side.

Wynn glimpsed a sword hilt protruding above his right hip.

It was too long, too narrow for any sword she'd ever seen, as if the blade's tang had been directly leather-wrapped instead of first fitted with wood for a proper hilt. The pommel was too dark for steel, even in the room's night shadows.

"What's happening?" she asked, about to look to either Chane or Shade.

Pawl a'Seatt lifted his hand from the counter and pulled on his blade's hilt. "I said get away from that thing . . . journeyor."

The strange blade slipped free.

"Undead!" Chane rasped. "Wynn, get out!"

She glanced at him, but what little light crept in only silhouetted him from behind. She couldn't see his face.

"Listen to Shade!" he urged. "Listen to her!"

"Move away," Pawl a'Seatt repeated coldly, and stepped through the counter's opened top.

At first Wynn thought she saw a long war dagger in his hand, like the one given to Magiere by the Chein'âs, the Burning Ones.

But no, this blade was larger, longer, almost the size of a short sword. Where Magiere's was made of the silvery white metal of Anmaglâhk weapons, the one in Pawl a'Seatt's hand was nearly black, as if made from aged iron.

It was well more than a handbreadth wide above the plain bar of its crossguard. Each of its edges tapered straight to the point. But those edges were strangely rough in an even pattern.

Wynn squinted and saw that it was serrated.

Shade's noise remained constant, like mewling beneath a continuous shuddering snarl, but she didn't rush at the scribe master. Wynn put a hand on the dog's back as she stared at Pawl a'Seatt's face.

Black hair hung straight around his features from beneath the wide-brimmed hat. The faint ribbon of light exposed skin not even close to Chane's pallor. His eyes were brown, though too sharp and bright for the color. They were not the crystalline of an undead.

"No," she whispered. "No, he can't be."

He'd been present when the guild had chosen his scribes as the ones to come work inside the guild. Pawl a'Seatt had come to the gathering before noon, in daylight.

"I will not ask again," he said, but looked briefly out the broken window toward the street, where the conflict with the wraith had played out. "I will not allow even one of these *things*, let alone two . . . in my city."

My city? As much as that utterance puzzled her, Wynn was caught by something else.

Pawl a'Seatt knew what Chane was—knew what the wraith was, or had been.

"I tell you, he is an undead!" Chane hissed at Wynn. "Believe me!"

Shade began to physically shudder under Wynn's hand. Wynn sidestepped in front of Chane and pointed the crystal out like a spear's head.

"We were just leaving," she said.

Master a'Seatt shook his head.

"You go alone." He turned his gaze on Chane. "I watched you throw yourself through that black thing. The guards died quickly, yet here you stand. And you fled from the light that drove off another undead. I do not know how you mask your nature . . . your presence. . . . Only one other has ever done this. And he left here long ago."

Chane's hand tightened on Wynn's shoulder as he whispered, "Welstiel?"

Only the barest change registered in Pawl a'Seatt's expression—but it was there, that slight widening of his eyes in intensity, and Wynn caught it. The scribe master knew Magiere's half brother.

Welstiel Massing had been in Calm Seatt at one time? Did Chane know of this and hadn't told her? The ring was the only connection she could think of.

Magiere and Chap could sense an undead, but Welstiel had always eluded them. And he had often hidden Chane as well.

Pawl a'Seatt spoke as if he too could feel an undead's presence but had been baffled by the lack of such in Chane. But he never looked at Shade, as if she didn't matter. Even an armed man, like Rodian, had reacted a little at Shade's distress in the hospice ward. Shade's noise kept eating through Wynn's uncertainty.

She could remember one other time she'd heard this, but not from Shade.

Chap had reacted differently to Li'kän than to any other undead. He had told Wynn later that the ancient white female was not like other Noble Dead or vampires. Li'kän had left Chap cold and frightened instead of heated for a hunt.

Wynn found it hard to breathe.

Was Pawl a'Seatt another ancient one? Was she standing

before another of il'Samar's "Children"? And still, he had been out in daylight.

He looked alive enough to her. Even Li'kän couldn't conceal the telltale physical signs of an undead—though Wynn had once seen her walk straight through a shaft of daylight.

Chane, still young for a vampire, also had to be wary of close scrutiny by anyone.

"You will not touch him," Wynn managed to get out. "If you saw him in the street, then you saw what he did. He was protecting the city, protecting the guild!"

"He . . . you . . . simply accomplished what I would have done myself," Pawl a'Seatt countered, his tone hardening, "once I finally found it. Move aside now!"

Wynn thought she saw those brilliant brown eyes of his turn suddenly pale and glassy.

They glinted, but that wasn't possible. It was only faint street light catching in his irises, the brief spark seeming too much in a dark room.

If Pawl a'Seatt was what Chane claimed, he wouldn't hesitate to toss her aside. She could think of only one reason he hadn't done so already: She was one of the sages.

"The wraith isn't an isolated incident in our world!" she nearly shouted. "Chane and I are among the few who believe something from the Forgotten History is returning. We may be among the few who can hinder or stop it! I will take him out of the city, far from here. You will never see him again."

Pawl a'Seatt turned his head toward her. A hint of disbelief—or disdain—wrinkled his smooth brow.

"I have too much to learn . . . too much to do," Wynn rushed on. "If you saw us out there, you know I need him if I'm to stay alive long enough to uncover the truth. You are not taking that from me."

She slid her hand over Shade's face and shoved.

Shade backed toward the door, and Wynn retreated, backing Chane along until she'd gotten him onto the outer steps. Only then did she withdraw the staff and its crystal.

Master a'Seatt followed slowly, his hard gaze still fixed on her. He didn't close or strike, only maintained the same distance between them.

Wynn stumbled as she retreated down the shop's steps. She wasn't about to turn her back on this man—whatever he was.

Pawl a'Seatt stopped in the doorway.

Even as Wynn went to retrieve il'Sänke and Rodian, the scribe master never took his cold gaze off of her.

CHAPTER 20

D awn was a ways off when Ghassan il'Sänke climbed the steps to his quarters above the guild's workshops. He had never been so tired nor wanted to be alone more than now. He knocked briefly before entering.

A glowing cold lamp rested upon his desk. By its light, Wynn sat on the floor looking calmly at the scroll's blackened surface, with Shade lying beside her.

"Wynn," he said in warning, "you have not called your—"

"Mantic sight?" she finished. "No, I'm too exhausted. Whatever is left in the scroll can wait."

Through the room's rear open door, Ghassan barely made out someone upon his bed. Wynn's vampire lay still in the dark bedroom, though Ghassan did not know whether the undead actually slept. Chane had been injured in the conflict, although he bore no physical wounds. Wynn insisted they bring him back and that Ghassan get them all inside without detection. It had been tricky, not letting either of them know how the guards out front were suddenly gone from their post yet again.

Once Chane was put to bed and Wynn slumped upon the study's small couch, Ghassan had left them for a while. He had a more unpleasant task to face.

Now, as he closed the door, Wynn spoke up before he could offer an explanation of his whereabouts.

"You went to speak with High-Tower and Premin Sykion," she said, "about what happened tonight."

He sighed. "Yes, and I thought you would be asleep by now."

"Did they believe you?"

"Unfortunately, yes," he said, "though they have only my word . . . and yours. But we have broken more guild rules than I can name."

"What do you mean, 'unfortunately'?"

Ghassan did not want to explain, but it was better that she knew. "I would guess they have believed you all along."

The opened scroll began quivering in Wynn's hand.

"What you know," he said, "are things that no one outside our walls should ever learn."

Wynn stared up at him. She looked beaten down. In having been denied for too long, outrage flushed her olive-toned cheeks.

"They treated me . . ." she began, choking on her words, "like an imbecile, like an insane little child!"

"They could not afford the panic," he countered. "Or subsequent denial and denouncement of the guild, should others believe you—or learn what might be in those texts. Truth would not hold against the beliefs of many that the world has always been as it is."

"What about the captain?" she snapped. "He survived . . . He knows!"

Ghassan sighed again and shook his head. "True, he now faces a crisis of faith, but not as much as you assume. The history taught by his religion, so much like secular perspectives, is false . . . but the philosophical teachings of the Blessed Trinity of Sentience are still sound. If he can distinguish that, then he may realize he has not truly lost anything.

"But by his example, we should not be so forthright with those who do not wish to know, do not need to know. The guild is safe for the moment. Translation can continue in a more expedient fashion."

"Yes, the project," Wynn whispered spitefully, and lowered her head.

Ghassan still found her to be a puzzle. She knew far too much, yet always remained determined to do what was right, no matter the personal cost. At the same time, she did not really want to thrust the truth in everyone's face.

Wynn Hygeorht simply wanted acknowledgment from those who already knew. But she had received the exact opposite from the very people and way of life she cherished. It was stranger still that upon the edge of such dangerous times, Ghassan almost trusted in her judgment.

"You struggle over more than just the illusory blindness of your superiors," he said.

Wynn picked up her journal on the floor, the one in which she had scribed words from the scroll.

"This," she whispered, and held up the scroll as well. "I think you know—or suspect—more than you've said."

"It's no more clear to me than to you," he answered. "All poetic metaphor, simile, and symbolism."

And his instinct to silence her forever returned.

Even a rumored hint of such abominations as the wraith, and what it might represent, would create panic beyond control. Suspicion and paranoia would grow, along with heated denial and possibly open conflict between differing ideological factions. Ghassan had seen such things before within his homeland and the Suman Empire at large. But Wynn had served an essential purpose tonight. Perhaps that purpose was not yet completely fulfilled.

She opened the journal, scanned the scroll's copy page, and pointed to a brief string of ancient Sumanese, perhaps Iyindu and Pärpa'äsea. Her finger traced one haphazardly translated phrase.

"Can you guess at this at all?" she asked. "What is 'chair of a lord's song'?"

With a tired breath, Ghassan took the journal from her.

If Wynn's hasty strokes were accurate, the script indeed appeared to be Iyindu, both an old dialect and a writing system little used anymore in the empire. Fortunately it was not Pärpa'äsea, which was more obscure. But he did make out one error.

"You have the last of it wrong," he said. "It is not prepositional but an objective possessive adjective, a form not found in Numanese. The first word is not 'chair' but 'seat,' so it would read . . ."

Ghassan paused, studying Wynn's attempt at translation, and then he looked down to the corresponding Iyindu characters. The word *"maj'at"* meant "seat," but the final character of Iyindu script had been doubled. Had Wynn copied it wrong as *"maj'att"*?

"Fine," Wynn said, "so what does 'seat of a lord's song' mean?"

"Seatt," il'Sänke whispered, adding the sharpened ending of the last letter.

Wynn straightened, craning her neck, but she could not see and so scrambled up to peer at her scroll notes.

"Seatt?" she repeated. "Like in 'Calm Seatt' . . . or Dhredze Seatt, the Dwarvish word for a fortified place of settlement?"

Ghassan frowned. "Possibly . . . but the other part of your translation needs correction as well. Iyindu pronunciation changes according to case usage, though the written form of words remains the same."

Wynn huffed in exasperation.

"You translated based on *'min'bâl'alu,'*" il'Sänke continued, "which is not just a song but an ululation of praise for a tribal leader. In this case, and declination, the spoken pronunciation would be *"min'bä'alâle."*

Wynn stiffened, as if in shock.

Ghassan wondered if she was all right. Before he asked, a breath escaped her with a near-voiceless question.

"Bäalâle Seatt?" she whispered.

Ghassan had no idea what the truncated reutterance meant.

The phrase kept rolling in Wynn's mind.

"Do you know this term?" Domin il'Sänke asked. "Something you have heard?"

Oh, yes, she'd heard it twice before.

She'd never seen it written, except when she recorded its syllables in Begaine symbols within her journals of the Farlands. Even then, she knew the first part of the term wasn't Dwarvish as she knew it. If il'Sänke had read that one brief mention in her journals, he wouldn't have remembered it among the stack she brought home.

The first time Wynn heard of Bäalâle Seatt was from Magiere.

They'd reached the glade prison of Leesil's mother in the Elven Territories, and Magiere lost control of her dhampir nature. Most Aged Father had somehow slipped his awareness through the forest and into the glade's trees. He witnessed everything. At the sight of Magiere, appearing so much like an undead, terror-driven memories surged upon the decrepit patriarch of the Anmaglâhk. Magiere lost her footing amid the fight and touched a tree. Through that contact she'd slipped into Most Aged Father's remembrance.

Lost in his memories, Magiere heard one brief passing mention of a Dwarvish term.

Most Aged Father, once called Sorhkafâré, had been a commander of allied forces and alive during the war of the Forgotten History. He received a report of the fall of one "Bäalâle Seatt," and that all the dwarves of that place perished, taking the Enemy's siege forces with them. But no one knew how or why.

Wynn peered at the scroll. Here was that place-name again, hinted at in the obscure hidden poem of an ancient undead.

And the second time she'd heard the name of this forgotten place was far more recent.

A pair of black-clad dwarves—the *Hassäg'kreigi*, the Stonewalkers—had spoken of it as she eavesdropped outside of High-Tower's office. Then they were simply gone when she entered to speak with the domin.

And the wraith had come at her twice, wanting this scroll as much as any folio it had killed for.

"I need more!" she demanded. "You have to finish translating what I copied so far!"

"Wynn, no," il'Sänke said. "We finally have a moment's peace. This can wait until tomorrow, after we—"

"Now!" she insisted. "I need more so I can go to High-Tower for assignment. Something happened among the dwarves during the Forgotten History, and I'm going to

Dhredze Seatt across the bay. It's the only place to begin
and to find out what happened, or where . . ."

Wynn trailed off, for il'Sänke was shaking his head.

"In the morning," he insisted, but by his following pause,
she knew there was something more.

"We both go before the Premin Council—in the morning,"
he explained.

Wynn had nothing to say to this. What could one say
when one's way of life was about to end? They were going
to cast her out.

Did it even matter anymore? Yes, if she were ever to see
the translations again, or the original texts she'd taken from
Li'kän's library. None of the council knew of the scroll, but
that by itself wasn't enough, even when or if it was fully
translated.

"Sleep for a while," il'Sänke said. "We will rise early to
eat. Facing the council's formal summons is not good on an
empty stomach."

Wynn stood there numb as he retrieved the old tin case
from the floor and slipped the scroll away.

"And Wynn," he added, his tone colder, "remember that
whatever you have learned must be guarded . . . only for
those who can intellectually comprehend—and face—its
truth. It cannot be shared elsewhere."

Dropping on the couch, she looked up at him with her
serious brown eyes.

"I know," Wynn answered. "I think I truly do know that
now."

At dawn Rodian sat at his desk, exhausted and ill. He
should've rested, but throughout the night's remainder
he'd tried over and over to write his report. Most of those
dark hours had been spent merely staring at a blank sheet
of paper.

He was driven to finish it, even beyond his own
strength.

Upon arriving at the barracks, he'd gone to his room
and looked in a mirror. A few thin strands of light gray ran
through his hair, and more laced his trim beard. Remembering what had happened to Nikolas, Rodian wondered

how he was still even conscious and on his feet. Perhaps the brief touch he'd received was less than what the young sage had suffered.

And now he sat poised with quill in hand, trying to find words to explain it all to the royal family, via the minister of city affairs. The threat to the guild was over. The murderer had been destroyed. Yet what could he possibly say of the details?

What would the minister think upon reading of a black spirit that killed by touch as it sought out texts supposedly written by other "undead"? And all of it concerned a war that most believed never happened. Indeed, what would the duchess or Princess Âthelthryth have to say if he wrote such words? They trusted him to maintain order, peace . . . and sanity.

Rodian choked on a dry throat and sipped some water.

Garrogh was dead, and young Lúcan was unconscious in the infirmary with a fractured leg, looking little better than young Nikolas. They deserved to have the truth told, even if it would never be believed.

Rodian leaned forward, and a sharp pain grew in his chest.

He didn't know he was crying until sparse entries on the report suddenly blurred in the spots where tears fell. He crumpled the sheet and pulled a fresh one from his desk to begin again.

Attachment: Final Report
From Siweard Rodian, Captain of the Shyldfälches, Calm Seatt
To Lord Mikel Eävärwin, Minister of City Affairs, Calm Seatt

In regard to events surrounding the Guild of Sage-craft, beginning with the deaths of two journeyors, followed by a burglary and two subsequent deaths, the matter was resolved the night of the 26th of Billiagyth.

Assisted by two of my men—Lt. Leäf Garrogh and Guardsman Taln Lúcan—I attempted to apprehend and arrest a suspect outside the Upright Quill scriptorium. In the ensuing conflict, Lt. Garrogh was killed and Gm. Lúcan was severely injured, both from combat wounds and other injuries consistent with those of previous victims in this case. No arrest of the perpetrator was possible.

During the conflict, while attempting an arcane practice, the perpetrator—presumed to be a mage of unknown practices—may have miscalculated. He was rendered to ashes. No specific motive or identification is possible; it has been determined that the perpetrator is deceased. I conclude that this individual and the murderer sought in the deaths of sages, who sought information being translated by the guild, are one and the same. Refer to related reports previously filed in this case.

I request that both Lt. Garrogh and Gm. Lúcan be cited for gallantry, with the according marks engraved upon their sword sheaths. I will deliver Garrogh's personally to his next of kin. I further request that the maximum monetary death compensation be awarded to Garrogh's immediate family.

I hereby declare this case closed as of the 27th of Billiagyth, 483 of our common era.

It was the sparsest, most unspecific—unprofessional—report he'd ever written.

Scores of questions were left unanswered, and the omissions would be plain to anyone who cared. But no one would ask. The report would be promptly filed, and he would be commended for settling this disturbing matter.

His future was intact.

Closing his eyes, Rodian saw Wynn's defiant face glowering at him, challenging him to believe in her.

He buried his face in his hands.

"It is time," someone whispered.

Wynn awoke with a start upon the couch and found Domin il'Sänke leaning over her.

She sat up quickly. By the light filtering through the one

curtained window, it was well past dawn. She'd slept too late.

"You seemed to need it ... by your snoring," il'Sänke said. "Breakfast will have to wait."

She didn't even remember falling asleep. As she lay in the dark upon the couch, her mind had filled with all the pieces of these past days, some of which didn't yet fit together.

Shade stirred on the floor beside her and stretched out with a yawn before rising to all fours. Her shoulder seemed better by the way she paced. Perhaps she healed as quickly as her father. Shade finally settled at the chamber's front door.

"All right," Wynn said. "I'll take you out in a moment."

Shade whined.

Wynn headed immediately to the rear door and peeked in at Chane.

He lay on his back, stretched out upon the bed, completely still with his eyes closed. His reddish brown hair was a mess around his face, but he seemed peaceful enough. The brief respite of such a sight slipped away when she noticed that his chest didn't rise and fall. He lay there as still as a corpse.

"Come," il'Sänke whispered, and on their way out he locked the door.

After Shade finished her morning business in the bailey's northern grove, they headed straight to the keep's main doors. The council chamber was on the third floor, and Wynn led the way in silence. Whatever might happen this morning, she had already grown certain of her path for the future.

She was tired of submission, obediently waiting until others allowed her answers.

They reached the double doors of the council's chamber, but before Wynn could knock, il'Sänke rapped lightly on the wood with one knuckle.

"You may enter," Premin Sykion called from inside.

Wynn shoved the doors open, stepping in first. This stone chamber had once been the master bedroom of the king and queen when the ancestors of the royals had resided in the first castle. In place of any large bed, chests, or wardrobes, only a long, stout table sat before the room's far end. It was surrounded on the far side and two ends by plain high-backed chairs, all of which were filled with the five members of the Premin Council.

Wynn was barely halfway into the room when her determination faltered.

Premin Adlam, in the sienna robe of naturology, sat at the table's left end. He was turned a bit away, speaking in a low voice to portly Premin Renäld of sentiology, robed in cerulean, who sat on High Premin Sykion's left. And Sykion, head of the council, seated at the table's center, was studying a document.

On her right, Premin Jacque of conamology had his elbows on the table. With both hands laced together, his forehead rested against them, hiding his face. The sleeves of his teal robe had slipped down, exposing muscular forearms.

Last, at the table's right end, sat Premin Hawes of metaology. She glanced sidelong at the visitors, and the cowl of midnight blue revealed hazel eyes almost the color of the wall's stones. Her stern glaze slipped coldly from Wynn to il'Sänke as the domin stepped forward in his like-colored robe. Then she glanced down at Shade, but her expression didn't change.

And Wynn was startled at the sight of one last person in the room.

Domin High-Tower stood near a window behind the council.

He wasn't looking outside or at the council or even at her. His head hung forward, beard flattened against his broad chest. He seemed almost cowed, or something well beyond weary.

Had he also been called before the council?

As much as il'Sänke and High-Tower didn't care for each other, their paranoia over involving outsiders had led to several ill-conceived ploys. Miriam and Dâgmund had lost their lives, and Nikolas was a mental invalid.

Wynn swallowed hard.

The council could do no worse to her than what she'd already suffered since her return home.

Premin Jacque raised his head. His blockish features filled with sadness as Premin Sykion began.

"We recognize your good intentions in what happened last night, but soundness of judgment has been . . . lacking in conduct. Our actions should not be driven by fear, or our security is sacrificed in such ill-conceived attempts to protect it."

High-Tower turned fully away toward the window.

"However," Sykion added, "as the cause of our great losses has finally been put to rest, we can move forward."

High Premin Sykion settled back. She carefully folded her hands in her lap, out of sight.

"Domin il'Sänke, you have been invaluable in our efforts. Our sibling guild branch in the Suman Empire should take pride in you. Having fulfilled our need, your stay should not be further drawn out. You are free to return home to family and friends."

Wynn squeezed her eyes closed. She heard not a sound from il'Sänke at those delicately phrased words. Her one confidant within these walls was politely being told to get out. Had they done the same to High-Tower? No, he wouldn't have remained if that had happened.

"Journeyor Hygeorht . . ."

Wynn's eyes snapped open, but Premin Sykion faltered with a sad frown. Wynn's resolve waned again in the dead silence.

"Considering your exploits in the Farlands," the premin finally continued, "you have accomplished much more than most journeyors in such a short time. But there is still concern over your well-being."

Wynn's anger returned. After all that had happened, and here in private where no one else could see or hear, she was still treated as mentally unfit. The lie was perpetuated, regardless that they knew the truth of what she'd told them all along.

"We wish you to take Domin Tärpodious as your new master," Sykion said.

Wynn's mind went blank. She wasn't being cast out?

"As he is a close friend of your former master, Domin

Tilswith," Sykion continued, "Tärpodious's tutelage would further shorten your steps to master's status in the guild. Your experience in far cultures, with new languages and knowledge, would be a great—"

"No!" Wynn cut in loudly.

Premin Sykion's eyes fixed upon her as High-Tower spun about. The worry on his face confirmed Wynn's suspicion.

"What are you doing?" il'Sänke whispered. "Do not give them a reason to be rid of you!"

He didn't see what this was really about, but Wynn did.

They offered her a new journeyor's assignment, to continue her training. To sweeten it further, they dangled a carrot before her, hinting that she might achieve master at a younger age than any before her. But there was a price.

Stuck in the archives, cataloguing and referencing with old Tärpodious, she would be well out of sight, with no need to ever leave the guild grounds. They could keep her under watchful eyes, controlling everything she did . . . everything she had access to.

"I'm interested only in the texts," Wynn said. "Where are they?"

Premin Jacque exhaled heavily, leaning his head on his hands once again.

Premin Hawes's hazel eyes narrowed as if in warning. "This will never work," she snapped.

"The debate is over," Adlam responded. "Leave it alone!"

Hawes leaned on the table, glaring along its length at Adlam. Sykion raised a hand before either spit another barb, but her gaze had never left Wynn.

"The texts are not your concern," Sykion answered. "Captain Rodian has assured us—again—that no charges will be brought against you for your interference. But if seeking suit to regain the texts is still your intention, it will do you no good, considering—"

"That the texts are not even here?" Wynn finished.

Sadness washed from High-Tower's face. His dark pellet eyes fixed on her. He was always so stern and self-possessed, but Wynn could swear she saw fright in his stony expression.

"Your lack of good judgment is reason enough," Sykion said.

That wasn't an answer to her question. And along with High-Tower's reaction, it confirmed Wynn's belief: What she wanted wasn't even being kept inside the guild.

Wherever the texts were, they were being brought in and out, so no offered journeyor's "assignment" would ever get her near them.

She was now an unnecessary pawn in their little safety game—their hope that they could forestall facing an opponent returning from the Forgotten History. Wynn couldn't help remembering wayward friends whom she'd longed for often in the past two seasons.

Magiere had been born in the worst of ways to be the leader of forces for the Ancient Enemy. Leesil, raised and trained by his own mother, was to be the instrument of dissidents among the Anmaglâhk and strike at that Enemy they knew almost nothing about. And Chap . . .

Having chosen to be born into flesh to guard them both, he had no idea how much his own kin, the Fay, had kept hidden from him. Beneath lies and omissions, all the Fay had truly expected from him was to keep Magiere and Leesil from taking any action at all.

And now it seemed the council wished the same for Wynn.

All this caution, this driven paranoia to do nothing for fear of doing the wrong thing—what did it amount to?

Wynn knew what each of her dear friends had done in the end.

"Give me the key to your study," she said to il'Sänke. "I need to get my things left there if I'm to proceed."

The domin looked at her with doubt and then appeared relieved that she no longer fought the council's plans for her. He handed over the key, and Wynn reached into her own pocket.

She pulled out her cold lamp crystal—the emblem of journeyors and higher ranks among the guild.

Wynn approached the council, directly in front of High Premin Sykion, and tossed her crystal upon the table.

Sykion's eyes widened at the implication even before Wynn said a word.

"I resign," she whispered.

It was still loud enough to hear in the chamber as the crystal's tumble finally came to a halt.

Wynn finished gathering her things from her own room. She arranged it all inside her pack, leaving behind the gray robe in favor of the elven clothing she had worn all the way from the Farlands. Wearing the robe would be a lie, for she was no longer a sage.

Shade watched her, occasionally following her around the small room or sniffing in the trunk.

Wynn tried not to think as she finished up.

This was too much like facing a death, and yet still left walking the world. She tried to keep her mind on one thing—Dhredze Seatt, the "Seafoam Stronghold" of the dwarves across Beranlômr Bay.

The only "outsiders" who'd come and gone unseen from the guild—who seemed to possess real knowledge of the texts—were High-Tower's brother and the other elder *hassäg'kreigi*.

The translation project would go on without her—had proceeded without her. Hopefully, since she'd said nothing of her plans, the guild would see no need to change the current location of the texts. Wherever the texts truly were, the city of dwarves was the only place to begin her search.

She picked up Magiere's old battle dagger from where she'd tossed it on the bed. The sheath was seriously weathered, and the blade itself needed tending. She'd never cared for weapons and knew little of caring for them. Chane would have to teach her.

Wynn lashed the dagger's sheath straps to her belt and retrieved the sun crystal, gripping its staff. Then she remembered to check for one thing—the pewter-framed spectacles. She found them still in her cloak's pocket.

After all of il'Sänke's effort and the expense to the guild, she had no business taking the staff as her own. The notion of walking off with it, before anyone could stop her, didn't sit well, but neither had many recent necessary choices.

And she would be traveling with an undead.

"Come, Shade," she said, and opened the door.

Shade trotted out, and Wynn glanced one last time around her old room. She could've stayed until nightfall, when it would be safe for Chane to go outdoors. But another long day in this room, no longer hers, was too much to bear. No, it was better to wait in il'Sänke's study until Chane awakened.

She shut the door and headed down the passage. One door along the way was open.

As she traipsed by, a cluster of apprentices sitting on the floor inside looked up. Wynn tried not to glance their way. Soon enough the whole guild would know they no longer had to put up with Witless Wynn Hygeorht and her fantastical tales.

She passed others as she came out into the courtyard. A couple of craftsmen, perhaps wheelwrights, made their way to the main building. Young initiates and a few apprentices scurried about, heading every which way to whatever tasks, lessons, or gatherings were planned for the day by their superiors.

Wynn stopped midway in heading for il'Sänke's quarters. Upon hearing lively voices in the crisp air, she turned, strangely mesmerized by a common sight.

"Come now, young ones," Domin Ginjeriè called. "We need to get these hung quickly."

Ginjeriè carried a large basket in her arms. She was followed by two apprentices and ten initiates in a double line, all bearing similar baskets filled with damp blankets. The initiates babbled and jostled each other, a few nearly toppling one another's burdens.

Wynn remembered herself once partaking in the late-autumn "washing" ritual. At the close of each fall, one domin oversaw the laundering of as many blankets as possible before winter set in, when drying them outdoors became impossible. Wynn should have smiled at such a fond memory, but she didn't.

"Domin, he's pushing me!" a little girl shouted.

"Marten, do you wish to walk alone . . . in front of me?" Ginjeriè called without looking back.

Wynn watched the double line of initiates trotting behind the domin, and her gaze fell to their moving feet. One domin, two apprentices, and ten initiates walked step by step toward the gatehouse tunnel. Wynn kept staring as words from the scroll echoed in her head, along with what she'd seen in the translations.

Six and twenty steps . . . to five corners.

She'd wondered about five ancient Noble Dead uncovered by name, who had "divided"—and the strange mention of "five corners" in the scroll. Li'kän was locked away beneath the ice-bound castle, and hopefully Häs'saun and Volyno were simply no more. That left only the other pair of the five—Vespana and Ga'hetman.

But another grain of truth began to dawn upon her, and it was so much worse.

The double column of sages, thirteen in count, fell into shadow as they tramped out of daylight into the gatehouse's tunnel.

"Oh, no more of this . . . please!" Wynn whispered to herself.

Not five corners for five ancient Noble Dead. Not six and twenty—twenty-six—steps taken, as some metaphor of distance. Whatever the five corners meant, the other measure was for pairs of feet—two by two, totaling thirteen.

The Children numbered thirteen.

How many of the other names she'd read were those of other ancient undead, possibly still somewhere in the world? It was bad enough that the one she'd banished with the sun crystal couldn't be one of them. The Children were ancient vampires, and the wraith had been some new spirit form of Noble Dead.

And Wynn thought immediately of Pawl a'Seatt.

The stoic master scribe with the odd family name had claimed to have been hunting undead in *his* city. He'd implied that he had sensed the wraith's presence, though he hadn't been able to find it. Magiere was the only other person Wynn knew of, besides Chap, who had such ability. Chane had been fervent in claiming that Pawl a'Seatt was an undead, yet Wynn had seen the scribe master in daylight. None of it made sense.

He couldn't be a dhampir, not for what Wynn knew of Magiere's singular birth and what great efforts that had taken. He couldn't be one of the Children, if Wynn's guess that Li'kän's forced servitude was common to all such.

Who—what—was Pawl a'Seatt?

The only other thing Wynn knew was that none of the Upright Quill's staff showed any fear of the shop owner, beyond his strange actions on the night of Jeremy's and Elias's deaths. Pawl a'Seatt wasn't guilty of those deaths. He had always been protective of his employees, watching over them each night when they left the guild grounds. And he had a long-standing and respected relationship with the guild.

Wynn turned toward the keep's main doors, rather than heading on to il'Sänke's quarters. She had one more stop to make.

When she reached the hospice, Nikolas was reclined against the bed's headboard. He gazed up, perhaps at the ceiling or at nothing at all. At the sight of his lost eyes, Wynn almost wished she'd just slipped away instead. But she couldn't be so cruel, and she had something important to tell him.

Shade trotted in on her heels, and thankfully, Domin Bitworth wasn't present.

"Your color is better," she said.

Nikolas rolled his head toward her, only then realizing someone was there, and he half smiled.

"Do I still have gray streaks in my hair?"

She pulled over a stool and sat beside him. "You may be stuck with those, but they make you look distinguished."

Then he noticed her clothing and the pack, and any hint of happiness drained from his fragile features.

"You're leaving?"

"Yes, I have an assignment," she lied. "I just came to say good-bye . . . and that I'm glad to have your friendship."

He rolled his head back and focused on the ceiling again. What else could she say? This poor young man had more demons in his past than the memory of the black-robed wraith. His few friends here had either died or left him.

"Nikolas, listen to me," she said. "Look at me. If anything like this ever happens again . . ."

She grabbed his hand.

"If something . . . unnatural ever plagues you or the guild, don't waste time going to Sykion or High-Tower or even Captain Rodian. They cannot help."

At this Nikolas's brown eyes filled with confusion.

"Go to Master a'Seatt," she insisted, "at the Upright Quill. Tell him everything. He will know what to do."

Nikolas blinked and then nodded once as he squeezed her hand.

"I have to get going," she said, and stood up, shouldering her pack.

"But you'll come back?" he asked quickly.

Wynn glanced back from the doorway. "When I can."

She hoped that wasn't a lie as she headed outside into the courtyard with Shade.

Wynn blindly made her way through the northwest door, down the hallway through the storage house, and into the workshop building. She had barely rounded the hallway's end and climbed the stairs, pulling out the key to the quarters, when she spotted il'Sänke in the upper passage.

"Where have you been?" he shouted.

The domin's dark-skinned face glistened with perspiration. His eyes looked wild with panic instead of the anger in his voice. He looked her up and down, taking in her pack and traveling attire, then shook his head.

"You . . . you idiot!" He rushed at her.

Shade snarled in warning, and Wynn had to grab her.

Il'Sänke snatched the key from Wynn's hand and turned back to unlock his quarters. He slammed the door inward with his palm.

"Get in here!"

Wynn still felt shamed for what had happened to him before the council. But she'd just had a horrible revelation, and she was sick of being told what to do. She just stood in the passage, returning his glare in silence.

"You do not even know what you have done," he hissed. "How much danger your dramatic gesture could bring you. Nor what you might have done instead!"

And Wynn grew so very confused.

"Inside," he said, and this too was not a request.

Wynn slipped silently past il'Sänke into the study, with Shade rumbling all the way.

Domin il'Sänke tossed the key onto his desk. His robe's hood fell back as he ran both hands through his dark brown hair. Then he jammed one hand into his pocket and pulled out a cold lamp crystal.

"Take this back!" he demanded, and thrust it out.

Wynn looked at her crystal and shook her head.

"I cannot," she said. "I won't be shut away, left to do nothing, while they do little more than that."

"Why let them?" he said. "You can choose not to."

There was something in il'Sänke's gaze that unsettled her, as if her next denial might make him more outraged or frightened or both. Thundering footsteps rolled down the passage outside, and Domin High-Tower barreled through the open door, his bushy red hair disheveled.

"Wynn," the dwarf exhaled. "Think, girl! You have pushed things to the limit, but do not throw away all you have—"

"She does not have to," il'Sänke snarled over his shoulder. "You . . . and your council gave her all she needs to see to that."

Wynn looked up, at il'Sänke. "Make some sense . . . please!" she said.

He shook his head, gritting his teeth. "Can you not see it for yourself? Any rope they try to bind you with can be pulled on both ways."

"The guild does not play at politics!" High-Tower snapped.

"Oh, spare me!" il'Sänke spit back. "This is all about politics, the politics of fear." And he fixed on Wynn. "You can choose your own assignment and still remain one of us. In the end, the council will have no choice but to accept this."

Wynn barely grasped what he was getting at. When she glanced at High-Tower, the dwarf's face was flushed, but he remained silent. That was strangest of all, that he didn't even try to cut il'Sänke off. As if he wanted her to hear this but dared not say it himself.

"They are afraid of you," il'Sänke added, "with all you

know ... stepping beyond their reach. They fear what you might reveal to others, once free of your oath to the guild. They need a hold on you, or at least that is what they want you to believe."

Il'Sänke shook his head, and the hint of a smile spread on his face. Somehow it wasn't comforting.

"You can do anything you want," he added.

"The council will never agree," High-Tower said, but it seemed weak and less than a true denial.

"Then do something, you dried out mound of mud!" il'Sänke countered. "Or I will. I have no doubt I can procure her a place in my branch the moment I arrive there."

"I'm not going to the Suman Empire!" Wynn cut in.

High-Tower sighed. "She must present a proposal for approval ... if she wishes to request her own assignment."

"Then write it yourself," il'Sänke returned. "And sign it! Tell the council she has changed her mind about resigning. They will agree to anything in that event."

"The specific assignment has to be outlined."

"No, it does not," il'Sänke answered.

High-Tower closed his eyes, and il'Sänke held out the crystal once more.

Wynn's head was spinning as if she stared at these two through her mantic sight. But the nausea in her stomach was now from fear that this small hope might not be real. She reached out and quickly snatched the crystal before it might vanish.

Il'Sänke slumped in exhaustion, bracing a hand on the desk.

Wynn still had no idea why the foreign domin was so frightened by the idea of her resignation, as if her action might force him to do something horrible.

"I will need funding," she said.

"You will get it," he assured her. "If not from them, then through my branch ... and no, you will not have to go to the Suman Empire."

Wynn gazed down at the crystal in her palm.

She was still a sage.

*   *   *

Near midnight, Wynn sat on the second bench of a hired wagon with Chane. He carried the scroll in one of his packs, along with Wynn's brief translations, and she held on to the sun crystal's staff. The driver, paid double for the three-night journey, steered a course along the bay road as they headed for the far peninsula peak of Dhredze Seatt.

In truth, Wynn didn't care how they traveled, so long as this search led to answers—and the texts.

Glancing back at Shade stretched out in the wagon's bed, Wynn knew that someday, possibly soon, Shade would discover that Chane was undead. The ensuing scene would be unpredictable—probably ugly—but she would leave that until it came.

She glanced over at Chane. What would happen when he grew hungry?

But again . . . she would deal with that when the moment arrived.

Chane and Shade were the only ones available who believed in the reality of the Noble Dead—and possessed the ability to face them.

To her left, beyond dark trees obscuring the bay, she could hear small waves lapping at the rocky shore.

"It may be hard for you, traveling only at night," Chane said.

She jumped slightly, as he hadn't spoken for most of the night.

"I'll adjust," she answered.

But would she, to any of this? She traveled at night with a vampire and a majay-hì to Dhredze Seatt to learn . . . what?

To find the texts, and to learn of a forgotten place, another dwarven seatt, lost in a forgotten time. And why had the wraith, whoever it had once been, desired information from the scroll and folios?

She glanced up at Chane's clean profile in the darkness. No matter what he might be, she could count on him while she uncovered the truth.

"I'll adjust," she repeated.

EPILOGUE

The gaudy and worn painted sign above the scriptorium's front door read, THE GILD AND INK. But the night street was empty, and the only person inside was busy in the back workroom.

There, a portly bald man stood before a tall wooden table with his back turned to the open door leading to the shop's front room. He wore a rich velvet tunic over a linen shirt. The quill in his hand was poised above a stack of freshly scribed parchments.

Master Shilwise never noticed the darkness within his shop's front room intensify as something bulged inward *through* the front wall.

A figure in a black cloak and robe wavered and then vanished. Its transparent form reappeared, wavering yet again, as if struggling to become real. Once wholly solid, it slid silently along the floorboards, through a stand bearing a displayed book, and into the rear workroom.

And still Master Shilwise was poised unaware above the parchments—until he shivered. The air had turned suddenly chill. He spun around, and his eyes widened as a hiss filled the workroom to its rafters.

"Reverent One!" Shilwise whispered, and swallowed hard. "I'm relieved to see . . . I heard that you were . . ."

"Destroyed?"

With that one word, the hiss became a voice surrounding Shilwise. And the black figure went on.

"Or had you simply hoped so?"

The question seemed to coil about Shilwise, squeezing him with frigid cold.

"No!" he whispered, shaking his head. "I would never. You've been more than generous for what you've asked of me!"

"And still, no one suspects?"

"That I can read the sages' symbols?" Shilwise finished. "No, not even my own scribes. And with the way you ransacked my shop"—and a touch of bitterness leaked into his voice—"I'm the last person anyone would suspect to have aided you."

The black-robed figure floated closer. Shilwise quickly slipped out of its way.

It approached the table, and its large, sagging cowl tilted downward over the parchments. Hands and fingers wrapped in frayed black cloth extended from the robe's sleeves and gripped the table's edge.

For an instant Shilwise thought he saw the table's wood through one of those hands.

The black figure wavered, its whole form turning translucent.

"Are you . . . all right?" Shilwise asked.

The visitor ignored this question. "All of them are here?" it asked, still looking upon the parchments.

Shilwise nodded. "All the extra copies I made, in plain language . . . both from what my shop processed, and what you acquired from other scriptoriums."

"And what of the female journeyor?"

"I don't know," Shilwise answered. "I've heard nothing. And you asked me to have her watched only two days ago."

"Has your spy learned anything of use? Where are the original texts?"

"Only hints and whispers, Reverent One."

"Hints of what?"

"Something concerning dwarves," he answered, "some visitors glimpsed once or twice on guild grounds, wearing dark gray or black attire. But they weren't actually seen coming or leaving; they were just there. But . . . now that Pawl a'Seatt is the only one working for the guild, I'm uncertain how to proceed."

The black figure appeared to sag, one hand slipping through the table, and then it straightened.

"Reverent One?" Shilwise asked, uncertainty thick in his voice.

"No . . . you have been fully hindered and can go no further."

The hand that had slipped lifted up.

Shilwise watched as those wrapped fingers extended before the black cowl's opening. Some effort seemed to be applied, for the hand became solid once more. It lowered but slowed before reaching the table . . . and shot straight for his throat.

Shilwise's face twisted, eyes and mouth widening to their limit.

All that came from his throat was a strangled gargle, then a choke, and not another sound. He tried to claw at the figure's wrist, to break that grip. His hands kept slipping straight through the figure's, and merely thrashed in the air.

No one else was there to watch the color fade from his flesh and hair, nor look into his eyes as his irises whitened as well. There was no one to watch the figure's form solidify as Shilwise's life faded completely. When it released its grip, the scribe master dropped straight to the floor.

Shilwise's body twitched briefly in a last spasm, like a bloated, pallid frog.

And the figure flexed its seemingly solid fingers.

The hiss rose again in the room, filled with strange relief. Its hand settled upon the sheets, carefully turning them one by one. Then its noise laced with frustration. What it sought was not here—there were only names no one should know. . . .

Jeyretan, Fäzabid, Memaneh, Creif, Uhmgadâ . . .

The figure's cowl turned toward the ashen body left crumpled on the floor. Its purchased servant could not be found in this condition. The city guard and officials already believed the "sage killer" was dead and gone. And better to stay dead—though that twisted double meaning brought it no humor. No one could know it had not been so easily finished, at least until it found the young journeyor, misfit among her own kind. She might yet lead it to the texts, and to what any of this had to do with "dwarves."

As it reached for the oil lantern on the table, more names scattered across the pages made it stop.

Li'kän . . . Volyno and Häs'saun . . . Vespana and Ga'hetman . . .

The figure snatched up the lantern and slammed it upon the floor next to Shilwise's body.

The black figure turned over the last sheets, gathering up the stack as flames began to spread across the floorboards. But as it headed for the workroom's rear, it paused again with its cowl tilted down over the parchments.

One name had been missed in its hurried scan—one on the very first sheet—and a moan threaded in its hiss.

The sound rose above the fire's crackle until the rear window's pane rattled. The black figure shattered that window and pulled the parchment stack through the opening as it slid out through the shop's rear wall.

That one name had been kept hidden, as carefully as himself, for a thousand or more years.

His name . . . Sau'ilahk.

ORDER	REALM	ELEMENT[1]	COLOR[2]	FIELDS[3]	DUTIES
Metaology	Existence	Spirit/Tree/Essence	Midnight blue	Metaphysical sciences and philosophies; theology; cosmology; religion and magic; folklore, myth, and legend.	Interaction with public groups and organizations to areas of emphasis.
Cathology	Knowledge (between greater Existence and Awareness/Sentience)	Fire/Flame (Light)/Energy	Gray	Intellectual (informational) sciences and philosophies; ethnic geography and history; languages and linguistics; literature; archaeology scholarship and pedagogy; etc.	Interaction with groups involved in knowledge in general, as well as intercultural communication and translation. Oversees all guild branch affairs and population.
Sentiology	Awareness (Sentience)	Air/Gas/Wind	Cerulean (pale blue)	Social sciences and philosophies; sentience sciences; political and economic geography and history; customs and laws; statistics; politics and government; economics; the arts; etc.	Interaction with national and regional bodies. Known to assist in international and intercultural negotiations.

ORDER	REALM	ELEMENT[1]	COLOR[2]	FIELDS[3]	DUTIES
Conamology	Endeavor (between Sentience and the Natural World)	Water/Wave/Liquid	Teal (green-blue)	Applied sciences; technology; mathematics; medical research; education; engineering; farming; trades and crafts; etc.	Interaction with trade guilds. Oversees guild- and kingdom-sponsored services, such as public schools. Physicians can be found among this order.
Naturology	The Natural World	Earth/Mountain/Solid	Sienna (light brown)	Natural and earth sciences; physical geography and history; astronomy; biology; anthropology; zoology; etc.	Interaction with groups and populations in relation to daily life and well-being. Healers can be found among this order.

1. As known within the guild by their conceptual or symbolic references according to the three Aspects; other arrangements and/or descriptive terms for the five Elements vary among differing cultures.

2. Chosen during the guild's founding for pragmatic reasons related to material and dying process rather than as a direct association to an order's associated Element.

3. As general modern references and not to be taken literally; considerable overlap can be found among the orders, as evidenced by emphases listed.

THE RANKS OF THE GUILD OF SAGECRAFT

Student Anyone studying formally at a guild branch who is not seeking to become a sage.

Initiate The first rank, requiring three to four years of study before testing for apprentice status. Initiates do not belong to an order and wear tan-colored robes. Upon completion of initial studies and testing successfully for apprentice status, they declare which order they wish to join. This requires approval from a domin of the selected order. Upon acceptance, they take the robe of appropriate color.

Apprentice The second rank, requiring three to four years under the tutelage of a master or domin of the order before seeking and testing for journeyor status. During apprenticeship is the only time one may seek to change order. If so, the process is the same as that for an initiate who has just completed initial studies.

Journeyor The third rank, requiring three to five years before seeking and testing for master status; most take closer to five years. A journeyor receives one or more assignments abroad in their native territory (though not always), providing public and private service to hone their skills. Once all assignments are completed, journeyors may petition for master's status—with permission of their domin. The petition process is arduous, involving verbal and written examinations and interviews, as well as a review of all personal development and accomplishments. The process must be completed in one season, on a schedule chosen by the journeyor. If denied, a journeyor must continue service in the public sector for another year before repetitioning. Only three attempts at this process are allowed.

Master   The highest rank achievable through study and work; few make it this far. Master status is required to be considered for the titled posts of either domin or premin. Masters are free to work within the guild or seek pursuits elsewhere. Some are occasionally encountered in service to ruling individuals, governments, and occasionally large trade, craft, and other guilds and organizations in the Numan Lands.

Domin   A special titled position for a master sage inside a branch of the guild; it is offered and assigned by the Premin Council, and there is no petition or application process. All domins of a particular order and branch (if there are more than one) collectively manage the order's affairs under the direction of their premin. A title of position rather than rank, it is somewhat equivalent to the head of one major department within one college of a university, though this is a very loose comparison.

Premin   A special titled position for the one and only head of an order in a single branch of the guild. In most cases, only a domin is selected for this position, though some masters have achieved this status. Selection is done by the remaining four premins of a branch's other orders, along with input from the domins of the order in question. Somewhat equivalent to a chairperson or president of an entire college at a university, though this is a very loose comparison.

Premin, High or Grand

Each guild branch is administrated by its Premin Council, composed of the five premins of its orders. Among them, one is head of that council and bears the title of high premin. This individual is selected from among the currently sitting premins. The selection is made collectively by all premins and domins of the branch, regardless of their order. Most often, the premin of the Order of Cathology is selected as high premin, for this order manages the collected knowledge that the guild safeguards, and thereby has the greatest interaction with all orders. However, exceptions have occurred. The selection process can be lengthy, arduous, and highly political—doubly so when selecting the grand premin.

All sitting high premins of the three established branches are also members of the Premin Grand Council for the entire Guild of Sagecraft. Among them is selected a primary administrator, who is titled grand premin. This selection process is made only by premins of the three branches. Again, the selection has most often been a cathologer, a premin of the Order of Cathology, at one of the branches. Exceptions occur more often than with selection of a high premin in a single branch.

NEW IN HARDCOVER

THROUGH STONE AND SEA

A Novel of the Noble Dead

by Barb & J.C. Hendee

Wynn journeys to the mountain stronghold of the dwarves in search of the "Stonewalkers," an unknown sect supposedly in possession of important ancient texts. But in her obsession to understand these writings, she will find more puzzles and questions buried in secrets old and new—along with an enemy she thought destroyed...

Available wherever books are sold or at penguin.com

National Bestselling Authors
Barb & J.C. Hendee
The Noble Dead Saga

DHAMPIR

A con artist who poses as a vampire slayer learns that she is, in fact, a true slayer—and half-vampire herself. And her actions have attracted the unwanted attention of a trio of powerful vampires seeking her blood.

THIEF OF LIVES

Magiere and Leesil are called out of their self-imposed retirement when vampires besiege the capital city of Bela.

SISTER OF THE DEAD

Magiere the dhampir and her partner, the half-elf Leesil, are on a journey to uncover the secrets of their mysterious pasts. But first their expertise as vampire hunters is required on behalf of a small village being tormented by a creature of unlimited and unimaginable power.

Available wherever books are sold or at penguin.com

Also Available from
National Bestselling Authors
Barb & J.C. Hendee
The Noble Dead Saga

TRAITOR TO THE BLOOD

The saga continues as Magiere and Leesil
embark on a quest to uncover the secrets of their
mysterious origins—and for those responsible for
orchestrating the events that brought them together.

REBEL FAY

Magiere and Leesil were brought together by the
Fay to forge an alliance that might have the power
to stand against the forces of dark magics. But as
they uncover the truth, they discover just how
close the enemy has always been...

CHILD OF A DEAD GOD

For years, Magiere and Leesil have sought a long
forgotten artifact, though its purpose has been
shrouded in mystery. All Magiere knows is that she
must keep the orb from falling into the hands of a
murdering Noble Dead, her half-brother Welstiel.
And now, dreams of a castle locked in ice lead her
south, on a journey that has become nothing less
than an obsession.

**Available wherever books are sold or at
penguin.com**